Prologue

Annie Lebeau sat on the sagging steps of her back porch, her bare toes curled in the damp, dark Louisiana earth, her threadbare dress hiked up to expose her flabby thighs. A single light bulb dangled from a cord over her head, casting a yellow glow, a bug light that kept the insects at bay. She shifted the corncob pipe in her lips and cackled through her few remaining teeth. Cocking her head to see better with her good eye, the old woman again counted the money the man had left her.

"*Couillon, el vugh,*" she muttered the obscenities, referring to the man who had just visited her shanty. Once more satisfied the amount was what she had asked, plus a little *lagniappe*, she reached inside her bodice and pulled out a cloth bag pinned to her one-piece undergarment. Unhitching the sack, she tugged its drawstring apart and tucked the wad of cash inside, then put her moneybag back where it belonged, snugged safely between her pendulous breasts.

The hot, humid air was still, and the night was silent except for the low chatter of night bugs in the cattails and weeds lining the bayou. The moon appeared to be ringed with a haze, a harbinger of rain. A heavy, musky smell hung over the swamp. The waters of the bayou lapped sluggishly at the pilings of her dilapidated dock, where only the prow of a submerged pirogue was visible. Nearby, a couple of night birds called to each other, courting or hunting.

Annie rested her elbows on her knees and puffed on her pipe. The smoke wreathed her grizzled head, and she sniffed appreciatively at the odor of the expensive cherry-blend tobacco the man brought her. A large gray tabby cat emerged from the darkness and wound itself around her ankles. She absent-mindedly petted the creature.

"*Mais ye*," she mumbled, thinking about the rich Creole man who'd just left. *He knew he better pay me good to do what he asked, him.* Aloud she spat, "*Fils de putain.*"

Annie had no use for the man or the others like him who sneaked out to her shack on Bayou Ombre and paid for her services. The rich bastards who knelt in their churches and prayed to their Christian saints and then slipped around to ask her to work spells for them, using her Voodoo magic. Just like their ancestors had done with the women in her family for almost two hundred years.

"Sons o' bitches, ev'ry one of 'em," she muttered in English this time. But she'd take their money.

Something large and clumsy-sounding made a sucking, snuffling noise as it wallowed through the mud, before splashing into the water near the old dock, but Annie ignored it.

The photograph the man left lay on the steps beside her. She picked it up and studied the face of a four-year-old child, now a young woman. She muttered around the pipe, "I fix you, me. An' not do it fo' de money...but fo' money, mo' *bien.*" She squinted through the smoke. A more recent picture would've been better for identification purposes, but Annie could see the girl had the look of the St. Cyrs about her. Dark hair, olive skin, those emerald eyes. And the old woman knew her name, would not likely forget it. Annie would have her posse on Laurette St. Cyr's trail from the moment she arrived in New Orleans.

The old black woman rose stiffly to her feet and shuffled across the weathered floorboards. She had work to do. Her late-night visitor didn't know for certain when the girl he paid Annie to put the *fix* on would be arriving, but he told her it would probably be in the next couple of weeks. No matter. Annie would have the airport covered, along with most the best hotels in the Crescent City. The *petite cocotte* would not be hard to find.

She paused and took the pipe out of her mouth, narrowing her eyes. *What if the girl didn't fly to New Orleans? What if she drove herself here?*

The tabby on her heels, Annie opened the back screen door and went inside, letting the door slam behind her. Never to mind. She stuck the pipe between her lips and puffed. She'd find the little hussy, no matter if she arrived on angels' wings. But considering the girl was a St. Cyr, the angels' wings weren't a likelihood.

Chapter 1

The New Orleans heat and humidity slapped me in the face like a wet washrag, as I wheeled my luggage through the doors from the Louis Armstrong Airport to the concrete strip where taxis idled, waiting for passengers. I hadn't been in the city for twenty years and had forgotten the terrarium-like ambience of the Deep South. My nose twitched at the smell of the place, a long-dormant, yet familiar odor...woodsmoke, swamp rot, the big river.

Another odor, stale sweat and cigarettes, assaulted me, as a small, wiry man, his steps paralleling mine, brushed against me. I'd caught a glimpse of him eyeing me at the baggage carousel. My skin prickled, and I stepped aside to avoid him. Mama always warned me to stay away from people like him.

A burly black man leapt out of his big black SUV, a taxi logo on its side, and offered his services. A diamond-studded gold tooth flashed in his smile. "Let me help you with those bags, ma'am." His deep voice held a distinctive New Orleans accent, an echo of familiar voices from my childhood.

As he was about to take my luggage from me, the skinny stranger suddenly appeared at my elbow and tried to latch onto one of my bags. "I tote them bags, missy."

The creature looked like a mangy ferret, and I turned the wheeled suitcase aside to keep him from touching my belongings. "No thank, you." I glared at him.

I didn't like his weasely looks. His light brown skin had a sickly, grayish tinge, and he just didn't look clean; whereas, the big man had a friendly smile and wore pressed slacks and an immaculate blue shirt with his company's logo on the breast pocket.

"I got dat, podnah." The smaller man grabbed a bag. "I already seen dis lady inside the airpo't, me."

The big cabbie showed his diamond-studded tooth in a nasty grin. "Back off, jackleg. I got this fare."

I shrunk from them, gripping my luggage handle. I was afraid a fist fight was about to break out over who had the privilege of driving me into the city.

"I tole you I seen dis lady firs'," the smaller man insisted, baring tiny pointed teeth.

"This my fare. You hear what I'm sayin'?" The larger man glowered. "You get yo' butt whipped, you mess wi' me."

"I already seen...."

"You, get!" The cab driver snatched the bag away from him.

The smaller man "got," and the first driver to offer his services picked up my bags and stashed them into the cargo compartment of his vehicle.

"Fine lady like you don't need to be ridin' wi' trash like that. He's only part time...works on his own, not for a reg'lar cab comp'ny." He nodded toward the man, who was getting into a ratty-looking, beige sedan and casting dirty looks our way. "Don't think he's washed that heap in recent mem'ry."

The near altercation had given me a start. "I noticed him inside the building and didn't like his looks." I pulled my pink shirt away from my chest and fanned myself with my hand. I was sweating.

"He's jus' trash. Knows not to mess wi' me." He flashed another smile and held out his hand to help me climb into his vehicle. "What brings you to our fair city, ma'am, if you don't mind my askin'? You a long way from Seattle."

Obviously, he'd noticed the tags on my luggage.

"I'm here to see my family and check on some property." I wasn't comfortable discussing anything personal with a stranger, but I felt it would be rude not to answer his question. "And just see the city. I haven't been to New Orleans since I was a small child."

The cab driver walked around his SUV and jumped inside. "You got fam'ly here?" His tone was friendly, not pushy or nosy. "I prob'ly know some of 'em. I was born and raised right here in N'Awlins. Know mos' ever'body, me." He settled behind the steering wheel and buckled himself in, then pulled away from the passenger pickup area.

I leaned forward and saw the sedan pull into traffic behind us but didn't mention it to my driver. After all, the streets were public property. "My family's name is St. Cyr. I'm Laurette St. Cyr."

As the driver swiveled his head toward me, I caught a scant frown on his face. He paused a beat before commenting. "My pleasure, ma'am. I'm LaRondell Duclose."

"Nice to meet you," I nodded, wondering at the expression that had passed momentarily over his face. Maybe it had nothing to do with me. Maybe he'd noticed the man in the sedan tailing us.

"St. Cyr, huh? The St. Cyrs live out on Bayou Ombre…Shadow Bayou. 'Course some of 'em live right here in the city, too. Which ones you close to?"

"Etienne St. Cyr was my father."

"Oh, my. He jus' passed, him. So sad. I'm sorry for your loss, ma'am." He crossed himself at the mention of my father's death.

Before I could ask, he said, "I didn't know yo' daddy person'ly, but any time you lose yo' mama or daddy, it's bad."

"Yes, it is" I agreed. In my case, death came as a double whammy. I'd lost both my parents within months of each other, in a matter of speaking. My mother had died only six months earlier. On the other hand, the father I'd believed dead for the past twenty years had passed only a few weeks earlier, according to the letter tucked safely in my tote. The Letter…capitalized, as I had come to think of it…

from a lawyer named Claude Landrieu, had turned my life upside down. My father had left me a plantation called Shadow Cove on Shadow Bayou. I had come back to Louisiana, a place my mother had taken me from when I was only four…come back to claim my inheritance, whatever it might turn out to be. For all I knew, it was a shack in a swamp; although, I had vague memories of a large, white-pillared house, surrounded by trees dripping Spanish moss. "You've lived here all your life?" I wanted to change the subject.

"I sho' have. Wouldn't want to live no place else. Ain't got the Saints and Drew Brees no place else. 'Sides, I play in this band, and I wouldn't want to give that up, no."

"What kind of band do you play in?"

"We play blues mostly, some jazz, a little rock. We call ourselves The Blues Juice. We get gigs all over the Quarter." He pronounced it *Qwahtah*. "We're usually booked up way in advance, so I reckon folks like us."

He swung the cab off the road from the airport and into the traffic on I-10. He drove fast but expertly. He chatted amiably about growing up in the city, playing football in high school, and dating a girlfriend who was studying nursing.

I listened with half an ear as I gazed out the window. Closely packed subdivisions lined the highway on both sides. We passed a few large commercial buildings, a couple of clinics, a tall water tower. I craned my neck to see if the tacky sedan was still behind us. If it was, there were so many cars on the interstate that I didn't notice it.

"This yo' firs' time back in our city in a long time, you gonna find all kinds of things to do and see." He grinned at me in the mirror. "Katrina changed some things, but this is N'Awlins. Ain't nothing gonna keep us down fo' long. And you gonna find some of the fines' food you ever put in yo' mouth. Make you wanta slap yo'mama." He boomed a laugh.

"That's what I've heard. New Orleans is famous for food and music…and those cemeteries I've read about." The road curved, and now I saw graveyards coming up, bounding the interstate on either side. "Is that what we're seeing right here?" I leaned forward to get a better look, as we sped down the road. "Those old cemeteries?"

"These aren't the real old ones you've read about. One of the old ones, St. Louis Number Two, is just a couple blocks out of our way to the hotel. If you like, I'll swing by there and let you take a quick gander."

"Okay." I almost laughed out loud. I remembered my mother saying "taking a gander" at something, a Southernism for taking a glimpse. "I read in a guidebook that you should never go to the old cemeteries alone. Are they really that dangerous?"

"Yes'um, they are, so don't you be doin' that, no. I ain't gonna stop, just cruise by and let you get a look. Even in the daytime, you don't want to venture near 'em, unless you with a group. You need to get on one of the guided tours to visit 'em properly. They're right interestin'."

The cabbie kept up a line of chatter about the sights I needed to see in his hometown. He pulled off the interstate near the cemetery.

A brick wall surrounded the graveyard. LaRondell slowed in front of an iron gate, where a man in a red wife beater was selling tee shirts.

"Seems like I'm the only one in N'Awlins not sellin' souvenir tees." The cabbie chuckled.

Through the gate I gaped at a city of the dead. Row after row of ornate tombs flanked narrow paths laid out like streets. I moved closer the window to get a better look.

As I twisted in the seat, I looked out the rear of the cab. Slipping along slowly in our wake was a dirty tan sedan, a hatchet-faced man at the wheel. When we'd left the airport, I'd thought the skinny man might be simply returning to the city, but now it was obvious he was following us.

"This place so wet, we don't bury people, les' they pop right back up." LaRondell laughed. "Out at your fam'ly's place, they have their own cemetery…like with most of the old homes."

"Do the ones outside the city have the aboveground tombs, too?" I was nervous about the man tailing us but didn't comment on it. Maybe he had a beef with LaRondell.

The driver slowed to a stop and turned in the seat to face me.

He must have seen the sedan behind us, but he gave no indication other than drawing his brows together. "*Mais ye*. It's wet all around N'Awlins. If we didn't put folks in these tombs, we have a big rain storm, like with Katrina, we have coffins in the streets, along wi' snakes and 'gators."

"Oooh." I made a face at the image his words conjured, and he bellowed his rich laugh.

When he pulled onto Canal Street, I gawked. Three, or was it four, lanes were marked for traffic...but vehicles churned in at least five lanes. The wide boulevard looked like something I'd seen in pictures of cities in the Middle East. A few camels and donkey carts wouldn't be noticed. Cars and SUVs of all sizes vied for space with trucks, motorcycles, Mopeds, bicycles, and people on rollerskates. The closer we got to the Mississippi River, the more crowded the street became. People carrying what LaRondell told me were called *geaux* cups, pronounced "go," filled with cocktails, wove in and out of the traffic, paying no attention to the vehicles.

Again, I swiveled around to see if I could spy the dirty sedan. There it was, three cars back. The man from the airport was definitely following us. He didn't know me, so he had to be looking for a fight with LaRondell. Considering the cabbie's size, the other man was on a fool's errand for sure.

The people swarming the street wore everything from bikini outfits to evening dress, even though it was only late afternoon. Some even wore costumes, although it wasn't the season for Mardi Gras.

The driver rolled down the window and hollered to a bearded man wearing a pink tutu. "Yo, Maxie, whereyat?"

"Yo," the man yelled back. "I see you at Tipitina's, me. Later."

LaRondell rolled the window back up. "Tipitina's is a blues club. Sort of a landmark. You won't want to miss it."

I held my breath when we made the U-turn across the neutral ground, as the median separating the traffic lanes on Canal Street is called, and crossed the street car tracks. The driver drove as though he expected cars to get out of his way as he executed a tricky maneuver that brought us into the right lane to enter the Canal Street Marriott's parking garage.

"Here we are. Safe and sound." LaRondell handed me from the cab and waited as a covey of valets unloaded my bags. "I've enjoyed havin' you for a customer, ma'am, and I do expect you'll enjoy your visit to our city." He handed me a business card. "You be needin' a driver, just give me a call."

I thanked him and gave him a generous tip, saying nothing about the man in the dirty sedan. He was not my problem, and LaRondell was certainly big enough to look out for himself. I felt safe now that we'd reached the Marriott. The place had Security, and I would keep my door locked.

Chapter 2

I checked into the hotel and was quickly whisked up to my room. The friendliness of the service people amazed me. They all acted as though they were delighted to have me visit their city. My mother had left me well-situated financially, and I could have afforded one of the small boutique hotels, but the big, elegant Marriott was conveniently located and had all the amenities, and it wasn't like I was planning to take up residence in the place.

I'd brought only a few clothes with me, so it didn't take me long to settle in. I showered and picked out something to wear to dinner.

Claude Landrieu, the St. Cyr family lawyer, had told me he would be out of town a couple of days but would pick me at the hotel Monday morning, so I was on my own this Saturday night and all day tomorrow. I was actually looking forward to prowling around the Quarter and playing tourist before settle down to the business of being an heiress.

Not sure of the dress code, for Dickie Brennan's Palace Café, if any, I'd donned a pair of black pants with a bright cranberry stripe running through the fabric and a sheer black and cranberry print shirt, adorned with sequins, worn over a slinky camisole matching the stripe in the pants. The outfit was dressy, but not too.

As I left the hotel, a warm mist was dampening the streets, and the August sky was still light, beginning to turn a deep blue. A *mélange* of tourists and locals milled about under the Marriott's *porte cochère*. Lights glowed all along Canal Street, street lights, varicolored lights on the buildings, the stores and hotels, Harrah's Casino. The wide boulevard glittered like a carnival midway.

Dodging tourists with shopping bags, *geaux* cups in hand, I started up the block toward the restaurant.

I noticed an old woman, with prune-like skin, standing on the corner. She wore a black blouse and a multicolored skirt that hung to her ankles and held a corncob pipe between her gums. Some kind of amulet dangled around her wrinkled neck, and a dozen gold bangles decorated each scaly wrist. Even in the motley crowd common to the streets of New Orleans, the crone stood out.

She stepped into my path, blocking my way and staring at me curiously. I almost stumbled to avoid walking into her. One of her eyes was milky, the iris invisible. The old woman did not accost me or say a word to me. Her stare was unnerving. She cocked her head to favor her good eye, and I was reminded of a large, ugly bird, as she leaned toward me peering one-eyed. She studied me as though she were memorizing my features.

Her breath smelled of tobacco and rot.

I flinched from her.

Even though she had stepped into my path, not the other way around, I mumbled an apology and moved around the odd creature. I looked over my shoulder and saw her continuing to track me with one bloodshot eye. I averted my gaze, avoiding making any further eye contact with her, and hurried toward the restaurant.

When I stepped from the curb, I heard a hiss behind me. "St. Cyr." I whirled around.

The old hag had vanished.

I was sure I heard her whisper my name...or at least I thought I heard her. Perhaps the sound had just been a trick of my ears in the foot traffic squishing on the rain-damp *banquette*, as the New Orleans sidewalks are called. A chill ran up my spine.

Chapter 3

Dickie Brennan's Palace Café was hardly the bistro the name implied. The restaurant was multilevel, with an air of casual elegance, so my outfit was appropriate. I was seated at a table near a front window. I asked for a Bloody Mary to sip while I perused the menu of exotic sounding food. I took my time and admired the original artworks decorating the restaurant's walls. The wall-sized paintings displayed famous characters from the Big Easy's past.

The Crab Claws Bordelaise and the Café Spinach Salad appealed to me for starters. Something called Shrimp Tchefuncte sounded intriguing as an entrée. I wanted to save room for the pecan pie that, wondering if it was as good as Mama's. A bottle of a moderately-priced *sauvignon blanc* could accompany the entire meal.

My seat facing Canal Street afforded a perfect site from which to watch the crowds meandering along the wide boulevard. While flying across the country, I'd read a current New Orleans guidebook. The more I read, the more fascinated I became by the City that Care Forgot. It was hot, humid, dirty, and stinky, but I was already falling in love with the place.

I settled back with my cocktail.

Louisiana was like a foreign country to me. Mama had never talked about the home she left so long ago. I'd leapt into the future in a place I knew little about. Instinctively I knew I belonged here, and here I would stay.

I pondered some of the tasks ahead of me. I had no idea what awaited me at this plantation I'd inherited, but it was mine. The cab driver had mentioned a family cemetery. Now I had a place for my mother's ashes, where she belonged, with her husband and my ancestors. I would have her cremains shipped with the rest of my things. Cemeteries never held much interest for me, but there was something morbidly fascinating about a graveyard full of my ancestors.

I propped my chin on my fist and gazed out the window. Beyond my reflection, people meandered and cavorted along the wet sidewalk.

The heat and the light mist of rain created a sauna in the sultry New Orleans air. The humid heat combined with the coolness of the cafe's air conditioning caused the windows to be frosted like the tall glass holding my cocktail. Droplets wriggled down the glass panes, making the street scene waver.

I glanced up from the crab claw appetizer the server placed in front of me and saw the old woman I'd encountered outside the hotel. The old hag stood just beyond the cluster of empty bistro tables in front of the restaurant. The unmistakable figure appeared wavy in the condensation running down the glass. *What is she doing here, standing outside in the drizzle?* I looked away, not wanting to make eye contact with her. When I looked back, she'd disappeared again. I shivered and pulled my light blouse-jacket closer around myself, and finished my appetizer. I wouldn't let her appearance unnerve me. She was just another of New Orleans's infamous street people. All big cities had them. Surely she wasn't following me. This notion brought to mind the unsavory-looking man who had tailed my taxi from the airport.

The two things had to be coincidences. Nobody had any reason to follow me.

I nearly choked on the final bite of the shrimp in *meuniere* sauce, when I looked up and saw the woman again. The old witch had come closer to the window and appeared to be mouthing something at me. I grabbed my napkin and held it to my lips. She made a curious sign in the air with her fingers, pointing at me, while shaking the amulet she wore.

"Are you all right, ma'am?" The waiter materialized at my elbow. "Is there something wrong with the food?"

I blinked my eyes against the glare of the multicolored lights of vehicles and advertising signs on Canal Street. Because of the moisture beading on the windows, I saw the scene as though looking through warped antique glass.

The woman had vanished again.

"No." I shook my head. "I thought I saw someone. No. I *did* see someone. I'm sure of it." *Am I?*

Okay…I'd enjoyed a Bloody Mary and most of a bottle of wine. Now I was seeing things, or imagining I was. Good thing I didn't have to drive back to the hotel. The pecan pie and the rest of the wine still needed to be consumed.

"A friend, someone you know? The *banquettes* are busy at this time of evening."

"This might sound a little crazy." I turned toward the young man. "But there's been some old woman standing outside, and it looks like she's talking to me and making strange signs."

The server chuckled. "It's just Annie Lebeau." He scraped the French bread crumbs on the table cloth into his palm. "I'll be happy to close the curtains if you like. A lot of people like to sit by the windows and people-watch." He made as if to close the curtains, but I stopped him.

"No. It's my first trip to New Orleans, and I'm enjoying doing just that, people-watching. I was just starting to feel like I'm going crazy. I see the old woman one moment. I blink, and she's gone."

"You're not crazy…*she* is. She's an old Hoodoo woman. Lives out on Bayou Ombre…or Shadow Bayou, as it's called in English… comes into town just to hustle the tourists."

I felt the hair rise on my neck. "Shadow Bayou. Do you know where it is?"

"Of course. I'm a N'Awlins native," he drawled. "It's up the river about twenty miles, just across a creek where Frenchy's Landing's located." He had a coffee-with-cream complexion and eyes a shade of greenish-gray. His hair was a cap of light brown, tight curls.

New Orleans held a large number of citizens of mixed race... mulatto, quadroon, octoroon. I wondered which one he was... and how did people keep that sort of thing straight? "Is Frenchy's Landing a town?"

"A small one. It used to be a place the trappers brought their furs to from the swamps so they could be shipped downriver to N'Awlins."

"You said this Annie was a 'Hoodoo woman.' What's that?"

"Hoodoo, Voodoo," he said. "Whatever you want to call it. Some people consider it a religion."

"Isn't it more like some kind of black magic?"

"In a way, I guess you could call it that. Hoodoo came here from Africa with the first black slaves and got a big dollop of Catholicism dumped into it. The people who still practice it pray to the Catholic saints, right along with working spells with the African gods. You'd be surprised at how many people still believe in it." He straightened the folds in the hand towel on his arm. "Some use it to cast spells on people...or claim to, anyway." He flashed a smile, as if to say, *you can believe what you want.*

"And this Annie person practices this *Hoodoo*?"

"*Mais ye*, it's not too uncommon, mostly among people who live way out in the swamps," he explained. "She claims to be a descendant of Marie Laveau."

"I've read about her...famous witch or something?"

"Voodoo priestess, actually." He gave a short laugh. "If all the local Hoodoo believers who claim to be descended from her were real, that poor old woman would've had to have birthed about two hundred kids."

The server's assistant brought the pecan pie, and the server poured the rest of my wine.

I took a bite of the dessert. "Oh, my God. This is divine." I closed my eyes in ecstasy.

"I'm glad you like it. It's one of our specialties."

"It's every bit as good as my mama's." I dabbed my lips with my napkin. "Go on with your story about that Voodoo queen or whatever she was. I'm fascinated."

"Well, to say the least, old Marie Laveau didn't have two hundred babies," he went on. "In fact, she had only one daughter, same name as her mama, Marie. She toddled around town with her mother and later joined her mama in doing ladies' hair."

"She was a hairdresser?"

The young man's eyes sparkled when he laughed. "I guess she liked to have something to fall back on if there were lean times in the Voodoo business."

"I read about some country music singer who did the same thing," I told him.

"There's plenty of literature around town about Marie Laveau, and you can visit her tomb if you want to, but only go with a tour group. Our cemeteries are famous, but don't ever go into them alone."

"My cab driver told me the same thing about the cemeteries."

"There are some gangs who prey on the tourists who go there alone, so don't ever do that." He picked up my plate, which now held nothing but crumbs. "Can I get you a cup of coffee to top off your meal…something with a chocolate topping?"

Chapter 4

Annie Lebeau was nowhere in sight when I left the restaurant, heading back to my hotel. The old woman was probably off annoying some other hapless tourist.

I waded into the throng, people moving toward me, alongside me, away from me, carrying me along with them. I felt like I was caught up in some human stream, gently buffeted from all sides, gliding along with little of my own volition. A big city girl, I kept my purse clutched tightly to my abdomen.

I had no doubt the *banquette* was as crowded at nearly ten o'clock at night as it had been at two o'clock in the afternoon or ten o'clock in the morning. Clearly, New Orleans was a city that never slept. The crowd thinned out, and I tottered on my spike heels the block or so back to the Marriott, squinting against the glare from the car lights and the lights spilling out of the stores along the short route. Apparently, Canal Street was lit up like a parade was in progress every night, all year long, and was just as noisy. Crowds of people laughed and jostled each other, meandering in both directions all along the *banquette* and right out into the lanes of traffic. Some carried *geaux* cups of liquor or were weighed down with shopping bags, even at this hour.

A new influx of people surged from Chartres Street, and I almost stumbled into a big, redheaded man decked out in frizzy dreads and wearing a New Orleans Saints black and gold jersey. He laughed and apologized, although the blunder had been my fault.

Whew! I was about half in the bag. Disoriented, I wanted to stand still for just a moment and get my bearings, but that wasn't possible, with all the people jockeying for position on the *banquette*. Something akin to exhaustion swept over me. I hated flying, and the trip had been a long one. I felt as if I had sucked in a breath back in Seattle and held it until I felt the plane's wheels touch down in New Orleans. I was tired, and now I was drunk.

Mama would not approve. I giggled at the notion and put my fingers over my lips, lest somebody notice how snockered I was. Then I laughed out loud. *This is New Orleans...nobody will notice or care if I'm as drunk as an old sailor.*

"At least all that booze should guarantee me a good night's sleep." *Did I just say that out loud?* I cut my eyes left and right. Nobody was paying any attention to one more half-plastered tourist.

I approached the big glass doors on the Marriott's front. The sibilant sound of my name...*St. Cyr*...hissed, as if coming from a snake.

I whirled around and almost fell on my face.

"Whoa...there, ma'am...those spike heels don't work real good on these slick streets."

Strong arms gripped me above my elbows, and I stared up into a smiling black face. The Marriott's liveried doorman had caught me before I hit the pavement.

"Oh, I must have caught my heel." Past his shoulder, I caught a glimpse of Annie Lebeau, her gnarled fingers again working strange air signs in my direction. The old woman was shaking that amulet at me again and mouthing something, grinning maliciously around her few teeth.

The doorman held me by both arms. I shook my head, as if to dispel the disquieting vision of the old witch. I stuttered a nervous laugh and huffed out a breath. I allowed myself to be guided, all the while on the lookout for the old hag, who had disappeared again into the crowd.

"Let's get you up these steps." The man's grip was strong but gentle. He was laughing, and I had a feeling he had helped many a half-drunk tourist into the hotel. "You gon' be walkin' much in our city, ma'am, you best be wearin' flat shoes or just takin' a cab instead."

The shoes had not caused me to lose my balance. I was discombobulated by the combination of the liquor I'd consumed and by the spookiness of the woman I feared was stalking me.

Why is this old bag following me?

The doorkeeper helped me up the steps and into the hotel's massive lobby, where he handed me off to another attendant, who walked me to the elevator and saw that I got to my room in one piece. "I think you be needin' that first thing in the a.m., ma'am." He nodded toward a small corner table. "Complimentary coffee right over there. Plenty of ice water in the fridge, too."

Feeling foolish at getting so ripped, I thanked him for his help.

"If you want anything else, just give us a call." Grinning, the man refused a tip for his help and insured that my door was locked as he left.

When the valet left, I sagged onto the bed. "Jesus…I'm drunk as a skunk." I was thankful again the service people in New Orleans seemed to be exceptionally friendly.

I fixed myself a glass of ice water and guzzled it. I needed something to dilute all that booze. I didn't have much tolerance for alcohol…something inherited from Mama. One of few things she had told me about my father was that he "drank a bit," as she delicately put it. Like her, I was mostly a moderate drinker.

By the time I finished the second glass of water and got undressed, I felt like I could shower without falling on my face. I scrubbed off my makeup, showered, and toweled myself dry. Standing naked at the lavatory, I brushed my teeth. I was still a bit unsteady. As I reached for one of the hotel glasses to rinse out my mouth, the glass slipped from my fingers and broke on the countertop.

I tried to gather up the shards and cut myself. "Ouch. Shit."

Blood spurted from a slice on my forefinger. The red stream ran down my arm onto the countertop. I swiped at the mess with tissues.

Cursing, I grabbed a cotton ball out of a plastic bag, sank down onto the toilet seat, and pressed the cotton to my wound.

I leaned back against the toilet tank. Tired and aggravated.

I left Seattle at seven-thirty this morning and arrived in New Orleans at five-thirty. Less than six hours in this town, and I'd been stalked by a nutcase, accosted by a crazy Hoodoo woman, gotten drunk all by myself, and nearly cut my finger off.

What else is going to happen to me in this place?

"Welcome to N'Awlins."

Chapter 5

The next morning I fumbled my way out of bed and into the shower, surprised that my hangover wasn't worse than I'd expected. I gulped down four Ibuprofens. My mouth tasted like I'd been sucking on dirty gym socks, and I felt just a tad fuzzy. I don't usually drink coffee, so I'd brought packets of hot chocolate with me to wash down the daily supply of vitamins Mama always insisted on.

First on my Sunday agenda was mass at St. Louis Cathedral, then the jazz brunch at The Court of the Two Sisters. The rest of the afternoon, I planned to prowl in the shops of the French Quarter.

I shampooed my hair in the shower and dried it, while I drank my chocolate. Mass was at eleven, and I had plenty of time to make the six- or seven-block hike to the church.

By the time I'd dressed in a pair of jeans and a bright green tee shirt and had my makeup and hair done, I was feeling almost human. Along with Mama's six-carat diamond bauble I always wore on my right-hand ring finger, I slipped a heavy emerald ring on the right middle finger and a diamond pinky ring on my left hand. Little diamond ear studs completed my jewelry. I cocked my head at my reflection I the mirror and admired my bling. I love jewelry.

The hotel concierge had told me that casual attire was permitted in the churches in New Orleans and in the restaurants during the day. In keeping with the admonition from the doorman the previous night, I wore flat sandals.

Stepping out of the hotel, the sunlight was so bright I had to put on my sunglasses. The day looked like it would be beautiful, no cold, misty drizzle like I'd left in Seattle. I breathed deeply. Even in the morning, New Orleans had its own delightfully funky smell.

The streets were already crowded, and many of the bars I passed didn't look as if they'd closed all night, doors open onto the *banquette*. In one dive I passed, a couple of patrons sat at the bar eating fast food breakfasts and drinking beer. A man lay on the floor beside them, passed out. A pink-dyed toy poodle was eating out of a bowl on the countertop.

I stepped around a couple of men sitting on the curb sharing a bottle of Mad Dog 20-20. One man's skin was ebony; the other's milk white, though his hair was black and tightly curled against the part of his skull that wasn't shaved into the trademark New Orleans *fleur de lis*. My attention on the two men, I almost plowed into a woman who was clearly a "lady of the evening." She was tall and skinny and wore denim shorts with fishnet stockings held up by black lace garters. Sky-high wedgies, and a gold lame halter top completed her outlandish ensemble. Her black hair was a frizzy topknot and her skin the color of coffee with cream.

"Whereyat?" The woman addressed the men on the curb, as I stopped for a moment to look at my phone map.

"Who dat, *cher*. Ain't seen ya. Where ya stayin'?" The dark man flashed a gold-toothed smile.

"New crib in Treme." Deftly balancing a cup of coffee so she wouldn't spill it, the woman plopped down on the filthy curb with the men, her bony knees up to her chin. She reached inside her halter and pulled out a joint. Using a gold lighter, one of the men lit it for her in a surprisingly gentlemanly fashion, and the three of them shared the marijuana.

Nobody seemed to notice, or care, that they were openly smoking dope. After the blandness of Seattle, New Orleans was definitely a culture shock.

Glancing up, I used my hand to shield my eyes from the sun, as I admired the buildings with balconies overlooking the street. Some of these galleries held bistro tables, chairs, and potted tropical plants. People, still in their night clothes, sat under table umbrellas, having breakfast and reading the *Times-Picayune*, oblivious to the passers-by only a few feet beneath them. I glanced at my watch and stepped up my pace along Decatur Street, so I wouldn't be late for mass.

I passed the Jax Brewery building and turned left a couple blocks later, on the street bordering Jackson Square. Artists had already set up their outdoor shops in front of the church. Original paintings covered the fence around the park.

I've always had a fondness for old churches, and St. Louis Cathedral was awesome, its architecture and interior decorations bedizened with all manner of Baroque angels, harkening back to another era and even another country. After mass, I wandered around the huge church, admiring the incredible art work and the opulent decor. The nuns at the parochial school I attended had seen to it that my Latin was sufficient to read many of the inscriptions.

When I left the church, I automatically scanned the crowd surrounding Jackson Square. I sighed with relief when I saw no sign of Annie Lebeau. Maybe the old gal slept in on Sunday mornings.

I ambled down Pirate's Alley over to Royal Street and The Court of the Two Sisters, where I had reservations for the famous jazz brunch. The restaurant boasts the largest courtyard in the French Quarter, and the hostess led me to a table near a fountain. A large blackbird promptly perched on the back of the chair to my right. I tried shooing the creature away, but he gave me a look that told me he had dibs on the table.

Tiny lights were strung in the trees that grew up through the paving stones of the courtyard. I wondered why the owners didn't put a screen over the trees to keep the birds out. I wasn't crazy about sharing space with them.

My waiter approached and must have seen the expression on my face. He flapped his towel at the bird, who retreated to a tree limb. "Don't mind them. They're simply part of the *lagniappe*, or something a little extra, in the French manner."

"Birds aren't exactly litter box trained."

He raised an eyebrow. "This *is* N'Awlins."

His expression told me that explanation should be sufficient, so I let any further remarks slide and settled into the chair he held for me.

"My name's Sam, and I'll be looking after you today, ma'amzelle." He fetched me a glass of ice water while I perused the menu, deciding to try the brunch buffet.

I ordered a half carafe of white wine and allowed Sam to lead me back inside to the buffet line. I looked behind me and saw the avian demon had returned to my table. Not only that, but he calmly crapped right on the tablecloth, all the while eyeing me as if daring me to object.

"I'll change the tablecloth while you visit the buffet," my server told me, shaking his head. "Pick up a few shrimp on the buffet and give him the tails. Sultan will leave you alone if you give him a nibble or two."

"Sultan?"

"That's what we call him. He thinks he rules the place. Like I said, just give the old boy a little nibble, and he'll behave himself."

I gave the blackbird a nasty look, which he returned. After the meal I'd eaten the night before, I was surprised that my mouth was watering from the smells of the enormous spread laid out. I passed on the omelet station and moved on to the sliced rare roast beef and the spicy shrimp *etouffee*, the Creole shrimp and grits. I tried to decide between the crawfish and spinach pasta and the crab and spinach quiche, so I got a little of each.

An industrial-sized scoop was provided to shovel cold boiled shrimp onto your plate. I love boiled shrimp, and the restaurant had several dipping sauces to choose from. I got enough shrimp to share with the bird.

The smells from the table of freshly baked breads were incredible. Then there was the dessert selection. I ignored both for now and added a serving of salad greens to my plate.

Once I was seated back at my table, the blackbird perched across from me. As Sam suggested, I tossed the creature a shrimp tail onto the paving stones. The bird swooped to gobble up his treat and left me alone as long as I gave him the occasional handout.

While I ate, Sam stopped by and chatted with me. "I'm not a native...moved here from Dallas ten years ago. I love the city. I act in a theatrical troupe." Like the other service people I'd met so far, he was far more loquacious than his Seattle counterparts. "Our next gig is a play at one of the old mansions upriver...a ghost and murder play staged in a house on Shadow Bayou."

"My family's from Shadow Bayou ...the St. Cyrs."

A frown flickered across his freckled face. "St. Cyr?"

"You know them?"

"No, ma'am...but I know of them. Your family's well known." His tone was polite but guarded, his reaction much like that of the cab driver I'd met yesterday. Apprehension tingled up my spine. *What do people react to my family's name this way?*

I passed on dessert and paid my bill. I gathered my tote bag and left, fighting down the urge to let loose an unladylike burp.

Chapter 6

O n Royal Street, I looked left and right. Even on Sunday, the street was working alive with people. Before I started prowling the shops, I needed to call Claude Landrieu and let him know I'd arrived. I found a park bench right across the street from a building that discretely advertised itself as a police station. The renovated mansion certainly didn't look like any police station I'd ever seen, but then, as I was learning, "This *is* N'Awlins."

I dug the phone out of my tote and punched in a number.

"M'sieu Claude's looking forward to seeing you again after all these years," the woman who answered the phone told me when I identified myself.

The lawyer's name had been tickling my memory ever since I'd seen his signature on the letter. "He knows me?"

"*Mais ye*, but he hasn't seen you since you were a *bebe*, so he's so excited about seeing you."

Something tightened inside me. This man had known me when I was a child.

"And Sharla…she's about to bust a gut, her."

A memory slammed into my brain. A pretty caramel-skinned woman, with eyes like bright turquoise jewels. I could hear her voice, singing to me in French. I could smell her skin, feel the softness of her body. Sharla. My beloved nanny. How could I have forgotten her? "Sharla?" My voice sounded strangled. "Where is she?"

"Why she's at Shadow Cove, *cher*, where she's always been, and she's dying to see her *bebe* again," the woman who had herself as the Landrieu housekeeper Dihanne Forchet told me.

"Oh," was all I could manage. Claude and Sharla, only wisps of memories from my childhood, people my mother would never mention, along with anything else pertaining to our old life in Louisiana.

"Your *oncle* Claude was so sorry he had to be out of town when you arrived," the Forchet woman said. "He will be in late tonight and will fetch you at the hotel tomorrow morning as planned."

"He offered to have a car pick me up at the airport," I told her, "but I told him I'd be fine using a cab, so if picking me up is any inconvenience...."

"*Mais, non, non, non.*" Her laughter tinkled. "*M'sieu* doesn't want to fret on you gettin' lost, him. *Non.*"

I smiled at her friendly tone. The way she sprinkled French words into her speech, her curious way of turning a phrase reminded me of my mother's way of speaking.

We finished our conversation, and I had to just sit for a few moments, my heart thudding, while I sorted out what I'd heard. The people the housekeeper had mentioned. I'd known them, and they'd known me well. She'd referred to the lawyer as my <u>oncle</u>, uncle, Claude. These people had been my family, and my mother had never talked about them. Why?

Tucking my phone away, I got to my feet and ambled down Royal Street, forcing my thoughts to focus on the present...for the moment anyway. I browsed in the antique stores and gift shops, most of which were open on Sunday. In a shop specializing in estate jewelry, I spied some beautiful gold and diamond earrings set in a *fleur de lis* design. I couldn't resist them. Besides, I needed a keepsake to celebrate my return to my native soil.

On the next block, in an art gallery, a charming young man, his inky black hair pulled into a glossy ponytail, gave me a tour of the store. He told me his favorite painting was one of King David crying. I agreed that the portrait was certainly unique.

I picked up a couple of tee shirts at a shop on the corner of Toulouse. I also bought a package of pralines. I missed my mama's pralines. I crammed everything into my tote and hefted it onto my shoulder, as I headed down Royal once more.

The day couldn't be more beautiful. The sun was glorious. The air smelled of the flowers blooming in pots set out on the *banquettes* and the spicy foods cooking in the restaurants that seemed to be almost as numerous as the bars. The bars had their own sweaty, sour smells that wafted out of open doors, along with the strains of everything from Dixieland Jazz to old Motown and rap. Underneath this *mélange* of aromas was the smell of the big river itself. You couldn't get away from it. The faint odor redolent of fish and garbage. It was a unique New Orleans smell and reminded me of long ago afternoons in the Quarter with Mama. Everyone seemed to gravitate toward this oldest part of the ancient city.

Smiling to myself, I thought it would be cool if I ran into one of the celebrities who frequented the area...movie stars, musicians.

Trying to decide where to go next, I pulled my phone out of my tote and checked my map. I looked up. Annie Lebeau glared at me from the opposite side of the street.

Chapter 7

I consider myself a pretty nonconfrontational sort of person, but this was ridiculous. That old sow was stalking me, and I had no idea why.

"Crazy old bat," I hissed and shoved the phone back into my bag. I hiked the tote higher onto my left shoulder and gripped the straps with a white-knuckled fist. Anger pulled my lips into a tight line. My heartbeat quickened as I started across the street, heading in Annie Lebeau's direction. I was going to find out why this old hussy was skulking around behind me.

Somebody grabbed hold of my tote so violently I was nearly jerked off my feet. In my fury, I'd tightened my grip, so I automatically yanked my bag toward myself. The black youth hanging onto my gear slammed into my body, and I was assaulted by his pungent body odor. I elbowed the creep away from me, but he hung on like he had fish hooks for fingers. I stumbled and almost lost my footing on the uneven stones of the *banquette*, dragging the kid with me in an awkward dance.

He was about fourteen, wearing his street uniform of baggy

shorts with his underdrawers showing, unlaced sneakers, and a wife beater with BADASS printed on the front. He used both hands to grapple with the big canvas carry-all, trying to wrest it from my grip

In a split second, without even thinking, I shot out my right fist and clipped him under his left eye. "Get away from me!" The big emerald ring on my right hand opened a gash in his face. I slammed another blow into the side of his head, cutting him again. Blood streamed down his face.

"Bitch!" He hollered and fell to one knee on the rough paving stones, grabbing his face where I'd hit him. He lunged and clawed at me, his britches sliding down towards his now bloody knees.

I danced away from him, causing the next unseen blow to hit off center on my back. Otherwise, the shove would have knocked me down.

Without even looking, I rammed my left elbow backward and slammed it into another body. I whirled around and faced off with a boy of about twelve, silver pegs piercing both ears, a grinning skull emblazoned on his black tee shirt.

The kid screeched and stumbled away, holding both hands to his battered, bloody nose, mumbling curses.

Pain shot upward from my knuckles. I shook the hand that had done the damage, but I wasn't about to back down. "Get away from me, you little bastards," I snarled.

A third boy, maybe fourteen, awkwardly cavorted around his two buddies and this small woman who was whipping their butts. He looked like he wasn't sure he wanted to continue the assault. He shook a headful of dreads at me and backed away, holding his open palms out to his sides, eyes wide, gold-capped teeth bared. I'd wrapped the strap of the tote around my wrist and swung it to use as a weapon as I headed toward him. The thing weighed a ton, and I might've decapitated him had he not decided flight was the better part of valor and turned tail and fled.

The first attacker yelled at me, "You ho' dawg cunt." He tried to get to his feet, stumbled over his britches and fell again, and scuttled on the pavement like a black crab.

I lunged toward him, swinging the tote. "Get away from me, you little asshole. I'll bash your head in."

Cursing me soundly, the trio of thugs staggered off down the street, the youngest one leaving a trail of blood in his wake.

I snapped my head to the right to look back across the street. Annie Lebeau had disappeared.

Several people had stopped to watch the attack but did nothing except stare. A couple of them had their phones out filming the entire fracas. Panting, I glared at them. "Assholes," I muttered at the rubberneckers, not caring if they heard me.

I clutched the tote bag to my breast, using both hands to hold onto it like it was a life jacket. I was shaking like I'd just been tumbled in a concrete mixer. I took a deep breath to calm myself, glad I'd taken the doorman's advice from last night and worn flat sandals. Otherwise, I had no doubt I would be face down in the gutter right now, my bag and all my money and credit cards stolen.

Chapter 8

"**A**re you all right, ma'am?"

I turned to face a light-skinned, neatly dressed black man, of perhaps sixty, about six feet tall and fit for his age. A constellation of tiny moles dotted his tan skin on either side of his nose, and his gray-green eyes mirrored his concern.

He placed his hand on my elbow, as if ready to support me in case I chose this moment to do the ladylike thing and faint. He shook an ornate walking cane in the direction of the boys' retreating backs and hollered something in French. I didn't understand the words, probably a profanity or two.

"Yes. I'm fine. Thank you." I huffed to catch my breath. My heart was still pounding. I don't usually relish being touched by strangers, but the warmth of his hand on my arm was comforting. His fingers were strong, and I could see corded muscles running up his arm. He wore nicely pressed trousers and a short-sleeved, yellow, window-pane checked shirt.

"Those little thugs don't normally operate this close to the police station." He nodded toward the building nearby on the opposite side of the street. "That boy's ears gon' be ringin' like the bells in St. Louis church, and the other one'll need a nose job. You packed quite a wallop."

"I guess when you're as small as I am, your survival instinct tells you to shoot to kill…so to speak."

"Why don't you step inside my shop right here and sit down for a moment," he suggested. Keeping his hand under my elbow, he navigated me into a small bistro. "I'll treat you to a cup of coffee or a little glass of wine." He nodded toward the back of the shop. "The Ladies' Room is right that way, if you'd like to freshen up."

"Thank you." I took a deep breath. "Umm. I'd like just a glass of ice water, please, if you don't mind." I followed his directions back to the restrooms.

Leaning on the lavatory, I studied my reflection in the mirror. My face was flushed and sweaty, so I wet a paper towel and held it against my skin. I let the cold water run over my wrists to help me calm down. The necessities taken care of, I returned to the main room.

The small deli-type shop had a couple of bistro tables set out on the *banquette*, but I chose a seat at a table just inside the open French doors.

My rescuer puttered behind the counter that ran the length of the bistro. Mardi Gras masks were arranged around an ornate mirror on the wall behind him, flanked on either side by glass shelves holding bottles of wine and containers of gourmet coffees. The other walls were decorated with posters advertising the annual Jazz and Heritage Festival and a couple of other upcoming entertainment events. A pair of large oil paintings depicting the bayou country hung on one wall.

In a moment, the shopkeeper returned with a tray holding my glass of ice water, in addition to two glasses of red wine and a piece of soft cheese and some crackers and a spreader. He deftly balanced the tray in one hand, while using the other to hold his walking stick. He moved with a slight limp. "I hate to see a visitor to our fair city getting a poor opinion of us." He seated himself across from me and stretched out his left leg.

"Thank you so much." I gratefully drank down most of the glass of water in one gulp.

"My name is Roland Dubois," he said. "My wife Giselle and I own this little shop."

"It's very nice." A garden of potted tropical plants encircled a tiny fountain in one corner, and the ubiquitous ceiling fan turned slowly in the early afternoon air. Like many of the French Quarter shops, the bistro relied on ceiling fans and open French doors to keep the inside cool. A couple seated across the room were having a snack, and a man seated alone at another table was drinking coffee and reading a newspaper. None of them appeared to have witnessed the attack on me. Of course, it happened very fast and was over just as quickly. My heart rate had slowed, and my breathing was back to normal. I sipped the wine. "This is delicious."

"It's a very nice St. Emilion, one of my favorites, in fact. We sell a select number of special wines and cheeses and deli meats, some special-order coffees." He nodded toward the counter. "We like to keep our merchandise unique, so we get more business from the local people than from the tourists."

"This is my first visit to New Orleans since I was a child," I told him. "Oh...I'm sorry...my name is Laurette St. Cyr."

He paused in taking a sip of his wine. "I suspected that's who you were when I first saw you."

I set my glass down. "What?"

"Don't look so alarmed. I know your family well and heard you were comin' to town." He chuckled and flapped his hand in dismissal. "You have the look of the St. Cyrs stamped all over that beautiful face. I would've recognized you anywhere."

I felt my face flushing. *Now that he rescued me, is he trying to hit on me?* My expression must've reflected my thoughts.

He raised his eyebrows. "Now don't go lookin' at me like that, *ma petite, non.* I have a daughter about your age. Your father and I were old friends." He nodded toward the cheese. "Eat a little bit. It'll help as the adrenalin rush subsides." His eyes crinkled. "Trust me on that."

"You knew my daddy?" This information relieved my suspicions a bit, but I wasn't ready to let down my guard. I spread a little cheese on a cracker and nibbled it. I wasn't really hungry after that huge brunch, but I ate just to be polite. It was the wine and the water I really needed.

"*Mais ye*. Etienne and I went to school together, friends all our lives. I still have family on Bayou Ombre."

My mother used the term *mais ye*, and I knew it meant *but yes* or *certainly* in the Creole and Cajun dialect.

He nodded toward me. "Please accept my condolences on your father's passin'. He was a better man than many people realized."

What a curious thing to say.

"I was honored to deliver one of the eulogies at his funeral." He sighed. "He will be missed. He was a fine man, but in many ways I suppose his passin' was for the better."

"Why do you say that?" Strangely enough, I felt a twinge of grief at his mentioning my father's death, the father I barely remembered. It was nice to know this man had a kind word for him. Tears welled in my eyes, but I fought them down.

"As you might know…or maybe you don't…he had been…well, ill…for a number of years."

"Actually, I don't know anything about him. How was he ill? Did he have cancer or something?"

He didn't answer my question, but instead drew his brows together, causing furrows to plow across his forehead. "What about your mother, Celine Renard? Is your *mama* still alive?"

"No." I swallowed the lump that suddenly clogged my throat. "My mother died only a short time ago, earlier this year, a cranial aneurism. I found her on the kitchen floor." I grabbed a napkin and dabbed the tear that slipped from my eye. "She was only forty six."

"*Pauvre bebe*," Roland patted my hand. "As with your father's family, I knew your mother and am acquainted with most of the Renards, too." He cocked his head. "So you're all alone?"

"Just me."

He twitched his lip in a cryptic smile. "Just you and the rest of the St. Cyr family and the Renards." He eyed his wine glass and turned it around on the table a couple of times. "Bless your heart."

I'd heard my mama say "bless your heart" often enough to know it was a Southern expression with several meanings, most of them not particularly good. My mouth felt dry, so I drank the rest of the water. "Mama never talked to me very much about my family. I know virtually nothing about them. I don't even know how my father died. You said he was ill...."

He raised his hand. "Ill wasn't the right word, I don't think. It wasn't exactly that he was ill...but he was not himself. Not the man he once was." He cleared his throat. "I think it's best that you hear the story from Claude Landrieu or one of the family."

I shook my head. I was getting annoyed. "I don't understand. What's this big mystery surrounding my father?"

"Now don't go gettin' het up, young lady." He raised an eyebrow and pointed a finger at me. "It's simply not my place to tell you these things." He sighed and leaned back. "I can understand your confusion, Laurette." He eyed me. "I'll tell you this much. There was an accident a long time ago. Honestly, I don't know all the details. It happened just before your mother left with you."

"My father was hurt? Was he incapacitated or something?"

"Something like that." He rested his forearm on the table. "He never fully recovered."

"Then why didn't Mama ever tell me this? Why did she let me think he was dead?"

He shook his head. "I honestly don't know...and she's not here to tell you."

We sat in silence for a few moments. "You mentioned Claude Landrieu. I guess you know him, too."

"Quite well. He's a fine gentleman. You'll like him. I went to school with him, too." He wagged a finger at me. "You can trust him. He's a good man."

The customer who'd been reading the paper got up to leave. He passed our table. "Have a good one, Roland. Gotta get my butt back to work, even on a Sunday."

"Take care out there, Frank. Must be tough, looking after other people's money."

"Dirty job, but somebody's gotta do it," the man replied and headed out the French doors and down the street.

"Well, I also have some work to do, supplies to order," he huffed and raised his glass in a tiny salute. "Let's hope you don't have any further misadventures like that of this mornin'."

"I hope not. I've just now stopped shaking." I wanted to ask him what he meant about my being alone with the St. Cyrs and my mother's family, but instinct told me he wasn't going to say more about them. Something in his tone set off alarms in my mind. I knew little or nothing about these people, and it was obvious he knew them all well. I didn't want to offend him by pressing him for more information. And he did have a business to run. I started to gather up my tote. I wondered just who Roland Dubois really was. There was a confidence about him, something that said he was more than simply the owner of a bistro. "I can't imagine what's going on with that Annie Lebeau creature, why she keeps following me."

Roland finished his wine. "I came out to water the plants on the *banquette* and saw Annie watchin' you from across the street just before you headed in her direction. I have to admit, I stopped to watch what would happen. Call it an old man's curiosity." He shook his head. "I certainly didn't expect you to be attacked."

"What's wrong with that woman? She's been stalking me ever since I arrived yesterday evening."

His eyebrows climbed. "Annie's a Hoodoo woman, lives out in the swamp of Bayou Ombre...or Shadow Bayou as it's called in English. She's mostly harmless...mostly."

I didn't miss his pause.

"She makes a little money hustlin' the tourists, doin' readin's, sellin' potions, that sort of thing."

"I swear I'm not imagining it. She's following me around."

"It's possible. As I said, I'd just stepped outside to finish waterin' my plants when I noticed her." He nodded toward the street. "I saw her shadowin' you as you were walkin' along the street. She was on the other side, but watchin' you and keepin' pace with you."

"I didn't see her until I came out of the tee shirt shop and started up this way. I was going to go over and give her a piece of my mind. Then those little creeps tried to snatch my tote bag."

"I didn't connect those boys as bein' with her until they attacked you. Had I suspected them of anything, I would've intervened, but they were fast little devils."

"They were that all right. Scared me half to death."

"They wound up on the short end of the stick." He chuckled. "I'm just glad you weren't hurt."

He took one of the business cards out of the condiment container, wrote some numbers on the back, and handed it to me. "Those are the numbers for the local po-lice station. Ask for Sergeant Cormier and tell him you know me, if Annie gives you any problems. The second number is my cell phone. Call me if you need me...or call the store. Giselle always knows how to find me."

What is he up to?

Dubois smiled, exposing fine teeth with tiny spaces between each one. "I'm a retired po-liceman, detective actually. This used to be my beat. I know most of the characters around here, past and present, since my little business allows me to watch the street."

A policeman. A wave of relief washed over me. That's why I sensed an air of confidence about him. Something that made me trust him instinctively. I nodded toward his leg. "Did you get hurt and retire?"

He kept his left leg extended straight out and had propped his walking cane against the wall beside the table. "Got my knee bummed up chasin' a bad guy. Shot me in the leg." He shrugged. "So I took my retirement, and Giselle and I opened this little place. We both enjoy runnin' it, and it lets me keep up with what's goin' on in the Quarter. I'm a nosy son of a gun, just can't seem to help it."

"That probably made you a good policeman."

"I'd like to think I was one of the good guys." He smiled, and his eyes crinkled at the corners, then he shifted gears. "Are you stayin' out at the house, Shadow Cove?"

His eyes were a greenish gray, with a tinge of blue, not brown like those of most black people. His skin was a light tan, and his graying dark hair held a hint of red. "No. Right now I'm at the Canal Marriott. In fact I've never been to the place. Mr. Landrieu is picking me up and taking me out there tomorrow."

"From what I've heard, Claude has pretty much been runnin' things at Shadow Cove after your daddy got to where he couldn't handle the place, after the stroke. And of course, there's Sharla."

My interest piqued again at Sharla's name. "She was my nanny, wasn't she? I barely remember her."

"Sharla's a marvel. The best. She'll be delighted to see you after all these years. She loved you like you were her own."

A quiver of anticipation ran through me. Now I was more eager than ever to see the home I had left. Someone who had loved me waited there.

"Sharla looked after both your grandparents and took care of your daddy until he died. She's devoted to the St. Cyrs."

"Daddy had a stroke on top of an accident?"

Roland twisted his lips in a wry smile. "The luck Etienne enjoyed in the days of our youth seemed to have run out for him."

"You seem to know a lot about the goings on at Shadow Cove, even if you don't want to talk about them."

"Probably no more than a lot of other people, and my family's been friendly with your family for years." He shrugged. "Retired cops hear things, and the place is only a few minutes up the road from the city. I've got some people who live in Frenchy's Landin', a couple of cousins. Of course, in and around N'Awlins, we all seem to be related somehow."

"So I've heard. I've already been told New Orleans is a small town."

"Um, hmm. In a lot of ways, and the same families've been here forever. So many of us are related to each other in all kinds of twisted up ways...black, white, and everything in between."

That accounted for the colour of his eyes. Like a number of other people I'd already encountered, Roland Dubois was clearly a man of mixed race.

As if reading my mind he said, "My granddaddy was a white man, and my *grandmere* was half and half on my mama's side, and both of my father's parents were mixed, but mostly black...so I have light skin and green eyes. The races have always mixed in N'Awlins." He grinned. "A lot of black people here are as light-skinned as you are, but they're still considered black."

I fished my sunglasses out of my tote. "You call your grandfather 'granddaddy' and your grandmother by the French word?"

"It's like everything else in N'Awlins, all mixed up. French, English, American, a little Spanish, Irish, some German and Italian...whatever." He grinned. "Our city is the ultimate meltin' pot. Most of us black folks from the old families are part French, too, and grew up speakin' the language."

I laughed. "This place is like another country all by itself, but it's the friendliest city I've ever been in...except maybe for the attempted mugging."

"We pride ourselves on our friendliness, and we want our visitors to enjoy themselves and not have any problems while they're here. That's why I gave you my card." He peered at me closely. "I meant what I said. If you get into any trouble or need any help, call me."

He gave me another admonishing wag of his finger. "My daughter's twenty-three, so I know young ladies today pride themselves on their independence, but often you're more naïve than you think you are. You're in a strange city, and no matter how friendly it may seem, there are probably more crazies right here in the French Quarter than there are in the whole of the town you're from, wherever that may be."

"Seattle. And it's a pretty big city."

"Ummm." He got up from the table. "Like you said, N'Awlins is like another country." He drew his brows together. "Seattle, huh? Sometime, you'll have to tell me how your mama wound up there?"

He walked me toward the *banquette*.

"Does this Annie actually know who I am?"

"*Mais ye*. I have no doubt. She knows everything that goes on in this town."

45

"But how...and why...is she interested in me. How'd she find out I was coming here?"

"I'm sure the servants at the homes of some of your St. Cyr relatives talked, and she heard about it and found out when you'd be arrivin'." He leaned on his walking stick and squinted into the sun. "Then she asked the help in the hotels or at the airport. It's not hard to find out things about people when you know people in the business of providin' services."

I remembered the man at the airport. Maybe he had been following me and not the cab driver. "So like a doorman or a waiter or one of the hotel cleaning people, someone like that could have tipped her off."

He nodded. "Of course, when you don't realize that, it makes her look spooky, doesn't it?"

"Yes...as a matter of fact. And she just seems to vanish into thin air."

"As you said, 'seems,'" he pointed out. "Those boys' jostlin' you was no accident. They're workin' with Annie. When you started across the street to confront her, they grabbed you and distracted you so she could get away." He gave a short laugh. "You're so small and defenseless lookin', I doubt they expected you to knock the starch out of 'em."

I couldn't resist a tiny smirk. "Because I'm small and look sort of helpless, I took some courses in self-defense. Seattle may be a pretty blah city compared to New Orleans, but a girl has to watch out for herself."

He threw back his head and laughed, a rich sound. "Good for you. I insisted my daughter Nicole do the same thing when she was still in high school."

"You said Annie doesn't like the St. Cyrs. What's that about?" This whole business was just too bizarre. I'd never been involved in any sort of sticky situation before.

"Crap that goes back between families over a hundred and fifty years," he answered. "You know how some folks just won't let an old grudge die...or a new one, for that matter."

A couple of tourists wandered into the shop.

As much as I enjoyed talking to Roland Dubois, I needed to let him get to work. "I'd better be going and let you tend to business. And thank you again for helping me...and for the chat."

"Now I meant what I said about callin' me, if you need me," Dubois said. "And when you get settled in out there at Shadow Cove, come on back down here and let me know how things are goin'. I'll be lookin' for you."

Chapter 9

Roland Dubois smiled, watching Laurette continue on her way down Rue Royale. He had no doubt her presence would turn the St. Cyr bunch upside down. The Shadow Cove property was worth millions, and Laurette was the only heir to the fortune. The St. Cyrs would be after her like a pack of gators after a wounded fawn.

Etienne St. Cyr had been one of Roland's best friends when they were young men. Time and circumstances pushed a wedge between them. Roland's job took up a major part of his life, and Etienne's wild ways and tumultuous marriage, then his accident, distanced them. Giselle, Roland's wife, could scarcely abide Celine St. Cyr. After Celine left, the elder St. Cyrs invited the Dubois couple for the occasional dinner, though they didn't entertain as much as they once did, due to Etienne's unpredictable condition. He knew Pierre and Helene St. Cyr appreciated his stopping by and playing cards with their son, taking him for a ride into town, and chatting with him about their old friends, even though Etienne's mind often did not absorb the tales Roland told.

Roland had been a pallbearer for his friend's funeral, and he missed his infrequent visits with Etienne.

The former cop considered Etienne's parents fine people...or as fine as a St. Cyr could be. Dealing with most of them was like herding a nest of water moccasins. They had no loyalty except to themselves...and they could be fierce in this loyalty. But they would turn and bite each other as quickly as they would strike a stranger. They treated the people working for them fairly, but they were not people you wanted to be involved in a business deal with. They would cut your throat if they thought your interests were not the same as the family's interest.

Laurette was an innocent...or so she appeared...being thrust into tangle of serpents.

He would like to have told the young lady more about her father's accident and a lot of other things about her family, but it was not his place. He'd keep an eye on her. His police contacts here in the city and on Bayou Ombre were still in place.

He'd bet more than a few of her relatives would have their noses out of joint because of her arrival, a situation that would bear watching.

Heaving a sigh, the shopkeeper turned to look after his customers, taking their orders and placing a cup of imported espresso in front of one and a glass of white wine before the other. Their colorful tote bags identified them as tourists. Roland made small talk with them, welcoming them to the Big Easy and answering their questions about what to see in the Quarter, but his mind was strolling down the *rue* with Laurette St. Cyr.

Now the mystery was solved as to what had become of Etienne's wife and daughter. Even with the new-fangled computers the police force had employed, Dubois had been one of a team of cops unable to locate Celine and her child. Laurette's St. Cyr grandparents enlisted his aid in finding their daughter-in-law and grandchild shortly after Celine's disappearance, but to no avail.

Roland suspected Celine had run off to Europe. She'd been given enough money to hide herself and her child.

He wondered how much Claude Landrieu knew but didn't tell. Knowing the canny lawyer, Dubois suspected Landrieu knew when the cow ate the grinding stone...probably saw the handle go down. He wondered if Landrieu had known the whereabouts of Celine and Laurette all along and told no one. Perhaps feeling they were safer a long way from the bayou. The attorney had a well-deserved reputation for discretion.

Roland wiped down the countertop with a damp rag. He'd been friends with Etienne St. Cyr and Claude Landrieu most of their lives. Etienne had been a good man, as far as looking after his family went, but the rich Creole had a wild, rebellious streak, not uncommon to the St. Cyrs. Then there was her mother. Celine Renard would've been a fine mate for the Devil himself.

Laurette was a special young lady. A smiled tickled the ex-cop's lips. *What will Laurette think when she sees the portrait at Shadow Cove?* The painting was the reason Roland recognized her immediately when he saw her walking toward his shop. Purely St. Cyr, she bore little resemblance to her mother.

He ran his fingers over his chin, pondering what Celine had been doing in Seattle all these years. Surely there'd been another man in her life. Celine was not the type of woman to live without a man's attention. Could she have remarried...even knowing Etienne St. Cyr was still alive? Roland wouldn't put anything past Celine Renard. He'd ask Laurette about that the next time they met, and he would keep an eye out for her. A frown creased his forehead, and a wry smile twisted his lips. Here he was, Sir Roland Dubois, a sixty-seven-year-old, black, gimpy guardian angel, or knight.

Chapter 10

"That gal's gonna be trouble. I can feel it." Robert St. Cyr fumed. "She's nothin' but an outsider. Her mama hauled her off and never came back. She don't know shit about how we live down here in Lou'siana. Probably thinks it's all mint juleps and magnolia blossoms, like what she's read in romance novels or some such shit as that."

"Now, Robert." His wife, Regina or Reggie to most people, gave his name the French pronunciation, Ro-bare. "She'll only be trouble if you let her. She's what twenty-one, twenty-two years old?"

"Just turned twenty-four, accordin' to my man's report." He slapped the file folder he'd been perusing down on a side table and stalked over to a barred window overlooking Conti Street. Robert pulled aside the drawn curtain and peered unseeing at the street scene of tourists ambling and locals hustling along the brick *banquette*. The shaft of sunlight danced off the crystals of the room's chandelier, its tiny lights glowing even in midafternoon.

He leaned closer to the window, spying the mail-carrier making his way down the narrow street.

"Well, I for one am not going to be intimidated by a brat like her. From what that detective told you, she's nothing but a mama's girl, doesn't know her ass from her elbow about life." His wife set down her glass of white wine, uncurled her long legs from the seat of the wing-back chair, and walked over to the table. She picked up the manila folder and flipped it open, turned the photographs of Laurette this way and that, cocking her blond head. "The childhood pictures are good. Too bad the ones that detective took don't show much more than dark hair and sunglasses. I wonder if the girl's turned out to be as beautiful as her mother. Celine St. Cyr was beautiful and mean as a snake, from what I've heard."

"I barely remember her," Robert grunted. "But she was a bitch."

The small main salon in the elegant townhouse belonging to Robert and Regina St. Cyr was furnished with heavy brocade- and velvet-covered sofas and chairs, harking to another era. Handcrafted antique tables and sideboards crowded the limited space, attesting to the lady of the house's affinity for anything old and expensive.

A small, exquisite brick fireplace, faced with white marble, fought for its life in the cramped surroundings, squeezed on either side by curio cabinets holding Reggie's prized Eighteenth Century figurines. From above the fireplace, a collection of miniature portraits of long dead St. Cyrs maintained stoic watch over the cluttered room.

The double doors to the entrance hall were open, and Robert heard the mail drop through the metal slot on the front door into a box on the interior. He muttered, "There's the mail. I'll get it." He let the curtain fall back into place.

The main doorway, banded with sturdy wrought-iron hinges and locks, was recessed into the front wall immediately off the *banquette*. The former carriage way had been converted to a large entrance hall, which opened into the main salon and led to a courtyard, around which the two-story mansion was built, with many of the rooms facing the paved garden and its tropical plants and fountain. At the rear of the house, the former slave quarters were now a four-car garage, opening onto an alley behind the big house.

"I still can't believe Nonc Etienne left everything to Laurette. Hadn't seen her since her mama took off with her for parts unknown," Robert grumbled, coming back into the main salon and sorting through the stack of mail. He was a tall man, quickly going to fat, his dark hair streaked with silver although he was only a few years past forty. His smooth face wore a perpetual pout and lacked the angularity that marked most of the St. Cyrs' features. He wore a pair of Dockers that had seen better days, a light blue golf shirt with a country club logo, and felt bedroom slippers.

By contrast, his wife was decked out in rhinestone-studded, designer jeans and a pink silk shirt. She'd kicked off the *faux* jewel-encrusted, high-heeled sandals she'd worn to lunch at Broussard's with her *clique*.

Reggie shrugged. "She's still his daughter." She continued looking at the photos inside the folder. "In these old pictures, she has St. Cyr stamped all over her, doesn't look a thing like Celine." She turned toward her husband. "Suppose the Renards know she's coming back to Louisiana? If they do, I'll bet they're having a shit fit."

"Her mama's family? I damn sure haven't told them. Hell, I don't even know if they know Celine died."

"Landrieu probably told them...doing the decent thing and all that."

Robert drew his thin lips into a narrower line and tossed the mail onto a sideboard. Walking in a circle, he smacked his fist into his palm. "Damn. Papa Pierre treated that bastard like he was family, lettin' him run everything. Me...his own flesh and blood...I could've taken care of that place and the business."

"The proviso in the will says Little Miss Muffett will have to live at Shadow Cove for one year before she can actually inherit the place," Reggie reminded him, with a scant smile. "Maybe we can arrange for her to not want to live here, make her want to leave as fast her feet can carry her." She raised her carefully groomed brows above her azure eyes and pursed her lips.

Robert marveled at the cryptic way her mind worked...much like his own...not wanting to confide that he'd already started some wheels in motion. "That might be somethin' to work on." He snorted a short laugh and carried on with his own train of thought. "Our efforts to get Nonc Etienne declared incompetent didn't work. He'd already arranged to have Landrieu put in charge if he got to where he couldn't take care of things."

Reggie interrupted him. "Actually, old Papa Pierre did that before *he* died. He and Big Mama looked on Claude as their son and made no bones about it. They both trusted him more than their own true blood kin...obviously."

"Claude's mama was a St. Cyr, Papa Pierre's second cousin, so in a way, he *is* family. When his daddy died, my granddaddy took him under his wing and looked after him and his mama, sent him to college and everything."

"Are Angeline and Jason as upset as we are? I know how your sister can get."

"Yeah. You should've heard Sissy rantin' when we were talkin' about that party Sharla's throwin' so we can meet Laurette. She and her husband want to be there to hold the tail out of the way, along with the rest of us."

"Too bad your daddy isn't around to handle things." Reggie laid the folder down. "We wouldn't be in this mess about who'd be running the plantation. Surely your grandparents would've trusted their younger son with that responsibility if he were still alive. This has put you and Angeline both in an awkward position."

Robert huffed. "I don't think my daddy was thinkin' too much about me and Sissy when he was gettin' his weasel greased down in the Quarter and wound up gettin' his ass shot by that colored woman's main man. Hell, me and Sissy were still in high school when it happened. Embarrassed the dogwater out of everybody. Mama took to her sick bed, and Aunt Denise wouldn't even allow anybody to come visit her for at least two weeks. Went to the funeral wearin' one of them head to toe black things like them A-rab women wear. You know how she gets."

"I talked to Aunt Denise this morning. She's about to pass a squealing worm," Reggie drawled. "I can't wait to see her lock horns with this Laurette creature. Denise will make a mouseburger out of her."

Robert curled his lip. "Tanglin' with Aunt Denise is like stickin' your head in a wood chipper. I don't imagine this little ol' gal is up to the challenge."

"Unless she's like her mama. Then it will be like two scorpions with their tails raised. You know what a scrapper Celine could be. She and Etienne were always at each other's throats about something, even when he had good sense."

"Yeah. Nonc Etienne hadn't been right in the head ever since he took that header down the stairs years ago, just before Celine took off with her kid." Robert stopped pacing and stuck his hands in his pockets, jangling his change and keys. "That always seemed strange to me. I mean her husband fell down the stairs, nearly killed him, and she just packed up her kid and her shit and left for parts unknown. Nobody ever heard from her." He stalked over to a sideboard holding an array of liquor bottles and decanters and poured a stiff bourbon. "I've always thought the whole damn family was coverin' somethin' up, savin' face, and all that."

"You've always said you thought Celine pushed him down the stairs when they were having one of their knock-down-drag-outs. So you know if that's really what happened, they were just trying to avoid a scandal. I'll bet Claude has known where Celine was all along, and so did Papa Pierre and Big Mama. Maybe Nonc Etienne knew, too, not that he would've had sense enough to deal with it. But to leave everything to his kid he hadn't seen in twenty years. All that property, the business, the big house…." Reggie caught her upper lip with her bottom teeth and shook her head. She picked up her glass and took a swig, then plopped back down into the chair she'd vacated. "Well, I personally don't give a damn about living in that derelict house. I'm happy right here in the Quarter. On the other hand, it would be a wonderful challenge to renovate it. We could turn that old barn into quite a showplace."

"It isn't the house. It's the land that's worth a lot of money."

Reggie studied her fingernails and narrowed her eyes. She

pursed her lips, her expression revealing that the mechanism in her head was working on a new venture. "But we could have a good time fixing the house up. I could turn it into quite a showplace. Melisande Bouchard would be pea green."

Robert waved aside her remark about her socialite friend's envy, sloshing whiskey onto the Aubusson carpet and earning him a dark look from his wife. "Court Delacroix would love to add it to his holdin's. Rip up all them damn cane fields and build houses on 'em. He'd pay us top dollar, too."

With a sigh of aggravation, Regina heaved herself from her chair and fetched a roll of paper towels from the cabinet holding liquor and glasses. She squatted down and blotted the carpet. "Has he mentioned it?"

"Just hinted…but you've seen what he's done with Fleur d'Or… him and his daddy. Hell, they knew there was no money in cane anymore, unless you let a big conglomerate run it for you. They've got themselves rich all over again, subdividin' their plantation and buildin' minimansions." He swallowed a mouthful of bourbon. "Why don't you let Filene clean up that rug?"

"It'd take her an hour to waddle her fat ass in here. Besides, I have her busy helping Kenisha in the kitchen, and I don't want that stain to set." Reggie stood up. "I wish you'd quit being such a damn pig and slopping liquor all over stuff. That carpet came from Rao's, not Walmart." She returned the paper towels to the cabinet and wadded up the used ones and tucked them into a small wastebasket under the counter.

Robert paced the carpet, being careful with his drink. "Whatever," he muttered.

His wife returned to her chair and folded her lean body into it. "I don't know why there wasn't just an offer of some money to the little hussy, this Laurette. Pay her off and be rid of her." She raised her eyebrows. "You don't suppose that was done, do you? And she turned it down?"

"Damned if I know. Claude wouldn't share anything with any of us, other than tellin' us what we'd been left…or not left, I should say."

"We got a little chicken shit two million dollars, same as Angeline. Denise got five million, and her two kids each got two million, same as us."

Robert only grunted.

"But the prize is Shadow Cove itself. It's priceless, according to some people...the historic preservation people." Reggie drank off the last of her chardonnay. "Maybe a gator will get little Laurette while she's visiting."

Robert wasn't about to tell his wife about his visit to Annie Lebeau's shack a few days earlier, not yet anyway. Not that he didn't trust his spouse, but Regina liked to run her mouth, and he couldn't afford to let her bragging screw up his plans. Annie hated the St. Cyrs almost as much as she loved money. He could count on her greed to entice her to do what he wanted...nothing lethal, not yet anyway.

The information Robert's detective garnered on Laurette was mostly worthless...just education and work stuff. No arrests, no rumors or gossip. The girl's slate was squeaky clean.

Robert had fed Annie Lebeau what little he knew. Annie had her ways. Laurette had been away from bayou country so long, she'd be easily spooked by the old woman's Voodoo act. Annie should be able to scare Laurette into abandoning her inheritance and heading back to Seattle like her panties were on fire. If Annie's spells didn't work and scare the girl off, well, accidents happen, especially to folks unfamiliar with the swampland. Robert's lips curved upward.

Chapter 11

I was too exhausted by the ordeal with the street thugs and overstuffed from my late lunch to go out to dinner. I'd nibbled on the cheese and crackers in Roland's shop and grabbed a chocolate ice cream cone from a street vendor at the French Market. Everywhere I turned in this town, food was on display.

In my room, I spread out the treasures I bought during my stroll around the Quarter. In addition to some tee shirts, I bought a couple of miniature Mardi Gras masks, a crawfish-shaped spoon holder for the kitchen, a pair of roof slates painted with old French Quarter scenes.

My arms ached from carting my finds around. I had to reign in my buying, reminding myself that I really wasn't a tourist. Even if this plantation turned out to be a derelict and looked like too much for me to handle, I'd decided to stay in New Orleans. I had plenty of money, thanks to Mama, and could get myself a nice house. I could come back to the Quarter and shop any time I wanted. This place felt like home to me. If things didn't work out at Shadow Cove, I was going to live in this wonderful city. With my degree in architecture,

I should be able to get a job, not that I needed one. Working for a company that restores old buildings sounded like fun.

I tried on my *fleur de lis* earrings and admired them.

I showered, washed my hair, and ordered some crab-salad rolls and a bottle of chardonnay from room service. When dinner was delivered, I settled down in front of the TV. I needed to be bright-tailed and bushy-eyed, as Mama used to say, to meet the family lawyer the next morning.

Chapter 12

Claude Landrieu's call from the hotel lobby came through at ten o'clock sharp.

I wore casual clothes, suitable for hiking around the grounds of Shadow Cove Plantation, a pair of stylishly faded jeans, my ugly Ecco sandals, and one of the souvenir NOLA tee shirts I bought the day before…this one bright yellow, with a big green, gold, and purple-sequined *fleur de lis* on the front. I pulled my hair into a ponytail and put big gold hoops in my ears. I'd removed Mama's diamond solitaire ring from its accustomed place on my right hand and placed it on my left ring finger. My right hand was sore and a bit swollen from the blow I'd struck the would-be mugger the previous afternoon. I flexed my tender fingers and grinned. *I taught that little bastard a lesson.*

Landrieu was waiting for me as I got off the elevator. I'm not much for physical displays of affection in public, but before I could protest, he grabbed me in a tight hug and kissed me on both cheeks.

"My goodness, you're a lovely young thing." Beaming, he held me at arm's length and surveyed me like I was a fairy princess he'd found on a toadstool. "Nobody left you on the St. Cyr doorstep. I'd recognize you anywhere. Those eyes, that hair. That little dimple in the chin, just like your daddy's." He touched his forefinger to the middle of my chin.

Flustered by his effusive demonstration of affection, I attempted to return his smile, while I checked him over.

Landrieu was about five foot nine and trim. His silver hair was well-styled, his skin had a light biscuity tan, and he was immaculate in his pressed jeans and blue and white striped knit shirt. Sky blue eyes twinkled behind silver-framed glasses.

Roland Dubois told me he'd attended school with Daddy and the lawyer, so I figured he must be the around the same age as Daddy, although he could easily pass for a man in his early fifties, not sixties.

A couple of women turned to look at him as he escorted me to the huge hotel garage. Claude Landrieu was a dapper, handsome man. He handed me into his silver-blue Jaguar sedan, all the while chatting about how delighted he was to have me here in Louisiana.

"I feel like I should remember you," I said. "Things are still coming back to me."

He laughed. "You've been gone a long time, *cher*. Your Uncle Claude remembers enough for the both of us."

"Did I call you 'Uncle'?"

"*Mais, ye*. It's a Southern thang, in case you've forgotten…calling people you aren't related to 'aunt' and 'uncle,' regardless of color or the fact that there's really no blood relationship." He pulled out of the Marriott's garage and headed up Canal Street. "However, we are, in fact, related…distant cousins. But then everybody around N'Awlins seems to be related to everybody else…except the Yankee transplants."

"That's what I've heard."

"Sharla's about to pee in her pants, she's so excited."

"I barely remember her, but my instincts tell me I'm going to be happy to see her, too."

"*Mais ye, cher*. You're coming home to people who love you."

Trepidation skittered through my head. I hoped he was right.

Chapter 13

Once we were out of the city, the flat land we passed through on the way "up river," as my new "uncle" called it, was a far cry from Washington State. Gray Spanish moss festooned all the trees and shrubs, lending a misty, surreal appearance to the surroundings. Blooms on the flowering bushes were brilliant, the grass a delicate shade of green, the soil sinfully black. Ancient Creole-style brick and stucco bungalows, wood-frame Victorian houses, and quaint old shotgun cottages sat alongside modern concrete block homes in the neighborhoods we passed.

My host explained that most of the newer homes had been built since Hurricane Katrina had devastated the Gulf Coast.

Slowing through Frenchy's Landing, he told me the place was once a trading post and boat landing for fur traders. The part of town nearest the Mississippi River exuded the ambiance of a Nineteenth Century village, with weathered wooden buildings built high off the ground, a defense against flooding.

In the town itself, many of the buildings were traditional redbrick, with green shutters framing French windows. Trees and flowering crape myrtle bushes lined the narrow streets. I took it all in, my new home town. A quaint restaurant, its deck holding chairs and umbrella tables, sporting a *faux* weathered sign advertising Cajun Cookin'. A tourist trap bar and lounge, a couple of gift shops, three antique shops, a garage that actually sold gas, and a general store, complete with rocking chairs on the front porch. Beyond the "Historic District," a Holiday Inn Express stood next to a chain grocery store, with an affiliated gas station out front.

Set back from the road, down a long graveled driveway lined with tall trees, I could see what appeared to be a country inn, the Cozy Cajun Bed and Breakfast.

"That's a nice little place, run by friends...the Lesieurs," Claude commented. "You'll meet them soon, along with everybody else. The Landing's not that big, so everybody knows everybody and their business. Most of the people who live here work in N'Awlins."

Farther from the river, the first convenience store made an appearance, then a tire store, a strip mall, with the usual dry cleaners, beauty shop, pizza parlor, and discount drug store. About two miles out of town, Claude turned off the main road onto a two-lane blacktop. The trees met overhead, forming a long, dark tunnel.

On the backside of the borders of oaks, I could see skinny green stalks towering above the car, in seemingly endless rows, their narrow leaves fluttering in the breeze. "What are those plants?"

"Sugar cane. You don't remember, *cher?*" Landrieu cut his eyes away from the road. "The very life-blood of the plantation you're inheriting." He waved a hand. "You own all that."

"I had no idea it grew so tall." I craned my neck to get a better look. The fields went on as far as I could see. Then his words sunk in. "You mean all this is part of Shadow Cove?"

"It is...and it all belongs to you." He reached over and patted my arm, as we rattled over a bridge and turned onto another narrow road, small clusters of frame houses lining either side.

"Then the plantation is still profitable?"

"Very, and don't let anybody try to tell you otherwise. Shadow

Cove Plantation is doing more than holding its own." He cut his eyes toward me. "It's a multimillion dollar-a-year enterprise."

I tucked my bottom lip under my teeth and digested this information, wondering if he was suggesting someone might try to tell me the land was worthless, perhaps in a bid to wrest my inheritance from my control. Unease chilled me. I was no businesswoman, but I had a feeling I was going to have to learn to be one in short order.

So far the people I'd met only casually in New Orleans reacted in a peculiar manner when they learned who I was...except for Roland Dubois. But then Roland knew all about my family. Even he had dropped hints that Shadow Cove might not be a plantation taken from the pages of a romance novel...perhaps something more Gothic. I'd sensed an undercurrent of caution in the remarks, warnings of something out of kilter. I didn't want to imagine something downright evil was afoot, nor did I want to face my new home with these negative notions. I would do as Mama would suggest, were she here, keep my guard up and trust no one until I determined the lay of the land.

The vast surrounding acreage had been in my family for generations. I owned all this. A newfound determination rolled over me. I straighten in the seat, my mind made up. I would stay at Shadow Cove and accept the responsibility for overseeing its operations. This land, this plantation was my heritage, the property a land grant from French King Louis XIV...one of few things I remember Mama telling me about the place. I was not going to be run off. Never before had I been in control of anything. Until her death, Mama made all my decisions for me. Now this was all mine, and I had to take care of my life and my future by myself...with the help of trusted friends, as soon as I could sort out who they might be.

Lost in my own thoughts, I paid little attention to the lawyer's running commentary. His snippets of gossip and remarks about Louisiana culture and politics in general were white noise in my head. I gave myself a mental shake and returned my attention to his words. He knew all the dirt on everybody and had an amusing way of telling a story. He asked me very little about my mother and made only noncommittal comments on my replies to his questions. I had an idea he already knew far more about my mother and me than he was letting on. In fact, I would bet he'd known our whereabouts for years and kept this information to himself for his own reasons, whatever they might be.

My contribution to our conversation was innocuous remarks about growing up in Seattle, the schools I attended, my job. "I never liked Seattle. It was always cold…always misty. I just always had a sense of not belonging there." I laughed. "When that plane touched down at Louis Armstrong, and I got my first glimpse, my first smell of New Orleans, I felt like I'd come home."

Claude picked up my hand and kissed it. "I'm so glad to hear you say that, *cher*. I want you to feel at home at Shadow Cove. It *is* your home and don't let anybody take it away from you."

Another chill raced up my spine. *What is going on here?*

Roland told me I could trust this man. But I didn't really know him. Didn't know Roland either, for that matter. I was flapping in the breeze, alone.

The Jaguar rattled over another flimsy-looking, two-lane bridge spanning a creek, the greenish water barely moving. A quartet of alligators lazed on the bank, enjoying the sun and ignoring the car.

"Laurette, your father was the brother I never had," Claude said. "I miss him terribly." He gave me a warm smile. "So in a way, I consider you a niece, and I would be honored if you'd continue to call me 'uncle' and think of me that way."

"Okay, Uncle Claude." I tried the words out and laughed. "I've never had an uncle before."

"Wonderful, music to my ears."

"I know you're expecting me to ask this, so I may as well get to it," I ventured, twisting around in my seat. "Why did my mother let me think my father had been dead all these years, and why did he never contact me?"

My new uncle paused for a moment. "*Cher*, I'm going to explain all of it to you today…or most of it anyway. There are so many questions that need answering." He shifted his blue eyes toward me. "Some of the answers are going to upset you, I'm afraid."

"Oh? How?"

"What *did* your mama tell you about your father and why she left?"

"Virtually nothing. She got very upset when I tried to question her, so by the time I was ten or so, I just stopped asking." I stared unseeing at the green countryside rolling by. "I guess I just assumed that Daddy's death had somehow traumatized her, and she felt like she had to leave Louisiana...like being there continued to haunt her or something." I shook my head and turned back toward him. "I suppose I concocted some sort of fantasy because I didn't know what really happened."

"So you know nothing."

"No. Until I received your letter, I'd thought he'd died when I was four. Then Mama left Louisiana, and we wound up in Seattle. I had no idea he'd been alive all these years until I received your letter."

Landrieu sighed. "Laurette, your father had an...accident...a bad one."

I didn't miss the pause in his words and didn't bother to tell him Roland Dubois had said much the same thing...the same way. "What kind of accident?"

"He took a tumble down the staircase... nearly died from the fall. The accident left him both mentally and physically...shall we say...challenged." He slowed to let a truck pass and put on his directional signal to turn left.

The flat tone of his voice told me he had recounted this story a number of times, and it just might not be entirely true. Like he'd memorized the so-called facts and was repeating them by rote. I kept quiet and let him continue.

"Etienne's injuries, both mental and physical, were intermittent. Some days, for several days at a time, he'd be perfectly lucid. Then with no warning, his speech would become impaired, he'd babble, couldn't remember things. He could no longer be allowed to drive. He stumbled into things, tripped over his own feet. Sometimes, he couldn't even bathe himself. Your grandparents took him to any number of specialists, but because of the nature of his injuries, their symptoms not being constant, none of the doctors seemed able to help him. Finally, the visits to the doctors and the treatments seemed so much like torture, Nonc Pierre and Tante Helene gave up and decided to leave him in peace."

"You call them 'uncle' and 'aunt.'"

"A sign of respect in the South. As I mentioned, we're distant cousins, and your grandparents always treated me much like a nephew or something." He returned to the subject of my father. "It pained me greatly to see Etienne's mind slipping, not recognizing people, not remembering things. And I'm still coping with his passing."

Silently, I digested his words. "He must've remembered me. I mean he left me everything."

"Honestly, I'm not sure he remembered you or your mother," he answered, his voice tight, flat. "His parents were the ones who made all the provisions for you."

"They knew where I was?"

He nodded. "They knew, and I knew. Your mama didn't want them to know, of course, but we tracked you down." He gave me a sidelong smile. "I've watched your progress, young lady, and I'm proud of you. Your grandparents thought it would be best if your father had no contact with you. I can't say I totally agreed, but I abided by their wishes."

"When did they die?"

"Nonc Pierre died seven years ago, but Tante Helene lived to be ninety-five. She passed only last year, only a few months before your father. By that time, your daddy's mental state had declined to the point where I doubt he could've absorbed any information about having a daughter, so I simply left things alone. In my heart, I knew he didn't have much longer." He reached over and took my hand and squeezed it. "Don't feel hard toward them, *cher*. They were old, and they were only trying to protect you, as well as their son."

Chapter 14

The shell driveway to Shadow Cove Plantation meandered for the best part of a mile from the highway through a forest of tall oaks. When Landrieu pulled the Jag into the clearing in front of the big house, I felt a sudden urge to cry. I fought down the tears welling in my eyes.

The memories of this place slammed into me with the force of a two-by-four upside my head. For a split second, I felt as though I'd never left.

The circular drive, with purple azaleas in the center flower bed, a marble fountain nestled among the shrubs, the big, white-pillared house, its wrought-iron grillwork surrounding the second story gallery. Pots of tropical plants on the front verandah, blooming gardenias on either side of the steps. Baskets of ferns hanging from the second story ceiling. It looked like an ad for a Southern travel brochure.

Long-forgotten memories flooded over me. Me, waiting on the upper gallery for my daddy to come home. I could hear his voice. *"Ma bouton. Ma bouton. Ou est ma bouton?"*

"*Ici*," I would cry and run down the stairs to his arms.

Shadow Cove.

My home.

In a near daze, I got out of the car without waiting for Claude to open the door. The sweet, exotic aromas of the flowering plants hung heavy in the humid air. The odors and the sultry heat assaulted me. The familiar smells, the feel of the air, the tinkling sound of the water in the fountain. I stood still and stared around for a long moment, until I realized Claude had gotten out of the car and was standing beside me.

I was home again at last. I was where I was supposed to be. Tears stung my eyes. My throat closed up, so I gave a short laugh, partially to hide the emotion that threatened to overwhelm me, then slung my tote bag over my shoulder and turned to go into the house. "Let's go inside."

Before I could take two steps, a small, very pretty woman with *café au lait* skin opened the front door and came out onto the verandah to meet us. She fairly danced off the steps and down to the driveway.

"You've brought our baby home, Claude." Her smile was wide, but there was a cautious expression in her turquoise eyes. Her hair was a short, crisp cap of dark curls, almost black, but with a reddish sheen, a shade that could not quite be called auburn, more like polished mahogany. She wore jeans, sandals, and a tee shirt.

Did I detect a catch in the woman's tone? Her voice resonated in my memory.

The dusky-skinned woman paused a scant foot from me and looked me over as though she were committing every visible inch of me to memory.

"Sharla?" I ventured. Was this the woman I remembered playing with, the woman who looked after me before Mama had taken me away from my home? She looked to be about the same age as Mama, mid-forties.

If possible, the woman's smile grew wider, and I could swear there were tears in her eyes. "You remember. You come give Sharla some sugar, *bebe*." She threw her arms around me and held me like she never wanted to let me go.

The familiar smell of her washed over me. The same light, spicy perfume, the aroma of her hair, her skin. That familiar smell that had comforted me when I was a baby. The warm firmness of her body against mine was like a safe cocoon. I hugged her back, trying not to start bawling like an infant. I'd lost my mama, but now I had Sharla back.

At last, she took my face between her palms and looked as though she wanted to devour my features one by one. "I declare you look just like your daddy...don't have his size though."

"No, I'm small, like my mama." She and I were on eye level, and I studied her face carefully, taking in the oval shape with high cheekbones, a small straight nose, a dimple in her left cheek.

"Yes. You are about the size of your mama at the same age." A cryptic tone tinged her agreement. She looped her arm through mine and led Claude and me inside. "Y'all come on in. I've got some groceries cookin', but we've got time to give you a quick tour of the house, your home, I should say." She smiled at me. "We do hope you're planning on staying, yes."

"Something smells good." The lawyer chuckled and held the door for us. "Part of the reason I spend so much time out here is so I can enjoy Sharla's cooking."

"Don't I know that's right?" She flashed him a grin over her shoulder.

The plantation house was big, as big as I remembered, but I'd not expected such an opulent mansion. Somehow, I'd been expecting it to be rundown, but it was even more imposing than I remembered. The two story entrance hall was tiled with black and white marble, a wide staircase curving to the second floor. A crystal and gilt chandelier was suspended from the second story ceiling. Tall windows on either side of the front door allowed sunlight to flood the room, while the verandah kept out the heat. Sharla told me the house had been renovated years earlier for central heat and air conditioning.

"I don't know how folks stood this heat way back in the Nineteenth Century," she commented, leading me into a parlor to the right. "This is the formal living room, or *salle de séjour*, but most of the 'living' is done across the hallway in what we call the family room."

Rather than being decorated with antiques, as I expected, the large room was tastefully and conservatively furnished with contemporary pieces. A long sofa upholstered in peach sat in front of a white brick fireplace. Facing the sofa were matching chairs in a peach and green floral print. In another furniture grouping, the peach and green color palette was repeated, giving the large room a fresh, airy ambience.

I walked over to the baby grand placed in front of the windows overlooking the front lawn and touched a couple of keys. Their tinkling sound brought back a poignant memory of sitting on Daddy's lap, while he let me pick out notes. Daddy had been an accomplished pianist…a talent I had not inherited.

Peach draperies flanked the tall windows, and I was already picturing how they would look with modern Venetian blinds. I turned back and took in the glass-fronted display cabinets on either side of the fireplace. They held enough bric-a-brac to outfit a gift shop. I was going to enjoy combing through this stuff and sorting out what to keep and what to get rid of. Some old, dark landscapes occupied the walls on either side of a large arched doorway between the living room and the dining room. I could probably get a good price for them in an antique store in New Orleans. Not that I was planning on getting rid of a lot of stuff right away. I had all the time in the world to sift through it.

I smiled to myself. I'd probably wind up keeping all of it.

Sharla waved a hand toward the dining area. "That's the *petite salle à manger*. We use that room for family dining. The large dining room where we have dinner parties is on the other side of the foyer, next to the family room."

"Two dining rooms. This house is huge."

"*Mais, ye, cher*, and it's all yours." She held out both her arms.

"The living room is beautiful. I was expecting something antiquey, like from *Gone with the Wind*." Glancing at the painting over the fireplace, I gasped and did a double-take.

I walked over and stood beneath the painting, stunned. I might've been looking into a mirror, seeing myself decked out in post-Civil War finery.

Claude came up and stood beside me, chuckling. "I was waiting to see your reaction to that painting."

"She looks like me...or I look like her. We could be twins."

"That's the original Laurette St. Cyr, for whom you were named."

"Her portrait hangs in a place of honor," Sharla added. "After the War of Northern Aggression, Laurette St. Cyr is credited with getting the plantation back on its feet. The entire place would've gone belly-up had it not been for her."

"The War of Northern Aggression?"

"What y'all were raised to call the Civil War or the War Between the States, way out there in the west...and in Yankeeland," she said. "Down here in the South, we still call it the War of Northern Aggression, because that's what it was. Southerners were simply asserting their right to withdraw from the Union, not rebelling. The damn Yankees came down here and destroyed our property, stole everything they could carry back with them, and left us destitute."

I gaped at her. Sharla was clearly of mixed blood, so....

"Don't give me that look, *cher*. I'm a daughter of the South through and through, regardless of color." She raised one eyebrow at me, a gesture I recognized all too well. My mother used to give me the same warning signal. "My grandma was the last black ancestor I had. I'm only one-fourth black."

"Known back in the good ol' days as a quadroon," Landrieu interjected.

"*Mais, ye*," Sharla agreed, her voice tinged with bitterness. "Way back yonder when, a white boy woulda paid my mama good money to enjoy my...shall we say...company."

I caught the cryptic look that passed between Sharla and the lawyer. *What is their secret?*

Sharla quickly changed the subject and moved into the small dining room, with Claude and me following her. "This furniture dates to the late 1880's. You wouldn't believe how much Tante

Helene was offered by a dealer in N'Awlins. But she would never have sold it." She gave me a look that said I'd better not be thinking about getting rid of the beautiful table and twelve chairs or the gleaming sideboard and China cabinet that occupied the *small* dining room. I wondered what the *big* dining room was like.

"Tante Helene and Nonc Pierre were your grandma and grandpa." Sharla smiled. "You called them Big Mama and Big Daddy. Child, you've missed out on a lot, not having a Southern upbringing. I imagine you have no idea about the relations between folks down here. We call people we're close to, but may or may not be related to 'nonc and tante,' uncle and aunt, as a sign of respect...and their color doesn't have anything to do with anything." Sharla reiterated Claude's words

That made sense, in a way, to these people at least. I wondered if I was supposed to call her Aunt Sharla but didn't ask. Instead, I walked back into the living room and looked at the painting of the other Laurette again. "How am I descended from her? I mean we have the same name, but...?" I looked to both Claude and Sharla to provide an answer.

"Come on back through the house to the kitchen," Sharla said. "I need to stir my gumbo"

"Laurette married her overseer, a man name Kyle Tanner," Claude told me. "She had no brothers, just a sister, Selena, who was crazy as a loon."

"Selena? And my mother's name was Celine. How odd."

Sharla turned back and looked at Claude. "That *is* odd. The spelling's different, but the names are almost the same. I'd never thought of that."

"Neither had I," Claude agreed. "What a curious coincidence."

"You said this Selena was crazy?" I wanted to hear the story.

"On account o' that Hoodoo woman," Sharla put in. "That woman ran her plumb crazy. She still haints the cemetery."

The hair on the back of my neck stood up. Another Hoodoo or Voodoo woman? And haints? "You mean Shadow Cove is haunted?"

Sharla laughed. "Now, *cher*, what good's an old Southern mansion without a ghost or two?" She cocked that eyebrow at me. "Of course the place is haunted…if you want to believe it is, anyway."

I wasn't certain if she was kidding. "This Voodoo woman, she wasn't related to that Annie Lebeau I saw in New Orleans, was she?"

Sharla and Claude both stared at me, then at each other. "You know about her?" Claude asked.

"She was stalking me." I looked from one to the other. "What?"

"Oh, shit," Sharla hissed and took a deep breath. She looked at Claude, who nodded and drew his lips into a thin line.

"What?" I repeated.

"Annie Lebeau *is* descended from the Hoodoo woman who messed up Selena St. Cyr," Sharla told me. "That Hoodoo woman came to N'awlins from Haiti. Name was Odile Toussaint. She had some children and a man she abandoned to come to Shadow Cove to look after Selena. Later on, some of her descendants moved out here to the bayou onto some property the old master had left Odile as partial payment for looking after Selena."

"What was wrong with Selena?"

"Riding accident left her legs paralyzed," Landrieu answered. "Her daddy, whose name incidentally was Etienne, just like your daddy's, heard about this Hoodoo woman who might be able to cure her and brought her to Shadow Cove."

"Did it work?"

"Oh, it worked all right," Sharla said.

We entered the kitchen, and Sharla took the lid off a pot of gumbo and stirred it. The smell was so wonderful I thought I might faint. I'd skipped breakfast.

"The only problem was the two women fell in love with each other."

I gawked at her remark. "Selena and the Hoodoo woman?"

"*Mais, ye, cher.*" Sharla laughed. "They were doing those things back in the good ol' days."

"They didn't tell Laurette that Selena had regained her ability to walk, and the two of them conspired to kill Laurette so Selena could inherit the plantation," Claude said. "Laurette and Kyle suspected that the Hoodoo woman had been involved in the death of Laurette's father a short time after the woman came to Shadow Cove."

"What happened to him?"

"He was killed in another riding accident. Accidents like that were fairly common back then, like car accidents today."

"Etienne St. Cyr was dragged to his death by his favorite horse, and the man had been an expert horseman, so Laurette and Kyle were suspicious about his death," Sharla added.

I digested this bizarre tale of my ancestors. "I gather they didn't succeed in killing Laurette though."

"No. In fact, according to Laurette's journals, which is what we learned all this from, nobody's quite sure what happened, but Selena and Odile must've had a falling out and gotten into a fight," Claude went on. "There came up a big storm. The next morning Laurette and Kyle found the two women dead in the cemetery. A large tree had blown over on top of both of them, but nobody knows if that's what killed them. They were beaten and torn up like some wild animal had gotten hold of them."

"I wonder what they were doing in the cemetery during a storm in the first place," I mused.

"According to her journal, Laurette suspected they were in the cemetery to do some kind of Voodoo ceremony." Claude took a glass from the cabinet, stuck it into the ice dispenser, and filled it with water.

"Or maybe they just got into a catfight and took the fracas outside and wound up killing each other," Sharla said. She dipped a small spoon into her gumbo, blew on the liquid, and tasted it.

"Whew! That's some story." I crossed my arms over my chest and leaned against the kitchen counter while Sharla puttered among the pots and pans. "And am I right in assuming that somehow this Annie Lebeau blames the St. Cyr family for the death of her ancestor?"

"Right you are," Claude answered, rattling the ice in his glass. "She claims to be descended from the famous Voodoo priestess Marie Laveau, too. But that's just bull for the tourists. She was actually descended from Odile Toussaint."

I pondered this. "So she was stalking me to scare me or what?'

"That's what I'd like to know," he commented. He finished his glass of water and set it in the sink. "And how did she even know you were in N'Awlins?"

"I wondered that, too, but a man I met in the Quarter told me she more than likely had learned it from various service workers at the hotel and airport."

"Who suggested that? How did that come about?" His expression told me that he didn't like this turn of events.

I told him about my encounter with Annie and the ruffians and my rescue by Roland Dubois. "I'd given a couple of them a few good whacks, but then Roland appeared, and they took off running."

Claude smiled in relief. "Roland. Thank God. We've been friends for years."

"That's what he told me."

"Well, I'm glad he was on the scene to help you. Roland's one of the good guys, and he might be right about how she knew how to find you. But what I want to know is how she knew you were coming to N'Awlins in the first place. That was pretty much kept within the family."

"Roland suggested that perhaps some servants had talked," I explained. "He said Annie had a whole posse, as he called them, who did her bidding, so it was easy for her to find out when I was coming to town." A black cat meandered into the kitchen, and I bent down to pet it.

"To my knowledge, none of the servants knew about it. It wasn't like we put an ad on the front page of the *Times-Picayune*, no." Sharla was cutting up some French bread to put back into the oven to warm.

Her remark led me to believe Sharla did not see herself as a servant. I wondered exactly what the woman's status was in the household. She acted as if she were family.

"I might just have to ask Roland to see what he can find out. He still has his resources on the police force," Claude said.

Leaving Claude to decide how to handle the dilemma of Annie Lebeau, I returned to the previous subject. "I'm curious about something else…about that woman in the portrait, the one I'm named for. If there were no sons, and Laurette married a man named Tanner, how is it we have the St. Cyr name again?"

While she waited for the bread to warm, Sharla poured us each a glass of white wine, and we moved outside to the back verandah where she'd set the table for lunch.

"Laurette and Kyle's children…there were seven of them," the lawyer explained. "Hyphenated the name and called themselves St. Cyr-Tanner. Over the years, several of their descendants dropped the Tanner and just used the more prestigious St. Cyr. So you have a number of relatives around the bayou and in N'Awlins with the names of St. Cyr *and* Tanner."

"And few of them are what I'd call desirable." Sharla grinned and returned to the kitchen.

In spite of Sharla's words, a quiver of excitement raced through me with the knowledge that I had so much family that I hadn't known existed. I wondered if there was a family tree where I could discover who was who, but before I could ask, Sharla announced the food was ready.

Sharla spooned rice onto our plates and ladled up her special crawfish gumbo. She placed salads of home-garden-grown spinach in front of us and retrieved the French bread from the oven. *"A la mange."*

"Let's eat, y'all," Claude translated.

"I vaguely remember speaking French as a child," I unfolded my napkin and placed it across my lap. "Creole French, of course."

"Creole French is different from Parisian French, but if you speak one, you can understand the other." Sharla forked some salad into her mouth.

A number of New Orleans natives sprinkle their speech with French words and phrases. I decided not to mention that I'd studied French in school, so I could understand the local patois passably well. For now, I would keep this information to myself. *Who knows what I might overhear if people think I can't understand them?*

"You'll pick up some of the lingo again." Claude dug into the gumbo. "The most important words all have to do with food."

Sharla laughed her agreement and toasted him with her glass of wine. "Y'all save some room for that peach cobbler I made early this morning."

Chapter 15

Sharla insisted she needed no help with the cleanup, so Claude escorted me around the property near the house. "There are acres and acres of sugar cane, but you don't need to see that right now," he told me. "Seen one cane stalk, you've seen 'em all. I'll give you a guided tour in a few days, when my schedule allows." He wagged a finger. "Meanwhile, *cher*, don't go wandering in the fields alone. As I said, all the stalks look alike, and you could get lost."

We walked onto the dock and sat in the wooden chairs at the end, shaded by the gazebo I remembered from my childhood. "Daddy and I used to sit out here and feed the fishes and ducks." I looked down into the water and saw fish darting among the lily pads. A family of ducks glided by, mama duck in the lead. Nostalgia washed over me. I was four years old again.

"He loved to sit out here, even after his accident," Claude said, then paused. "Okay." The word came out on puff of air. "I told you I needed to tell you some things that might upset you."

His troubled expression made me steel myself for his revelations. I couldn't imagine what was coming and hoped I was ready for it.

"On the surface, your parents' marriage was a fairy tale…in the beginning," he said. "Etienne was the scion of the St. Cyr family, and Celine was raised like a princess, along with three brothers and four sisters, all with flaming red hair, just like hers." He chuckled, as if remembering some private joke. "Yes, indeed, Etienne was both rich and handsome, and Celine the most beautiful creature one could imagine. They appeared to have a charmed future."

Sharla came down the brick pathway from the house. She carried a tray with two ice-filled glasses and a pitcher of sweet tea. "I'm gonna leave y'all to catch up. I've got a dozen things I need to be doing." She poured us each a glass of tea. "Y'all don't stay out here too long. It's hot as blazes, even if y'all are in the shade."

"Yes, ma'am, I hear you." Claude's tone was amused, and he laughed at the face the quadroon woman pulled at him.

"Y'all just holler if y'all want something. I'm going back inside, me."

"Sad to say, your daddy was not the most faithful of husbands," Claude picked up where he left off. "In his defense, your mama was not the easiest woman on the planet to live with. Celine had been raised like a Nineteenth Century Southern Belle and tried to live up to some of the worst of those antiquated notions of womanhood. She had no idea about what marriage and being a wife and mother involved."

I started to protest but stopped, after all, he might've known Mama better than I did…in a very different way. She'd been gone for only a few months, and I was still grappling with the loss. I'd been looking back and seeing some things I didn't like to admit, but still this was my beloved mama we were discussing. My mother had been a very controlling, manipulative woman, using feigned dependence on a man to get whatever she wanted, but I knew Mama had loved me more than life itself.

"So we had a rich playboy and a diva trying to make a marriage work. Then there was the age difference. Your daddy was some twenty years older than your mama. He married her as soon as she graduated from Sacred Heart Academy in N'Awlins." Claude snorted. "Said he didn't want a wife with a 'history,' no matter what *he* had done up to that point." He made air quotes with his fingers and took a sip of tea. "I'm not speaking ill of the dead on either side of this equation. As I said, Etienne was the spoiled first son of a wealthy family. Celine's family had taught her to expect to get her own way about everything, too. So they often fought like alley cats."

"You mentioned Mama had three brothers and four sisters. What about Daddy? You said he was the first son. Did he have brothers and sisters?"

"Your mama didn't tell you anything, did she?" He raised his eyebrows at me.

"No, and when I'd ask, she'd either stonewall me or get very angry and have one of her spells."

Claude's smile was thin, and he shook his head. "Celine's *spells*." He barked a short laugh and set his glass on the table situated between the chairs. "Everyone who knew your mama was familiar with her so-called spells. She controlled people with her spells...her tantrums and temper fits. I guess it's supposed to be typical Southern Belle behavior. Her mama does the same thing...and her sisters." He pulled a sour face and nodded toward the house. "Your Aunt Denise, your daddy's sister, pulls the same crap."

I nodded, not unfamiliar with my mama's tactics to get her own way...and it always seemed to work. I never developed the talent, if that's what one would call such machinations.

The lawyer's expression was speculative.

I wondered if he suspected I thought the same thing about my mother's shenanigans. I turned the glass of tea in my hand, saying nothing, waiting for him to continue. I may not have Mama's charm, but I'd learned to keep my thoughts to myself and maintain a bland expression on my face, letting the other person do the talking and not revealing what I was thinking.

He took a deep breath and went on. "One of her fits resulted in your father's accident." He clutched and unclutched the hands he held in his lap. "Although, she wasn't entirely at fault."

He stopped talking and seemed lost for the next words.

"What happened?"

"It was about a woman." He sighed. "As I told you, Etienne was handsome and spoiled, and women found him irresistible." He gave a short, mirthless laugh. "I can't think of the number of times I had to extricate him from...shall we say...embarrassing situations."

"And Mama knew what he was doing?"

"Sometimes...this last time...or I should say the last time they had a fight about it, she accused him of fooling around with a woman I knew for certain was not involved with him in a sexual way. Things were not what she suspected." A confounded expression crossed his face. "Celine should've known better."

I waited for him to explain this last statement. Instead, he just shook his head and stared across the greenish-brown water.

A long-legged white bird flapped its wings and glided scant inches above the surface.

"They both had hot tempers. They'd get into some pitched battles...let me tell you...even threatened to kill each other."

I gasped, not that I couldn't believe my mother would say such thing in the heat of anger.

"I'm not so sure they meant it," he soothed. "But there were some occasions when other people heard the threats, which made things even worse."

My mouth was dry, and I was grateful for the tea Sharla had brought us.

"The last time, he was threatening to leave her...put her out, really, since Shadow Cove is his family's home, so he wasn't about to leave."

"He was going to divorce Mama?" I pressed a knuckle to my lips.

The lawyer nodded, then shrugged. "I don't know. St. Cyrs don't divorce, not as a rule, not the done thing in an old Catholic family. It was probably just empty talk, but they were having a ferocious row. He'd been drinking...her, too, not that Celine drank all that much. Everybody heard them." He paused. "When I say everybody, fortunately, it was just your grandma and a couple of house servants who've since died. I was spending the night at the house because Etienne and I were planning on going fishing early the next morning." He nodded his head toward the house. "Sharla was in the bedroom with you. She was worried the fight would upset you." He gave me the ghost of a smile. "You were her first priority… always."

I watched him closely as he sat for a moment, as if gathering his thoughts. I suspected he'd rehearsed his speech and didn't interrupt him.

He steepled his fingers in front of his face and patted the tips together. "They'd been yelling and carrying on for a half an hour or more. They'd come out of their own suite into the hallway. They were making a lot of accusations to each other, dredging up things that should've best been left alone. I came to the door of my room just in time to see what happened next." He reached for his tea and took a long gulp. "Things got physical when Etienne tried to shoulder your mama out of his way. She slapped him. He pushed her away, but she came at him again, this time with her claws bared. About this same time, your grandma came running out of her room. We both saw the initial blows exchanged." He frowned. "Etienne didn't actually hit Celine. He would've never done that to a woman, but he slapped her hand away when she tried to hit him a second time. He grabbed her wrist and twisted it and told her to leave him alone." His voice sounded like his throat was getting tight.

I put my hand to my mouth and continued to watch him. It was clear he didn't like talking about that night. He appeared to be reliving it all in his mind's eye. I deserved to know the truth, but maybe not all of it at one time. I said nothing, letting the silence hang as heavy as the humid bayou air.

For a few moments, the stillness was broken only by the sound of insects buzzing in the grasses growing along the water's edge. A fish popped out of the water, then disappeared beneath the surface with a splash.

Claude rattled the ice in his glass, then set it down on the table. "Etienne was trying to walk away from the fracas, but Celine wouldn't give it up." He gave me a look. "You know how she could be.

Nonc Pierre was in Baton Rouge that night, so he wasn't here to stop it. Etienne latched onto your mother, grabbed her by the shoulders and was shaking her and yelling at her that she needed to come to her senses…telling her she didn't know what she was talking about, what she was accusing him of. He looked like he was about to lose it, madder than I've ever seen him."

I was aghast at the horror story unfolding.

"I swear I could hear Celine's teeth rattling, your daddy was shaking her so hard, and she was screeching and clawing at his arms with her nails." He huffed. "Fortunately for all concerned, he was wearing a long-sleeved shirt, so she couldn't actually scratch him and leave any tell-tale marks from their battle."

Tell-tale marks? I leaned back in my seat, wanting and dreading to hear the rest.

"Tante Helene tried to intervene, tried to get in between them, but they wouldn't let go of each other. She had hold of Celine's arms from the back, trying to pull her from Etienne's grasp, and Etienne seemed to back off again." His recitation had taken on a mechanical quality. "I ran to help Tante Helene, just as Etienne shoved Celine aside. He turned away and started for the stairs. Before I could reach them, your mother pushed Tante Helene away and grabbed a big brass vase off of the table in the upstairs hallway. She screamed that she was going to kill your daddy. She ran after him and caught up with him right there at the head of the stairs. She swung that vase at his head so hard, she literally knocked him off his feet." The lawyer closed his eyes for a moment. "He actually left one of his shoes at the top of the stairs…knocked him slap out of his shoes. He pitched forward and fell down the stairs."

"She was defending herself." I bristled.

"Not really," he opposed. "As I just told you, Etienne had already backed off from the squabble. Said he was going down stairs and get himself another drink, not that he needed one. Just as he reached the top of the stairs, Celine ran up behind him and hit him with the vase."

I flinched, as if feeling the blow myself.

Landrieu picked up his glass and took another long drink, keeping his gaze fixed on the bayou water. "Tante Helene was screaming bloody murder, and Nathan, the butler, had come out of the back of the house to the foot of the stairs when the yelling first started. I remember catching a glimpse of him when I ran past the stairwell to reach your mama and daddy. So I know he saw the whole fracas…saw your mother hit your daddy, saw him fall. He even ran forward in an effort to catch Etienne, but he was old, and your daddy was not a small man. Nathan's wife, Astrid, was cowering behind the door and saw what happened, too."

"You mean it looked to everybody like Mama deliberately tried to kill him?"

Claude gave a little nod, then shook his head. "It looked like that, I suppose, and everybody heard what she said…you know, about killing him. Who knows what she was thinking? It all happened in a fit of anger. She hadn't planned it. Etienne was walking away from her, and she grabbed the vase and ran up behind him, just as he reached the stairs, and hit him, screaming that she would kill him." He repeated, like he was seeing it all anew. He seemed to study my face for along moment.

"Did any o' y'all try to help Daddy?"

He nodded. "We thought he was dead at first, but I was the one who felt for his pulse. We called Doctor Hebert. When got here, he called an ambulance. Etienne lay in a coma for weeks. The family claimed he'd had an accident. Not a word was said about Celine's actions. It was better to let people think Etienne had been skunk drunk and had fallen down the stairs than to allow it to get out that his wife had nearly brained him."

"The servants?"

Landrieu shook his silver head. "They wouldn't deliberately have said anything against the family. They were like family." He nodded toward the big house. "They lived in an apartment out back…a cottage. But I have no doubt they talked to the others, the ones who weren't there to see the fight. Then there was the ambulance crew, and they must've noticed the condition your mama was in. She came half way down the stairs and just sat there on the steps, silent, the entire time the ambulance people were there." He pursed his lips. "She'd thrown that heavy vase down the steps behind your daddy, and it was left lying right there on the floor beside him. It wasn't until after the ambulance left that Tante Helene thought to pick the thing up and wipe it off with the tail of her bathrobe and put it back where it belonged. I remember her examining it and finding a dent, so she turned it to the wall where nobody'd see it." He took a tiny sip of tea. "I never knew if the ambulance crew noticed the thing or not. As far as I know, nothing was ever said."

"The cover-up started that fast? And by my daddy's own mother, after what she'd seen? And my mama? What did she do?"

"She and your grandmother went to their rooms and got dressed. I drove them to the hospital." He raised his eyebrows. "We did what we had to do. Anything to protect the family's good name. But the fights between your mama and daddy had become common gossip. They were both flamboyant and not always as discreet as they should've been. Still, the story of Etienne falling down the stairs was maintained by the family, in spite of the rumors that abounded."

I leaned toward him. "And Mama just left, after what happened? She never tried to stay and make things right or do anything for Daddy?"

"Leaving wasn't entirely her idea, although she didn't fight it. It was better than facing the law if what actually happened were ever to leak out, especially if your daddy'd died. Not that something like that would've likely happened, a leak I mean. The family would've kept a tight lid on any sort of scandal. I think Celine was afraid of facing Etienne if he didn't die. Your daddy had a temper just as bad as hers."

"What happened? I mean I still don't understand what made her just up and leave?"

"Nonc Pierre and Tante Helene paid your mama some money…a lot of money. They told her to leave." His mouth twisted in a grimace. "They wanted her to leave you with them, but she wouldn't go without you. They didn't fight her over you. They knew she'd take care of you. But they had to get her away from Shadow Cove. Saving the family's reputation, and all that."

"How much did they pay her? I'm just wondering because she left me quite a bit of money, and I had no idea where it'd come from."

"Five million."

I sagged against the back of the chair. "So that explains the fat nest egg she left me. I wondered where she'd gotten hold of that much money. Five million dollars plus interest for twenty years, less some living expenses until she married Mercer, of course." I chuffed a laugh. "My stepfather obviously had no idea about that. I saw it in his face when the will was read. I was surprised he didn't try to sue me, when he found out she'd left me the money…being the spouse and all."

"It would've done him no good." He paused as if for effect, looking me directly in the eye. "Your parents never divorced."

I felt my jaw drop, and I sat upright. "You mean Mama was never married to Mercer Hollowell?"

"No." He shook his head. "If you remember, or maybe she never told you. They were 'married' on some island in the Caribbean, a place where they didn't have to prove anything, except their identities."

"Yes," I said slowly. "I remember Mama telling people they'd combined their wedding and honeymoon." Unconsciously, I cocked an eyebrow at him, a gesture that mimicked my mother's habit. "You mean you knew all about the wedding, too?"

"Of course. It wasn't really a wedding, but I don't guess Hollowell ever knew any different." Landrieu snorted. "But your mother knew exactly what she was doing."

"He was besotted with Mama." I looked away. "At first."

"She had that effect on men, a real charmer." Claude's tone relayed that he'd thought Celine somewhat less than charming.

"What did my grandparents tell people? I mean about why Mama left."

"In the beginning, they said she was so distraught over Etienne's accident that she just had to get away." He shrugged. "I can't guarantee that many people bought that story. This *is* the South. A wife stays by her husband's side. But Celine had a reputation for being a diva, one of those 'all about me' types. So nobody was really surprised when things got tough and she just got going…as the saying goes…more or less. Most people assumed she'd gone away for a while, and then they just stopped asking, out of respect for her parents and for the St. Cyrs."

"She never came back here. Never had any contact with anyone in all those years," I pondered aloud.

He shook his head. "Only three of us knew where she was, and two of them are dead. Your daddy was in no shape to run Shadow Cove, so your grandparents turned it over to me to hold until your father died, and then to turn it over to you, if you want it. To avoid a scandal, I promised your grandparents that I would keep an eye on you and make sure you were all right. When we deemed the time to be right, I would go to see you and tell you what had happened." He gave me a sheepish look. "To be honest, I'd been pondering going to Seattle to see you ever since Tante Helene died, but I really didn't want to tangle with your mother." He lifted his hands and let them fall in a helpless gesture. "I should've gone when I learned about your mother's death, but I kept putting it off. Your daddy would seem to be getting better, and then he'd get worse. I must apologize for not contacting you sooner. I shouldn't have waffled on the issue. I should've contacted you before Etienne died."

"I don't know that it would've made any difference," I said. "What about Mama's family, the Renards? Didn't they want to know what happened to her…or me?"

Landrieu sighed. "As I mentioned, two servants witnessed the fight between your parents. Even the most loyal servants will talk to their friends and families…not out of any sort of meanness, but people talk. Gossip got around that Celine had struck Etienne and tried to kill him. The Renards simply closed ranks and turned their backs on Celine…and you."

"Nice people."

"Snobbish, clannish is what they are," he remarked. "But I have to admit, I'm surprised at the way they simply shut her out. As far as I know, they acted as though she died twenty years ago. Never mentioned her name. She'd embarrassed the family, so they wanted nothing to do with her."

I leaned forward again and put my hands over my face, trying not to cry. My mother had not been perfect, but I loved her. "I had no way of knowing how to contact any of them when Mama died, and I didn't even try. I figured they must not've cared about her anyway. She was cremated. The urn is packed with my other stuff back in Seattle. I didn't know what to do with her ashes. I don't know exactly why I didn't have them put in the memorial garden at the church she and I attended, but something inside me kept telling me not to do that. Do you suppose I can have them put in the family cemetery?"

He reached and touched my shoulder gently. "Of course, your mama was family. She deserves to be in the cemetery with the St. Cyrs, right beside your daddy."

"Umm, did…uh…Sharla know where Mama was?"

He shook his head. "No. I never told her, not until your daddy died."

I struggled to compose myself and changed the subject. "You didn't answer my question about my father's brothers and sisters." I sniffed back the tears I'd so far avoided spilling.

"So I didn't. I got caught up in telling you what happened." He leaned back in his chair and quickly reeled off the roster of relatives. "Etienne had a younger brother Henri, who was killed in a shooting in the French Quarter a long time ago. His sister Denise lives in N'Awlins with her husband Mitchell Couliette. Mitch is a petroleum engineer…has his own consulting company. They have four kids, Junior, Chantal, Philippe, and Andre." He ticked them off on his fingers and twisted his lips in a wry smile. "Sweethearts every one of them."

His tone told me he thought otherwise. I rubbed a finger between my brows, concentrating on remembering the names.

"Henri had a son Robert and a daughter Angeline, now married to Jason Laporte, a stock broker or something like that…doesn't really have to work. Robert prefers to be called by the French pronunciation Ro-bare…" He paused and chuckled at this affectation. "He's married to a social maven named Regina Whitlock. They have five kids, Bobby Joe, or more correctly Robert Joseph." He gave the name the French pronunciation. "Then there are Simone, Desiree, and Jean and Jacques, twins." Again, he ticked more names off on his fingers. "And there's Henri's widow, of course, your Tante Simone. There was a third son between Henri and your Tante Denise… Maurice, but he died when he was only four years old…appendicitis."

"So I have all these relatives I've never heard of. Not to mention the ones on my mother's side."

He gave a short laugh. "When you meet them, you might wish you hadn't."

"That doesn't sound promising."

"Let me put it this way…why do you think your grandparents left me in charge of the estate and made sure everything was passed on to you?" He arched an eyebrow at me. "Young lady, you have stepped into a nest of vipers, and it'll be up to Sharla and me to see that you don't get bitten." He wagged his head. "Don't trust any of them."

The caution my mother instilled in me caused my interest to spark at his remark. Claude warned me not to trust anybody except him and Sharla, but I actually knew none of these people. *Why should I trust even these two?* For all I knew, they were in collaboration to rip me off.

Apparently the St. Cyr family was very rich, and Claude Landrieu had been managing the affairs of my grandparents and my father. *Why should he want to turn everything over to me? Surely he must have a tangible interest in the property…a share, a portion, or something. All his years of hard work and no part of the St. Cyr holdings being given to him? All left to a young woman who hadn't been raised here and knew nothing about the family business…while he'd been the one steering the family's finances all this time?*

I thought this must rankle. But if so, he'd given no indication. *What would I be feeling right now, were I in his shoes?*

I tried to maintain an expressionless mask. Oh, God, I wished

Mama were here now to tell me what to do. She hadn't been perfect, but I'd never had any reason not to trust her…until this business with the inheritance surfaced. Still, the fact that she'd put aside all that money for me spoke volumes about how much Mama had cared about me and my welfare. Celine might've appeared self-centered and flighty, but she hadn't frittered away a fortune on herself. She'd kept the money for me, her daughter.

Chapter 16

I rode back to New Orleans with Claude that afternoon. Sharla wanted me to stay at the plantation, but I hadn't brought any extra clothing with me. Besides, I needed time alone to absorb what Claude had told me. After the bombshell revelations about my family, I remained quiet, wrapped in my own thoughts for most of the trip. Claude also said very little. Apparently, he, too, was talked out...for the moment.

Although I was exhausted, I didn't want to appear ungrateful, so I allowed him and his partner, an optometrist named William O'Neal, to escort me to dinner at Arnaud's that night.

My first glimpse of the famous restaurant made me glad I'd packed a couple of dresses suitable for its elegant ambience. I wore a short silk emerald dinner dress, with thin straps. The bodice was dark green lace sprinkled with sequins. My mother's diamond and emerald earrings and matching necklace and strappy, black patent heels were the perfect accessories. I twisted my hair into a loose "up do."

Claude introduced me to the tuxedoed maître d', who personally escorted us to our table in the main dining room.

The décor of the elegant eatery made me feel like I was stepping back in time to when the restaurant was founded in 1918. The classic black and white checkerboard tile flooring, the pristine white table clothes, the beautiful beveled windows overlooking Rue Bienville harkened back to a more formal era. Potted palms lent a tropical ambience to the place. I was even enchanted by the uncomfortable cane-back chairs, another New Orleans staple.

A team of black-uniformed servers hovered discretely, prepared to attend to our every need. Claude told me their uniforms denoted their positions in the pecking order of the wait staff, and they all stood at military attention while taking orders, writing down nothing. These ladies and gentlemen were professionals, not college students waiting tables to make their car payments.

Arnaud's was definitely a place I could grow accustomed to.

While we perused the extensive menu, Claude told me he and Wills had been together for two years, following the death of his longtime partner Seth Fournier. "After Seth died almost five years ago, I decided I preferred to live alone, so Wills and I keep our separate residences."

"Having our separate abodes makes our time together more valuable." Wills beamed.

Both men were Louisiana natives; although, it was obvious Claude was the older by at least twenty years.

Claude had a home in the Garden District. "Do you live here in New Orleans, too?" I asked Wills.

"Right now I have a place in the Quarter, but I've been trying to decide whether or not I want to continue living here or move into the house my mama left me on Bayou Ombre," he answered. "Of course, it's more convenient to my office if I stay in the city. On the other hand, the house on the bayou is free."

"Is your house near Shadow Cove?"

"It's on the other side of Frenchy's Landing from your place." He grinned. "I grew up on Bayou Ombre. I'm a swamp rat."

"I'd hardly call you that." I laughed. "Or you're the most sophisticated rat I've ever met."

He grinned. "I can handle a *pirogue* with the best of 'em. I can wrestle a gator. I can catch a mess of mudbugs and cook 'em up like a Cajun, me." He faked a Cajun accent.

"But you're not Cajun, right? With a name like O'Neal."

He waggled his hand. "My family's mostly Irish, obviously, but I had a French grandfather on my mother's side, which is how I happen to own that property on Bayou Ombre."

O'Neal was about six feet tall with light brown hair, going gray at the temples, and mild blue eyes, I thought were set just a tad too close together. His finely chiseled features kept him from being merely pretty. He was strikingly handsome. Like Landrieu, he was immaculate in his dress and grooming and kept himself in exceptionally good physical shape.

"I'm very active in the New Orleans Center for Creative Arts and the Shakespeare Festival sponsored by Tulane. I do some acting with a couple of the local theatrical groups as well." Wills showed no reluctance in talking about himself. "I've done some work with the New Orleans Fringe and the Marigny Theater."

"You seem to have lost much of your native drawl," I remarked. "Did you take diction lessons to prep you for acting?"

"Oh, absolutely. I couldn't be a success in the theater, if I sounded like Jeff Foxworthy when I opened my mouth."

"Wills lived in New York for a short time and appeared in some off Broadway plays," Claude put in with a proud smile.

"I did not set the Great White Way on fire as planned." The optometrist turned his wine glass in his hand. "So I returned home with my tail between my legs and let Mama pay for optometry school." His tone was droll. "It's a good gig. I'm not complaining, but acting's what I love."

"And you're wonderful at it," Landrieu patted the younger man's hand.

Our server brought the appetizers. At the suggestion of both men, I ordered the Oysters Arnaud, consisting of one each of the restaurant's signature oyster appetizers. Since Wills had ordered the same thing, I figured it must be good. I tried the Rockfeller first and rolled my eyes upward in appreciation.

"Arnaud's food cannot be beaten anywhere," Claude intoned, tucking into his own smoked pompano.

Our conversation turned to various restaurants in New Orleans and the merits of each.

"This place is like Disneyworld for foodies," I said.

"All we're missing are the characters, but we have enough Goofies of our own," Wills quipped.

Following the first course, we enjoyed bowls of the wonderful shrimp bisque. "I'm going to weigh a ton if I don't watch out. But I do love food." I finished the soup, and the server poured another round of the Sauvignon Blanc Claude had selected.

Like any fine eatery, Arnaud's allowed its patrons time to sip and chat between courses, never rushing them. There was a stir at the entrance to the dining room, and I saw several heads swivel in that direction.

A very tall, lean, gray-haired man strolled into the dining room, followed by a half dozen hangers on, including a much younger beauty clinging to his arm.

A rustle at the tables nearby, murmurs.

"Isn't that…"

"Sure is," Claude interrupted. "After all those spaghetti westerns, he's now staying behind the camera. He's in town directing his latest opus. I had the honor of helping him with some legal questions about using some of our old buildings in the Quarter. He's quite a nice fellow."

The superstar spied Claude and headed our way, leaving his entourage to be seated at a long table.

Claude and Wills rose to their feet, and hands were shaken all around.

I was embarrassed at being speechless when I was introduced, but the movie star quickly put me at ease with his affability. My face burst into flames when he told me how lovely I was. Then he leaned down and kissed me softly on the lips, before turning and walking back to join his party. I could feel my blush spreading all the way to my toenails.

"Oh, my God. Oh, my God. Oh, my God." I babbled the mantra, carefully touching my fingers to my lips. "I can't believe I actually met him face to face, and he kissed me. I may never wash my lips again." I tried to stifle a giggle. "This would never happen in Seattle."

"Just one more reason to love N'Awlins, *cher.* You never know who you'll run into," Claude saluted me with his wine glass.

What an evening. Being fed like royalty in a world famous restaurant and meeting an international superstar.

The server placed a dish called Crabmeat Karen in front of me. The creation consisted of crab meat in white wine sauce, served in a puff pastry shaped like a large crab.

The men also ordered shellfish dishes, so the white wine Claude selected went with everything.

The server opened a second bottle and circled the table, pouring libations for us.

Dessert was slabs of dark chocolate cake with fresh strawberries dipped in more chocolate.

"I called ahead and ordered this dish special." Claude grinned. "I remembered you loved chocolate, just like your mama and daddy."

The conversation during dinner was not about my inheritance or much of anything to do with Shadow Cove. The men carefully steered the talk toward cultural topics or local, amusing snippets of gossip.

Claude ordered orange-spiced Café Brulot for everyone.

"Have you decided when you want to move out to the house?" Claude inquired, carefully dabbing his mouth with his napkin. "There's no sense in your staying at a hotel when your home is Shadow Cove. We even have cars you can use."

"I haven't decided whether to sell my Porsche Cayenne I left back in Seattle or fly back there and drive it here." I took a sip of the coffee concoction. "I really love that car, but it's such a long drive. Right now, my mama's lawyer's wife is keeping it in her garage. She's the realtor who found me a condo after Mercer put me on the street, after he learned Mama had squirrelled away all that money and left it to me."

Claude explained my windfall to Wills, who toasted me with his coffee cup. "Good luck for you."

"That Arnold and Janet Fowler you mentioned?" Claude asked.

"Yes. Nice people. I don't know what I'd've done without their help after Mama died."

"Why don't you check with this realtor and see if she knows somebody reliable who would like to drive your car to New Orleans for you, and you pay for their expenses along the way and their plane ticket back to Seattle?" Wills suggested.

"I hadn't thought of that. To tell you the truth, I don't have any good reason for going back to Seattle, other than to pick up my car. And I really haven't been relishing that long drive back here alone. The realtor told me she would take care of getting all my stuff packed and shipped if I wanted her to." I chewed my lip. "You know, the realtor, Janet, might like to drive the car here…with her husband…take a vacation."

"That would be a great idea," Claude agreed. "Why not ask them?"

"I think I'll do that."

Wills clapped his hands. "See there…another problem settled."

"As for moving out to Shadow Cove right now, I don't want to feel like I'm imposing on Sharla."

"I can assure you she won't mind at all," Landrieu answered. His blue eyes held a special twinkle. "You can't imagine how much she'll enjoy having you with her. Besides, she already has your room ready. She was convinced that once you saw the place, you'd fall in love with it and want to live there. After all, it *is* your home now."

"Looks like she was right. I do love the place already. Sharla doesn't live at Shadow Cove, does she?" In the back of my mind, I was feeling just a tiny bit uncomfortable about staying in the huge house on the bayou all alone. Surely, they must have some kind of security system, but maybe not, since the place was so isolated. And there was all that talk of ghosts and such, not that I believed in such claptrap. A cold shiver ran up my spine. As the natives say "This *is* N'Awlins," and I was quickly learning, any number of strange things could happen to a person here. Hoodoo women stalking, ruffians mugging, movie stars ambling by one's table.

"Oh, yes. Sharla lives there. She's had a suite there since before you were born," the lawyer said.

Her living at the house might seem odd, but after all, Sharla was the housekeeper...or something. I felt a twinge of relief knowing I wouldn't be alone in the house. "You mean she has no husband or family? She's so pretty, I just assumed she was married and just worked there during the day."

Landrieu shook his head. "She's a fixture, like a family member. She was Celine's maid, more like a paid companion really, before you were born. She and your mama were born only a few months apart and grew up together. Her mother worked for the Renards, your mama's people. Sharla came to live at Shadow Cove when your parents were married. After you were born, she looked after you, seeing as how she's a registered nurse."

"Sharla's a nurse?"

"And a very good one," Landrieu assured me. "After your father's accident, he needed 'round the clock care. Not that he was helpless. But, as I told you, he had bouts of mental and physical 'uncertainty,' I guess you'd call it, so there needed to be someone close by all the time. She became his private nurse, his girl Friday, chauffeur, and just did whatever needed doing."

"She didn't want to go with my mama when she left?"

"Your mother left abruptly. She didn't invite Sharla to go with her." Landrieu's expression was unreadable. "Sharla was needed more here and stayed with the St. Cyrs to look after your daddy."

As I'd felt earlier today, I sensed more going on behind the scenes than I was being told.

What a tangle. A beautiful mulatto woman living with a pair of newlyweds in the family home...along with an older generation, all those servants, watching and listening. The scion of the family injured and never being quite "right" again, his wife disappearing with their child. The tension, the mysteries, the strange relationships... lies, deceptions, undercurrents of passion. The St. Cyr family could be a television soap opera.

From their remarks and the way they acted toward one another, I'd picked up on a special relationship between the lawyer and the beautiful, mixed-race housekeeper. Now, sitting here with "Uncle" Claude and his lover, I realized there was not a sexual relationship between him and Sharla, but they shared secrets, the nature of which I could not yet fathom. Yes, I would be watching my backside with these people.

"Sharla has taken very good care of the St. Cyrs since your mama left, not only your daddy, but your grandparents as well," Claude said.

"And learned how to be a killer cook in the process," Wills added. "I'm secretly in love with that woman."

"Tell me she doesn't take care of that house all by herself."

"Hardly. There's a cleaning lady and her two daughters who come in twice a week and a quartet of yardmen. Sharla keeps a local building contractor on retainer to do occasional handymanning and look after the maintenance of the house and the outbuildings. She oversees everything to make sure the place is kept up properly. The house, like all old houses, always seems to need some upkeep." Claude nursed his after-dinner coffee.

"Which reminds me," Wills interjected. "If you want to make any changes, larger closets or other things to make you more comfortable, I would suggest you make use of the talents of Courtland Delacroix, the contractor Claude mentioned."

I saw Claude cut him a sharp look, as if to say his friend was overstepping his boundaries in making this suggestion, but he only sipped his coffee and murmured. "Yes, Courtland's very good."

"I'll have to meet him. Since I'm an architect, I know a lot about building maintenance, and I don't want to get ripped off."

"He's the best building contractor in the bayou, and he's trustworthy," Wills put in. "Claude's known him for years, but he and I met about three years ago in a nonprofessional way. Like me, he's an amateur thespian, and we work with the same groups."

"Not much of an actor, but then, what he lacks in talent he makes up for with his looks," Claude remarked.

Wills pursed his lips. "Yes, Court is quite handsome."

"Has to beat the admirers off him." Claude cast an unreadable glance at his partner over the rim of his cup.

Wills shrugged. "There is that."

This curious exchange piqued my interest, but I only asked, "Is this Courtland Delacroix from here?"

Claude nodded and started to say more, but Wills interrupted him.

"Court's family owned what used to be Fleur d'Or Plantation up the road from Shadow Cove. They got out of the cane business a while back, thirty-five or forty years ago, and started a land development and construction company. They've subdivided the property into five-acre tracts and build only custom homes to suit the owners…no spec houses."

"First quality homes, not McMansions, fortunately for the neighborhood." Claude saluted with his cup. His scant smiled didn't reach his eyes.

Wills nodded enthusiastically. "They're beautiful homes in keeping with the Louisiana plantation style and tradition."

"Delacroix Construction has a fine reputation, although I did hate to see Court's daddy parcel out property that was an original Louisiana land grant, just like Shadow Cove," Claude amended.

I sensed a peculiar tension between the pair and tried to lighten the mood with a laugh. "Well, I have no intention of doing anything like that. I'm going to last out the requisite year here and claim my inheritance, in spite of the ghosts that are rumored to share the place. And I'm going to keep the place intact."

"Excellent." Claude's returning smile seemed genuine. "I believe you can keep the ghosts under control, with whatever help you need from Sharla and me." He finished his cup and nodded to the waiter for a refill. "I was watching your face while we were giving you the grand tour. I could tell you have a special feeling for the place."

"Haints and all?" I grinned back.

"Yes…haints and all," he answered. "Besides, I think they'll enjoy sharing space with somebody who appreciates the old place."

"Well, if you're sure it won't be an imposition on Sharla, I think I'd like to go ahead and move out there. I've never really been a hotel person."

"*Cher*, it *is* your home, after all. You'll just need to sign all the paperwork, and you will be a Louisiana landowner, or will be in one year. And I'm counting you to be able to put up with the rest of the St. Cyrs that long."

"Are these relatives I've never met going to have their noses out of joint?"

"You have no idea." Claude grinned.

Wills patted his lips with his napkin, and I couldn't quite discern his expression.

Chapter 17

The nearly full silver moon rode low over Bayou Ombre. Its reflection spread on the dark, still water like a sheet of aluminum foil.

The terrified scream of a nutria signaled its capture by an alligator. From deep in the murky darkness came the cry of a big cat, possibly the offspring of a pair of black panthers rumored to have been released into the swamp before Hurricane Katrina came ashore.

Oblivious to the primitive yet familiar sounds around her, Annie Lebeau hunkered over an old fashioned iron washpot in the scruffy yard behind her shanty. The stench coming from the pot was dreadful, but Annie sniffed it appreciatively, as if she were concocting a delicacy worthy of Antoine's Restaurant in the Quarter. The skinned head of a dead cat bobbed to the surface of the roiling mess, and she pushed it back under the water with a wooden spoon.

Above her head on a clothesline strung between two cypress trees, hung the black hide of the hapless feline.

Parts of a chicken swirled in the disgusting stew, and Annie added a spoonful of filé and one of saffron, spices used in both

Creole and Cajun cooking, as well as in a number of Voodoo potions. Tiny glass bottles, stoppered with corks, lined the bench where she perched. Pieces of cloth, with string for tying them into bags lay alongside the bottles. One of the cloths held a tiny wad of dark brown hair and a ball of cotton with what looked like a spot of blood on it.

Annie was making a special *gris-gris*. The spell was powerful and deadly.

Chapter 18

"The little hussy's been here since last Saturday, and we've yet to meet her," Denise St. Cyr Couliette griped to her nephew Robert. Their table overlooked the courtyard in Commander's Palace in the Garden District.

"We haven't been summoned by the Queen of Bayou Ombre," he reminded her.

"I cannot for the life of me believe Mama left everything to that little fairy, Claude Landrieu, to administer. Not a word to me and Mitch. We could've handled everything. So could you, for that matter."

Robert snorted. "Hell, I talked to my own lawyer about it when Papa Pierre was still alive. He said there wasn't a damn thing I could do about it. All the arrangements had been made. He said Papa Pierre and Big Mama were both of sound mind, and they could do what they wanted to with their own property. Big Mama's nephew on her mama's side is a federal judge up in Baton Rouge, so that didn't help my case any."

Denise was sucking down the *paneed* veal and crawfish. "We'll just have to find a way to make Shadow Cove most unappealing to her." Like her nephew, she had the St. Cyr green eyes, olive complexion, and mahogany hair, although her hair was streaked with strawberry blond highlights, while his was starting to thin on top. She took excellent care of herself and looked a good ten years younger than her fifty-plus years. She was the baby of the family. Like her brother, Etienne, she'd married later than most of her generation. She and her nephew could pass for brother and sister.

He nodded, forking a chunk of grilled pork tenderloin into his mouth. "I know Courtland Delacroix would love to get his hands on that property, but I talked to a developer down in Miami. We could get the two competing with each other and get top dollar. The Miami dude, some rich Cuban…he's got more money than God…big sugar."

"*Mais ye*, we'd get more from him than Delacroix's able to offer. But we both know we need to keep the property close." Denise touched her napkin to her lips. "Sell off the land but keep the house and the cemetery property."

Robert took a swallow of wine. "Reggie has some harebrained notion of renovating the house and living there, but I have no interest in living out in there in the asshole of nowhere. I like it fine here in N'Awlins."

"That girl won't know squat about running a plantation. I'm betting she'll be more than willing to get out from under that place." Denise tapped her long red nails against her butter dish. "I mean… hell…she didn't even grow up here. I'll bet she can't wait to get back to Seattle. We should be able to talk her into splitting the property into shares. There's enough for all of us."

Robert flashed his aunt a cryptic grin. "I just have every idea she's going to get a bellyful of bayou living pretty damn quick and will be happy to share with us."

His cell phone rang. He pulled it out of his jacket and checked the display. "It's Landrieu." He injected a tone of joviality into his voice when he spoke to the lawyer.

Denise listened to a series of grunts and uh, huhs.

"She's right here. We're having lunch. Let me ask her." He

covered the phone with his hand. "Claude wants to know if you and Nonc Mitch are planning to come to the house for dinner Thursday night. He's already talked to Sissy and Jason, and they'll be there, but he says he hasn't heard from you."

"I still haven't asked Mitch." Denise looked perturbed. "This Thursday?"

Robert waved his hand in front of his face. "Not this one. *Next* Thursday."

"Well, that's still short notice for a dinner party." She frowned "That's why I hadn't called Claude back." She took her purse from the chair beside her. "I guess I misunderstood something."

"Claude says it's just an impromptu welcoming party for Laurette, nothing fancy, just a buffet."

Denise clucked her tongue and fished her phone out of her purse, then punched in her husband's number. A brief conversation confirmed that he could make the dinner. "Ask Claude if they're inviting the kids."

"Yeah. Wants us all there." Robert clicked off his phone. "It'll be a buffet style dinner, and casual dress."

"Buffet, huh, all right with me. Making it easy on Sharla," she commented, with just a touch of acid. "Wonder what will happen to that snotty high yella when this Laurette up and turns over the property to us and leaves. Suppose she's put some money aside?"

He wiped his lips on his napkin. "Don't know. According to Mama, the gal's always been uppity, ever since she came to Shadow Cove when Nonc Etienne married Celine, and she moved out there with her to be her maid."

"That's because she's nearly white...quadroon anyway...never has known her place." Denise sniffed. "I've often wondered if that story wasn't true about her and Celine having the same daddy. And her mama Bethany Williams *is* very light skinned."

"Wouldn't surprise me. Old Marc Renard was a tomcat." He snickered. "Still is...every chance he gets."

"I wonder if any Renards will be invited to this *fais do do*."

"Hmm. Claude didn't say. If they are, this could get interesting."

Chapter 19

My new uncle, Claude, picked up me up at my hotel the next morning, and I checked out. We stopped at his office so I could sign the paperwork, making me the new owner of the plantation. Then he took me to brunch at Brennan's before driving out to Shadow Cove. I'd packed light for my trip, so there was plenty of room in the Jag for all my stuff. The night before, I kept out a pair of tan cropped pants and a dark green knit shirt and sandals to wear. I quickly discerned that New Orleans was a very casual city before the sun went down, and right now the late morning sun was beating down on us as we walked to where Claude had parked his car.

"There's a Cadillac Escalade in the garage you can drive or the smaller Caddy SUV if you prefer. There's also a Mercedes sedan that was Tante Helene's vehicle of choice. I think Sharla usually uses the Escalade," Claude told me. "Well, actually, they all belong to you now, along with everything else on the plantation, so you can drive whatever you want."

We dodged around the street musicians set up on the intersection of Royal and Bienville. Claude dropped a couple dollars into the hat turned upside down on the *banquette* to collect donations.

"I'll probably opt for the little Caddy until my Cayenne is delivered. I called the realtor last night, and she's actually going to drive the car here herself, along with her husband. She says that'll give her a good excuse for a vacation in New Orleans. She's overseeing the packing and shipping of everything else."

We got into his car and headed out of the French Quarter. On this trip, I was paying more attention to the landscape and buildings we passed. Louisiana was like another planet compared to Seattle, with its squeaky-clean, environmental-friendly everything. There was an air of something I could think of as only genteel decay about the older sections of New Orleans, and even the newer buildings seemed to have a patina of age.

I turned my head to gawk, spying a two-by-four somebody had placed on the wrought-iron bannister of a second story gallery to support a window air-conditioner unit sticking out of a third story window. If the board slipped, the air conditioner could fall and brain somebody on the street below.

Claude saw my expression and laughed.

"This *is* N'Awlins," I mimicked the local patois.

"You're fitting in quick, *cher*."

"I called the bank where I stored my jewelry before I left, and they're sending my jewelry by special courier…like they're delivering the crown jewels or something. They wouldn't allow me to have Janet bring the jewelry with the other stuff."

"It's an insurance thing." Claude stopped at a redlight, and a couple of nuns in old-fashioned black habits crossed in front of us.

One of the sisters waggled her fingers at Claude.

He rolled down his window and called, "Whereyat, Brigitte?"

"What you doin' with that pretty girl, *matou*," the older of the two women called back. "You changin' your spots for stripes this late in the game?"

"*Ne jamais arriver, cher souer*," Claude answered, making a clawing motion with his hand, in reference to her calling him a tomcat.

Both nuns laughed, and they went on their way.

Still chuckling, Claude explained. "Brigitte...or Sister Marie-Jean, as she's now known...and I have been friends since we were children." He pulled the car through the light and returned to the subject we were discussing. "I suppose this Janet will deserve a tip on top of her commission for selling your condo, since she's decided to drive your car here from Seattle."

"If everything goes off without a hitch, she'll have earned it," I said. "And I'm footing her hotel bill while she's here and her other travel expenses; although, she already told me she and her husband will be responsible for their food and liquor bills. They're pretty nice folks. Not leeches."

"That's good to hear." He deftly maneuvered his car around a delivery truck parked in front of a souvenir shop. The ancient streets were barely wide enough for two vehicles to pass. "You'll need some help for a while, getting settled in and taking care of the business," the lawyer went on, stopping for another of the ubiquitous traffic lights. "And I'll be right here to help you as long as you need me." He reached over and squeezed my hand.

"You have no idea how much I appreciate that."

"I'm glad you made the decision to stay so quickly."

We'd gone over the plantation's finances that morning, and I'd seen nothing that raised a red flag or indicated that Landrieu's management of the property was ever anything except open and above board. "I saw no reason to dawdle about accepting what my father...um...I guess really my grandparents...left me." Mama would've warned me to keep my guard up, but I genuinely liked my "Uncle" Claude Landrieu. He seemed to be the true Southern gentleman his appearance and manners indicated. And in the matter of running the plantation, I could find nothing amiss. Plus, my grandparents had trusted him completely. Still, there was Mama's voice whispering in my ear to be on the alert.

As if reading my mind, he reiterated. "Your grandparents always treated me like one of the family." A grim expression passed over his face. "Certain members of your family resent that. That's the reason

I'm glad you took possession so quickly. It won't officially belong to you for another year, but in that time, there's nothing they can do to keep you from doing whatever you want on the property, renovations and so forth. You just can't sell it."

With the skill of long familiarity with the narrow streets clogged with tourists, carrying packages and *geaux* cups of liquor, Claude navigated the route out of the Quarter without mishap, turning onto a wide boulevard that would take us out of the city. I still wasn't sure I wanted to try driving in that part of New Orleans until I knew my way around. The oldest section of town was full of side streets, alleys, *cul de sacs*, and one-way venues, all constantly packed with people ambling aimlessly, drinking, and not watching where they were going.

"Do these relatives of mine feel like the plantation should have been left to them?"

"They want the place divided up, and each would take a share to do with as he or she pleases. They've been squabbling about it since before Etienne died." He chuckled. "They had no idea that I've known where you were all along. That's another reason I waited almost a month before contacting you. I wanted them to think that I was having to search for you." He waggled an eyebrow. "A good poker player never reveals all his cards at once."

"As I told you, Mama left me pretty well off. Apparently, she spent very little of that five million dollars of 'hush money,' I guess I should call it," I ventured. "Her so-called husband, Mercer, was rich, so the money just sat in the bank. I didn't...or don't...have to work unless I want to. But I'd wanted to work, since I'd gotten my degree in architecture. Now...I don't know. Maybe I'll be a Southern belle of leisure for a while."

"That architecture degree will come in handy with whatever renovations you want to make to the house."

"If nothing else, it will assure me that I'm not being ripped off." A burgundy vintage Rolls Royce pulled up beside us at an intersection, and I admired the gleaming automobile.

Claude nodded to the driver, a black man wearing a gray fedora.

The man grinned and returned the greeting, touching two fingers to his fancy hat, his smile flashing diamonds between his front teeth.

"Asphodel Delesseps," my uncle commented. "A client."

"Looks like a pretty rich one. What does he do?"

"Pimps, mostly."

My jaw sagged, and he burst out laughing at my expression. "Not all my clients are the most upstanding of citizens, but they pay the bills just like everybody else." He continued to chuckle. "Besides, I've known Asphy since he was a kid. He's not all bad, and he's quite the entrepreneur. He's spent a lot of money helping with the post-Katrina restoration projects."

"Oookay. As I keep learning, New Orleans is a place like no other."

"And I would live no place else," he commented with a grin. "You don't seem to have any qualms about moving here." He returned to the subject at hand.

"In spite of some of the things I'm seeing, I have no reservations at all. I'm actually excited about it. I told you I never really liked Seattle. Somewhere in my subconscious was this niggling memory of a warm place, lots of sunshine. I guess I always felt like a crawfish in a salmon pond."

He threw back his head and laughed.

Claude Landrieu had one of the most marvelous laughs I'd ever heard. Yes, I liked this man and hoped nothing would change that.

"I love this place. I even love the heat and humidity...the stink of the river...the wild and crazy people...all of it. I feel like Alice falling down the rabbit hole, and I never want to climb back out." I twisted around to face him. "Seattle is so clean, so environmentally perfect. Even the people look perfect, fit, healthy...not even the grunge element looks like the street people here. I always felt like I was supposed to be someplace else. I just didn't know where until I arrived in New Orleans." I fluffed up my hair with both hands. "I know it sounds weird, but I just felt like I was coming home, from the moment I got off of that airplane and got my first whiff of that

New Orleans smell, heard the voices of the natives. Something in me just clicked."

"You were coming home, *cher*. You just didn't know it."

We drove a few minutes in companionable silence.

"Nobody back in Seattle you'll miss?"

"Not really. I never had many friends in school, and I just broke up with first and only boyfriend a few months ago." I shrugged. "I never became close to anyone at work either. I knew they thought I was just a little diva, marking time until I found a rich man to marry."

"How did you get on with your stepfather?"

"Mama married Mercer when I was about five." My attempted laugh sounded strangled. "Pretended to marry I should say, after what you told me. I think he felt guilty about leaving his wife and marrying Mama. He was always decent to me, but no bond ever formed between him and me. He was Mama's husband, not my daddy." I gave him a thin smile. "He went back to his first wife after Mama died, and I've seen him only a couple of times, and there was a definite chill in the air."

"He was probably pissed about that money he didn't know about that Celine left you."

"No doubt, but my mama did look after me, in even in death." I heard the catch in my voice and was quiet a moment to compose myself. "He made all the arrangements for Mama's cremation, didn't consult me at all. He gave me all her jewelry and personal possessions." I licked my lips. "Of course, that was all before he and I found out about the money she'd left me. Had he known about that, I wonder if he would've been so generous." I huffed. "He was very quick to give me Mama's personal stuff, including the urn with her ashes. It was like he couldn't get rid of her…and me…fast enough, so he could run back to his first wife." I turned back in the seat and leaned my elbow on the window frame, twirling a lock of hair around my finger. "Right after Mama died, he took off for his cabin in the woods. I didn't see him or hear from him for three or four days. I guess that's when he was making arrangements to sell the house out from under me."

"He didn't even talk to you about it or ask if you were looking for a place for yourself?"

I shook my head. "Not a word. He simply turned all Mama's belongings over to me and told me he'd sold the house and I'd have to find another place to live. Like I'd just lost my mother, and now I was losing my home." I stared unseeing at the landscape whizzing by. "Then I got a call from Mama's lawyer, saying there was a will. That's Arnold Fowler. Mercer and I were summoned to his office, and it was obvious from the get-go that Mercer had no idea Mama'd hired a lawyer and made the will, leaving me all that money." I barked a laugh. "I don't know who was more stunned, but I wish you could've seen Mercer's face. She left him nothing, but it was like she wanted him to be at the lawyer's office so he'd know about the money she left me. Without my inheritance from Mama, I would've been out on the street with nothing except what was in my savings account."

"Bless your heart." He reached for my hand again and gave it another squeeze. "Mercer gave you nothing in the way of support in one of the worst times of your life."

I nodded. I'd thought the same thing but never mentioned it to anyone. I didn't want to sound like a whiner.

Landrieu grunted. "Well, she was never married to him in the first place. Wonder how long it'll take him to find that out, not that he can do a thing about it at this point."

"Knowing Mercer, he'll never tell a soul."

Claude chuckled. "You don't think so?"

"No. He'd never want anybody to know somebody had made a monkey out of him. I think that's why he stayed married to Mama… pride, ego. I knew they weren't happy with each other. She had a way of dazzling people."

"And then the new wore off," Claude said drily.

"Exactly. And he'd never have admitted to a soul that he'd made a mistake. He's very stiff- necked. We had this huge house, and he and Mama even had separate suites." As we talked, I could hear myself falling back into the slow cadence of the South, mimicking

Claude's speech patterns. "What a joke she played on him. They weren't even married, and he could've walked out any time he wanted to…but he never knew that." I drew my lips in a line. "Boy, my mama was a piece of work, and I never even realized it. If she weren't my mama, I guess I'd call her a brazen, conniving hussy. But she did look out for me."

"She did do that." He sighed. "Miss Celine was the ultimate Southern Belle. She would've been perfectly suited to the N'Awlins society of the Nineteenth Century, down on de ol' plantation, fanning and sipping mint juleps, while the servants stepped and fetched."

I laughed at his droll humor. "I know that's right. She was like some exotic bird in Seattle. There was no other woman like her there. I think that's why Mercer was so bowled over by her. His ex-wife was a very sporty type, into tennis and golf, always in jeans and sneakers. No way would you have gotten Mama onto a tennis court; she might've broken a nail. Of course, I have to admit, I'm a lot like that, too. I'm not athletic, find sports boring in the extreme. Except maybe football. It has a certain almost intellectual element to it."

"And then there are all those fine asses in those tight uniforms. Umm, umm."

I gave him a sideways glance. "Yep. There is that."

We both guffawed.

In spite of his being two generations older than me, I felt no awkwardness at his ribald joking. There was none of the dirty old man in Claude Landrieu.

"How did you wind up going into architecture? Doesn't seem quite fittin' for a belle in training."

"I like to work with home plans and designs and watch things being built." I cut my eyes at him, and my tone was mischievous. "Notice I said the words 'plans,' 'designs,' and 'watch.' I'm not what you'd call very handy, but I can put a very female spin on the design of houses, and it's women who actually buy the houses."

"Or gay men." He winked at me.

For the rest of the trip, we chatted about what we looked for in the design of a house and were not the least surprised that we had similar tastes.

"One of the first things I would do is put in a pool," Claude told me and turned off the highway onto the long driveway to Shadow Cove. "Etienne talked about doing that, but as Sharla pointed out, sometimes he became unable to control his motor functions, and she feared he might drown, so neither of us encouraged that project."

Claude pulled the Jag into the circular driveway. Again Sharla came out onto the front verandah before we reached the door. This time she was wearing denim shorts and a red cotton blouse tied at the waist.

"Are you psychic? You're here before we reach the door." I teased.

Sharla hugged me and then pointed to the tiny camera overlooking the front of the house. "From the kitchen I can monitor who comes to the door."

"A security system?"

"No." She shook her head. "Just a camera, so I can see who's at the front door. It's activated by pressure on the front steps…just sees people, doesn't record anything."

It took only one trip for the three of us to haul my belongings upstairs to the room Sharla had prepared for me.

"Etienne's room was the largest bedroom, a suite actually, but it's very masculine, and I thought you'd be more comfortable here for right now," Sharla told me.

The room was large and airy with two sets of French doors opening onto the upstairs gallery. White-painted wainscoting ran up half the wall, and the upper portion was painted a cool sage green. I liked the sage, white, and beige bedspread, but the bed would have to go. I didn't care for the old fashioned four-poster, nor did I find the dark Victorian paintings adorning the walls to my liking. On the other hand, a white fireplace centered in the wall opposite the bed gave the room a cozy ambience. A sitting area, consisting of a loveseat and two chairs, occupied the space in front of the hearth.

A large, flat screen TV sat in a niche on shelves beside the fireplace, and an at-home work station nestled along a wall in a corner.

"I had the computer installed as soon as I knew you were coming home," Sharla said. "I figured you'd have a phone and I-pad, but the computer would be handy, too."

Another portrait of the original Laurette St. Cyr hung above the fireplace. She looked very young in the painting. She wore a white lace gown, and a small magnolia blossom was tucked into the black velvet ribbon around her neck. The resemblance between us was uncanny, but I couldn't think of myself as being half as beautiful as the Creole girl.

I would leave the painting in place. I rather fancied having Laurette for company.

I felt a thrill of excitement at being able to revamp and decorate my very own permanent home to suit myself. I walked over to one of the French doors and opened it. Stepping out onto the upper verandah, I discovered the room overlooked the family cemetery.

Sharla followed me. "I hope you don't find it ghoulish that the room overlooks the cemetery. You can change rooms if you like. I thought you might like this one because it belonged to the original Laurette."

"Really?" I turned to face the quadroon. "That's totally cool. Maybe I can persuade her spirit to give me some guidance."

Sharla did that eyebrow-cocking gesture at me. "Don't make light. More than one person has sworn they've sensed her presence in various parts of the house, and she was what you might call a very formidable lady."

I swear the hair on my arms rose. "You seem to know a lot about her."

"*Mais ye*. As luck would have it, in one of the old chests full of family papers, your grandmother and I discovered some house plans, and they showed who slept in each bedroom. And they were marked up in Laurette's own handwriting. I've saved all the old papers, in addition to several packets of letters and other things. I'm something of a history buff."

We walked back inside together. "For now, I think I'll keep this room. I have plenty of time to decide where I want to sleep. And it *is* a nice room."

Sharla grinned and spread out her arms. "The whole house is yours to do with as you please. Knock out walls to give yourself more room, revamp the bathrooms, whatever your heart desires, *cher*."

"Claude said you have your own suite. Where is it?"

"It's down the hallway on the opposite side, across from Etienne's suite."

I pondered my next words. "I hope you don't think I'm being forward, but it seems odd that such a pretty woman as yourself would want to live out here. I'd think you'd want to live in New Orleans. It's not that far away."

"And I hope you're not planning on running me off." Sharla raised one eyebrow at me.

This time, the gesture caused an odd prickle to run up my spine. I had the same habit myself, and so had my mother, Celine. "Not at all. Like I said, I'm just being nosy."

Sharla chuckled. "I came here with your mama right after her honeymoon. I went to nursing school while I worked as her maid. Then I just fell into being sort of a combination lady's maid and paid companion; although, Celine never treated me like a servant." She paused, and a melancholy look flickered momentarily through her turquoise eyes. "Later, when you were born, I stayed to look after you. I was your nanny. After your daddy was hurt, he needed a private nurse, so I stayed to look after him, and the family paid me far more than I'd've made as a nurse in a hospital. I suppose your grandparents came to think of me as family."

"You've welcomed me here just like you are family," I told her. "As far as I'm concerned, you will be my family, and this is your home for always." Despite the warnings I suspected my mother would be giving me, I felt very warm and comfortable with both Sharla and Claude. I hoped my feelings would not be betrayed.

"I appreciate that. I'll tell you a little secret. Your grandparents always paid me well to look after Etienne. When they died, they left me enough money that I'd be secure for life should I choose to leave Shadow Cove...or be forced to leave the place. I love this house, and I can't imagine living anywhere else."

I hooked my arm in Sharla's, and we started out of the room. "You have no worries about being evicted. The house is your home… for the rest of your life." I suppose I felt such an immediate bond with the other woman because she'd looked after me from the time I was born, until Mama took me away from here. She and I were connected, and I couldn't imagine making her leave this place that was home to us both.

"Come on down here, and I'll show you my crib."

Sharla's suite was directly across the hallway from the one my father had occupied. It consisted of a large bedroom, with an adjacent sitting room and a private bath. The bedroom and sitting room both had French doors that opened onto the upper verandah, or gallery, overlooking the front driveway. The rooms were decorated in yellow and white, with touches of green, and prints of tropical flowers. A fireplace occupied the wall between the bedroom and the sitting room, serving both rooms. A comfortable sofa and chairs were arranged so the large, flat screen TV could be easily viewed. Ferns and an ivy plant flourished in large Oriental fishbowl pots on the floor beside the French doors. A bird of paradise spread its petals in a marble vase. Clearly, Sharla loved to nurture animals and plants…babies.

A white desk in one corner held a computer.

But it wasn't the machine that caught my eye. Silver-framed pictures occupied the shelves above the computer, and I strolled over to get a closer look. My breath caught. My own face smiled back at me from over a dozen pictures, photographs taken from infancy until I was four years old.

I picked up one of several pictures showing Sharla holding me and studied it. I looked to be about four, so the picture must have been taken shortly before my mother left Shadow Cove. My skin was only a shade lighter than Sharla's…probably from spending so much time outdoors in the Louisiana sunshine. Her love for me shined from her dazzling smile.

Sharla came up behind me. "You were my baby, too." A mist filled the quadroon woman's eyes.

She loves me still. This certainty gave me a feeling of security I hadn't experienced since Mama died...just knowing one person in the world truly loved me unconditionally. My smile trembled, and I felt a flutter in my stomach. "I remember you taking care of me and playing with me. I remember loving you so."

Her expression shuttered quickly, and she turned away. "Here, let me show you my boudoir."

With a final glance at the photograph of the two of us, I put the frame back in its place and followed her.

The bedroom was furnished much like the living room, painted yellow and white, with splashes of tropical colours. A large, calico cat snoozed on the four-poster bed, covered with a white eyelet spread. "This is Madame Queen, Queenie for short," Sharla introduced. "One of my other babies."

The feline allowed herself to be petted for a moment and then curled up to finish her nap.

"I love cats, but Mama wouldn't let me have one. Neither she nor Mercer liked animals. In fact I've never had a pet."

"Celine couldn't abide anything that might mess up her perfect surroundings." A melancholy look crossed her face, but she quickly banished the expression with a smile. "Well, you can indulge yourself as much as you like. I have several frisky felines I'll be happy to share with you. We have lots of room for dogs, cats, a giraffe if you want one. And, I repeat, it *is* your house, and don't let anybody bully you into thinking otherwise."

My primitive alarm system jangled at her tone, and I was reminded of the not-so-carefully veiled warnings I'd received from Claude. He told me virtually the same thing. Something was definitely rotten at Shadow Cove. It was with no little trepidation that I was anticipating meeting the St. Cyr clan.

Chapter 20

I spent the next few days getting settled in and exploring every nook and cranny of my home. I was having a wonderful time poking around the house and even in the family cemetery. I picked some flowers and placed them in a vase at the original Laurette's aboveground tomb, one she shared with her husband, Kyle Tanner. The graveyard was well tended by the yardmen, and I actually enjoyed moving among the marble mausoleums, running my fingers over the cool stone, a sort of communing with my long-dead family.

The huge carved angel adorning Laurette's resting place gazed down at me. In spite of her stony visage, I felt almost as though the angel was watching over me, welcoming me.

I passionately loved my new home and was determined nobody was going to take it away from me. I kissed my fingers and touched the angel's toes before heading back to the house. I promised Sharla I'd help her with the food for tonight's party, and I needed to decide what to wear for my first meeting with my family.

I'd quickly realized my Seattle wardrobe would not do in the

New Orleans heat and humidity, so I treated myself to a couple of shopping excursions. New Orleans had it all, Dillard's, Saks, oodles of specialty shops. I was in shoppers' hog heaven.

I had a little skip in my step, as I navigated the family tombs on the way back to the house.

Chapter 21

The evening of my "debut," as Sharla called it, arrived, and I found myself eager to meet those family members who'd been invited. The trepidation I felt earlier about being thrust amongst these unfamiliar people had abated somewhat. After all, I kept reminding myself, I was the legal mistress of Shadow Cove Plantation, whether they liked it or not. This was my roost to rule.

I'd spent most of the afternoon helping Sharla with the food preparation. I took a shower and washed and dried my hair.

From my newly purchased finery, I selected a pair of black slacks and a colorful, tropical print blouse, sprinkled with sequins. Sharla said the party would be a casual buffet dinner with family and a few friends.

"No white ball gown required." I laughed to myself, remembering Sharla's words. I donned the *fleur de lis* earrings I'd bought in the Quarter my first day back in New Orleans. I turned my head this way and that, admiring my reflection in the mirror, watching way the diamonds sparkled. The salesman had told me the earrings originally belonged to a member of the Lemoins family, another old Louisiana clan.

I frowned at the face looking back at me. Constantly in the back of my mind were the warnings from Claude and Sharla not to trust my family. I felt confused. The pair had been treated like family by my grandparents and by my father, none of whom I remembered with any clarity. My instincts were telling me to trust them and heed their admonitions. My *real* family I'd yet to meet, and I wondered who these friends were who had been invited.

A new wave of loneliness washed over me, a longing for my mama, and I forced myself to shake it off. I had to stop being a ninny…a mama's girl.

Sharla told me she was bringing in a few people to help her with the preparations and the cleanup. My honorary aunt, for I could think of no other way to explain our relationship, explained that she employed a network of temporary helpers when the family threw a *fais do do*, a local term for any sort of party or gathering.

As I descended the service stairs that led to the kitchen at the back of the house, I heard Sharla and another woman chattering in the kitchen.

"That chile had bes' be careful," an unfamiliar female voice said. "She don't know nothin' 'bout the bayou, and she sho' don't know nothin' 'bout these St. Cyrs. She have a bad accident, and won't nobody ever see her again. She be gator bait, her."

My breath caught in my throat, and I paused on the stairway. The words were like a cold draft wafting over me. I felt the hair on the back of my neck stand at attention. I eased down another couple steps to the landing, staying close to the wall, in case the old stairs creaked. My back against the wall, I pushed my head forward, closer to the doorway to hear better.

"I know that's right." This was Sharla. "I haven't wanted to scare her off, but I've warned her to watch her back. Etienne and his mama and daddy were good people, not perfect but good. But I wouldn't trust the rest of the St. Cyr tribe as far as I could throw them. I don't want to think they'd do anything to harm her, but I've lived with them nearly my whole life, and I know the kind of meanness some of them are capable of."

"Hmmph, I'd rather have a damn gator in my house as one of them people. That Robert has been a sneaky snake ever since he was a baby, him."

"They're better than her mama's people, the Renards," Sharla said. "And that's not saying much."

"*Mais, ye,*" the other woman spoke. "Yo' mama worked for them for years, so you know what they be like."

"Mama finally scraped up enough money to start her own house-cleaning service, when I left to move out here and look after Celine. She finally got shed of them…as much as she could anyway."

I heard cabinets opening and closing, dishes rattling.

"They treated you and yo' mama all right, didn't they?"

Sharla's bitter laugh carried to where I hunkered against the wall on the landing. "They had to."

"Let me get out there and get the dishes and silverware all laid out."

The door between the kitchen and the dining room flapped. I took a deep breath and smoothed down my blouse, then continued to make my way down the rest of the stairs. As I stepped into the kitchen, I forced my lips to stretch in a smile that I hoped wasn't a grimace.

Sharla must've heard me. She turned toward me, her face lighting up. "Don't you look the thing, *cher.*" The dusky-skinned woman wore a pair of cutoffs and had a "do rag," or "mammy rag," as I learned it was called in the South, tied around her head. A tea towel was tucked into the waistband of her shorts, flapping in front of her as she moved.

"I'm not sure if I'm overdressed or underdressed."

"You're just right. We're doing casual, but not blue jeans casual." She nodded toward the back door. "I've got Moline's husband, Jimmy, out back barbequing some chicken. He brought a bushel of oysters out from the city and has got them shucked and keeping cold on ice. I've got a pot of shrimp Creole cooking, along with a pot of beef ragout. Got the dirty rice keeping warm. I'm going to fry up some okra and some eggplant, too. That pot over there's got a mess of collard greens in it, and I've made a big salad. We're having my special chocolate bourbon pie for dessert, along with the pecan pies Moline brought with her."

"Oh, my God," I groaned. "I'm going to look like the Goodyear blimp by Christmas time."

The woman Sharla had engaged to help her for the evening bustled back into the kitchen, and Sharla made the introductions. Moline Roget was the color of milk chocolate, small and round, with a beautiful smile that displayed gorgeous teeth and deep dimples. She was close to sixty, but moved with an energetic bounce. She wore jeans and a white tee shirt with splatters of tomato sauce on it and, like Sharla, had a "mammy rag" protecting her hair.

"We'll all have to do a quick clean up and change clothes before the guests get here," Sharla instructed.

"No sense in dressin' up to cook," Moline agreed. "My Jimmy's been cookin' barbeque and shuckin' oysters. He stinks like woodsmoke and fish."

"I've got the batter and the bags of flour ready for the okra and the eggplant. So you can pop them into the fryer just before we're ready to eat," Sharla told Moline. "The crabs are in the fridge, ready for frying, too." To me, "You're going to love the deep-fried, soft-shell crabs. Little tiny things." She indicated the size of the crustaceans with her fingers.

"How many people are we entertaining?" I asked.

"Ummm…I invited twenty-six, twenty-seven, thereabouts. Some will bring some others, so we'll be ready for them. We'll have enough food for pharaoh's army because, in the bayou, when you say casual, you never really know how many will show up." Sharla paused to taste the Creole sauce. "The families, both St. Cyrs and Renards are invited; although, I invited only your grandparents and your aunts and uncles from the Renards, not the whole pack. There's just too damn many of them."

"That's what Claude told me. I had no idea my mama had three brothers and four sisters."

"*Mais ye*. And then there's all their offspring. I'd have to rent the Superdome to entertain them all," Sharla commented. "Only two of your Renard uncles and two aunts will be here…plus your grandparents. The rest of the tribe are either out of town or have other plans, but you'll get a sampling from the ones who show up."

Her expression had me wondering just exactly what this "sampling" was going to involve.

"Claude and Wills will be here, of course," Sharla went on. "And I invited the Delacroixes and the Lesieurs, too, and Paul Thibodeaux's got a mess of shrimp he's boiled up for us and put on ice. He's bringing that, although I didn't ask anybody to bring anything."

"His wife bringin' that killer buttermilk pie she makes?" Moline pulled a stack of napkins out of the linen pantry.

"She better, else I may not feed her," Sharla joked. "Their daughter Katie's coming with them, and Paul's brother Remy, who will probably show up with an entourage to look Laurette over. You know how the bayou boys are."

"Entourage." Moline snorted. "More like his pussy posse."

Sharla laughed. *"Mais ye.* That's a more fitting name for them, seeing as how that's exactly what they are. I was trying to be genteel, ladylike, if you will."

"Call it like you sees it." Moline cocked her mouth to one side. "We know how them boys are."

"Can I help with anything?" I was standing around feeling useless, and I felt a prickle of annoyance at the notion of being "looked over" by the local yokels, like some prized heifer at a county fair. On the other hand, their curiosity was natural…and probably meant to be flattering. After all, I was the new girl in the neighborhood. All the locals would want to crawl out from under the front porch and get a gander at me, as Mama would have phrased it. *Good lord, I'm starting to think like these people talk.*

"You can help Moline lay out the stuff for the buffet," Sharla told me. "Come on in the dining room, and I'll show you where everything is."

I followed in her wake and saw the table had been covered with a snowy cloth, and a pair of tall, ornate silver candelabra decorated each end.

"Katie Thibodeaux still moonin', after that Delacroix boy?" Moline carefully stacked the folded napkins on the end of the table next to the plates and silverware. "She been like a love-struck calf ever since she went to work at that buildin' comp'ny he and his daddy owns."

Sharla laughed. "Court is hardly a boy. He just had his thirty-third birthday."

"He needs to get himself another wife, him. Have some babies and spend some of that money he's makin'."

"Is this Court Delacroix the building contractor Claude told me about?"

"Yes," Sharla answered. "His family's plantation, when it was a plantation, was right next door to the Shadow Cove property. What did Claude say about him?"

"He just mentioned that I might want to use him if I do any renovations." I paused. "Actually I guess it was Wills who suggested it."

"That Court Delacroix is some kind o' fine," Moline cocked her head me. "*Cher*, you might want to cast yo' eye in that direction. You gon' be needin' a man, you." She turned toward Sharla. "You invite his cousin Cheyne?"

"*Mais ye.* He'll be here if duty isn't calling." Sharla wiped her hands on the towel at her waist. "Cheyne Delacroix is our sheriff."

"He ain't married either." Moline shook her head. "Don't know what ails them Delacroix men and the women. 'course Court's a widower, but he done brooded 'bout losin' that crazy woman long enough." She crossed herself at the mention of the dead woman. "Her family's from N'Awlins, but she was schooled up north. I always figured that's what ailed her."

"That might've done it," Sharla agreed.

"Well, hell, that right there'd be enough to drive a body nuts, puttin' up with all them northerners and they attitudes." Moline huffed. "I stay right here where I belong, me. Don't need no Yankeefied at'tudes messin' up my head, no."

"Courtland's wife killed herself," Sharla explained. "Nobody could ever understand why. Most people thought he was the perfect husband."

"Maybe not too perfect," Moline said. "I got my suspicions 'bout what went down wi' that, but I ain't sayin', me." She thinned her lips and nodded. "That Cheyne'd be another good prospect for you. 'course he ain't got Court's money, but he's still handsome as sin. Better man than Court. Ain't got no rich daddy to bankroll him, and he's a good man."

"Oh, my God. I'm hardly unpacked, and y'all've got me married off." The slow, sing-song cadence familiar in my childhood had seeped back into my speech.

"Moline just can't stand to see a woman happily single, or man either, for that matter," Sharla teased. "Y'all quit yammering and finish getting the dining room set up."

Chapter 22

While setting up for the dinner party, Moline told me she was a first cousin to Sharla's mother, Bethany Williams.

"Bethany's daddy and my daddy are half-brothers. 'course Bethany's mama was almos' white, what's called oc'troon," the black woman explained. "My mama was a woman of mixed color, too, but she was more black than white, her. My grandpa on my daddy's side was bright…could pass for white, him, but not down here 'round N'awlins, where ever'body knows ever'body else." She cackled.

My head was spinning with all these explanations of family connections and who was what part black and what part white. I wondered if somewhere back in the nether regions of my own ancestry I might be "tarred with the brush," as I'd heard the saying go, but with my mother's fiery hair and bright blue eyes, I thought it unlikely.

"Bethany went to work for yo' mama's people right out of high school," the maid went on. "Don't know how she stood 'em for so long. Them Renards definitely think they stuff don't stink. Treated the help like they was still down on de ol' plantation." Having laid out the serving pieces, she put the silver back in its place on the tall, carved sideboard. "Me, I'm not gon' put up with bein' treated like that."

"Why did Bethany tolerate it?"

Moline tossed me an arch look and didn't exactly answer. "Guess they all had to put up with each other."

The sound of two argumentative voices drew me through the dining room to the family room, from which I could see the entrance hall. Apparently, the front door was unlocked.

"Be careful not to break the heads off those stargazer lilies on the door jamb." Claude used his fanny to shove the door wider, and he and Wills jockeyed armloads of flowers into the entrance hall. "Thought y'all would be needing a nice centerpiece for the table, but Wills insisted we bring enough for a damn funeral," Landrieu announced. He and his partner went into the dining room and proceeded to arrange the flowers and candles on the dining table. "We've got more in the car for the rest of the rooms."

The odor of the beautiful lilies, called stargazers, almost knocked me down. I twitched my nose at the aroma of Mama's favorites, the gardenias. Roses of every color were piled high, waiting to be arranged.

Wills was already sorting through the boxes of greenery. "We know where all the vases are stored, so it won't take us long to arrange the flowers. Never mind us. We'll handle the posies."

I did some more of what I seemed to be cut out for…just standing around…while Moline and Sharla headed for the bathrooms to take quick showers and change clothes before the other guests began arriving. At least the men allowed me to help in placing the flowers and candles around the rooms where the entertaining would be done.

When the women came back to the kitchen, I was surprised to see Moline wearing a gray striped maid's uniform with a white apron.

She laughed at my expression, "*Cher*, I am a maid by profession and make no 'cuses for it, me. Housekeepin' and maidin' is what I do best."

Sharla, on the other hand, was wearing black pants and a black sleeveless shell, embellished with a sequined camellia on one shoulder. In a way, the ensemble was a uniform, conservative, something one might expect a modern housekeeper to wear.

"Don't I look fine, me?" Jimmy, Moline's husband appeared. He, too, had showered and changed from the cutoffs and tee shirt he'd been wearing to shuck oysters and barbeque chickens. He wore black pants, with a long-sleeved white shirt and a short, gray striped vest that matched Moline's dress. Hands out to his sides, he turned in a circle, so I could admire him.

"*Mais ye.*" I lapsed into the patois. "You do clean up good."

"In addition to being a first class oyster shucker and barbeque chef, I'm a bartender." He grinned at me, showing a gold-wrapped canine tooth.

The bar was in the family room, and Jimmy started laying out the glasses, shakers, and stirrers. His wife bustled from the kitchen, bringing him a supply of sliced fruit and veggies for garnishes.

A young woman wearing a uniform identical to Moline's hurried into the room, smoothing her apron. "I'm sorry I'm running a little late, Grandpa. My lab took longer than I thought it would."

I immediately noticed the strong resemblance between Moline and the newcomer. The younger woman was thinner, but she had the same beautiful smile and dimples.

"This is our granddaughter, Larissa. She going to Tulane...gon' be a doctor, her." Jimmy beamed. "We're right proud."

"Either that or I'll open my own catering business," the young girl teased. "I'm getting lots of experience in that." Without being told to do so, she started placing goblets and flutes on trays. The glassware would be filled with wine and champagne to be passed among the guests.

From the looks of things, the Roget family was accustomed to working for the St. Cyrs when the occasion called for their talents. They all seemed to know where everything was kept in the house, and they dived in and did what was needed with little direction. Again I felt a bit anxious at having so many people knowing so much about the house I lived in, owned actually.

Chapter 23

The sun was dropping behind the trees, and the lights on the front verandah and along the driveway illuminated the front of the house. The chandeliers in the entrance hall and the living and dining rooms, as well as in the family room, cast warm glows over the polished furniture and brought out the jewel tones of the carpets adorning the tiled floors.

I walked through the rooms, admiring how quickly the small staff had readied everything for a party. My excitement was tempered with a new wave of nervousness at the prospect of meeting my family for the first time in twenty years. So far, I gleaned that, while my father and grandparents had been held in some esteem, the rest of the clan were not well-regarded. I hoped I could judge them with impartiality and form my own opinions. After all, they were the only family I had.

"Do you suppose I'll measure up to the standards of both families?" I asked Sharla from the entrance hall. She was taking a last look at the flowers in the family room. "You said the Renards are bigger snobs than the St. Cyrs. What if they don't show up?"

"It's like mixing scorpions and rattlesnakes when you get the St. Cyrs and the Renards together." She came up beside me. "Everyone I invited RSVP'd. They'll all show up out of curiosity, if for no other reason."

The doorbell rang.

Sharla stepped ahead of me. "I'll get it, *cher*. It's probably Denise and her tribe. They always arrive early, so they won't miss anything." She winked at me. "Watch yourself with her. She's a bitch on wheels, so be prepared for her to try to bully you."

"Thanks for the heads up."

"Go on into the family room with Jimmy. That's where everyone will be gathering." She laughed. "Where the booze will be dispensed."

As Sharla predicted, the first wave of St. Cyrs consisted of my Aunt Denise and her husband, Mitchell Couliette, with their son Junior and his fiancée, Patsy Martin, in tow.

Another car was pulling into the drive way, and Claude took over the duties of introducing everyone to me, while Sharla manned the front door.

The resemblance between my aunt and my father was uncanny, the same dark hair, green eyes, strong, angular facial features, and she was a strapping woman, no little dainty thing. She sailed into the room like an Eighteenth Century man o' war. Mitch Couliette, on the other hand, was fair, with graying blond hair, and his girth displayed a fondness for Creole cooking. He walked three paces behind his wife. Junior was the image of his father and was already a good fifty pounds overweight, and not yet thirty.

His fiancée was pale and thin, with lank brown hair that had been tortured into some semblance of a "big hair" coiffeur. The bouffant "do" made the rest of her appear even more lifeless and wilted, but she sported what looked like a four-carat diamond ring. She was around my age and was decked out in an orange spandex mini with black ankle strap platforms and an armload of black and silver bangles that looked capable of snapping her frail wrist.

My aunt's green eyes remained flat and cold as she fussed over me, gushing about how I looked so much like my daddy. "There's no mistaking you for a woods colt, *cher.* You're St. Cyr through and through."

I felt my hackles rise at the "woods colt" remark, as if she'd been entertaining ideas that I might be an imposter. Keeping my face devoid of expression, I made a point of letting her see me make a careful perusal of her, from head to foot. The ankle-length, tropical print skirt, fuchsia knit top. and fuchsia wedgies were flattering and obviously expensive. Her hair and makeup were perfect. I hated to admit, she was quite an attractive woman.

Talking nonstop, Denise (I had trouble with the "aunt" part) made her apologies for the absence of her second son Phillipe who was on a cruise with his wife. Her husband and first son Junior muttered "how do" and headed for the bar. The Fiancée, as I was already thinking of the plain-faced Martin girl, stood around looking lost, while her future mother-in-law continued to fawn over me and jabber at me.

Sharla ushered in a young woman in full Goth regalia, her long black hair streaked neon purple. Her lips and nails were painted black, and her St. Cyr green eyes were outlined in thick black eyeliner. Rings pierced her upper lip, her nose, and one eyebrow and sparkled from several holes in each ear. She flaunted a black leather skirt and matching vest, with nothing under the vest, torn black stockings, and black boots. A spider was tattooed on her neck, and a hodgepodge of tats formed a sleeve on her right arm. This was Denise's daughter Chantal.

Her boyfriend, introduced as Toad, had candy-apple red hair and more piercings than a dart board. He wore tuxedo pants, a red velvet vest, and a wife beater with a sequined dragon on it. Tattoos covered most of his exposed flesh. I guessed they were both in their early twenties. From their garbs, makeup, and tattoos, it was hard to tell.

"They're in a band that plays in clubs in the Quarter." Denise waved them aside, clearly embarrassed by their bizarre appearance. "Where is Andre?" She demanded of her daughter.

"Parking the wheels, making himself useful." Chantal sulked. "So, can we get a drink or something?"

Andre Couliette slunk through the front door. "Y'all coulda waited for me," he groused to his Gothed-out sister. "It's not like I'm the hired help, ya know."

"This is the baby of our family." Denise beamed.

The "baby" was twenty-one and the only one who looked like a St. Cyr. He had his mother's dark brown hair and green eyes. He was about six feet tall and quite handsome, or would be if he hadn't worn the look of a kicked dog. His neatly pressed tan casual pants were paired with a red and tan striped knit shirt.

We shook hands, and he asked me about living in Seattle. "I'm planning a trip to the west coast to visit a friend in the Napa Valley. I'm hoping I can find a job there."

His mother sniffed. "Going off to find himself, he says. As if staying home and helping tend to the family business is beneath him."

"Mama, please. Let's not start." Andre seemed to sag into his socks.

So far Andre appeared to be the most normal member of this branch of my family. He dressed decently and had some manners. Denise's remarks told me she was not thrilled with her son's planned relocation to California.

"Go get yourself something to drink, son." Denise made a shooing motion with her hands. "Your new cousin and I have things to discuss." She turned to me, spreading her lips in a smile that bordered on lascivious. "So, *ma cher*, what were you and your mama up to in Seattle all these years? I can't imagine why she moved to that place."

While I wasn't fond of the city I grew up in, the way Denise pronounced the word sounded like Seattle had to be on a par with the seventh circle of Hell. "I suppose we lived as normally there as anyone would live anyplace." My answer was bland. I wasn't going to mention anything about my mother's second husband…who as it turned out wasn't really a husband after all. "I went to a small private school. Then I studied architecture in college and worked for a large firm…."

"You worked?" She snorted as if *work* was a four letter word.

Before I could answer, she forged on. "I'm surprised Celine would allow that."

"I had my degree and…."

"What about boyfriends?" Her dark eyebrows wiggled like two caterpillars getting ready to rumble. "Don't you have some special beau pining for your return? I'm sure he's eager for you to get back home."

Ah, that's it. She's trying to find out if I'm staying here. I put on my best Scarlett O'Hara simper. "Why, Aunt Denise, I just love it here. There's no way I'll ever go back to Seattle. I belong here at Shadow Cove. This is truly where my heart longs to stay." *Yeah, I'm laying it on thick.*

"You're planning to stay here…live here?" Denise St. Cyr Couliette's face matched her fuchsia blouse.

"I just love the bayou and New Orleans. I don't know why Mama ever left."

"Well, if you're thinking about running this plantation by yourself, you can't imagine what you're taking on. You know nothing about raising cane."

I might raise a lot more than cane. You mess with me and you're going to find out there's a lot of Mama in me.

"Not to worry, your Uncle Mitch and I will be here to help you along. So will your cousin Robert." She looked toward the entrance way. "He and his wife Regina…we call her Reggie…should be here any minute." She learned toward me and lowered her voice. "Now don't be letting any outsiders try to influence you. You can rely on Mitch and me to look after the family's interests."

My attention was diverted by a large, florid-faced man, lumbering through the door beside the bar and carrying a huge stainless steel tray loaded with shrimp. Behind him, Wills was bringing in bags of ice. The two men were setting up the shrimp cooler on the sideboard, covered with thick padding to protect the surface, while Moline bustled in with a tray of freshly shucked raw oysters on ice. "I got more of these trays in the fridge if you could help me with 'em, Wills."

I nearly laughed out loud when the maid cut her eyes at Denise and frowned. "We wasn't expectin' no guests for another twenty or thirty minutes, no."

Denise glared at Moline, who simply turned away, with a sniff of her little nose. "That gal's uppity. Always has been," my aunt snapped. "Now that you're here, you might want to make some staff changes. I'll be more than happy to refer some people to you. Like I said, you don't need to be depending on outsiders."

At that moment *outsider* Claude appeared at my elbow. "Excuse me, Denise. I want to introduce Laurette to Paul Thibodeaux."

"Thank you for the rescue. She's about has subtle as a tank," I murmured as he led me away toward the bar area.

We stepped around the Fiancée, Patsy Martin, standing alone and still looking lost.

"How are you this evening, Patsy?" Claude smiled and nodded toward the pale, quiet girl, then whispered to me. "She's Junior's third fiancée in five years. Odds are she won't make it to the altar with him either."

"She's wearing a nice ring. You suppose his parents paid for it?" Junior did not look or act like a ball of fire, so I wondered if he even had a job. He seemed as lifeless as the girl he was engaged to.

"Hardly." Claude gave me an arch look. "He's quite the entrepreneur, or so he thinks."

"Junior? He doesn't strike me as a future Donald Trump."

"He's one of the more successful purveyors...make that white purveyors...of illegal substances in N'Awlins." He gave me a jaundiced look. "I keep expecting him to get his cut throat any time, but then he doesn't do the deals himself, and his main supplier is a dude named Delmas Flynn down in Maybelline, Florida."

My mouth sagged open, and Claude grinned. "Sugah, there's virtually nothing that goes on in the St. Cyr family that I don't know about."

I closed my mouth and opened it a couple more times before any sound would come out. I was trying to wrap my mind around the idea that a member of my family was a drug dealer. "Do Aunt Denise and her husband know about Junior's business?'

"They pretend he's in real estate …but I'm sure they know what he's doing," Claude answered. "And be careful of those two. Mitchell Couliette's crooked as a birddog's hind leg."

"Isn't he a stock broker?"

"Uh, uh, that's Jason Laporte, your cousin Sissy's husband. Mitch is a petroleum engineer. He and Jason work on deals together, Mitch being a silent partner of sorts, along with your cousin Robert, which means they all have their own pipeline to some interesting oil connections in South America."

"Like oil cartels?" I said. "Like maybe tied to drug cartels?"

"Bingo." He pointed his finger at me like a pistol. "Robert lives off of his investments in a number of shell corporations…mostly off shore or in South America."

A fresh spate of the willies slithered up my backbone. This man did indeed know all my family's secrets, and I had to wonder if they knew how much he knew. Granted, he was a relative of sorts, but still, it made me uncomfortable to know somebody was privy to all my kin's secrets…and I was even more uncomfortable knowing the nature of those secrets. My thoughts skittered to Sharla. She knew the personal, intimate habits of the members of my family, from living with them. I wondered if she and Claude shared secrets and information. These two seemed awfully close. Being raised by a secretive, untrusting mother had honed my emotions to razor-sharp wariness. I reminded myself again that I didn't really know any of these people, blood kin, friends, none of them. "Jesus," I hissed.

"Pray to Him, baby girl. You'll need all the help you can get with these folks." Claude plastered a grin on his face and threw out an arm. "Thibodeaux, *mon ami*." He led me to where the big Cajun man was spreading the ice around the freshly caught and boiled shrimp.

"Landrieu, *tu crapeau!*"

"T'Paul, I want you to meet Laurette, Etienne's little girl."

"Ah, *ma p'tite*, you *are* a St. Cyr. You got de look, you," Thibodeaux boomed, and his gray eyes crinkled. "Sorry I got here a little late. I'd planned on being de first to arrive, so I'd have de shrimps ready for everybody."

"You're not late. You know the Couliettes," Landrieu provided in a stage whisper. "They have to get to everything early, don't want to miss anything or be missed by anybody."

Thibodeaux's chest rumbled in laughter. "I know dat's right." He winked at me. "I'll give you some sugar later after I get out of my apron. Don't want to get you smelling fishy, *cher.*"

He wore a big plastic apron over his party clothes and plastic gloves on his hands.

A daughter of the South, I remembered giving or getting "some sugar" referred to a hug and a kiss. I supposed I could handle sugar from him. Calling Paul Thibadeaux T'Paul, or *petit Paul,* was a misnomer. He was huge, like a big, rumpled Teddy bear. I instantly liked him.

"My wife Doralynne and our daughter Katie will be in tereckly," the big Cajun thundered. "Dey dropped me at de back do' wi' de shrimps. Said dey wanted to come in de front do' like white folks."

Moline was standing right beside him, and I cringed, but the maid didn't appear to take any offense. Instead she barked an order at him. "T'Paul, I need you to move yo' shrimps down a might. I want to put the sauces and crackers right there in between the shrimps and the oysters."

"Yes'm. Yo' wish is my command." Thibodeaux moved the big tray of iced shrimp down on the sideboard to make room for Moline's plates.

I was getting a hands-on course in Southern culture. Even in Seattle, I'd heard people make fun of the way Southern black people talked. From my mother's speech patterns, I knew "tereckly" translated to "directly" or "right away." I was picking up the cadence and realized Southern blacks and whites sounded exactly alike, and they didn't appear to get the least bit offended by comments and remarks that were considered politically incorrect in other parts of the country. I was not seeing any of the prickly attitudes between the races I'd anticipated.

Sharla was shepherding a new group of guests into the room. Leading the pack was Thibodeaux's wife, who introduced herself as

Doralynne. She turned to introduce her daughter Katie, who seemed unable to tear her gaze from the man beside her.

I had to stop myself from gaping. I'd never seen a man this handsome outside the movies. He was gorgeous.

Doralynne cut her eyes at her daughter then gave me an eye roll. She patted my arm and muttered, "Later. I got help to my man, me, and get this buttermilk pie in the icebox." She grabbed a shrimp as she passed the tray and headed for the bar, balancing a large rectangular plate that held her famous pie and asking Moline if she could help with anything.

Sharla stepped in to introduce me to Amboise and Henriette Delacroix, an older couple standing next to Mr. Gorgeous.

Katie Thibodeaux's big brown eyes grew even bigger as she gave me a full-body laser scan. Petite, brunette Katie was all too obviously sizing me up as competition for the attention of the man Sharla was introducing.

"And this is their son, Courtland."

Chapter 24

I found myself impaled by a pair of crystalline blue eyes framed by impossibly long black lashes. Courtland Delacroix stood an inch or so over six feet, had a thatch of sun-streaked blond hair, a golden tan, and was built like the proverbial brick outhouse. His smile was dazzling and roguish. He might have stepped off the cover of a lurid romance novel. His cream-colored, light summer jacket and yellow shirt set off his tan to perfection.

The man could've made a fortune in ancient Greece posing for statues. His manners and charm seemed to rival even his good looks. Courtland Delacroix appeared to be the epitome of the Southern gentleman.

Any Southern Belle worth the starch in her crinolines would've swooned. I might. He was simply too handsome for words, and he was still holding my hand he'd shaken. I would not've been surprised if he kissed my fingers.

Glancing past the luscious newcomer's shoulder for only a second, I noticed someone else gazing at Courtland, wearing the same rapt expression as Katie. I shouldn't've been surprised that we both found the man devastatingly attractive.

I answered his parents' polite questions about my life in Seattle and accepted their condolences for the death of my mother. The senior Delacroixes were both striking and elegant. Court's father tall, with curly, graying blond hair and those riveting blue eye, his mother only a couple inches taller than I, her blond hair stylishly cut, her green print sundress showing off her tan.

"Celine was the belle of every ball," Henriette assured me. "There was no one more beautiful or charming." She made a kissing motion on her fingers. "And your daddy, what a man." She chuckled. "A rogue, but then every man should have a little rogue in him, *n'cest pas?*"

Her husband threw back his head and laughed, the sound that of a man sure of his own supremacy and attractiveness. "Is that why you married me, *cher*? I thought it was my money." He put his arm around his wife. "Let's let these young people get acquainted while I have Jimmy build us a couple of martinis."

Katie attempted to cling to Courtland Delacroix's sleeve, but he was ignoring her. His attention was riveted on me, and I wasn't totally comfortable with what I took to be a bit of rudeness on his part, despite his charming manner toward me.

Court, as he instructed me to call him, flicked Katie Thibodeaux off of his sleeve like a fly. Taking me by the elbow, he steered me toward the opposite end of the room. "All this greeting must be making you thirsty," his baritone rumbled in my ear, sounding remarkably like Clark Gable playing Captain Rhett Butler. "Allow me to get us both a glass of wine from the bar, *cher.*"

Does everybody call everybody cher? I felt as if I had been dropped into a play of manners in the South of another era. I needed a lace fan to flutter. Before I could generate a tiny simper, I looked away from Court and found myself skewered by the daggers shooting from Katie's eyes. "If looks could kill" barely covered the murderous expression on her pretty face.

A chatter of voices at the front door caused me to shift my

attention from the spiteful face of the Cajun girl. A second wave of St. Cyr relatives were being led toward me by Wills.

"Laurette, honey, this is your cousin Robert St. Cyr and his wife Regina." Wills made the introductions, then shooed their offspring ahead of him, like he was herding cats.

Sharla had described both Robert and Regina, and I knew my cousins were a generation older than I, in their early forties. Unlike his deceased younger brother, Henri, my daddy married relatively late in life, so I was closer in age to my cousins' children. I had little recollection of Robert and none of Regina.

While Robert displayed the dark St. Cyr coloring, with the family's trademark green eyes, Regina was a tall, slim blonde, her hair upswept into an elegant French twist. Her studied air of sophistication was undermined by the calculating gleam in her sharp, brilliant blue eyes that seemed to dissect everything in their path. She was wearing a neo-Pucci print pants outfit in turquoise and hot pink. Giant beads of turquoise and pink dangled from her neck and ear lobes. Pink stiletto sandals boosted her five foot nine inch frame to over six feet. She talked as though her jaws were wired together and gave the impression of her looking down her nose at everybody from her considerable height.

"Do call me Reggie, *cher*. Everybody does." Those razor-sharp eyes sliced and diced me from head to toe. "Those earrings are *tres charmant*." Regina sprinkled her conversation with French words, as if to solidify her position as a member of an old Creole family, while her maiden name was the very American Whitlock.

My finger immediately went to my ear lobe to touch the diamond and gold *fleur de lis* baubles. "Thank you."

"Mama Simone, don't you love these earrings?" Reggie turned to the older woman at her elbow. "This is Robert's *mama*, your Tante Simone."

I was given another eyeball strafe. "So good to see you again, *ma cher*." My aunt leaned forward, I thought to kiss my cheek, but it was to examine my jewelry. "I have a shop in the Quarter, so I know jewelry. These appear very nice indeed."

"Mama's quite the expert on jewelry," Robert informed me. "I guess you take after Aunt Celine in your fondness for things that sparkle."

"I do like jewelry," I admitted. "I found these in a shop on Royal Street. They're estate jewelry. I thought I might as well buy myself a memento of my return to New Orleans."

Something in Reggie's supercilious expression wavered as she admired the gems. "Oh, then your trip is a mere visit, *n'est-ce pas?*"

I didn't miss the gleam, both avaricious and hopeful, that sparked in my cousin's eyes. "No. I'm not visiting. I'm here to stay." I flashed a pleasant smile and wasn't surprised to see Reggie's eyes narrow and her lips freeze in what was more a grimace than anything that could be called a genuine smile.

Regina nodded slowly. "*Vraiment? Nous allons voir.*"

I gave her only a quizzical look, thinking, *oui, cousine, we shall see indeed.* My French might be rusty, but I clearly understood the words spoken in a syrupy tone.

My Aunt Simone was speaking to me again. "So you're staying here at Shadow Cove, *cher?*"

"Yes. I love it here. I had no idea how much I'd missed my home."

The older woman rewarded my remark with a supercilious sniff. "Well, be careful you don't bite off too much." Her smile was wolfish. "Of course, Robert will be happy to help you find your way through the tangled mess I'm sure you'll find your *papa* left."

I had no intention of telling her that Claude had been over all the paperwork dealing with the plantation, and I'd found nothing amiss. I wondered what she was up to.

The older woman turned to introduce a young lady of about seventeen "This lovely creature is my granddaughter and namesake, Robert's older daughter. And this is number two daughter, Desiree."

The younger girl looked to be fourteen or so.

Before either girl could greet me, they were nearly knocked aside by their brothers, twins, Jean and Jacques. The boys did not bother to speak, but headed straight for the shrimp and oysters.

Neither their mother nor their grandmother made any move to correct their behavior. A young man in his late teens brought up the rear, and Reggie introduced me to her eldest son Bobby Joe, who barely nodded and zeroed in on the food.

I kept my smile in place. On the outside, Robert's crew looked more respectable than Denise's tribe, but their manners were nothing to brag about. So far, none of their offspring had said diddly to me. The teenage girls gave me a silent once-over, and the boys appeared to have nothing but food on their minds.

I was surprised to see Bobby Joe, who couldn't be more than nineteen, snag a glass of wine from the tray on the bar and down it in one gulp.

I looked over the elder Simone St. Cyr, my father's younger brother's widow. She was of medium height and slim, with perfectly coiffed silver hair and dark blue eyes, flat eyes, almost lidless, reptilian, I thought. Her features had a soft, smoothness to them, and my cousin Robert's face reflected their relationship, rather than exhibiting the St. Cyrs' more angular bone structure.

Glancing back at Robert, I caught him studying me. Although his eyes were the St. Cyr green, they had the same flat, lidless, lizard-look as his mother's. I shivered.

"It's so wonderful to see Etienne's baby girl again after so many years. I've thought of you often, *cher*." Tante Simone, as she insisted I call her, wore a white silk shirt and rhinestone-encrusted jeans with rhinestone-decorated wedgies. Her smile was no warmer than that of her daughter-in-law, so I took her words with a grain of salt.

"That's sweet," I murmured, my words matching hers in their insincerity.

"I'm a bayou girl born and raised," she went on. "I was a DuBey before my marriage. Our family owned a sugar mill upriver from Shadow Cove. "Like others, we sold much of our property, but still we're all like one big family." She put an arm around her granddaughter, the younger Simone.

The teenager continued to peruse me without speaking. I detected a sullen undertone in her silence. She resembled me, with the St. Cyr green eyes and long mahogany hair. She wore black jeans and a colorful, sleeveless print top, with a jeweled neckline, and black wedge sandals. The other girl, Desiree, looked much like her mother, and was decked out in a green and blue print sundress and white sandals. Huge white hoops decorated her ear lobes, and a dozen skinny white bangles adorned her wrists. She had an unappealing *hauteur* about her, influenced no doubt by her mother's behavior.

Bobby Joe St. Cyr, who was downing another glass of wine at the bar, was tall and thin, with dark brown hair and his mother's piercing blue eyes, eyes that never stopped moving. I had the impression those eyes missed nothing, and they had already pierced me like daggers.

I must truly pose a threat to these people.

The ten-year-old twin boys had been only a blur of thin bodies and pale blond hair. They were already attacking the shrimp, and one threw a shrimp tail at the other.

Moline pounced on them and grabbed them each by an arm. She hissed. "You two hellions, you mind yo' manners in this house or I be takin' both yo' butts out back fo' a beatin', and don't y'all think I won't."

Cousin Reggie, the boys' mother, seemed oblivious to the children's bad behavior or to their chastising by the maid. I noticed she was far more interested in the couple just arriving than in the antics of her sons. Regina St. Cyr's eyes were slicing into the newcomers like twin scythes.

Chapter 25

Sharla escorted Tommy and Lucille Lesieur over to meet me.

Her face a mask of hatred, Reggie's eyes tracked the petite, dark-haired Luci Lesieur.

What is that all about? I'll ask Sharla.

In any case, I took an instant liking to the Lesieurs, who owned a bed and breakfast in Frenchy's Landing. They were in their early thirties, and Sharla told me the Lesieur family and the St. Cyr family had been long time friends. Luci's mother was a cousin to Tante Simone St. Cyr.

Tante Simone had just told me we were all family. I'd heard plenty of jokes about the interrelationships among Southern families, and it seemed to be true.

As if reading my mind, Sharla interjected. "Nearly everybody in the bayou and around N'Awlins seems to be related to everybody else, white, black, French, American, Irish…you name it."

Luci chuckled. "And sometimes, we sure Lord don't want to be admitting it."

"I know that's right," Sharla agreed and directed the newcomers toward the bar and appetizer buffet. She pulled me aside. "I invited some of our neighbors to this *fais do do,* so you wouldn't have to put up with your family all sniping at each other, and I thought you might like to meet some people."

"What's with Reggie and Luci? I couldn't miss the looks Reggie was giving her, and she seems like a very nice person."

"Luci's a doll, as far as her personality goes, but she's hot to trot. She had a fling with Robert way back yonder in the dark ages. And Reggie never forgets a hurt, although she's hardly in a position to throw stones."

I raised my eyebrows. "Oh, Miz Creole Society has a secret?"

"Not much of one." Sharla snickered. "Miss High and Mighty Reggie got caught making the beast with two backs with Paul Thibodeaux's younger brother Remy in one of the boats he keeps down by the dock at his house. And let me tell you, Remy Thibodeaux is some kind of fine."

I added my own snicker. I'd taken an instant dislike to Cousin Reggie.

"Guess who caught her?" Sharla did not wait for an answer. "Luci Lesieur. Probably down at the boats looking for some action with Remy herself."

The doorbell chimed, and Sharla moved to greet the newcomers and bring them to me. I felt a bit like a queen, or maybe a crown princess, being introduced to my court and subjects, and they were all making no secret of sizing me up.

"This is Sarah and Rodney Chester. Rodney's a Sociology professor at Tulane, and Sarah's a poet of some renown in the Quarter," Sharla told me. They were both dressed like 1970's hippies and were a friendly, outgoing pair.

"Ah, and here's our padre. You missed meeting him Sunday," Sharla reached out to hug a short, handsome, silver-haired man wearing a black shirt with a Roman collar. The priest had come in with the Chesters.

"I had pressing business in Palm Beach, m'dear." Father Gerald O'Malley might've spent most of his life in the Louisiana bayou country, but he still retained his melodic Irish accent. His bright blue eyes held a distinctly Leprechaunish twinkle.

"Uh, huh. How'd you do in the golf tournament?" Sharla teased.

He wagged his palm. "Not bad. Came in third." He grinned and hugged me. "Always glad to welcome a new parishioner. Of course, you're not exactly new to me. I christened you." His smile was broad. "I've known the St. Cyrs practically since I got off the boat from Ireland."

"By way of the Vatican, and it was a jetliner, not a boat, Father Gee," Sharla amended with a laugh.

"The fact that I got here is what counts, m'girl," he countered. "Now where can a man of the cloth get a drink?"

As if by magic, Larissa appeared at his elbow with a glass of scotch on the rocks. "Laphroaig, Father. Per your standing order."

"Bless you, m'child."

The house was rapidly filling, and I knew I'd never remember the names of all these people. So I'd concentrate on remembering the names of family and maybe call everybody else *cher.*

A woman bearing a striking resemblance to my cousin Robert came toward me, a mane of blonde-streaked, mahogany hair cascading to her shoulders. The first thing I noticed were her cold, flat, lizard eyes, St. Cyr green, but still reptilian. Angeline, call me Sissy, St. Cyr Laporte did not wait to be introduced. She waved her hand toward the man trailing her. "This is my husband Jason. He does the Wall Street thing, only in N'Awlins." Her thin lips stretched in what I assumed was a smile, but there was the same warmth I would expect from a snake. Those flat eyes gave me a better body scan than I could receive in an airport.

Sharla had told me the couple had three teenagers, and Sissy made her apologies for their absence.

I felt no great sense of loss at not meeting them.

Angeline's white lace sundress was expensive and tasteful, as were her white accessories, sandals, earrings and wrist bangles. The purity of the white outfit did not fit the vibes I was getting from her. I was glad neither she nor her husband tried to hug and kiss me.

Jason Laporte was a caricature of a sleazy 1950's con man. He had to be at least fifteen years older than his wife, with slicked-back, dyed-black hair, black eyes that never met mine when he spoke, swarthy, oily skin. He was thin and wiry, and his designer shirt and pants looked too big for him, the kind of man who would look like an unmade bed no matter how expensive his attire. His sleazeball appearance would've made me wonder how he'd snagged Sissy, who was quite good looking, had Sharla not already told me his family was old New Orleans money...lots of it. His smile held no more warmth than that of his wife.

"You'll probably need some help figuring out your financial situation." He got to the point in a voice that reminded me of Jack Palance's menacing whisper. "You can depend on me to help you, *cher*. After all, we're family. No need to go looking to outsiders for help." I saw his eyes slip toward Claude Landrieu.

He creeps me out like The Walking Dead, and he's wasting no time trying to get access to my inheritance. What a family. They have all the subtlety of a force-seven hurricane.

The pair excused themselves to get to the bar, and I wiped the hand Jason shook on my pants.

So far the St. Cyrs I'd met gave me no reason to trust a single one of them. They were a pack of ravenous wolves...*loup garou*...as the locals called the werewolf. The Renards were yet to arrive, and from what Sharla said, she might need to get out a whip and a chair to keep the two factions from killing each other.

Courtland Delacroix managed to insinuate himself next to me and was making small talk with the Chesters who had stood quietly by, ignored by Angeline and Jason. In addition to being handsome as sin, he was smooth and charming. He was bright and seemed to be one of those people who could talk to anybody about anything. Mama would've adored him.

I did a double take when I spied the man Sharla was escorting into the room.

From a distance, Courtland Delacroix and the newcomer could pass for twins, but as the man drew nearer, I could see there was a vast difference in the two. If anything, he was even handsomer than Court, and he seemed to fill the room with his presence.

"This is Court's cousin, Cheyne Delacroix," Sharla introduced. "Cheyne is our parish Sheriff."

Once again, I had to tuck my tongue inside my mouth before I made a fool of myself by drooling.

"I'm really glad he was able to make it this evening." Sharla gave the man an arch look. "We usually have to catch him on the fly for any kind of social event. Sometimes I have to wonder if we bore him or if he's just that dedicated to crime fighting."

"No man with his blood still coursing would find you boring, Sharla." His laugh rumbled. "I'm just not much of a gadabout, and you know it."

The two Delcroix men looked to be around the same age, early thirties. They had the same sun-streaked blond hair and crystal blue eyes, the same straight nose, and perfect white teeth. But Cheyne was taller than Court, several inches over six feet, and was built heavier. I'd bet he weighed around two hundred fifty pounds…solid muscle. Even in high-heeled sandals, the top of my head barely reached his jaw. This was one big man. And he looked as hard and unyielding as a solid concrete pillar. His dominating presence seemed to suck the air out of his surroundings.

He wore neatly pressed black slacks and a pale blue knit shirt that clung to his toned chest, abs, triceps, biceps, and a lot of things I was trying not to think about.

Unlike Court's smooth, cultivated charm, Cheyne's manner was rough-cut, a bit colder and harder, his voice a deeper baritone. His eyes were just as blue, but they held a wariness, like he was always distancing himself, summing up whoever he was talking to. There was a hint of suspicion in them, cops' eyes. Still, his tone was friendly when he spoke to the Chesters.

A prickle ran up my arms when we shook hands. His smile would've been beautiful, if there had been any warmth in his eyes. *Is this man really so cold? He might be. Would I like to thaw him out? Hmm. Mama would not approve of him. Too big, too rough, too intimidating, too primitive male.*

"So how's the so-called crime fighting going on the bayou, podnah?" Court asked, his tone indicating he really didn't care about the answer. He sipped his white wine from a crystal glass.

"Same old same old, mostly petty stuff," Cheyne answered curtly.

Electricity sparked between the cousins. These men did not like each other.

Cheyne paused to thank Moline for bringing him a drink, unrequested. This time, his smile reached his eyes.

"Virgin Mary," the maid commented.

"Now, Moline, gimme a break. I'm off duty as of an hour ago."

"I lied," she cackled. "That Mary ain't no virgin…she just the way you like 'em, hot and spicy."

I would never admit to a soul the direction my mind travelled at the maid's saucy remark. I had a feeling Cheyne Delacroix was pretty hot and spicy himself, not nearly as cultured and cultivated as his cousin Courtland. I wondered why that notion appealed to me. I'd always followed Mama's lead and paid attention to men who were polished. Mama would be quick to tell me the handsome sheriff should not be the man who sent my heart racing, but I couldn't ignore the surge of warmth that rushed through me when our elbows brushed each other.

I had to tread carefully here. My experience with men was minimal, nothing like what I assumed was normal for a young lady my age. At twenty-four, I suppose I was a semi-virgin. My three experiences had been with my only serious boyfriend. And I sent him packing when I learned he cheated on me. I never told my mother I'd been to bed with him.

At Moline's remark, Cheyne looked pointedly at me, a tiny smile tickling his lips. "Are we talking about drinks here, Moline?" He cut his eyes back toward the maid.

"We talkin' 'bout yo' taste in lotsa things, Mistah Po-lice man. I know yo' kind."

"Quit flirting with me, woman. Your man's giving me the evil eye."

"That case I better get my fine self back to work, me. Don't want to give Jimmy no cause to whup yo' butt."

I could just imagine the lanky, sixty-something bartender attempting to take on a man the size of Cheyne Delacroix.

The sheriff's laugh was hearty and genuine.

Maybe he isn't such an iceberg after all. Mama always told me the way to get a man's attention was to focus on what was important to him. I wasn't much of a belle, but I gave Mama's advice a try. "It seems pretty peaceful out here. I wouldn't think there would be much crime." I continued Court's line of conversation regarding crime fighting.

He shrugged his massive shoulders. "Mostly petty stuff, in-fighting amongst the locals."

"Petty crime, petty squabbles?" I said.

"Mostly. Not a lot of murder and mayhem, like you see in N'Awlins." He raised his eyebrows above the rim of his glass. "And I can do without all that. I'm a peaceable sort."

Somehow I doubted that. I could detect a suppressed aggressiveness wafting off him like pheromones.

"Ha. You love getting into stinks." Court confirmed my suspicions. "Peaceable, my aa…ahem…foot." He waved a hand. "We should be talking about something else in front of a lady."

M my hackles rose at his condescending tone. "No really, I'm interested. I'm used to a big city, so I'm curious about what goes on here. It *is* my new home." I cut my eyes at Court. "We ladies aren't nearly as delicate as some men seem to think we are."

A tight smile played on the sheriff's lips, as if he enjoyed my jab at his cousin. "Umm, well, I can't tell you anything confidential, but as a for instance, I just left the LeRoi's house. Marie had a stall at the street festival last weekend, and she swears one of those damn Lebeaus…they're basic trash…stole some jewelry out of her display. So of course I have to check it out. That's mostly the…."

"Annie Lebeau?" I interrupted.

Cheyne observed me from his towering height. "You already know about her?"

"Yes, she was following me around while I was in New Orleans. A man named Roland Dubois more or less rescued me after I cold-cocked one of the street brats she had with her."

The sheriff's booming laughter filled the room. "You did what?"

I felt my face flush, but I told him about my encounter with the boys in New Orleans and how I'd knocked one of them silly and bloodied another's nose.

"Remind me not to piss you off, sugar," Cheyne chuckled. "Roland's a good man, good cop. I'm glad he was there to help you."

"You actually fought them off?" Court's eyes widened. "My God. You could've been hurt. You should've let them have the purse and reported the attack to the police."

"They might've actually hurt her worse had she not fought back," Cheyne snapped. "The police aren't always Johnny-on-the-spot when you need them, so people need to know how to look after themselves." He raised his glass to me in a toast. "Sounds like you done good."

"I took some courses in self-defense when I was in high school, and I continue to keep in practice," I answered. "A girl never knows when her knight in shining armor may not be available to fight a dragon for her."

"Those little bastards are part of Annie's posse who run interference for her when she's picking pockets and just generally harassing people," Cheyne said.

"That's what Roland told me."

Cheyne laughed again and shook his head. "Knocked the shit out of 'em, did you?"

I joined his laughter. "I'm not sure how well I would've done if Roland hadn't stepped out of his shop about that time. There were three of them and one of me."

"Roland's a good man," he repeated. "I've worked a couple of cases with him."

Court cut off his cousin's cop-shop reminiscing. "I'm sure Laurette would like to have more interesting things to listen to than your cop stories." He made a *moue* of distaste. "Most women don't want to hear man talk."

"Hey, my man, she's the one who asked about the crime fighting." Cheyne gave his cousin a jaundiced look, and pointed the index finger of the hand holding his glass at the other man. "After *you* asked."

Before I could intervene and say I actually found police work interesting, Rodney Chester spoke up. "Y'all mentioned Annie Lebeau. I've heard of her, but I've yet to meet her."

"Yeah, our homegrown Hoodoo queen," Cheyne commented.

"You know…or maybe you don't…I teach a segment of my Sociology class on Voodoo. You know, how it was brought to New Orleans with the original African slaves, the influence it's had on the culture of the city. I'd really like to round up a genuine Voodoo practitioner to give a talk to some of my classes." He pushed his glasses up on his nose.

"Do you and your wife live in New Orleans? From things I've heard just since I arrived here, there are a number of so-called Voodoo practitioners right there in the city," I remarked.

"After our home was destroyed by Katrina, we took the insurance money and sold our house in the city and moved out here. Got a bigger piece of property and a bigger house, for the same money," the teacher answered. "And yes, you do hear a lot about the so-called practitioners. They mostly pander to the tourists." He shrugged. "But I gather this Annie person is the real deal."

"You don't want Annie Lebeau," Cheyne said. "She's mean as a snake and more than a little crazy. Besides, you really need to be careful with those people. They've been known to do some strange things. I've had more than my share of dealings with them. Voodoo's supposed to be a religion, but it can be a nasty business."

"The waiter at the Palace Café told me a bit about Voodoo, when I told him Annie had followed me to the restaurant. He said a lot of people still believe in that stuff. Now you're saying the same thing?" I remarked to our sheriff.

"Oh, come on. That Voodoo malarkey's not real. It's all smoke and mirrors," Court broke in before Cheyne could answer. "You'll scare Laurette all the way back to Seattle with that clap-trap."

"You and I were raised around N'Awlins, Court," Cheyne said. "We both know there's more to Voodoo than meets the eye. Some of it is power of suggestion, planting scary ideas in people's heads. But how do you account for the things that happen to people who don't even know they've had a curse put on them? I've seen it happen."

I saw Court's skeptical look, but Rodney broke in again. "You know, I've read a number of stories about exactly that happening. I've attended some Voodoo ceremonies, and those people really believe in what they're doing."

"Oh, for pity's sake," Court groused. "First it's police talk...now it's Voodoo. Don't you think our new neighbor would like to hear about the more pleasant aspects of Louisiana life?"

"Life ain't all purty, *podnah*," Cheyne mimicked his cousin's use of the familiar Louisiana address. "Besides, this little lady strikes me as the type who might enjoy a little spice in her life, talking about something other than church and children."

Luci Lesieur stepped up to our group. "I heard y'all mention that old harpy, Annie Lebeau." She turned her brown eyes up to Cheyne. "Honey, you're gonna have to do something about her. I had to run her off our property at gunpoint just a couple days ago. Tommy got the gun away from me before I could fill her flabby butt full of buckshot."

"You should call me, Luci," the sheriff answered. "Don't go taking the law into your own hands." He took a swig of his drink. "And I know how tempting it is to want to wring the old girl's neck."

"I know that's right," I put in. "She's spooky."

"Well, her Voodoo shit is more than just spooky," Luci added. "That old bitch is mean, just plain mean."

"I never heard much of anything about Voodoo until I got to New Orleans, and to tell you the truth, my interest has been sparked by that old woman following me around. Roland told me a little bit about how she operates...the things she does to make it look like she has some kind of occult powers." I looked at Cheyne, who placed the hand not holding his drink on my elbow. "Roland said she uses people at the airport and in the hotels to get information about visitors. I guess they're part of her posse."

"That's exactly what she does, but don't underestimate her and don't let your guard down." Cheyne somehow maneuvered us away from the others and over to the bar. He picked up a glass of white wine and handed it to me, as he thanked Jimmy for the Bloody Mary he was nursing.

I noticed he managed to lose his cousin in the crowd. More people had arrived since I began talking with our sheriff. They just seemed to be wandering in on their own, and some didn't bother introducing themselves. Of course, I wouldn't remember all the names anyway. "So how long have you been sheriff? I thought most sheriffs were older."

"Why, thank you, ma'am," he drawled. "I graduated from LSU and didn't have a clue as to what I was going to do with myself. I had a couple of pro football offers, but I'd simply had enough of the rah rah stuff and getting the dogwater knocked out of me every weekend. I was ready to go out and make my fortune, so to speak, but I wound up back home." He offered me a sardonic lift of his eyebrows as he paused to sip his drink. "The sheriff's department had an opening, so I hired on as a deputy. About two years later, our sheriff got himself shot up by some drug dealers. Nobody else seemed to want the job replacing him, so it sort of fell to me. I got elected...been sheriff ever since, so I guess I'm doing an okay job."

"You big hulk, you're monopolizing our Laurette," Wills O'Neal interrupted, putting a hand on each of my shoulders. "The girl must mingle."

Wills deftly steered me back toward a group that included the handsome sheriff's cousin. Once again Katie Thibodeaux clung to Court like a sandspur. I had the distinct feeling I was being manipulated into keeping company with Court rather than Cheyne and wondered what this was about.

Chapter 26

A commotion erupted at the front of the house. Raucous laughter echoed from the entrance way.

Court grimaced. "Oh, God. Don't tell me Sharla invited Remy Thibadeaux and his friends."

"They're friends and neighbors, Court." Claude joined the group and gave him a withering look. "But they're not the only new arrivals." He leaned toward me and murmured. "Gird up your loins, *cher*. The opposing contingent has just arrived…almost late as usual, so they can make an entrance." He plastered a smile on his face and took my elbow. "Come, child."

The contingent, as Claude called the Renards, consisted of four men and four women, several with flaming hair the exact color of Mama's. These people had to be my mother's brother, one of them anyway, and two of her four sisters. An older man, his red hair touched with gray at the temples, I assumed was my Renard grandfather.

Before my Renard family could reach me and be introduced, a startlingly handsome young man knifed through the cluster of my relatives and grabbed my hand, kissing it thoroughly. *"Ma'amzelle, permettez-moi. Je suis Remy Thibadeaux."*

Taken aback, I was speechless.

Paul Thibadeaux's younger brother was nearly as tall as Cheyne Delacroix, but leaner, sleek like a panther. He had hair so black it was blue, tanned skin, and eyes so pale a shade of gray, they appeared almost colorless. As Sharla said, he was a certifiable hunk, as were the two young men hovering at his side, ravenous lupine expressions on their faces.

And I felt like a lamb caught in the brambles.

Before I could gain any sort of composure, Remy swept me into an embrace and planted kisses on both my cheeks.

"Cher," he rumbled. "We're not related, so we'll have to be kissing cousins, you and me." Laughing, he turned to introduce the two men with him. "My real cousins, Denis-Jean Chaisson and Jacques Dumas."

The other young men were nearly as handsome as Remy and had the same dark hair and flashing white smiles. They both grabbed me and gave me "some sugar." My face was flaming, and I felt myself stiffen. I was trying to accustom myself to the habit of these people hugging and kissing everybody in sight.

Obviously untroubled by his interruption of the introduction of my Renard relatives, Remy hugged Claude, *"Mon ami,* we were nearly run off the road by that cow Annie Lebeau in that rattletrap she drives. She nearly hit us right at the end of the driveway."

My ears perked at the sound of the Voodoo woman's name again this evening.

"Was she on Shadow Cove property?" Claude's words were sharp.

The handsome Cajun shook his head. "No, but she looked like she was prowling, so I thought you should know. Something needs to be done about the *ancien cocotte.* She's a nuisance."

"Does she live near us?" I turned toward the lawyer.

"About three miles up the road, then off in the swamp," Landrieu answered. "But she has to make a detour to drive past the house. She has no business skulking around here."

"Somebody needs to drown the old *putain* in the bayou, her," Denis-Jean commented, and his cousins agreed.

"She gives me the creeps." I shuddered. "I had no idea she lived so close by."

"Not to worry, *m'petite*," Remy assured me. "You're surrounded by big strong men. We'll keep the boogie woman at bay. For now, we need some liquid refreshments." He gave my hand a squeeze and led his friends toward the bar and the appetizers, pausing to dispense yet another hug, this one to Sharla, who'd just come out of the kitchen. She wore a frilly apron over her black pants and top.

I didn't hear what he said but the housekeeper threw back her head and laughed, flapping her apron at him.

The flirtatious Cajun put both hands over his head and did a little dance step toward the bar, and I heard Sharla say, "*Plus tard, coquin.*" I wondered what Sharla had in mind for later with the rascal, as she called him.

The noise level rose several decibels, as laughter rang out from around the bar, welcoming Remy and company. Everybody seemed to know everybody else, and they all seemed to know where everything was in my house. I wasn't sure I liked this last notion. I was accustomed to a high level of privacy.

Claude left my side for a moment and escorted my Renard family toward me, telling them, "You know how effusive Remy can be. He might be a bit rambunctious, but he's a good boy."

Some boy. Several of the women guests are salivating.

"Laurette, *cher.*" Claude nudged me. "Look who's here."

The older woman I assumed must be my Renard grandmother drew her lips down in a *moue* of disapproval, and I heard her mutter, "*Salaud.*" Had I not known the meaning of the word, my grandmother's expression would have been translation enough. Scum. But she was directing her words at Remy, not at me.

The man I figured was my grandfather snorted but didn't appear particularly annoyed at the interruption by Remy and his pals. Indeed, he hadn't taken his eyes off me since entering the room.

"Laurette, this is your grandfather Marc Renard and your grandmother Madeleine," Claude said.

My attention was split. I was perturbed about Annie Lebeau being nearby and wondered what the men meant about "dealing with" the old woman. Surely they wouldn't harm her. I forced myself to pay heed to the introductions. I wasn't sure what to do, shake hands, hug…what? My grandmother certainly did not look huggable.

Marc Renard solved my dilemma by stepping forward and embracing me. "*Ma bebe*, we've thought of you so often, your *grandmere* and I. We're delighted to have you back home safe and sound."

The expression on Madeleine's face told me she didn't exactly share her husband's sentiments. Neither of them said a word about the loss of my mother…their daughter.

My grandfather was a handsome man, despite his age. His flame-colored hair bore only distinguished wisps of gray at his temples. His fair skin was smooth and unlined. He was of medium height and had eyes the color of a cloudless summer sky. My grandmother was not nearly as attractive, possibly because of the expression of petulance pasted to her face. She was petite, and her hair was completely white. I saw little of Mama, in my grandmother, until the older woman speared me with the same cold blue eyes. Madeleine's eyes could freeze a person in his tracks, cold, calculating…Celine's eyes, my mother's cold, cold blue eyes.

Marc turned and introduced me to Uncle Louis-Charles and his wife Cornell, along with my aunts Marie-Therese Coutant and her husband Larry and Lise-Francoise Rivier and her husband Terrence. "We call him Terry-Paul."

I seemed to be one of few people in the place who answered to only one first name.

The usual polite exchanges made the rounds, as Sharla joined the group. "*M'sieu* Marc." She nodded to my grandfather.

Renard grinned. "You look lovely, as usual, *m'petite*." He leaned forward and kissed her cheek.

His tone and the simple kiss were a greeting between two people who have known each other a long time and were fond of each other. No surprise, seeing as how Sharla had grown up in his house. I almost thought no more of it until I saw my grandmother's eyes narrow. Fury was written all over her pinched face. *What's this about?* I had an idea the woman had not wanted to accept the invitation to meet her granddaughter on St. Cyr turf...or maybe not at all. And the animosity her face revealed at Sharla's presence was all too clear. I did not like this Renard grandmother and wished my St. Cyr grandmother were still alive. Both Claude and Sharla spoke lovingly of that old lady.

Another stir at the front door announced the arrival of Roland Dubois and his wife. I was delighted to see him again and to meet his lovely wife. Giselle Dubois was tall and elegant-looking, with skin so light she could pass for white. Her hair was black and wavy, her eyes a lustrous chocolate, filled with good humor. She wore a cream lace top over a sky blue slip dress.

Giselle turned toward a beautiful young woman who'd entered with her and her husband, but was hanging back to greet someone. "That's our daughter, Nicole."

Nicole Dubois stopped to speak to a couple other guests, seeming to know everyone, then hurried over to meet me. She was about my age, but at least six inches taller, slender but muscular, an indication of regular workouts. Her coral shift, with a short, flirty hemline, showed off her figure to perfection. The matching sling back heels boosted her to over six feet. She had her mother's light complexion and dark brown eyes. Her hair was bleached and tumbled in a curly cascade half way down her back. Nicole was one of the most beautiful women I'd ever seen.

She laughed good naturedly when I asked her if she'd ever modeled. "I get asked that all the time, I guess because I'm so tall and skinny. To be honest with you, I always thought modeling would be the height of boredom. The closest I've ever come to anything like that is doing some amateur theater. I belong to one of the local acting groups. So do Wills and Court...but that's just for fun."

Wills had mentioned to me that he did some acting. With her looks, I imagined Nicole would be in demand.

Looking at her father, Nicole grinned. "I graduated from Tulane and will be finishing up at the police academy right shortly. I'm going to be a cop, like my daddy…just what I've always wanted to be."

Giselle put an arm around her daughter. "You can't imagine how proud we are of her."

It was hard for me to imagine a woman so beautiful not capitalizing on her assets, but there was a lot to be said for following one's dream.

A few St. Cyrs proceeded to mingle with the new Renard arrivals, and the usual pleasantries were passed around, but I detected an undercurrent of hostility between the two families. *Well, I'd been warned.*

Clapping her hands to get everyone's attention, Sharla called out, "All right, y'all. Before y'all get pizzle sprung on all this liquor, we've got a lovely buffet laid out in the dining room, so let's grab it and growl, just as soon as Father Gee says the blessing."

Chapter 27

I would've enjoyed talking to Cheyne some more about Voodoo and crime fighting in the bayou, or any other subject he might choose to discuss for that matter, but his equally handsome cousin Court was sticking to me like cat hair to a black velvet dress.

We filled our plates with the delicacies Sharla and Moline had cooked and walked out to one of the side verandahs, where we joined Tommy and Luci Lesieur. The priest, Father O'Malley, also was seated at the table.

Except for the big front verandah and upper gallery, all the porches were screened in to keep out the bugs, and outdoor lights resembling carriage lamps were affixed to the walls. The bulbs in the light fixtures were low wattage and cast a yellowish glow over the diners, lending the atmosphere a touch of the antebellum South.

"I wonder where Henry Toussaint is," Luci remarked.

"Maybe Sharla decided not to invite the hired help." Court commented.

The priest eyed him for a second over the rim of his glass of whiskey, and I detected a flicker of annoyance at Court's comment about hired help. "He and Alma are on an Alaskan cruise...they're twenty-fifth anniversary." Father's bland tone gave no hint of what he thought.

"Who's Henry Toussaint?" I looked from one to the other.

Father Gee answered. "He's the one who keeps the plantation running. In days of yore, he would've been called an overseer. Today, he's a plantation manager, sees to the maintenance of the fields and all the equipment used in the cane business...keeps the crews running year 'round." He took a drink of his expensive scotch. "He's a pretty indispensable cog in the machine of running this place, as I'm sure you'll find out."

"Or so he thinks." Court smirked.

The priest's tone was chilly. "Henry's a good man." He glanced toward me. "He takes good care of your interests, m' girl. He's worked for the St. Cyrs for over twenty-five years."

Larissa chose that moment to deliver a round of drinks to the table.

I looked around at the other tables and was relieved to see the St. Cyrs and the Renards were not segregating themselves. My Renard grandmother was seated beside the elder Simone St. Cyr. They appeared to be having an amiable conversation, displaying their diamond bracelets to each other. Aunt Denise and her husband were chatting with my mother's brother and his wife. The others were mixing and mingling with the guests, many of whom I still hadn't met.

The party seemed to be a success. Cousin Sissy and her sister-in-law, Regina, had their heads together a couple tables away from where I sat. They must've felt me watching them. They looked up simultaneously, scowling in my direction. Instantly, their sour expressions turned to Cheshire cat grins. They even raised their wine glasses to me. Unsmiling, I returned the gesture, feeling like some kind of gauntlet had been dropped.

I was perturbed when Cheyne came onto the veranda and chose to sit with Rodney and Sarah Chester, along with a Jamaican doctor and his wife, although there was a vacant chair at our table. He barely glanced in my direction.

I knew I was being childish. He'd been nothing more than polite to me, and a man as handsome as Cheyne more than likely had a steady girlfriend. I don't know why this idea annoyed me so much. He was not my type. He was too big, too macho, too rough. I forced myself to turn my attention to his more refined cousin Courtland, who was equally appealing on a physical level and certainly fit my image of a Southern gentleman, handsome, educated, cultured, charming, and rich.

So why am I so attracted to his cousin Cheyne? Can it be more of this rebelliousness I've been experiencing since my mother's death? A subtle urge to kick over the traces?

Forcing myself to listen to the conversation at my table, I learned Court was doing some renovating on the bed and breakfast the Lesieurs owned.

Father Gee started telling me about all the places he'd lived as a priest. I'd heard the Irish were great story tellers, and he was no exception. He'd lived in a number of places, including doing a stint at the Vatican before coming to Bayou Ombre some thirty years ago. He had some hilarious tales to tell. Golf was his passion, and his sense of humor was irreverent. "You grow up in Ireland, you either dig potatoes or become a priest."

He was an avid reader of mysteries and was fond of one of my favorite writers, James Lee Burke, whose novels often were set in Louisiana.

"Julie Smith's Skip Langdon mysteries are set in New Orleans, too," I told him. "You might enjoy them. She doesn't write 'girl' books." I used my fingers to make air quotes.

Chapter 28

After dinner, everyone meandered around the house, carrying their desserts on little plates and balancing cups of coffee or after-dinner drinks. I was getting tired of Court's overly solicitous behavior and his constant yammering about himself and his business, but Mama would've been proud of me for keeping my Southern Belle smile in place. I was relieved when he suddenly excused himself. I figured he must be visiting the restroom and secretly hoped he'd stay there a while so I could mingle with some of the other guests. Most of the invitees were members of my family, and I'd like to have more than a nodding acquaintance with them.

I probably shouldn't have done it, but I plucked another glass of wine off the tray Moline was passing around. Somewhere between the dirty rice and the fried okra, I'd accepted an invitation to dine with Court in New Orleans the next evening. Now I chastised myself for being so quick to accept the invite…but I wasn't sure why I felt this way.

I tracked him with my eyes as he started toward the rear of the house. He was lithe and graceful in all his movements, the way a model or actor moves. He stopped to whisper something to Nicole Dubois. She gave a smile and shrug before walking away. I saw him follow her with his eyes, then he turned and disappeared into the bowels of the house.

Does he flirt with all the women?

Now I spied Katie following in the direction Court had taken. At least I wasn't so desperate for attention as to trail a man to the restroom. *But where is Cheyne? There he is, talking to Tommy Lesieur, facing me but not looking at me.*

Several times during the evening, I caught Cheyne watching me with an amused expression. I had a feeling he knew his cousin was boring me and was enjoying the spectacle. And not once had he tried to intervene in the conversation with Court. In fact, he seemed to be pointedly ignoring me. Anger zipped up my spine, followed by a spark of aggravation for my own silliness. Again I wondered if he had a girlfriend. *But if he has a girlfriend, why hadn't he brought her to the party. Perhaps Sharla had not invited her. I'll have to ask Sharla about that.*

I covertly watched him, while pretending to pay attention to Aunt Marie-Therese, Mama's sister. *More than likely Cheyne has a "main squeeze," rather than a steady woman. He probably prefers to spend his time at football games or hunting and fishing with his buddies. He's a man's man. He would want a woman for convenience. Apparently, he likes to flirt with a woman and then turn and walk away. He shows only a surface interest and probably couldn't remember a woman's name five minutes later, much less the color of her eyes or the scent of her perfume.*

I gave myself a mental shake and gave a physical nod to whatever my aunt was yammering about. *I'm being childish. I'm acting like that pathetic Katie Thibodeaux with her mooning over Courtland Delacroix.*

"We'd love to have you join us at the theater one evening," my aunt was saying. "Our youngest daughter, your cousin Avril, is turning out to be quite a good little actress."

"I'd enjoy that," I answered automatically, but my mind was bouncing between the Delacroix cousins.

To give Court his due, he wasn't only drop-dead handsome, he was very polite and had seemed quite impressed with my knowledge of architecture. He was familiar with Shadow Cove house and offered several excellent suggestions for updating and remodeling the place. Right now my attention wasn't focused on Court's excellence as a building contractor. I sipped my wine and surveyed the room. Cheyne had disappeared. *Where has he gone? Like his cousin, he has vanished.*

I slipped between the clusters of people, not sure where to look for the elusive Cheyne Delacroix. My other guests milled about, wandering in and out of the rooms to sit on the verandahs encircling the house or just lounge in one room or another. A half dozen had climbed the stairs, and I could hear their laughter coming from the upstairs gallery. Nor did they stay with the parties they arrived with. Wills had vanished, and Claude was deep into a conversation with Luci Lesieur. The handsome Thibadeaux cousins flitted from one pretty woman to another, leaving gales of laughter in their wakes. I discovered the monster St. Cyr twins ensconced in a sitting room watching television. I breathed a sigh of relief that the hellions were not running around the house breaking things.

Several other people had arrived after the dining began, and I barely caught their names, but everybody seemed to know everybody else. The Cajun accents and Louisiana drawls bounced and pinged off my eardrums, making me feel somewhat off-center, trying to keep up with so many unfamiliar terms, often laced with French or Cajun slang. The noise level rose, as more people arrived and more liquor and wine were consumed.

Sharla told me she'd invited fewer than thirty people, but now at least a hundred people crowded the rooms and the verandahs. When I remarked on this to her, she seemed nonplussed. "That's why I always fix plenty of food, *cher*. I know how our neighbors love a party, and they always invite their friends." She laughed and disappeared into the mob.

Larissa replaced my nearly empty wine glass with a full one, before I had a chance to protest. I wasn't used to drinking as much as these people obviously did. A trifle light-headed, I perused the guests, still trying to put faces with all the names that had been tossed my way.

This was some party.

Rodney Chester perched on a sofa chattering to the older Simone St. Cyr and another woman whose name I didn't remember, while two more men whose names I didn't recall either were talking animatedly beside the main salon's fireplace. From their gestures, I figured they were talking about golf.

Still no Cheyne. Well, I wasn't about to wander around looking for him.

The Fiancée, Junior Couliette's girlfriend, was wallowing on Remy Thibadeaux before the two disappeared onto a verandah. "Hmmm."

One of Remy's cousins, I wasn't sure which, had cornered the younger Simone St. Cyr. The intent of the couple was clear as they eased themselves out of the house through a set of French doors.

I gave up trying to keep up with who was with whom and where they were, much less what they might be doing outside in the sultry darkness. I pondered why so many plays, movies, and books had been written about torrid sex in the steamy South. Since arriving I'd felt something shift inside myself, not quite sure how to describe it. The slow, languid cadence of the voices, making innocent words purr, sounding intimate, enticing, almost lewd. The casual use of endearments, like private invitations.

There was something about the smell of the place, fecund, ripe, a subtle muskiness, the dark rich soil, the not-unpleasant odor of bodies, the film of sweat that never seemed to evaporate, always leaving the skin feeling moist under the glide of fingers, flesh on flesh. The damp, flushed feeling that remained just under the surface. There was something wicked about the Deep South. Not evil...not exactly... just the emanation of an almost playful wickedness, with a touch of danger, that permeated the goings on between male and female, or male and male or female and female. I stifled an audible laugh at the path my mind was wandering on. *I'm sure as hell not back in Seattle anymore. Maybe I need another glass of wine...or maybe I've had too much.*

I spied Sharla deep in conversation with my newly introduced grandfather, Marc Renard. They were off to the side, in a corner of the huge main salon, clearly not wanting to be overheard. It was clear from his flirtatiousness Renard was a player, even at his age, but surely the old *roué* wasn't hitting on the housekeeper. I gave a mental snort. I certainly couldn't imagine Sharla leading him on, although I'd picked up on a strange sort of intimacy between them.

The two faced each other, their foreheads nearly touching. The light from a lamp behind them created a red penumbra around both heads, glinting off Marc's flaming hair and bringing out a tinge of red in Sharla's. I caught myself staring fixedly at them, as my brain tried to comprehend what my eyes were seeing. Their profiles were similar, the same small, straight nose, the chin, the way they held their heads as they bent toward one another. The silhouettes were all too familiar.

I couldn't stifle my gasp. *No. I cannot be seeing what's right in front of me.* Something cold crawled up my spine. Sharla had talked about her mother, Bethany Williams, who'd been the Renards' housekeeper, but she never mentioned her father. Her light skin, the reddish tinge to her hair, the blue-green eyes all advertised that she was of mixed birth, a fact she never sought to hide. She mentioned being a quadroon, only one fourth black. *Could what was right before my eyes be possible? Could Marc Renard be Sharla's father?* In profile, the resemblance was uncanny. I felt my heart skitter. That identical profile belonged to my own mother, Celine. Sharla and Celine could be twin silhouettes.

The air slowly left my lungs. That would mean Sharla and I were related. Sharla might be my aunt. I took a deep breath and shifted my eyes away, looking around the room. My gaze skidded to a halt. I wasn't the only one watching the pair in the corner. Madeleine Renard looked mad enough to murder someone, or, given her age, wealth, and social position, have someone murdered.

If what I was seeing was true, it was clear my grandmother knew all about Sharla.

I knew how Alice in Wonderland must have felt. Things just kept getting curiouser and curiouser. I needed to be alone, take a walk outside down to the bayou dock, get out into the fresh air. Nodding vague greetings to those I passed, I started down the darkened back hallway toward the kitchen and the back porch beyond. As I rounded a corner, I spied cousin Regina slipping inside through the back door, letting it close silently behind her.

Not wanting to be bothered with more of her smug, inane prattle, I stepped aside into the shadowy recess afforded by a large cabinet hugging the hallway. Peering around the corner of the massive piece of furniture, I watched my tall blonde cousin pause and look around, her furtive expression illuminated by the lights on the back porch.

Reggie touched her fingers to her crotch, her lips curving into a lewd smile.

I thought the gesture, the smile, the clandestine behavior were odd in the least. *What is afoot here?* I caught my lower lip. Reggie sneaked into the half-bath off the back porch. The bathroom door snicked shut. I started to resume my trek to the backyard but quickly stepped back to my hidey hole, as I heard the back door open again and saw Remy Thibadeaux enter the house.

He tapped on the door through which Reggie had just vanished. The doorway opened, and he, too, disappeared into the small room.

I came out from the shelter of the cabinet and leaned against the doorjamb. "I'll be damned," I whispered. The last time I'd seen Remy he was making for the verandah with Junior's fiancée clinging to his arm. Before I could sort this out, a rhythmic thumping sounded from the bathroom. I stifled a giggle. I needed to put some gone between the back porch and myself, so I turned to go back into the main part of the house where the party was in full swing.

A muffled squeal emanated from the other side of the bathroom door, followed by a growl, animalistic enough to have come from a bull gator. "Jesus," I muttered and retraced my steps toward the front of the house, as the bumping and thumping in the half-bath continued.

The Gothed-out kid called Toad and Chantal, Denise's daughter, rounded the corner and nearly collided with me. They were both glassy-eyed, and the odor of weed wafted in their wake. They mumbled an apology and forged on toward where the food was laid out. I wasn't sure they'd even recognized me.

"That old Hoodoo woman, Annie, better stay away from Shadow Cove, or Cousin Robert might have her ass shot," Chantal said, as the two shambled along. "Mama says he's not gonna...anybody interfere...their plans to...."

The girl's words were lost, as the pair rounded another corner in the labyrinth of hallways and small rooms at the rear of the house. I waited in the darkness, digesting her remarks.

Annie Lebeau again. What was Chantal talking about? What was my cousin Robert's interest in Shadow Cove? What plans could he be hatching for what he might consider his family's homestead, the homestead that now belonged to me? Where did I figure into his plan? A cold ribbon of fear snaked up my spine. I really didn't know any of these people or what they were capable of.

I heard the door to the half-bath opening, heard Remy and Reggie emerging, their laughter muffled. I didn't care that Reggie might have caught me eavesdropping on her assignation with the studly Cajun, but I really didn't want the aggravation of having another relative with an ax to grind. I slipped back toward the party, my head spinning with the strange goings-on I'd already witnessed tonight.

Chapter 29

I eased back into the dining room. Toad and Chantal were piling food on their plates and paid me no mind. A couple of people I'd met but whose names I didn't remember also were getting refills of food. They smiled at me, and I nodded politely in their direction.

The sound of a fiddle being tuned wafted from one of the verandahs.

Someone called, "Where's Remy? We need him to sing?"

"I got de tambourine, me," Paul Thibadeaux boomed. "And I can sing as sweet as dat pretty boy brudda o' mine."

This declaration was met with laughter and a few catcalls.

"*M'sieu* Marc and I will help you out. We make a trio of songbirds, us."

Standing beside the bar, I recognized Sharla's voice. Apparently, the liquor was loosening up all the factions of my family.

"Sounds like everybody's gettin' along. Better than 'em fightin' like they usually do." Jimmy poured me a fresh glass of white wine, just as the singing and fiddle playing began.

"Thank God for that." I turned around and almost bumped into Remy.

He was tucking his shirt tail into the back of his pants, grinning like a fool. "Hey. I'm on my way. You don't start without me." He called loud enough to be heard on the verandah.

I could smell Reggie's perfume on him and stepped aside, remaining between the bar and the hallway door. I gave him a fast once over, then quickly looked away. I didn't want this bayou tomcat to get the notion I might be interested in him. From what I'd heard and seen, he had enough women on the string.

"You best get out dere, you," Jimmy told him. "Somebody's gon' steal yo' thunder."

Remy accepted a glass of bourbon from the bartender and laughed. "Naw. Dey don't call me de Cajun canary for nuttin'." He broadened his bayou accent and headed for the verandah. "You come listen, *cher*, and we dance." He winked at me and made for the French doors leading outside.

"You watch dat one, Miz Laurette," Jimmy warned. "He thinks he's got de *buljoos*, him. Not a bad boy, but he go through women quicker'n a crawdad through mud."

"Believe me, I'll heed your warning. A Louisiana lothario is the last thing I need."

Reggie St. Cyr slithered through the door from the hallway. She stopped abruptly, seeing me standing directly in her path. She fingered the tendrils of hair that had come loose around her face. "It's so warm inside. I needed a breath of air." Her voice sounded shaky, and she fanned her face with her hand. "I need a fresh drink, Jimmy."

"It does get a bit warm in close quarters, especially out back." I smirked and raised my wineglass in mock salute.

Reggie's face turned bright red, and she looked everywhere but at me.

I sipped my wine and did that cocked eyebrow thing Mama did so well, letting her wonder if I'd seen her and Remy together. Might knock some of the snottiness out of her if she suspected I was aware of their tacky assignation in the bathroom.

Chapter 30

The old Voodoo woman watched the couple in the graveyard and chuckled low in her chest.

Seeing a party in progress at the big house at Shadow Cove, Annie had driven her ratty old Ford truck off the road and slipped through the trees and across the cemetery to spy on the revelers. A long blacksnake slithered over her foot, but she didn't move, transfixed by the scene playing out only a few feet away. Neither the night nor the creatures inhabiting the darkness bothered her. She was one with the night, preferred it to daylight.

A nightbird flapped by her face and perched in a tree above her head. The bird cooed a couple of times, then settled down.

Annie moved closer to the pair embracing near the big tomb with the spread-winged angel on top. The angel looked fierce, a sword stretched toward Heaven. This was the final resting place of both Etienne St. Cyrs, the master who died almost a century and a half ago and the one interred only a few weeks earlier. She wondered what they'd both think of the carryings-on she was witnessing.

From her position, she could see heads bent as the pair tongued each other's mouths, hands slipping inside clothing, caressing the bare skin, wandering to fondle crotches and buttocks. She was close enough to hear their moans, hear the unmistakable slide of a zipper.

She knew what would come next, but she liked to watch debauchery, especially among those who thought themselves better than her and her kind. "*Fils des putains*," she muttered, as she saw one's knees touch the concrete apron around the tomb and heard the other's sharp intake of breath.

"Oh, my God, *cher*, that's so good."

They were panting like young dogs with heartworm.

"Get up, get up and turn around. You know what you want." The words came out on gusts of fevered breath.

"Yes. Hurry."

A chuckle. "I know how you like it, doll." Another rustle of clothing being shunted aside. "A little rough, eh?"

Annie licked her lips.

"Ahh, God." A gasp. "Hurry, hurry."

"Uh, uh. It's too good to hurry. God, you're tight."

"I've got to get back. Uh…ooh…ooh…good God."

On the opposite side of the tomb where the lovers humped and groaned, Annie spied a white face peering at the couple from behind a tall marble vase, a pair of eyes wide with shock.

A bark of pleasure that sounded nearly painful. "Uh, uh…I'm coming. Uh. Uuuhh."

Annie grinned at the accidental voyeur's expression. The other gawker backed away, faded into the surrounding foliage. The old woman cocked her head to see better with her good eye, as the gasps and moans subsided and the sated pair began to rearrange their clothing. With nothing more to watch, she turned to leave…and stepped on a fallen branch.

The snap echoed through the darkness like a jalopy's backfire. Two faces jerked toward the sound. Both wore stricken expressions. Fearful. Caught.

The moon chose that moment to blink from behind a cloud, and Annie found herself spotlighted by the full silver orb. "*Merde*," she

At last, the guests began to leave. Courtland Delacroix was back at my side, but it was Cheyne I searched for and did not find. He hadn't been among the dancers. *Maybe he doesn't dance.* I hadn't seen him since shortly after dinner.

I politely ushered Court to the door, assuring him that I hadn't forgotten our dinner date for the following evening...actually for this evening, since it was past two o'clock in the morning.

I found Sharla perched on a bar stool, her shoes on the floor beside her, a final glass of wine on the bar in front of her. We were alone in the house. Even Jimmy and Moline had left.

"The Rogets will be back in the morning to clean up," she told me, yawning.

"What happened to Cheyne? He disappeared right after dinner."

"Oh, he told me to give you his regrets for having to leave so early." Sharla rubbed her feet. "He said he had to sit in on a video conference with some honcho in Baton Rouge first thing in the morning...or this morning, I guess I should say." She gave me an arch look. "Seems like you've piqued the interest of both the Delacroix men, the most eligible bachelors in the bayou, according to the *Times-Picayune*."

Chapter 32

The maître'd at Broussard's Restaurant on Rue Conti led Courtland and me through the elegant cream and black tiled entryway to the back of the building, where a band played in the flagstone courtyard. The main dining room was furnished in an updated décor, in neutrals, cream on cream, rather than reflecting the style of yesteryear. Antique chandeliers lighted our path through several dining rooms. Paintings of tropical scenes, decorated the walls, maintaining the French Quarter ambience. The back of the old building was redbrick, with arched windows cut into the façade. An upstairs gallery overlooked a courtyard surrounded by lush plants, the scent of their blooms heady on the sultry night air.

"Since this is your first visit to N'Awlins since you were a child, I thought you might enjoy dining in the Quarter again. I know Claude took you Arnaud's the other evening, but we probably have more restaurants in the Quarter than any other place of comparable size. And better restaurants I might add," Court told me after we were seated at one of the wrought-iron tables. "You may as well enjoy being a tourist before you settle into being a resident."

"I was never a fan of oysters until arrived here. It appears the restaurants in New Orleans can't devise enough ways to serve them." I looked over the menu. "I think I'll try the Oysters Broussard."

"Excellent choice," he assured me.

"This crab and melon salad sounds good and the Tournedos La Louisiane."

Court ordered the Taste of Rue Conti sampler plate, the Broussard's Salad and the Creole Spiced Ribeye.

He selected pricey wines, a Pinot Gris to accompany the appetizers and salads, and a St. Emilion to go with our entrees. I wondered if he was trying to impress me with the expensive wines… and why. "Do we need to save room for dessert?"

"Personally, I think Broussard's has the best selection of desserts of any place in town," he told me. Responding to my earlier comment about oysters, he added, "So far, I don't think the chef has created an oyster dessert."

"I'd never been a fan of the things until I got back home, and I've discovered they're wonderful."

Court waggled his blond eyebrows at me. "Ever wondered if what they say about oysters is true?"

"What's that?"

He chuckled. "Surely you know they're supposed to be an aphrodisiac."

"Oh." I felt a bit foolish. Everybody knew that about the bivalves, all the way back to the Stone Age. He must think I'd just crawled out from under a rock. I wasn't sure I liked the direction his mind seemed to be taking. I tried to cover my nervousness with a laugh. "Yes. I guess I did know that. I just hadn't exactly been thinking about it."

He took my hand. "Well, believe me, *cher*, no man would need that kind of stimulation with you. Just looking into those big green eyes is enough to set any man on fire."

He's smooth, but he gets to the point. He's not wasting any time… but why? How would Mama handle this situation? I hadn't inherited her flirtatious nature. Surely this man didn't think he was so devastatingly attractive that I would fall for this line of hooey and jump into bed with him. I smiled and said nothing.

Court's fingers gently massaged my palm, while he continued to gaze into my eyes. His fingers were smooth and soft, not the hands of a working man.

I couldn't deny my attraction to him. Still, my skin prickled. I just wasn't accustomed to men treating me in such a blatantly sexual manner. *I sound like a Jane Austen character. Twenty-first Century women are not supposed to be shrinking violets. Many of my contemporaries are downright aggressive and think nothing of making the first move. But that just isn't me. Maybe I really am a throwback to another era, as some of my former classmates had chided. I'm just not good at playing this game, and I know it. I'm not an accomplished belle, much less a hottie.*

My mind flitted to the memory of Cheyne Delacroix's hand on my elbow. His skin was hard, a bit rough. The hands of a man who knew how to do something besides toy with a wineglass, as Court was doing with the hand not holding mine captive.

Court's rush roused my suspicions, but suspicions of what, seduction or something else, something more material? He was smooth and not at all offensive in his approach, but he was coming on fast...too fast. I knew I was reasonably attractive. Some people even said I was pretty, but I was no beauty, hardly the *femme fatale* my mother had been. My face was not likely to launch a thousand ships, or even *pirogues* for that matter. And here this luscious Louisiana charmer was treating me like I was as sexy as Scarlett Johansson.

His finger traced a circular pattern on my palm, and he continued to gaze into my eyes, as if he could mesmerize this poor foolish female. *I might be naïve, but I'm not a total idiot.* In spite of his seductive words and his come-hither look, I sensed there was more going on here than a man wanting to get into my knickers.

His expression was downright predatory, cold and calculating. His smile showed too many teeth, like an alligator stalking its prey. For the first time, I noticed that his canines were just a tiny bit too long, too sharp, giving his smile a wolfish quality, part alligator and part wolf. Louisiana was the land of the *loup garou,* the werewolf, the land of Anne Rice's vampires, with their pointed canines. Nightmare creatures, not dreamboats. A smile twitched my lips, and I coughed to cover the laughter I felt welling up in response to the comic book creature my fancy was creating…an over-sexed gator-werewolf.

I pulled my fingers from his grasp to grab my napkin and touch it to my lips. He'd probably fall out of the chair if he knew what I was thinking about him. I imagined most women swooned right into his arms…he was handsome, rich, charming, but my "bullshit alarm," as my mother would've called it, was jangling on full alert. Mama'd been a flirt, but she'd never been a fool.

I put my napkin back in my lap and picked up my wine glass. "My, my, you Southern gentlemen do know how to turn a lady's head." The words leaving my mouth sounded just like Mama, but she would've enjoyed this kind of banter…I did not. I was out of my league with this man. He was cosmopolitan and sophisticated, while I was neither. Throughout the sumptuous meal, he continued to insert sexual innuendoes into the conversation, and I felt ill equipped to deliver any sort of witty repartee. I decided not to try and just cut him short. "This has been a lovely evening, Court, but I'm afraid I'll need to get up early in the morning. Uncle Claude and I have another business meeting."

Chapter 33

I deftly managed to sidestep Court's efforts at indulging in a necking session in the front driveway. We kissed a couple of times, and I have to admit it was a toe-curling experience. I had a feeling this man definitely knew his way around a woman's body. But petting in a parked car in the driveway struck me as a bit juvenile. I hopped out of his dark green Porsche before he could get a firm grip on me for anything more than a kiss or two. He probably expected to be invited in for a nightcap, but I didn't make the offer.

Sharla was still up when I walked into the kitchen. "I wasn't waiting up for you, *cher*. One of my cats has gone missing. Lafitte. He's a tomcat, but he's been neutered, so it's not like him to miss his dinner, and he's not out looking for a lady friend, him."

"Oh, do you want to look for him a bit longer? Want me to help?"

"No. I'll just make one final turn around the yard. I can't imagine where he is."

She seemed discombobulated and didn't ask about my date, so I headed up to my suite. After showering, dressed in only my nightgown, I walked down the hallway to Sharla's suite. "Did you find your cat?"

"No, and I'm worried about him. It's not like him to prowl. He's a big baby."

"Which one is he?"

"The black one, a big ball of black fluff, not a white hair on him. In the dark, all you can see are his eyes."

I'd been pondering talking to Sharla about a couple of things. I wanted to get her opinion on why Courtland Delacroix was giving me the rush. I also wanted to ask her about my suspicions regarding the identity of her father. On this second matter, I'd begun to wonder if maybe I drank too much wine at the party and my mind was playing tricks. Surely my grandfather would not have gotten his housekeeper pregnant and then allowed the child to be raised right under his wife's nose. That was just too bizarre to imagine.

I needed to postpone both of these discussions. Sharla was upset and distracted by worry about her pet. I'd never been allowed pets, but I liked animals.

Perhaps the tomcat would show up the next morning.

I returned to my own room and stepped out onto the gallery. Below me, the family cemetery spread, a white marble city in miniature. The aboveground crypts of the long dead St. Cyrs stood out in sharp relief in the silver moonlight. I leaned against the bannister and listened to the faint murmur of the water in the bayou. A screech, almost human, broke the stillness... the sounds of one nightbird calling to another. The evening was cool, the air moist.

Far beyond the boundaries of the graveyard, I caught a glimpse of a flash of light. Like a firefly, it flickered and disappeared. What could it be? I saw it again and leaned over the railing, peering through the thick foliage. Again the light flickered. It was a good distance from the house, maybe as far as the river on the opposite side of the cemetery. A boat on the river? That seemed logical, but why did the lights flash? I would think running lights on a boat would remain steady.

A shadow moved among the tombs beneath where I stood, and I straightened up. Except for the lamp beside the bed, the lights were off in the room behind me, and my nightgown was purple. I was probably nearly invisible, but I moved closer to the gallery's wrought-iron upright, hoping to blend in with the climbing vines. I scrunched my eyes and tried to see what had moved in the graveyard and beyond. Nothing. No movement, no light. Just black on black.

I wondered if it could be Sharla's wayward cat and was tempted to go downstairs and investigate.

I stared into the darkness for several more minutes but saw no further movement. I didn't see the light again. Could it have just been the moonlight glinting on a piece of metal in the far distance?

A breeze caught the Spanish moss streaming from the trees and made it dance in the moonlight.

I sighed and leaned back. All I'd seen was the shadow of the long beards of moss waving in the wind and probably just a piece of metal or plastic caught in a shaft of moonlight, turning and flickering in the moonbeam…no intruders, no mysterious flashing lights.

Still, the hair on the back of my neck quivered, and I felt a queer tingle up by backbone, like tiny cat's feet tripping lightly up my spine. The breeze felt unnaturally cold, and I fairly scuttled back into my room and closed the French doors behind me.

I started for bed, then turned back and locked the doors, even though I was on the second floor.

The temperature in the room seemed to plummet, and I shivered. I sensed I was not alone.

My heart thudded. Rooted to the carpet, I glanced around me. Saw no one.

My eyes were drawn to the portrait of the original Laurette above the fireplace.

Some invisible string tugged me toward the hearth. My feet moved as if with no conscious volition.

I stopped in front of the fireplace and looked up at the portrait of the other Laurette St. Cyr. Reaching out my fingers, I touched the glass protecting the painting. Instead of feeling cold, the glass was warm. I could swear it felt soft, like touching flesh. I gasped and jerked my hand away.

The portrait's enigmatic smile did not waver. Something moved inside me. *Only the fluttering of my heart?*

I backed away from the painting and hurriedly got into bed, pulling the comforter up to my neck. I'd never been afraid of the dark, but I was afraid to turn out the light. I took several deep breaths. I was being foolish. The painting was nothing but a portrait of a woman long dead. The peculiar sensation of touching warm flesh was my imagination.

The talk of ghosts, haints, cemeteries, Voodoo over the last few days...and now Sharla's missing cat...had unnerved me. And I'd drunk too much wine at dinner with Court.

I reached for the lamp and switched it off. I probably wouldn't sleep a wink.

Chapter 34

Sharla's scream jolted me awake. I leaped out of bed and grabbed my robe, running barefoot down the hallway. Over the bannister above the entrance hall, I could see the front door standing open, so I flew down the stairs.

Sharla stood on the porch with her hands over her face, sobbing.

I ran to her and stared at the mess on the floor. A piece of red material was spread on the boards, with what looked like chicken bones arranged in a pattern. In the middle of the bones was a small skull...a cat's skull. The black tail of the cat had been cut off and was wrapped around the head, secured with a red ribbon.

"That bitch! That horrible old bitch!" Sharla was crying and cursing. "She killed my poor little cat...my baby."

I drew her to me, tucking her face into my shoulder. "What's that mess on the floor?"

"It's a Voodoo spell. That old bitch is trying to hex our house. I came out to get the newspaper and found it."

"Let me get a garbage bag and get rid of it."

"Don't let any of it touch you," Sharla warned.

"You don't believe in this crap, do you?"

"I know what these Voodoo women can do." Sharla was trembling.

I turned to go back into the house and saw a tiny sack stuck to the door with a tack and scratch marks marring the perfection of the old varnished oak. "What's this?"

"Don't touch it."

"Bull. I'm not afraid of this nonsense." I snatched the sack from the door. It was made out of some flimsy material and tied with a red ribbon.

Sharla stood still, her fingers steepled, covering her mouth, her eyes wide with fear.

I jerked the ribbon off the sack and emptied it onto one of the wicker tables. A stoppered bottle holding dark fluid tumbled out, along with a tiny figure made of what looked like a corn husk. A scrap of red cloth was twisted around the figure. A wad of dark brown hair topped the effigy, and a cotton ball was stuck to its breast with a long pin. The cotton was covered with what looked like blood.

We need to call Cheyne." Sharla's voice was strangled.

Chapter 35

"I'm not going to tell you to ignore this bullshit," Cheyne Delacroix said. "It's serious business."

Sharla and I had gotten dressed, and the three of us stood on the front verandah.

"That horrid old bitch killed my cat." Sharla's voice quivered.

I put my arm around her.

Cheyne rested his balled fists on his hips and shook his head. "That's a pretty awful thing to do, even for her." He sighed. "It probably wasn't aimed at Sharla. She's trying to get to you through her." He wagged his head at me.

"But why? Neither of us has done anything to her?" I put my fingers over my lips. "This is horrible. Killing Sharla's poor little cat. And this crap about trying to put a hex on our house."

"Why would she do such a thing?" Fresh tears leaked down Sharla's cheeks.

"My guess is somebody's paying her. Annie doesn't do anything for free." Cheyne furrowed his brow and looked at each of us in turn. "Don't discount that old woman. She's as deadly as a moccasin. In spite of what my cousin Court was trying to tell you," he said to me. "Voodoo's very real."

The conversation was interrupted by the sound of Claude Landrieu's car crunching across the oyster shell driveway. The lawyer got out and came up the steps. He and I had an appointment in New Orleans with the factor for Shadow Cove. The factor is the agent who handles prices for harvesting and selling the cane. He's a business manager, a negotiator. "What's this, a welcoming committee?" Claude's smile faded when he saw Sharla's expression. "*Cher*, what on earth has happened?" He held out his arms and folded the housekeeper into them.

Sharla started crying again, so I explained the situation. "I'm going to gather that mess up into a garbage bag and throw it as far as I can into the bayou. Of course, Sharla wants to bury her cat's head and tail in a flower garden...poor little creature."

"Annie Lebeau is a mean old heifer. I wouldn't put anything past her." Claude held the back of Sharla's head, cradling her trembling body.

Cheyne shook his head at me. "You leave that stuff alone. I'm booking it as evidence. Evidence of what, I'm not sure yet. Criminal mischief to start with."

"And then there's that stupid Voodoo doll." I snarled. "More evidence of stupid crap nobody with any sense believes in?" He was talking down to me, and I didn't like it.

Sharla stepped out of Claude's embrace and dabbed at her eyes with the handkerchief he handed her.

"Don't ignore this Voodoo warning." Cheyne's expression was grim. "Don't discount Annie Lebeau's so-called powers. I've seen enough of Voodoo to know it's not the harmless fun stuff they sell in the shops in the Quarter, the love potions and all such shit as that."

"She came on my property and left parts of a dead cat and this other stuff," I said. "I don't believe in her spells and junk, but she has no business trespassing on my property."

Cheyne used what looked like a small pair of tongs to pick up the primitive doll. He turned it over and studied it. "I wonder what's with this cotton ball with blood on it. Where'd she get it? Is this your hair, do you think?"

"It looks like mine." I studied the wad of hair atop the effigy. "Roland Dubois told me Annie has a number of people working for her who work in the hotels. That hair could've come from my hairbrush, and I cut my finger the first night I was here and stopped the bleeding with a cotton ball. I'll bet somebody got that stuff out of my hotel bathroom."

"Um, hum. I'll bet that's exactly where it came from." Cheyne rocked back on his feet. "I'm going to check it out, but I doubt we'll find out which one of the hotel staff did this. With the turnover in cleaners, the hotels themselves have trouble keeping up with who's working where, and half of them will fall back on the old 'no speaka English' when you try to talk to them."

"What about talking to Annie herself?" I suggested.

"Oh, I intend to." Cheyne's smile was thin. "But the old bitch will just stonewall me." He put the doll in a plastic bag. "Y'all go on and take care of your business," he told Claude and me. "I'll stay here and help Sharla bury her pet."

Chapter 36

"Following the meeting with Marcel Rutledge, the factor, Uncle Claude treated me to a late lunch at Brennan's, continuing my tour of the finest restaurants in the French Quarter. My turtle soup and the beef and mushroom tartine, a sort of open face sandwich, were delicious, but the awful events of the early morning at Shadow Cove had taken the edge off my appetite. Claude was uncharacteristically somber. Neither of us was in the mood for dessert, both wanting to get home and be with Sharla.

It was nearly three o'clock when Claude turned off of the main road onto the long drive to the big house. Shell dust from another vehicle a hundred yards ahead of us boiled in the air. "I wonder who that is," I commented. When we pulled into the driveway, I saw the rear end of the Escalade Sharla usually drove vanishing around the corner of the house.

We parked out front and made our way through the house.

I heard Sharla talking in the kitchen, her words a mixture of Cajun French and English.

"I wonder who's here."

"Don't know." My new uncle raised his brows.

We entered the kitchen, and I placed my purse on the table.

Sharla's back was to me, but I could see a cat carrier sitting on the counter. She turned toward me, grinning, while she unlatched the pet container. "Look, it's my baby, my Lafitte." She pulled the black tomcat from the carrier and cuddled him. His hind leg was bandage, and he wore a plastic saucer-like guard around his neck. "He got his leg torn in some kind of trap. I'm going to have the yardmen go over this yard with a fine tooth comb." She kissed the top of the cat's head. "And this gentleman is going to stay inside from now on."

The cat mewled a feeble protest. He was obviously doped up from his trip to the vet and slumped bonelessly to the tabletop when Sharla set him down.

Without being asked, Claude fetched an old towel from the adjacent laundry room and spread it onto the countertop.

Sharla moved her pet to the soft mat.

The tomcat immediately closed his eyes and fell asleep as fast as only a cat can.

"Oh, my God. That's wonderful. He's all right. How did you find him?" I scratched the cat's ears.

Claude reached around me and stroked the injured animal's flank.

"After Cheyne left, I just walked around in the yard for a while, and I heard him crying," Sharla answered. "When I was looking for him earlier, he must have been passed out from the pain." She stroked the cat. "The poor baby had dragged that awful trap almost to the house. I guess he smelled me or just sensed me and started crying for his mama." She teared up again. "And Mama came to the rescue."

"Bless his heart," I said.

Sharla plopped down in a chair at the kitchen table. "I called Cheyne when I left the vet, and he said he'd be right behind me. That old bitch has got no business on this property. It might not have been my animal she killed, but she still slaughtered some helpless creature to use in her damned Voodoo crap."

As if on cue, the front doorbell rang. "That must be Cheyne," Sharla said.

"I'll get it." Claude hurried to admit the lawman.

"I went out to Annie's house as soon as I left here, but she's not home."

My ears perked at the sound of Cheyne's voice, but I heard another man speaking, too. The voice was vaguely familiar, but I didn't recognize it.

"What on earth's going on out here? I just dropped by for a quick visit, to see if Laurette would like to have dinner with us one night."

When the men hove into sight, I was not overly happy to see my cousin Robert with Claude and Cheyne. I'd met him and his wife only once and was not crazy about them. My suspicion meter increased a couple of degrees at the pending dinner invitation, because I sensed my feelings were reciprocated and wondered why he was making nice-nice. It had to do with the inheritance. I had it, and they wanted it. Claude told me my relatives made out quite well in the will my St. Cyr grandparents left, but I received the lion's share of money and all the property. No matter how much some people have, they want more. And they resent other people getting anything.

I was sure that described this situation. I wondered why Robert had driven out here from the city, when a simple phone call would've sufficed. His next words answered my question.

"I could've called, but I had a bit of business to see to, so I was in the neighborhood. I saw Cheyne turning into the drive just ahead of me." Robert came into the kitchen a few paces ahead of Cheyne and Claude. As if sensing an uncomfortable ambience, his lizard eyes darted around the room. The corrugations on his forehead told me he was rapidly assessing the situation. "Y'all got some kind o' problem?"

Cheyne nodded at me, pretty much ignored my cousin, and went directly to the injured cat.

Sharla gave Robert a quick rundown of the morning's events.

I watched my cousin's face for any reaction. After all, Cheyne said it was likely somebody paid Annie Lebeau to kill that cat and do some sort of spell. For all I knew, Robert could be the culprit.

My cousin just twisted his face in a frown. "You said you'd talked to her?" His lidless eyes bored into Cheyne.

Cheyne went to the counter and poured himself a cup of the coffee that had been sitting in the pot since early morning. "No, she wasn't home, but I'm going back to see her. I don't expect her to admit to anything. She's not that stupid." He took a sip and shrugged as if the taste was palatable...just barely. "You said it was an animal trap of some kind?" He asked Sharla.

"*Mais ye*. In fact, I took him to the doctor with the trap still on his leg. I was afraid I'd do more damage if I tried to take it off."

"I'll need the trap as evidence." Cheyne returned to the injured cat and stroked it along its back.

"The doctor said my boy was lucky. The thing had snapped shut on a little branch along with his leg...so it didn't break his leg, just cut him badly," Sharla said.

I watched Cheyne petting the cat. I wondered if he was as rough as he seemed on the surface.

"We need to do something to keep her off of this property." Claude sniffed the coffee left in the pot and made a face. He poured the offending liquid down the drain. "I guess a cop will drink anything." He gave Cheyne a sour look, which the lawman returned with no rancor.

Claude took a fresh packet of coffee beans from the cabinet and filled the grinder.

The machine overwhelmed any conversation until it finished its business, so we all just stood around and watched Claude, as he bustled about the kitchen like he owned the place. When the grinder shut off, he closed his eyes and inhaled the aroma of the freshly ground beans and started a new pot of coffee. "You heard Remy say she nearly ran him and his friends off the road right at the end of the driveway the other night, and she has no business at Shadow Cove," he reminded.

"Well, short of putting up an electrified fence with razor wire around the top of it and maybe hiring a couple of armed guards, I don't know how you can keep her out," Cheyne said. "You might think about getting a couple of dogs…big ones."

"Plenty of room for dogs, if the old sow doesn't try to poison them," Robert commented. "But dogs are pretty easy to distract."

I pulled a chair out from the table and joined Sharla. "Sharla and I were talking about getting some dogs the first night I was here. I've never owned one. What would you recommend?" I asked Cheyne.

"German shepherds," he answered. "Get a pair of white ones. You can see them in the dark."

"Or maybe black ones, so Annie *can't* see them in the dark," Sharla suggested, with a lift of her brows.

"One of each," I put in. "Of course, I'd want to get puppies and raise them, so they wouldn't be much use until they were grown and trained."

"There is that," Cheyne agreed.

"An alarm system might be better." Robert leaned against the counter. "And you wouldn't have to feed it."

He seemed to expect us to laugh, but three pairs of eyes just stared at him.

"Lot of property to try to cover with an alarm system." Cheyne poured out his stale coffee and helped himself to a fresh cup.

I drummed my fingernails on the table. "I'm not going to put up with that old hag. Everybody else might take her harassment for granted, but I'm not going to sit idly by and let her run around killing helpless animals and making threats to people."

The sheriff gave me a thin smile. "What do you intend to do, shoot her?"

"The idea occurred to me, but I left my gun packed with my other stuff back in Seattle." I wondered if it was my imagination or if my cousin's interest perked when I mentioned a gun. Then I saw his mouth twitch when I said the weapon was still in Seattle. "Of course, there's a whole rack of guns in the library. I could take my pick."

Robert's lip twitched again.

"You have a license? You know how to use a gun?" Cheyne cocked his head at me, his expression dripping skepticism.

I wasn't sure if this man liked me or not. He certainly wasn't smooth and flirtatious like his cousin. I detected more than a tiny bit of disdain in his attitude toward me, even though he'd been nice enough so far. "Don't look at me like that?" I glared at him. "As a matter of fact, and against my Southern Belle mama's opinion, I did buy a gun, and I did learn to use it at the Seattle Police Department's firing range." I shrugged. "Of course, I couldn't bring it on the plane with me, saw no need to anyway." I chuffed a laugh. "Not until I got to Shadow Cove, anyway."

"Hmph." Cheyne sipped from his fresh cup of brew. "You are full of surprises."

Claude got cups from the cabinet and poured a round for everybody. I passed and went to the fridge for a Coke.

"I could've told you Laurette was surprising." Sharla smirked at Cheyne. "She's already told me how she went against her mother's wishes and became an architect, took self-defense training her mama told her was unladylike…."

"And which might've saved my life or at least kept me from being robbed," I interjected. I flopped back down at the table and poured my Coke over ice.

The sheriff eyed a plate of beignets, Creole donuts, Sharla had cooked the day before and helped himself to one. He wagged the sugar-coated pastry at me. "That's true. I just don't want you to go popping off about shooting Annie Lebeau or anybody else."

"How about if I just beat her death?" I sagged in the chair and crossed my arms over my chest, giving him a stubborn, sullen look. "I want that old hussy to stay off of my property, and I intend to find a way to keep her off."

"Short of shooting her or beating the crap out of her, I hope." Cheyne wiped the powdered sugar from the beignets off his fingers with a paper napkin.

Chapter 37

Leaving Shadow Cove Plantation, Sheriff Delacroix drove his department-issued SUV down twisting lanes, out to the shack where Annie Lebeau lived. The roads were built up through the swamp, with deep ditches on either side. Thick underbrush lined the pavement.

A fox darted in front of Cheyne's vehicle, and he slowed down. He had a bad habit of driving too fast, not a good thing for a lawman. He was an impatient man…another bad trait for a cop, even a good one, and Cheyne knew he was a good cop…but he wanted to find out who was paying Annie to harass Laurette, and he wanted to find out soon. He had no doubt the old woman was doing this, and she didn't do anything for free.

Cheyne had his suspicions about the identity of Annie's customer, but he wasn't prepared to share his notions until he had something concrete, like an admission from either Annie or the person paying her. Annie hadn't been home earlier, but Cheyne was going to continue returning to her shanty until he rousted the old battleax.

He waited for a blue pickup truck to pass and waved at the driver,

Matt Pierce, before turning off the two-lane tarmac onto a narrow, unpaved road leading deeper into the swamp. Cheyne knew just about everybody on Bayou Ombre and knew the Old Pierce Place, as Matt's property was called, was only a quarter mile or so farther down the paved road. The Pierce homestead abutted the parcel owned by Annie, and Matt had had his share of problems with the old woman. Cheyne might want to talk to him later, see if he'd noticed any recent visitors to Annie's abode…anybody he might've recognized.

The sheriff turned again at a big oak tree, with a cornhusk scarecrow, dressed in a red shirt and overalls, nailed to it. The effigy was a marker to direct customers to the Voodoo woman's house. Spindly limbs, trailing long beards of moss, brushed against the sides of his vehicle as he navigated the rutted path.

Her old truck was not parked in its usual spot.

Cheyne pulled his SUV to a halt, cut off the motor, and got out. On his first visit, he'd merely ridden by and noticed she wasn't home. This time he decided to do a quick walkabout, nothing requiring a warrant.

Heat and humidity assaulted him, and he huffed out a breath. "Damn, it's hot," he muttered, pulling his shirt away from his chest and fanning himself.

A tabby cat perched on the front porch mewled at him.

"Yeah, I guess you're hot, too." Cheyne noticed a bowl of water on a table between two rocking chairs. He walked around the front porch, reaching out to pet the animal as it paralleled his steps and tripped lightly along the edge of the weather-beaten wood.

The cat leapt to the ground and tagged along with the sheriff as he walked around the side of the shack. Shards of pottery and old rusted cans littered the ground. Stalks and shreds of herbs and vegetables Annie used in her potions were scattered amongst the debris. A pungent, but not unpleasant, odor emanated from the drying plants.

The policeman stopped behind the house, hands on hips, and surveyed the backyard, looking for nothing in particular. An old iron washpot sat on a makeshift grate, fashioned from an iron bedstead, above a cold fire. A clothesline sagged between two trees. Scraps of cloth in a variety of colors fluttered from the line like pennants at a used car lot. He saw nothing to indicate any sort of Voodoo rigmarole had taken place around the premises, but then he didn't figure Annie would be careless.

A tattered wood and chicken-wire fence separated the backyard from the marshy ground along the bayou, and a dozen or so chickens scratched in the weeds around a henhouse on stilts.

The tabby jumped on a rickety table near the old fire and purred for attention.

Cheyne scratched the cat's head. The little creature was sleek, clean, and well-fed. *Strange that Annie has a pet, yet she thinks nothing of sacrificing animals to use in her Voodoo spells.*

He spied a tiny scrap of red cloth on the ground and picked it up. The material looked like the piece of cloth attached to the doll left on Laurette's verandah. He took a small plastic bag from his pocket and tucked the cloth inside.

Leaving the cat grooming itself in a patch of sunlight on the old table, he retraced his footsteps to the front of the place. No telling where Annie was, but she'd be back…and so would he. She might be in New Orleans. She did a surprising amount of business with people in the city.

He got back into his SUV and cranked up the big engine, relishing the gust of cold air blasting from the air conditioner. His clothes were damp with sweat from just the short time he'd spent walking around Annie's yard. A new cardboard box, with a picture of a microwave oven on it rested next to her garbage can at the edge of her front yard, waiting for trash pickup.

Cheyne cocked his head and peered out the windshield, squinting into the lowering sun. A television dish sprouted from the roof on one side of the dilapidated building. "Hmmm." He rubbed his finger over his upper lip. *Probabaly has a huge TV, a fancy sound system, and even a computer in that shack…all the comforts of home.* He'd been in plenty of firetraps that looked like the next wind would blow them down, to find all sorts of expensive electronic gadgets. *But never air conditioning.* He pulled his shirt away from his skin and fanned the cloth.

Not for the first time, he wondered if, just maybe, Annie didn't supplement her Voodoo business with selling drugs...and the junk she sold, potions and such shit as that, could not be technically construed as dope. Wouldn't surprise him, but so far he had no concrete reason to suspect her of dealing.

Bayou Ombre was no different from anyplace else when it came to drug problems, and the creeks traversing the marshy land provided an easy venue for delivering the product. He was acquainted with all the local dealers and heard gossip that Junior Couliette, Denise St. Cyr's son, was moving up in the hierarchy of purveyors of illegal substances around New Orleans. So far the booger hadn't been caught. He twisted his lips in a wry smile. It was just a matter of time. Junior was too stupid not to get caught, seeing as how he was rumored to be in cahoots with one of his relatives, the equally dimwitted Percy Arline, a member of the white trash branch of the Couliette family.

Damn near everybody whose families went back for generations in and around New Orleans was related. And rumors abounded amongst the family connections, the St. Cyrs and Couliettes included.

The St. Cyrs, rich as Renaissance princes, were involved in all sorts of mischief throughout the years. Most of the old families, including his own, had not made all their money legally, and it was common knowledge.

He put the car in gear and headed back toward the hard road. His thoughts ricocheted to the beautiful young woman who had invaded his world. Laurette St. Cyr didn't appear to be the simpering Southern Belle her mother was reputed to have been. The kind of woman who would bat her eyes and pretend to be so soft and helpless and then slip a knife between your ribs when you least expected it. He'd had his fill of women like that. No. The lovely Miss St. Cyr seemed very straight forward, honest, unpretentious. Cheyne hoped he was right.

He found himself drawn to her as he'd never been attracted to a woman before, and it wasn't just about sex…it was something more. She wasn't just beautiful. She was smart, after all, she was an architect… and he'd detected a wicked sense of humor. His lips twitched in amusement. He liked that. He also liked the feeling of wanting to protect her, care for her. In spite of her feistiness, she had an appealing vulnerability. *Okay, so I'm a macho man. Most women like that even if they pretend they don't, or so I've been told.*

Cheyne drew his fair brows together in a frown. His cousin, Court, appeared equally enchanted with their new resident. Typical of Court, he'd already beat his lawman cousin to the draw in inviting her to dinner.

The sheriff rewound his ruminations and went back to the words "appeared enchanted," wondering what Court's true motives were. His cousin was a user of other people in every sense of the word, and his opinion wasn't just a response to his never-to-be-admitted jealousy of Court's superior financial situation, his success with women, and his Southern gentleman charm, which seemed to beguile nearly everybody who met him, male and female alike.

Yes, Court Delacroix was a user.

Cheyne had evidence to back up his feelings. Things that went all the way back to childhood.

The cop huffed a dry laugh. He knew his cousin, perhaps better than anybody else did, knew things Court only suspected he knew. Court had a streak of the bully in him, but he would not go up against his bigger, stronger cousin. No, Court's bullying took a different direction, something far more subtle than physical confrontation. Court was a cunning son of a gun…and ruthless.

The Delacroix second cousins had been born only three months apart. Court to the wealthiest branch of the Delacroix family, while Cheyne's parents were solid middle class. They'd been fiercely competitive throughout school, attending the same Catholic schools in New Orleans and graduating from Holy Cross High School, where Cheyne won a football scholarship to LSU in Baton Rouge. Cheyne stayed in Louisiana, but Court left to study architecture in New York.

Court came home from Yankeeland with the daughter of a Senator on his arm. However, on a visit to one of the French Quarter's clubs, something happened that sent the young lady high-tailing her fine self back across the Mason-Dixon Line, never to be seen or heard from again. Cheyne knew the club's reputation and had been surprised Court had taken his fiancée there, even though Court said it was her idea. True? Maybe. After all, the wicked nightlife of New Orleans is famous for providing exotic and flagrantly erotic entertainment. In the case of the nightclub in question, Cheyne didn't think the offerings would be something most well-bred young women would appreciate.

Within a few short months of his return to bayou country, Court married the daughter of a wealthy local family, but the marriage didn't last long.

Cheyne's lips twisted in a wry smile. His cousin surely didn't have much luck with girlfriends. He barked a laugh…he was one to talk. Past thirty and never been married.

Court's wife, Fabienne Marigny, had been educated at some fancy girl's school in Massachusetts, Wellesley, Smith, some high-toned place. She returned home with the attitude that she was "just a little bit better," as the saying goes. Her family had been snobs to begin with, and the exclusive school honed Fabienne's snotty instincts to razor sharpness.

Cheyne gave himself a mental shake and followed the curving highway back into town. He didn't want to allow thoughts of Fabienne to linger in his mind. No one knew for sure why she committed suicide. She'd been what was called high strung, a diva, unable to control her emotions. That reasoning never set well with Cheyne, given his own brief relationship with her.

He'd found it hard to believe someone so self-centered would kill herself.

Fabienne was a spoiled brat for sure. And a flirt…a little more than a flirt, actually.

Despite the entreaties of his conscience that he stay away from his cousin's wife like he would avoid an inferno, the young sheriff had not been impervious been her brazen interest in him and had succumbed to her charms. Even while the short-lived affair was going on, Cheyne felt like he was being manipulated to make her husband jealous...or perhaps he was just timber to stoke the flames of her ego. For a while, he was consumed with lust for her. She was so beautiful, and when it came to sex, she was insatiable. No one was more exciting or innovative that Fabienne Marigny Delacroix. Cheyne wondered where she'd learned the skills at such a young age.

Unbidden, the crotch of his pants grew tight.

"Shit," he cursed aloud. The very thought of her could arouse him still. He ran his hand through his hair and shifted uncomfortably on the car seat. He didn't need to be thinking about her, but he couldn't stop. Her death still gnawed at him.

He stopped at the traffic light on Main Street and waited while a young preppy-looking couple, burdened with huge backpacks, pushed their bicycles across the intersection. Cheyne nodded in acknowledgement of their smiles and waves. The street was mostly deserted. Only tourists and cops were out in this heat. Even though he'd cooled down, his shirt was still stuck to his chest.

His mind fought against memories of his former paramour and lost. Fabienne had been a vixen, a schemer. There'd been no woman like her. She would lie and cheat and couldn't be trusted, but over a year after her death, Cheyne wasn't entirely certain she hadn't been telling him the truth about some things.

She and Court fought like pit bulls. According to her, their marriage was like both sides of hell.

Fabienne wanted a baby...and the autopsy disclosed she was pregnant...with Cheyne's child or Court's or somebody else's? Cheyne heard rumors that he wasn't her first or her only lover since her marriage to his cousin. He broke off his own affair with her after less than three months, three months in which he hadn't been sure if he was living in heaven or hell, so passionate was his obsession with her.

When he confronted her with his knowledge of two other men she was seeing, she laughed and told him she liked variety. And he told her...well...he'd behaved as something less than a gentleman at the time.

Two months later, she was dead.

He still carried a burden of guilt about cuckolding his cousin and about Fabienne's death. Neither he nor Court had ever spoken of her infidelity with Cheyne. In fact, Cheyne wasn't entirely certain Court knew, or if he did know, he didn't care. Cheyne didn't break up his cousin's marriage. Court needed no help in that department. If what Fabienne told Cheyne was true, he knew the reason she died... even if nobody else did...and her suicide never made sense to him.

He pulled his mouth into a tight line. *If Fabienne killed herself,* his mind reiterated for the thousandth time.

His mind trawling through the past, he almost missed the car pulling out of the long driveway leading to Court's house.

Cheyne almost waved, but the driver ducked down suddenly, as if looking for something in the seat, the lightly tinted windows partially obscuring identity. The furtive movement caught the sheriff's attention. A prickle of something like foreboding tingled along his skin.

"I'll be damned," he grumbled. He knew why the driver did not want to be identified by Cheyne. There was nothing illegal about a visit to Court's house, but Cheyne knew precisely why his cousin's visitor would prefer not to be recognized.

He had to admit he was surprised. The situation might bear watching.

Chapter 38

Until we had an opportunity to go to a kennel and buy a couple of puppies or get a fence installed, Sharla and I decided the best course of action to keep Sharla's cats safe was to latch the kitty door and keep the little critters inside.

"They can get plenty of fresh air and sunshine on one of the screened verandahs," Sharla said. "That way, I'll know they're inside and safe."

"I just wish there was something we could do about that hateful old woman."

"You mean short of killing her?"

"That idea has some merit?"

"Killing who?" Claude stepped from the mudroom into the kitchen, Courtland Delacroix in tow.

I was startled at their sudden appearance. *How had they gotten into the house unnoticed? Did one of them have a key or did people around here not lock their doors in the daytime? Either way, having someone come into my home without announcing themselves by knocking or ringing the doorbell made me uncomfortable. One more thing I needed to talk to Sharla about.*

"Annie Lebeau," Sharla answered, obviously nonplussed at the appearance of the two men. "I'm sick of putting up with that old sow and her shenanigans."

"Wouldn't be any great loss to the world if somebody killed her, *n'est-ce pas?*" The lawyer quirked his lips, then waved his hand toward his companion. "I had Court meet me out front to take a look at that door. It's a mess after what that old hussy did to it. I figured he'd know how to get it repaired. Then we came around the back of the house, so I could show him that loose gutter."

Court smiled and stepped over to me and put an arm around my shoulders. "And how is the loveliest new belle of the bayou this morning?"

Giving him a scant smile, I stepped out of his embrace. "I'm as well as can be expected with all this Voodoo business going on." I nodded toward the latched kitty door. "We're keeping Sharla's cats in the house until we feel safe from that Annie creature." Court had invited me on another date, but I declined. I had a lot to do, getting settled in and having my belongings shipped from Seattle. The truth was I felt like he was pressuring me. True he was handsome and charming as the devil himself, but I just wasn't prepared to jump into a hot romance…and there were just things that bothered me… things I couldn't put my finger on…about the rush he was giving me.

Sharla's eyes flashed quickly between the two of us, as though sensing something amiss, but she only said, "Will the door have to be replaced, or can you repair it? It's beautiful, and it's been a part of the house forever. Came from England, I think."

"I know a guy in the Quarter who does beautiful restorations, and you don't want to replace that door. It's priceless," Court answered.

"Absolutely." Claude was quick to agree. "That door is almost a hundred and fifty years old, solid oak, hand-hewn and carved. Sharla's right. It was imported from England right after the end of the War of Northern Aggression."

I felt a bit annoyed that these people were making decisions regarding my home without consulting me. I stifled my sigh of *pique*. They were far more familiar with my new home than I was.

Chapter 39

The sounds of the carpenters restoring the front door drifted from the front of the house to the kitchen, along with the steady beat of the music from the blues station the men played on their radio. Etta James was wailing that she had found true love *At Last*.

Claude made the arrangements through Court, and the master craftsman, Pierre Jones, assured him he could do the work of repairing and restoring the heavy door. Jones's workmen had the door laid out on sawhorses on the front verandah. They'd placed a piece of plywood over the opening to keep the cats inside and the bugs out.

"We can trust Court to find the best craftsman when we need work to be done," Sharla said. "His daddy's construction business is one of the best around, started by *his* daddy, after they got out of the cane business."

"So the Delacroix family has been around as long as the St. Cyrs?" I leaned on the countertop, watching Sharla roll out pastry for her crawfish pie.

"*Mais ye.* The St. Cyrs had their plantation, Shadow Cove, while upriver the Delacroix family had their Fleur d'Or. And both families have more skeletons rattling in their closets than Carter's got peanuts."

"More ghosts and haints and such?" I'd said nothing to Sharla about my peculiar experience with the painting in my room. In retrospect, I felt foolish. More likely I simply drank too much wine that night, and my imagination ran wild.

Sharla chuckled. "More like just a bunch of crazies."

"I've already figured out my family is strange. What about the Delacroix clan? Are they weird?"

"No more than is normal in Louisiana families."

I laughed. "You said Court's a widower. What about Cheyne?"

"Never been married. He was engaged once, but it didn't work out. All their siblings are married, but not those two."

"What was Court's wife's suicide all about? Do you know? That must've been awful for him."

"She's only been dead a little over a year." Sharla cast me a baleful look. "Court bounced back pretty quick, which would surprise nobody who knew him all his life. With Court, it's all about himself. Don't get me wrong. He's gentlemanly and well-behaved and an excellent building contractor...probably more honest than most, when it comes to his business." She rolled the dough out in a circle. "But he's also a very self-centered man. And his wife was cut from the same bolt of cloth. It was 'all about me,' with both of them, so you can imagine what they were like together." She paused in her work and faced me. "Then there was the rumor that his precious wife, Fabienne, was sniffing around other men, including his cousin Cheyne."

I nearly dropped my glass of Coke, and cold fingers gripped my stomach. "Was Cheyne fooling around with his cousin's wife?" I certainly hadn't pictured him as that kind of man. Of course, I pegged him as a man who saw women as little more than a convenience. But playing around with a married woman was pretty low in my estimation, and messing with his cousin's wife knocked him down yet another rung, even if the woman had been throwing herself at him. On the other hand, Sharla said the stories were only rumors.

"Well, nobody ever saw anything for certain, far as I've heard. But I noticed the two of them together at a party one night, and if they weren't gettin' it on, they were missing a helluva chance. That girl's panties were on fire for Cheyne Delacroix."

A twinge of jealousy twisted my gut, even though the past object of Cheyne's interest was dead. "Was she beautiful, this Fabienne?"

"Very. Real magnolia blossom. Dark hair and eyes, pale skin. Too beautiful for her own good."

"So maybe our sheriff's armor just might have a little rust on it?"

Sharla shrugged. "Not as far as I'm concerned. He's still a better man than Court, so that could've been what it was about. Maybe Fabienne thought Cheyne was a better man, too. And it could've been nothing more than a flirtation. As my mama said, 'There was some sniffing and tail wagging going on, but I'm not sure any pussy ever exchanged hands'."

I put my hand over my mouth to keep from spraying Coke. "Oh, my God. You've got such a delicate way of expressing yourself." I grabbed a napkin and wiped my hand and mouth. "How did Court's wife die?"

Sharla rinsed her hands under cold running water in the sink, scrubbing off the flour. "Nothing very exotic. She went out in the bayou and shot herself with one of Court's pistols. I remember hearing there were some bruises on her body, and she was pretty scratched up, but the coroner said that could have happened with her stumbling around in the dark. And she'd been drinking, nothing unusual for the oh-so-proper Madame Delacroix, according to the house servants. I gather she had something of a problem with the sauce and anything else that could send her to la-la-land. If she could drink it, smoke it, or snort it, she liked it."

"Not your traditional Southern Belle, huh?"

"She played the role, but it was all a front." She wiped her hands and arms off on a paper towel. "She was a wild little thing."

"And she wound up killing herself." I shivered. "That's awful."

Sharla twisted her mouth. "I wondered about that. Nobody ever suggested it was anything but a suicide...not officially anyway"

"Was Cheyne sheriff when it happened?"

"*Mais ye,* but he wasn't involved in the investigation because of his relationship to Court." Sharla picked over the crawfish she took from the fridge. They'd been peeled and were ready for baking. "Some cops from New Orleans handled the case."

"You said 'not officially.' You think there was something fishy?" I pulled a chair out from the kitchen table and sat down.

She pointed to the bowl of crustaceans. "Fishier than them mudbugs, if you ask me. It just seemed odd to me that a girl that self-centered would kill herself...and I wondered why. I never thought her and Court's fairy tale romance was all that lovey-dovey in the first place. I wondered why she even married him, except he had more money than her family did. She always thought she was all that and got even worse after she married a Delacroix."

"Her family wasn't rich, too?"

"They were well off. Old money, but her daddy had a taste for gambling and had pissed away a fortune. They were still rich, but not Delacroix rich."

"So what was Court's attraction to her, other than her looks?"

Sharla twisted her lips to one side and frowned. "Personally, I think it was because she needed him...his money...and he knew he could use that to manipulate her." She shrugged. "And he just needed a wife. A social thing, you know."

"Manipulate her, in what way?"

"Oh, it's just a feeling I've always had about Court. It's like he's only interested in people for what he can get out of them and what he can make them do for him." She got a Coke from the fridge and filled a glass with ice. "I think he only wanted a wife for a convenience. And she filled the bill, or appeared to anyway."

"Did she do anything...work or whatever?"

"Hardly. Too good to work, if you know what I mean." Sharla cocked that eyebrow and poured the Coke over ice and took her glass to the stove. "She was a snobby little piece of baggage." She picked up the bowl of crawfish and folded them into the sauce simmering on the stove. "I never paid much attention to her." She turned and gave me a brittle smile. "I didn't travel with her fancy set."

I leaned on my fist. "Would you have wanted to...hang with them, I mean?"

She chuffed a laugh. "It made me sorta glad I was only the hired help and much too old for those sweet young thangs to include in their circle. All they did was shop, lunch, and gossip." She held up a finger. "And drink more than was...or is...good for them."

"I never wanted to fit into that sort of crowd either. Just as well, I suppose." I twirled a lock of hair around my finger. "I was a bit of a misfit...Mama's girl, or so everyone thought. And I guess I was."

"I've always been close to my mother, too." Sharla's laugh was tinged with bitterness. "Guess I had to be. No way could I have been a DG like most of those chicks."

"DG?"

"You know...Daddy's Girl."

I wondered if now would be an opportune time to ask Sharla about her father, but she saved me the trouble.

"Everyone's always suspected that Marc Renard is my father, and *M'sieu* Marc, as I was taught to call him, has never done anything to dissuade them from that notion."

"Umm...is he?" My gut clenched when I asked her this all too personal question.

"My daddy?" Sharla gave me a long look, as if deciding how to answer. "Of course he is, and all the Renards know it. That's why Madeleine hates the sight of me."

"My grandmother?" Her casual revelation sucked the air out of me.

"*Mais ye.* But then I can't really blame her. I can only imagine how I'd feel if I had my husband's bastard child and his half-black mistress underfoot in my own home." Sharla put the lid on the sauce pan and sat down at the table. "I grew up in the Renards' house, played with Celine and the other legitimate young'uns, even went to school with them." Her lips quirked in a thin smile. "For all her faults, Celine was always much nicer to me than the other girls were...my other half-sisters. She pretty much treated me like we really were sisters, which of course, we were, and our birthdays were only a few months apart, less than a year. In most every way, we became each other's best friend."

"How did my grandfather treat you?"

Sharla raise one shoulder in a miniscule shrug. "The plain truth is I've never had anything to complain about with him. He was always good to me. *M'sieu* Marc paid my tuition at Sacred Heart right along with the bills for his 'real' daughters."

Mama had mentioned the school she attended in New Orleans. "You went to Sacred Heart Academy?"

"Um, hmm. You'd've gone there, too, had your mama stayed in N'Awlins." Sharla sipped her Coke, eyeing me over the rim of the glass. "*M'sieu* Marc, he even paid for me to go to nursing school. Bought me my first car, a little Mustang...brand new...bright red. Always gave me spending money. I never actually wanted for anything." She narrowed her lips. "Damn white of him, wouldn't you say?"

I remembered how my grandfather, Sharla's father, seemed quite cordial with his illegitimate daughter the evening of the party at Shadow Cove. Her comment didn't need an answer. "And so everybody knows? I mean, that he's your daddy?"

"Well, I've never worn a sign around my neck, and he never put an ad in the *Times-Picayune*, him, but I'm certain all the Renards know. With everybody else, it's just highly suspected." Sharla wagged her head. "And of course your grandparents and Etienne knew... and Claude."

It suddenly dawned on me. "You're my aunt, then. Aren't you?"

Sharla looked at me for a long moment and said nothing.

I saw her eyes mist over, but she quickly pushed her chair away from the table and got to her feet. "I've got to get this crawfish pie baking, me."

Chapter 40

Claude and Wills arrived a few minutes early for dinner. Claude brought the fixings for a new drink he wanted to show off. The ingredients included champagne, elderflower liqueur, and something called *crème de violette*.

I was never much of a drinker, but I'd already learned that in New Orleans, people drank for any occasion and at any time of the day. Getting a hangnail trimmed could be a good enough reason for a celebration.

Not that we were celebrating anything, but Paul Thibadeaux had brought Sharla a hamper of freshly caught and peeled crawfish, so she decided to make her crawfish pie Claude loved.

"Guess who I ran into in the Quarter this morning." Claude held up a cocktail shaker and closed one eye as he measured and poured the ingredients for the exotic drink he called *Stormy Morning*.

I perched on a bar stool and watched him. "Since I know so few people in New Orleans, I'm limited in my guesses."

"Roland. Roland Dubois." Claude gave his concoction an approving eye, put the lid on the shaker, and shook it. "I ran into him and Giselle just as I was leaving this little café where I often have breakfast on my housekeeper's days off. Right down the street from his place."

"I intend to go see him as soon as I get settled."

"He asked about you, and I told him you were in love with N'Awlins and Shadow Cove. I'll see when it'll be convenient for Sharla to have them out to dinner one evening. He said they both enjoyed themselves the other night." He poured his drink mixture over ice and garnished the glasses with lime slices. "*Cher*, get in here and try one of these," he called to Sharla.

I loved the idea of seeing Roland again, but I was just a tiny bit annoyed with the way friends and family seemed to take it for granted that they could invite people to my home whenever they liked. Sharla didn't seem to let such things bother her. She was clearly more of a social butterfly than I. Oh, well, I gave myself a mental shrug. Having company all the time hadn't caused any problems so far. Besides, I told Sharla to consider Shadow Cove her home.

Following our conversation earlier, Sharla said nothing more about being my aunt...or half aunt...or whatever. I decided to say nothing more until, and unless, she raised the subject.

Wills came up behind Claude, a hand held to his stomach and a sour look on his face. He accepted a glass of his partner's fizzy concoction. "I hope the champagne in this stuff helps settle my tummer. I've been trotting all afternoon." He took a long draught and smacked his lips in appreciation. "Just had to make use of your facilities," he told me.

"We have six bathrooms, so help yourself. I hope it wasn't something you ate."

Wills sipped some more of the cocktail. "Might've been the sautéed chicken livers at lunch, but this should fix me up."

Sharla came in from the kitchen. "My crawfish pie's just what you need to help what ails you." She grinned.

"Oh, sugah, you know I could be dying, and I wouldn't pass up your crawfish pie." Wills drank most of the cocktail and held his glass out for a refill. "With all the spices in that pie, this drink just might bolster my innards."

Claude took his partner's glass and filled it to the brim, then shifted his attention to me. "By the way, just as we were turning in your driveway, we saw Annie Lebeau prowling the neighborhood. She looked like she was fixing to cut across your property, but I slowed to a halt and gave the old witch the evil eye."

"Cheyne said he was going to have a talk with her," I told him.

Wills snorted. "I doubt it will do any good."

"Yeah. I don't think anything short of a stake through her heart will stop her." Sharla sipped her drink, nodded approvingly, and held the glass up to the light. "Wonder why this stuff settles to the bottom like that."

"It's the *crème de violette*," Claude said. "It sorta swirls around and settles, looking like the sky on a stormy day. That's how the drink got its name."

"Hmmm. I think you'll need to mix up another batch." Sharla smacked her approval.

"That's why I brought three bottles of champagne." The lawyer waggled his eyebrows.

"Speaking of Annie," I said. "Sharla called a fence contractor this morning, and we're going to have a portion of the back yard fenced in, with an electric wire top and bottom, so the cats can't get out."

"They're used to being able to come and go at will, and they're going stir crazy in the house," Sharla explained. "We already have a doggy door in the back door for them. With the charged fence, they'll have to stay inside the fence, but they can get outside and do their cat things, and there are plenty of bushes out there for them to play in and stay safe."

Claude pointed his finger at her. "Good idea. And put some motion sensor lights out there, too."

"Anything to discourage that old hussy from coming near our pets," I said. "Until somebody can come up with a final solution to the problem with her."

"I still like the stake through the heart." Sharla finished off her second drink. "I'm not sure that crazy old bitch is human."

Chapter 41

Acouple of cartons of my belongings arrived late in the morning, so I spent the afternoon unpacking and sorting. Half the clothes were bound for the church charity bin. I set boxes of pictures aside to go through later. Sandwiched between two ancient photograph albums was the package I was really looking for, labeled "loose pictures of Mama and me." I carefully unwrapped it to get to the rectangular box within a box and unwrapped that.

I pulled out my Smith and Wesson and hefted it, loaded it from a box of cartridges snugged in the carton with the gun. I slipped the revolver into the bedside table and placed a box of tissues on top of it.

Heaving a sigh, I felt better just knowing that gun was close by. The repeated sightings of those lights on the river bothered me more than I wanted to admit. Fishermen? Maybe.

I still hadn't explored that part of my property, but when I did, I planned on finding out how much it would cost to install a fence out there. Okay, so maybe I'm a privacy freak, but I just don't like knowing there are no barriers to keep people off of my land. I suppose my feelings might come from being a city dweller, where boundaries are clearly delineated.

That evening, Sharla and I spent blessed time at home alone, no invited company, nobody dropping by. She barbequed some chicken on the brick grill behind the house. She placed sliced zucchini, yellow and white squash, and asparagus spears on a metal grill pan alongside the chicken. I made potato salad and mixed a batch of pina colada. Dessert was her famous pecan pie. We turned on the tiny outdoor lights strung under the eaves of the gazebo at the end of the dock and fixed ourselves a picnic.

The evening was still warm and humid, but the breeze off the bayou was pleasantly cool.

As the sun was disappearing, a shallow draft boat, with tall seats for two riders, roared around the bend in the creek. The driver spotted us and swerved in our direction. The peculiar-looking watercraft literally flew across the water, making a hellish racket.

"Airboat," Sharla shouted. "Powered by an airplane propeller mounted on the rear. They're used a lot in shallow water, like the creeks and bayous."

The driver powered down the motor, and the boat glided to a halt near the gazebo. It was Remy Thibadeaux and another young man he introduced as Josie Thibadeaux

Josie was nearly as handsome as Remy and had the same dark hair and gray eyes. I thought he might be twenty-two or twenty-three. "Josie's my brother Paul's boy, my nephew," Remy explained.

"This is the beauty you told me about?" Josie flirted. "*Tres bonne.* I come back and see you, me."

"I'm starting to think all you Cajun men flirt with anything that moves," I called to him.

"Only the prettiest girls," Josie responded.

"What are y'all doing out on the river this evening?" Sharla asked.

"We're heading upriver to have a couple drinks with ladies," Remy told her. "Sisters who just moved here from Lafayette."

"Nice evening for romance." Sharla took a sip of her drink.

"Always nice evening for romance, *cher*." Remy flashed that devastating grin. "You call me, you get lonesome, hear?"

Sharla flapped a hand at him. "Get gone, you *flagonarier*."

The Cajun man made kissing sounds. "I sweet talk you for real, *cher*."

"Bull." Sharla laughed, the sound drowned out, as he revved his motor and whipped the boat around in a tight circle. The flat-bottomed craft skimmed the water like a giant marsh bird.

I noticed the red rear lights on his boat were just like tail lights on a car or truck. Perhaps Sharla was right. The lights I was seeing late at night were just men going up and down the river, fishing or courting.

"Would that young man be Katie's brother?"

"*Mais ye*, but they look nothing alike. Katie looks like her mother's people."

"I'm surprised he spoke to me, considering how his sister feels about me...you know...about Court?"

Charla snorted. "He knows how his baby sister is. And he knows she doesn't have a chance of snagging Courtland Delacroix. She's been slobbering over him ever since she went to work for his company, doing secretarial stuff...right out of high school."

"She needs to find herself a young man her own age."

"I know that's right. She's way out of her league with Court," she commented. "And personally, I think he's a rat for leading her on. Ego trip I suppose."

After we cleaned up the kitchen, we watched an old movie on TV. We surprised each other with our mutual taste for action and adventure movies, not sloppy romances. Sharla even liked The Sopranos, a show my mother forbade me to watch, so I bought a boxed set and watched every episode about six times on the sly in my bedroom back in Seattle.

Before crawling into bed, I'd gotten into the habit of going onto the dark gallery outside my room and looking for the mysterious lights. Tonight nothing seemed be stirring on the river, so I locked the doors and went to bed, feeling a new kind of comfort, knowing my loaded gun rested in the bedside table.

A chirping woke me. I was so deeply asleep, it took several moments before I realized the noise came from the phone on the night table. As I grabbed the receiver, the ringing stopped, but I held it to my ear and heard Sharla talking to someone.

"I'll get her up. You're on your way?" Sharla's voice was clear, and I recognized the other one as belonging to Claude.

"I'll be there in about twenty minutes. I'm almost out of the city now."

They both hung up.

I sat up in bed and turned on the light. Before I could swing my legs over the side, I heard the wail of sirens.

Sharla flung open the door and ran into my room. "We've got to get dressed. Claude will be here in a few minutes."

I rubbed my eyes. "What's going on?"

"Somebody's tried to set fire to the maintenance barns where all the equipment is stored."

"I hear the sirens." I staggered out of bed. I was not one to hit the ground running...more like staggering. "What on earth?"

"Claude didn't have time to fill me in, but apparently one of the workmen was bringing some equipment in really late and caught the perps in the act." She ran a hand through her hair. "Just grab a tee shirt and some jeans." With that, she fled back down the hall to her own suite.

Chapter 42

We were on the porch waiting when Claude pulled into the driveway, driving a maroon Jeep Cherokee instead of his Jaguar. Sharla jerked open the rear door and jumped into the backseat, while I climbed in beside Claude.

In spite it being nearly two a.m., Claude was immaculate in a pink-checked cotton shirt and neatly pressed jeans. He was one of those men who would look perfectly turned out in a pair of red flannel long johns in the middle of an elephant stampede.

"I don't know much. Henry called me as soon as he got to the barns." He drove rapidly along the winding roads through the canes fields.

"Henry?" Sharla sounded confused. "I thought he was in Alaska on vacation with his wife."

"Alma's mama had a problem, and they had to cut short their trip. Just got back late this morning, yesterday morning, now, I guess."

I remember Father Gee mentioning someone named Henry as the plantation manager, so I assumed this was who they were talking about. Before I could ask, the wails of another emergency vehicle drowned out the conversation.

Claude veered to the shoulder of the road to let the firetruck pass.

On the horizon, I could see an orange glow and emergency lights strobing the sky above the tall cane.

Claude whipped his vehicle back onto the roadway and navigated the route through the cane fields. He spun into the parking lot of a redbrick building. A sign out front proclaimed the place the "Shadow Cove Maintenance Barn." The facility was backlit by a roaring fire. Smoke boiled into the dark sky.

I scrambled out of Claude's SUV right behind him and Sharla. The heat from the barn fire assaulted me.

An eight foot chainlink fence, topped with razor-sharp cantina wire, was attached to the rear of the building and enclosed several acres of flat land. An array of maintenance and harvesting vehicles were arranged with military precision in rows along the right side of the property. I sucked in a breath when I saw two gas pumps only yards from the barn that was on fire. Men were spraying chemical foam around the pumps, isolating them from the fire.

We raced through the open fence gate.

A huge flatbed truck sat just inside the gate. Some piece of monster equipment was secured to the bed with thick chains. At least a half dozen police cars, their red, white, a blue lights flashing, and three fire trucks were parked haphazardly, one rolling to a stop just ahead of us. Pickup trucks and SUVs were parked in any available space. Claude said these vehicles belonged to volunteer firemen and just neighbors who showed up to help when they heard the sirens. "It's a small town Southern thing, *cher*. We show up to help each other."

Two ambulances idled side by side. A grime-smeared man sat on the rear of one, being tended by a female paramedic. Men ran everywhere, shouting at each other. Overhead lights around the fenced perimeter glared, dispelling the gloom caused by the roiling, oily smoke.

The odor of smoke and burned gasoline hung heavy in the air.

Cheyne Delacroix's massive physique loomed in front of us, with a uniformed, female deputy at his side. "Don't even have to speculate about arson," he nodded toward the man on the rear of the ambulance and walked us in that direction. "Rand here caught them in the act."

"Sons a bitches shot at me... nicked me." The man called Rand puffed on a cigarette. "I fired back. Think I nailed one of the bastards."

"Rand Morrissey...this is your new boss, Laurette St. Cyr." Cheyne made the introductions, barely looking in my direction.

"Ma'am." The wiry-looking man nodded.

"You think you shot one of them," I asked.

"Might've." He worked on that cigarette, grimacing as the paramedic patched him up. "He dropped the gas can, and I saw him staggerin', tryin' to run." He shook his head. "Too damn bad he made it to the fence."

"Looks like they cut through the fence on the far side." Cheyne waved a hand in that direction. "There's a weak spot over there where it looks like one of the maintenance vehicles struck it from inside, and they took advantage of it. Scoped it out ahead of time, no doubt. Might even be somebody who works here and knew about the weak spot."

"They got the barn nearest the gas pumps. I got out the fire extinguishers and started hosin' down the pumps. We'll have a hell of a mess if them underground tanks blow."

"Looks like the guys've got the tanks sealed off," Cheyne said. "Hope so anyway."

Another man, almost as large as Cheyne lumbered through the web of firehoses that were churning the dirt to mud, wiping soot and sweat off his face with his forearm. "You okay?" He asked the man named Rand.

"Yeah. I'm a tough bastard."

The newcomer barked. "Hell, I know that's right."

"How's Alma's mama doing, Henry?" Claude asked the big man.

Even in the midst of a crisis, Southerners took the time to inquire about a family member's health.

The man called Henry tapped a spot on his massive chest. "Heart. She's been having problems, but the doc says he's got it under control."

"That's good to hear. Give Miz Yvonne my love and let us know if y'all need anything." Claude touched my arm. "Laurette, this is Henry Toussaint, your field manager." He wagged his head at the other man. "Henry, meet your new bosslady."

"I'd shake, but my hands are nasty, ma'am." Henry's smile was white in his grimy face. He was only an inch or so shorter than Cheyne, barrel-chested, with olive skin and graying black hair. His voice sounded like it started down in his belly and gained momentum rumbling upward.

The deputy accompanying Cheyne moved to stand beside Morrissey, her notepad at the ready.

"So what happened? What were you doing out here at this hour?" Cheyne asked.

Morrissey lit another cigarette and gestured toward the big flatbed truck. "Had to run up to Baton Rouge and pick up that thing this mornin', a heavy duty sprayer...uh...yesterday, I guess now. You know how it goes when you get to one o' them places...hurry up and wait...so I was late gettin' on the road. Then the damn water pump went out on the truck. By the time I got the thing fixed, it was black-ass dark and headin' toward midnight, so it was after one-thirty when I got here to the barn."

All the men bobbed their heads in understanding.

"Just one fuckin' thing after another." A pained expression flickered across Rand's face. "'Scuse me, ladies."

"We've all heard the word before," I said. The other women just nodded their agreement. We weren't a bunch of old maid Sunday school teachers.

Morrissey cocked his head to one side. "When I pulled my rig in the gate, after I got it unlocked, I spied somebody over yonder by Barn D. 'course, they'd already seen me and was startin' to haul butt…but one of 'em stopped and tossed somethin'…probably a cigarette lighter. That's when the fire started."

"Good thing you got here when you did," Henry said.

"I know that's right." Morrissey worked on his cigarette. "I hollered, and the next thing I knew the bastards were shootin' at me. I grabbed my own piece off the seat and fired back." He jerked his head toward his injured shoulder. "Like I said, they just nicked me." He examined the bandage the paramedic finished placing on his upper arm. "I called the fire department and got our own fire equipment goin'…got one side of the barn hosed down pretty good, but the fire was still spreadin' when the fire guys got here." He hacked a cough and sucked in a lungful of smoky night air. "They were here quick, got right on it."

"Lucky." Henry huffed a laugh. "Tonight's poker night at the fire house."

"Umhp. Yeah." Morrissey took another deep drag off his cigarette. He squinted through the smoke. "I heard the one by the fence holler somethin' to the other one…yelled a name I think. Beau or bro." He shook his head. "I dunno."

I snapped my head toward Cheyne. "Lebeau?"

Cheyne's eyebrows climbed, as he looked at Morrissey. "Could he have called the name 'Lebeau'?"

The injured man pondered this notion. "Could've been. The fire was roarin' and all…but that might've been what he yelled."

"Annie Lebeau." I crossed my arms on my chest.

Cheyne nodded. "Could be. The bayou is full of her kin…thirty-five or forty of them right here on Bayou Ombre."

"I wouldn't put anything past that old bitch," Sharla snarled. "But somebody's paying her. She doesn't work for nothing."

"There is that," Claude said, and Cheyne nodded his agreement.

"I'll check around," Cheyne said. "But don't expect any confessions. That tribe sticks together, and they won't rat on each other."

"You be in the office in the morning?" Claude asked Henry.

"I'll probably be here most of the night with Cheyne, but come on by when you want to," the field manager answered. To me, "Sorry to get you out of bed, Miz St. Cyr."

I stood with my hands on my hips. "This is my property. I want to know everything that goes on at Shadow Cove."

He gave me a curious look, and Claude laughed. "This young lady's going to be tagging after you for a while, Henry. She wants to know everything about running a plantation, and you're just the man to teach her."

Henry's smile was slow but broad. "I'll be glad to help you any way I can. I've worked for the St. Cyrs most of my life." He cleared his throat and studied the ground at his feet for a moment. "I'm really sorry about your daddy's passing. He was a good man, and I'm happy to hear his daughter's taking an interest in the place. None of us was sure what would happen after your daddy died, what with your grandpa and grandma being gone and all."

"And I'm glad to hear you say that." Like him, I looked down at the soggy dirt for a moment, touched more than I would've expected at the sincerity of his tone. I raised my eyes and looked at him steadily. "Now that I own this place, I want to learn everything about growing cane and running the business, get to know the people working for me."

He met my gaze and nodded. "Good, good."

The firemen wouldn't allow us any closer to the barns, so we could do nothing but go back home.

Walking back to the car, Sharla asked Claude, "You spending the night at the house?"

"May as well. I'll need to take Laurette back out to the barns tomorrow for a look-see, after the fire department gets through. Maybe Cheyne's people will've gathered their evidence by then."

By these remarks, I learned that Claude kept some clothing in *his* room and often spent the night at the big house.

Chapter 43

We slept late, and Sharla opened some canned clam chowder and made a salad for lunch before Claude and I headed back to the barns to see how bad the damage was.

She'd already baked a batch of brownies before Claude and I got up. She tucked half of them into a metal tin and told me to give them to Henry and the people working in his office.

Munching a brownie and sipping from a plastic glass of Coke, I followed Claude to his SUV and climbed aboard.

"Before we go to the barns, let me give you a quick tour of the cane fields, not all of them of course, but enough to give you a feel for what it all looks like." He laughed. "You've been here going on a month, and I just haven't had the time to really show you the place. Now's as good a time as any."

I'd been wanting to explore the place but had no idea where to start and wouldn't have known what to look for in the first place. I'd been all over the house, poking into every nook and cranny, but I still hadn't seen much of the plantation itself. "That suits me. I'd probably get lost out here alone. One cane stalk looks pretty much like another."

"True. It would be pretty easy to get lost."

We followed curving, shell roads through the tall stalks of green cane. I was surprised at how high the plants grew. The stalks were planted right up to the edge of the roadway, which was barely wide enough for two vehicles to pass each other. I felt just a bit claustrophobic and was glad I hadn't come out here alone.

I'd put on minimum makeup and swept my hair into a ponytail. Claude and I both dressed in fresh jeans and tee shirts. Sharla put everything we wore the night before into the washer before we went to bed, saying our clothes smelled like a skunk had been barbequed in them.

"This is where the property abuts the Delacroix land."

He crawled the vehicle along a twenty foot tall earthen embankment that stretched left and right as far as I could see. A hedge of bushes grew along the top. Midway up the slope was a high chainlink fence topped with razor wire.

I lowered my window and craned my neck. Just beyond the top of the embankment, between the tree limbs, I could make out barrel-tiled roofs. "What's over there?"

"That's where Court and his daddy are building their development, minimansions. They put up that embankment and the fence to keep out the riff-raff and so the homeowners wouldn't have to look at the cane fields and the men sweating their asses off working for a living."

I had a feeling Courtland Delacroix and his father were not Claude's favorite people, even though he used Court's services for maintaining Shadow Cove. "That fence looks like something out of a concentration camp."

"I know, but it can't be seen from the houses, and it's on the Delacroix land on this side." Claude smirked. "We just ignore it."

"Umm…I didn't say anything at the time, but now that I know you better…."

Claude interrupted me with a chuckle. "You can ask me anything you like, *cher.*" His eyes held a twinkle.

"Oh, I just sensed a coolness between you and Court's father when you introduced him to me."

My uncle barked. "You picked up on that, huh?"

"Sorta," I answered slowly.

"Amboise is a homophobic asshole," he explained, laughing.

I flapped my hand. "Oh, is that all it is? I thought it was something serious."

"He's homophobic, dislikes anybody who's not lily white, and thinks women should keep their biscuits in the oven and their buns in the bed. He's like some kind of throwback to what he calls a kinder, more genteel era, when people knew their places." He raised a finger. "But he hides it all behind a cultivated Southern gentleman front. I've been around him often enough to know his true feelings."

"Does Court share his daddy's prejudices?"

"Court has his own quirks, but he's equally good at hiding his feelings...not good for business, doncha know?" He cast me a sidelong glance with a knowing look. "And Court's all about what's good for lining his pockets."

He turned to the right away from the embankment.

"Did the Delacroix family sell all their cane property?"

"Uh, huh, and Court has been champing at the bit to buy some parcels of Shadow Cove land."

My mind immediately travelled to the way my handsome neighbor seemed to be attempting to rush me into a relationship with him. Despite his Southern manners and charm, subtlety wasn't his strong suit, and now I saw clearly what he was after. *It's not me he's interested in, it's my property.* "Not going to happen. I'm not planning to sell a square inch of Shadow Cove. This is my inheritance, and I intend to keep it."

"Good girl." Claude reached for my hand and raised it to his lips.

"You said Court and his father own a development company. Where does Cheyne fit into this?"

"He doesn't." He took a sip of his cup of coffee he'd tucked into the console holder. "His father and Court's father are first cousins. Cheyne's side of the family isn't nearly at ritzy as Court's. Cheyne's daddy, Jean-Michel, owns a half-dozen small hardware stores. He does pretty well, catering to people who get disenchanted dealing with the big box stores. He sells everything from fishing tackle to washing machines and also rents equipment."

"Equipment...what kind?"

"Small stuff...like you need a backhoe but you don't want to buy one, Michie will rent you one."

"Oh."

"Cheyne's mama, Catherine, has her own business. She's a CPA. One of his sisters works with her, and the other sister and her husband work in his daddy's business. They're all what I guess you'd call upper middle class...for bayou society anyway."

"Odd that Sharla invited Court's parents to that party, but not Cheyne's."

He shrugged. "Not really. Cheyne's family chooses not to associate with what they consider the muckety mucks of bayou society."

"Like us St. Cyrs?" I wondered how Cheyne really felt about my family.

"Um, hmm. Might say they're sorta reverse snobs. Like our families, they've been in Louisiana forever, so they're not impressed by anybody else's bloodlines." He slowed the vehicle at a crossroad. "They're decent people. They just aren't into socializing much."

I remembered Sharla's remarks to Cheyne about his being hard to catch for a social event and wondered why he came to the party.

As if reading my thoughts, Claude commented. "Cheyne's a bit more into getting to know everybody...seeing as how he *is* the sheriff...and he's not quite as clannish as his parents. Still, they're decent folks...keep to themselves and run their businesses."

"So Cheyne didn't want to go into either business, his mama's or his daddy's?" I watched a huge spraying machine moving down a row of the cane plants as we cruised by.

"No. His interest is in law enforcement." Claude stopped the car to let a strange-looking machine cross the road in front of us. The driver waved his thanks at Claude, who returned the salute.

I had no idea what most of this equipment was or did, but I was going to find out.

"He's been taking pre-law classes at Tulane, which has a very impressive law school." He finished the coffee and dabbed his lips with a paper napkin from a holder on the console. "I've already offered him a job if he decides to pursue the law."

Cheyne's sheriff's vehicle was parked in front of the maintenance office when we arrived. In smoke-free daylight, the building looked like a ranch-style house, redbrick, with dark green shutters, a front porch with a couple of rockers, and carefully-tended flowerbeds out front.

The secretary, Marlene Crutchfield, took us back to Henry Toussaint's office.

Both Henry and Cheyne had changed out of their smoky, dirty clothes and showered and shaved, but both sported dark circles of exhaustion under their eyes.

From the two men, we learned little we hadn't known the night before. Rand Morrissey spotted two men on the property. The intruders brought the standard red gasoline cans with them and left both. Fingerprints were being checked. The tire tracks outside the fence indicated the vandals drove a big pickup, a Dodge Ram or a big Ford or Chevy. There had been some blood on the fence links, and it was being analyzed.

"What was their point do you suppose?" I asked, fearing I actually knew the answer.

"Could be just simple vandalism, but my gut tells me otherwise," Cheyne answered.

Henry toyed with a yellow pencil, dancing it across his knuckles. "I have to agree with that. We've never, ever, had any sort of vandalism here at the plant, and I've worked here over twenty-five years...started just before me and Alma got married."

Marlene brought coffee for the men and a Coke for me.

I gave her the box of homemade brownies to pass around. "It's me, isn't it? I'm the reason this stuff is happening."

The three men looked from one to the other, their expressions telling me they weren't sure they should let me know they agreed with me.

Cheyne spoke. "That's my opinion. I think somebody's wanting to scare you into leaving, trying to show you how difficult it might be for you to run this place."

I chewed my lip. "I have Claude and Henry here to help me, and Mr. Rutledge, our factor in New Orleans, to help me out on that end." I drummed my fingers on the chair arms. "I'm a rather determined little hussy, in case nobody's figured that out yet. I'm not letting anybody run me off, and I firmly believe somebody in my family...or with ties to my family...is trying to do that."

Henry Toussaint leaned back in his chair and eyed me, a smile twitching at his lips. "You got a lot of your daddy in you."

"A lot of my mama, too. She was hell on wheels when you crossed her."

Cheyne shook his head. He bit into his brownie and talked around it. "You've inherited genes from the devil himself on both sides, the St. Cyrs and the Renards."

I wasn't sure if he was being complimentary. "I'm not going to take any crap from anybody."

Cheyne washed down his brownie with coffee. "With that attitude, I have no doubt you're going to be able to handle this place, and God help anybody who gets in your way."

Chapter 44

W hen Robert dropped by the house a few days earlier, ostensibly to invite me to dinner with him and his wife, Reggie, he included Sharla in their invitation. I was glad my new best friend was going along. I didn't really want to face those two rodents alone.

My cousins pulled up out front of Shadow Cove in a Maserati Gran Turismo MC Centenniel. My eyes bugged. I knew the car cost close to $300,000. My ex-boyfriend back in Seattle drove one. The vehicle was screaming red and had virtually no backseat.

Sharla and I were each only five foot four, but we had to pretzel ourselves to get inside.

The two of us were outfitted for the occasion in dinner dresses, mine a pale rose, worn with ruby and diamond jewelry and dark red Jimmy Choo spike heels. Sharla was decked out in a sky blue outfit sprinkled with sequins. Tiny diamonds sparkled in her earlobes, and black sling-back heels boosted her height several inches.

Dressed to the nines in a lime green, silk dress, with a plunging neckline and a scalloped hem, diamonds glittering at all the appropriate locations, Reggie looked us over and commented approvingly on our ensembles, her tone implying she'd expected us to show up wearing bib overalls.

"I don't know why Robert didn't bring the Bentley." Reggie talked through her clenched teeth, as was her habit. "I told him there was no room in his new toy,"

"As you said, hon, it's my new toy, and I want to show it off." He slid behind the steering wheel and cranked up the 454 horsepower engine and revved it. The car sounded like it was about to become airborne. "Only had this baby three days."

I cringed and looked at Sharla as we contorted ourselves to fasten our seat belts. I was glad I'd shaved my legs; otherwise, I might've gotten knee-bristle burn on my chin.

Surprisingly, Robert drove the car at the speed limit and did not take chances, so my sphincter had relaxed somewhat by the time we reached the world-renowned Antoine's Restaurant in the French Quarter.

The interior of Antoine's was much like that of Arnaud's, tiled floors, white table cloths, cane-backed chairs. The walls of the main dining room displayed photographs of famous people who had dined at the eatery and framed awards the restaurant had received. The restaurant was founded in 1840 and is still owned and operated by fifth generation descendants of the Alciatore family.

When we were seated, I chose the *chair de crabes au gratin*, crab in cheese sauce, for a starter, and Sharla and I decided to share the chateaubriand for two as our entrée.

Robert, with what I assumed was his usual lack of subtlety, dived right into the subject of the vandalism at the maintenance barn and how running a plantation was way beyond my capabilities.

His spouse was no less artless in her remarks. "*Cher*, you should find yourself a nice condo or townhouse in the city. A place that requires little upkeep and leaves you plenty of time for socializing." She sipped from a glass of $400 cotes du Rhone.

"Just sell off that place and be done with it," Robert agreed. "Find yourself a rich husband."

And divvy up the proceeds among the family, per the stipulations of

the will. "I have no intentions of leaving or of selling Shadow Cove."
I forked a mouthful of the bubbling hot crab concoction. "I'm totally
enchanted with the place. And it *is* my inheritance."

Robert's nostrils flared. The skin grew pinched around his
lidless eyes.

Reggie pursed her lips. "But there will be so much to do...so
much business to attend to, and you really know nothing about cane."
She waved an escargot impaled on a tiny fork at me.

I dabbed my lips with my napkin. "I have some excellent advisers,
the factor, Mr. Rutledge, and of course, Henry Toussaint and Uncle
Claude."

"'Uncle' Claude?" Robert frowned his annoyance. "He's hardly
our uncle."

"It pleases him for me to call him that." I gave a little smirk.
"Besides, I understand it's an old Southern custom."

"I'm not sure I'd trust Henry Toussaint from here to across the
street," Reggie put in.

"He's worked for the family forever," Sharla said. "I never heard
Nonc Pierre or Tante Helene say a word against him."

I fought not to smile at her referring to my grandparents as
"uncle" and "aunt."

"Well," Reggie finished her snails and pushed the plate aside. "I
imagine Robert could recommend a much more efficient manager.
He has some marvelous contacts."

Robert preened. "And there's not much I don't know about the
cane business either."

Sharla gave him a look that said he was full of horse hockey, but
said nothing.

"Oh, look, *cher.*" Reggie touched her husband's sleeve. "There're
Marcel and Reba Chartrand. We must speak to them."

Robert turned and bellowed at the well-dressed couple arriving,
causing several people to turn and stare.

Sharla and I exchanged eye rolls.

The newcomers veered from the path to their own table to come
over and greet us, while their server waited for them. There was

much hand-shaking and air-kissing, with introductions between the couple and me.

"Come join us," Robert invited. "We can have another table pulled up."

Before either of the Chartrands could agree, my pushy cousin was directing the staff to move another table next to ours.

Truth be told, I was actually glad the couple joined us, since their presence might forestall any more efforts on the parts of Robert and Reggie to give me business advice. The rest of the evening proceeded pleasantly enough, with the new additions to our group regaling us with stories about their recent trip to Italy.

When our server brought the dessert menu, I ordered the vanilla ice cream with toasted meringue and chocolate sauce. I vowed not to eat another bite for the next three days.

Chapter 45

A fine mist was wisping through the French Quarter, as we left the restaurant. We waited only a moment under the overhang of the wrought-iron balcony facing St. Louis Street until Robert's new Maserati glided to a halt in front of us. The liveried valet held the door for Sharla and me, and we contorted ourselves to coil into the backseat.

Before the parking attendant could hand Reggie into the passenger's seat, the young man was knocked roughly aside by another man. The valet careened into Reggie, who squawked and grabbed hold of him to keep from being thrown to the damp pavement.

The sound of something heavy hitting the left side of the car caused me to jerk my head in that direction just in time to see another man shove Robert away from the car. My cousin stumbled backward, windmilling his arms, and grasped one of the ornamental, horsehead hitching posts on the opposite side of the narrow street, whirling around it like a pole dancer, trying to keep from falling.

A black youth, wearing a knit watchcap, leaped into the driver's seat.

His partner, long dreads bristling, scrambled into the passenger's side. He brandished a pistol and ordered the two '*hos*...Sharla and me...to keep our mouths shut. He tried to twist around in his seat to keep an eye on us, dangling the gun like he wasn't sure what to do with it, while reaching for the open car door with his free hand.

With a growl worthy of an enraged female panther, Sharla sprang forward. A registered nurse, she knew how to hurt people, despite her small stature. She grabbed a handful of dreadlocks and wrung his head nearly off his neck. Wrestling to get a hold on the gun hand, she climbed over the seat, her butt in the air, twisting his wrist and shoving his hand between his legs, the gun pointing at his crotch.

The carjacker squealed in pain, bucking to get away from his attacker and kicking at the open door, which kept flapping back and forth.

The driver hadn't had a chance to put the car in gear, before I had one of my four-inch Jimmy Choo's in my hand, whipping it against his head. He was yelling, and his buddy was screeching like fat woman with her titty caught in a washing-machine wringer.

Blood was splattering from my victim's head, when the gun went off. Two shots in rapid succession. One bullet smashed into the glass in the passenger's side window, shattering it.

"Mah dick...mah dick...you done shot mah dick off!" The howling kid dropped the gun and tried to use both hands to get Sharla off him. "Bitch!" He tried to swing his fist in the close quarters, but Sharla gave him a shove that propelled him half way out of the car.

"Fuck! I'm blind!" My victim squalled and slapped a hand over his eye, blood cascading down his face.

I continued to flail at the man in the driver's seat, the cramped seating of the car working to my advantage. I was small and could get some leverage behind my strokes. That expensive shoe was proving its worth, the sharp heel digging trenches in the man's face.

Blood was pouring down Dreadlock's leg where the bullet struck him in the groin. He staggered from the car, holding both hands to his crotch and wailing about "mah dick."

"You honkey muthah fuckah. I'll cap yo' ass fo' this shit." The man I was pounding yelled in Robert's direction, as he floundered from the seat. The carjacker fell to his knees, but quickly regained his footing. He slammed his fist against the rearview mirror and smashed it, leaving it to dangle by the wires, then kicked the side of the vehicle. "Fuck this," he hollered at his cohort. "Haul ass."

Red, white, and blue police lights strobed from the end of the street.

The pair stumbled off into the darkness, one hopping and holding onto his damaged reproductive equipment, still wailing about his penis.

Sharla and I clambered out of the backseat, me exiting on the passenger's side right behind her, and falling into Cheyne Delacroix's arms. Antoine's maître d' had hold of Sharla.

"What the hell's going on?" Cheyne bellowed. "We could hear the yelling and the gunshots inside."

I gaped around. My cousin Robert stood at the far side of his car, his hands out to his sides. He was shaking his hands like they had flypaper stuck on them and he was trying to shake it off, babbling about his new car.

"Look at that mess," Reggie screamed. "There's blood all over the fuckin' car. No way I'm riding in that thing." She flailed her arms. "Goddamn bullet hole in the seat, window blown out. What the fuck."

My, my! My high-toned cousin could sure cuss.

Two pairs of New Orleans's finest rolled their cruisers to a stop, blocking the street, and bailed out.

One of the officers recognized Cheyne, who told him. "Hell, I don't know what happened. I was inside having dinner for my mother's birthday, when we heard all the ruckus. I gather somebody tried to carjack Robert's Maserati, and..."

"And Laurette and I beat the shit out of them," Sharla interrupted, tugging on her dress to straighten it. She waved her hand. "They ran off that way."

"What was the gunshot?" Cheyne asked.

"One of the little assholes had a gun," Sharla answered. "I wrestled it around so it was pointed at him, and he shot himself in the crotch." She wagged her head toward the car. "Looks like the bullet just winged him and got stuck in the seat."

Cheyne barked a laugh. "I heard him squalling 'mah dick' when I ran out here."

One of the cops talked into his collar communicator, while chatter from the car radio erupted in the background. "Two of 'em. I'm about to get the descriptions."

I quickly related what the pair looked like. "Sharla and I were in the backseat when they got into the car, so we both just sort of jumped on them and started beating."

"Hoo Ha, baby girl!" Sharla whooped, and we high-fived each other. "We bayou girls kick ass."

Fists balled on hips, Cheyne roared a belly laugh. "It'll be a while before those two pull another stunt like that. You two are a pair."

"We rock," Sharla told him.

I grinned my agreement.

"This was one of the times when fighting back worked out," the New Orleans cop taking our statements remarked. "Might've saved your lives." He turned to speak to the policeman interviewing Reggie.

"My new car," Robert whimpered. "Look at the inside. It's ruined. Two hundred ninety-two thousand dollars…shot to hell."

"There's blood all over it, and be damned if I'm getting back in that thing." Reggie was not talking like her jaws were wired shut, and her snotty uptown accent had fallen by the wayside. "Damn car's nothing but a piece of shit now."

"My new car."

"Oh, shut the fuck up, Robert." Reggie was fuming mad, not seeming the least bit concerned that the car had almost been stolen with Sharla and me in the backseat.

A small crowd gathered…not nearly as many people as would have converged on the site of a possible carjacking in Seattle. But as I silently reminded myself, *This is N'Awlins.*

The police cordoned off the area, leaving one officer to stay at the crime scene until the tow truck arrived. The others loaded us into their cruisers to take us to the police station, only a few blocks away.

Cheyne told me he would go back to his dinner party and make his apologies. "I'll take you and Sharla home and give Robert and Reggie a lift back to their house." He grinned. "I'll have to hand it to you, you're a feisty little Southern belle. That's two fights you've won in the French Quarter." Chuckling, he shook his head. "Meet you at the station house."

Chapter 46

Cheyne stopped by the house next day at noon.

Sharla was making some egg salad and had a pot of what she called semi-homemade pea soup bubbling on the stove. "Campbell's secret recipe...and I added some chopped ham and a dash of sherry." She fetched another can from the pantry, opened it, and dumped the contents into the pot.

Our sheriff helped himself to a glass of iced tea and sat down at the kitchen table. "The New Orleans police called me this morning."

I turned from chopping some lettuce for the sandwiches. "Any news about our would-be carjackers?"

"Yeah. That's why they called. The one Sharla nearly emasculated had sense enough to get himself to the hospital."

"Nearly emasculated?" Sharla cast him a baleful look. "You mean the little puke is still able to reproduce?"

Cheyne chuckled. "I'm sorry to say he is. The bullet missed his vital equipment by only an inch."

"Too bad," Sharla grunted.

"He tried to tell the people at the ER some cock and bull story about being shot in a drive-by, but the police had already alerted the ERs around the city to be on the lookout."

"So he had to tell them the truth?" I asked.

"I'm sure medical people wouldn't want it to get around, but they have ways of making the bad guys tell the truth when they come in for treatment." He eyed me over the rim of his glass.

"I know that's right," Sharla agree. "While I was training for my nurse's license, I learned more ways to inflict pain than a member of the Spanish Inquisition…not that we do that sort of thing."

"So what happened?" I put the plate of chopped lettuce and sliced tomatoes on the kitchen table.

"When the police arrived at the ER, the doctor 'encouraged' the young man to tell him how he happened to be involved in a carjacking." Cheyne made air quotes with his fingers. "Seeing as how he has a rap sheet as long as my arm, but he'd never done a carjack before."

"And?" Sharla ladled the soup into bowls and placed them on the placemats.

I took sliced, toasted French bread from the oven, transferred it to a plate, and set it on the table. I joined Cheyne, who'd sucked down half his glass of tea.

"According to him, he was just the second-stringer." Cheyne salted and peppered his soup, like most Southerners do before they taste any food. "His buddy," he wagged his spoon at me. "The one you nearly brained with that shoe, made all the arrangements. Somebody hired him to boost that Maserati."

"Like somebody had a buyer and wanted that particular kind of car? I've read about that happening with high-end cars." I sipped my tea. "I have to wonder how they knew the car would be at Antoine's."

"Could be they were just on the lookout, but more than likely they were tipped off by somebody working at the car park or even the restaurant. Saw the car and made a couple of quick calls. The people who do this crap are incredibly organized, and cell phones enable them to be in touch with each other in a minute's notice." Cheyne dumped a dollop of egg salad on a slice of bread and smeared it around. "It's not too unusual in carjackings. I have to wonder why they didn't just steal it from the garage where it was parked."

Something flickered in my brain. *What was it one of them said as he fell out of the car?* I tried to grab onto the words. It seemed like it was something significant I forgot to mention at the time.

"It just strikes me as odd that they waited until you two were in the car before they tried to steal it." Cheyne interrupted my ruminations.

A cold chill ran up my spine as the carjacker's words flitted away, to be replaced by a new concern. "They might've gotten out of the city and killed us."

Cheyne grunted his agreement.

"Did the little turd tell the police who hired them?" Sharla pulled out a chair and sat down at the table with us.

"Uh, uh. The other guy made all the arrangements. All this one knew…or claimed to know… was it was some rich white dude, who told his buddy he'd skin him alive if he scratched that car."

"Hmmm. Sounds like somebody was paying him a lot of money to steal that car, and they wanted it in pristine condition." I started building my sandwich. "It scares the pea-turkey out me to think what might've happened if Sharla and I hadn't decided to jump them."

"You two ladies did the right thing in fighting back."

"So this guy never saw the man who was paying them to steal the car?" Sharla spooned her soup.

Cheyne shook his head. "So he says. And even if he's lying, he'd fall back on the old 'all y'all whities look alike to me' ploy. So we'd still get nothing out of him."

I almost choked on my sandwich as I burst out laughing. "I know it's awful, but I just can't get over the look on Robert's face and the way Reggie was cussing him out."

Sharla hooted. "Miz High Society was showing her true colors."

Chapter 47

After we finished lunch, I walked Cheyne out to his police vehicle parked in the roundabout. A flap from a canary's eyelash could have knocked me over when he invited me to dinner. I had no idea he might have the slightest interest in me.

"I'm tied up with a political do tomorrow night, but I wonder if you're free the following evening."

I felt a tiny twinge of guilt at accepting, since I'd just refused a dinner invite from his cousin Courtland for the same evening. I'd met a few men like Court Delacroix, but Cheyne was unique. He intrigued me, but I couldn't exactly say why. Maybe it was just another aspect of that rebelliousness I'd been feeling since Mama died. She would not have approved of Cheyne.

He was as well-educated and clearly as intelligence as his smoother, more sophisticated-acting cousin. I slipped the word "acting" into my mental ruminations; after all, Court was an amateur actor.

Chapter 48

I was glad I accepted Cheyne's invitation to dinner. He talked about himself on the way from Shadow Cove into the city. But unlike his cousin Court, I sensed no bragging, and he told me some funny stories about his crime fighting career. He was a great raconteur and had a wicked sense of humor. Yes, he was definitely a different creature from his polished cousin, and I found him much more appealing.

Seated in the elegant Pelican Club restaurant, I felt my lips curl in a secret smile.

"What are you smiling about?" Cheyne eyed me above menu, which featured a painting of a pair of canoodling pelicans.

"Ummm. I was just thinking about how time seems to slow down in this place. New Orleans, that is," I lied. No way was I going to tell him I was cataloguing his charms and comparing them to those of his cousin. "It's like I've fallen through a hole in time to a kinder, gentler, more mannerly era."

"Careful. You're in what's been called the Wickedest City in the World." He returned my smile. "And it's mostly true. N'Awlins is wicked and seductive, and I wouldn't live anywhere else."

"It seems like everybody I've met here says they wouldn't live anywhere else."

He pointed a forefinger at me. "There you go."

"I already love the place. I never felt like I belonged in Seattle, but New Orleans and this whole bayou area suits me. I feel at home here." I gazed around the opulent room, which Cheyne told me was once a salon in a wealthy Frenchman's townhouse. The dark-paneled walls were decorated with original art works depicting New Orleans scenes. The muted glow cast by wall sconces leant the place a Nineteenth Century ambiance. "This is a lovely restaurant. I keep expecting to see Scarlett O'Hara come waltzing through the door, hoop skirt and all."

"I thought you'd like it."

"Can I tell you something?"

He laid the menu down and sipped his glass of bourbon. "I would hope so."

I snicked an embarrassed laugh. "When I told Sharla you were taking me to someplace called the Pelican Club, I expected it to be a fish and seafood shack. Good thing I told her, so she could give me a heads up about the dress requirement. I was prepared to wear jeans."

"I'm crushed." He put a hand over his heart. "You thought I was some peckerwood with no taste." He flashed a grin. "But I notice you accepted my invitation without knowing a thing about where we were going."

I raised my glass of wine. "There is that."

"I have a weakness for fancy food and elegant restaurants, and I indulge myself every chance I get."

This surprised me. I thought he would be a steak and potatoes or hamburger kind of guy. "I like nice places to eat, too. And I've developed a real fondness for oysters. I'd never eaten them before I came here." I pulled a face. "They're so yukky looking."

He laughed and nodded toward the menu. "Try their baked oyster appetizer. You'll like it."

"I'd already decided on that. How about the rack of lamb? Have you had it?"

"It's excellent. That's what I'm going to order for myself, but I want the Seafood Martini Ravigote for an appetizer." He waggled his eyebrows. "It has lobster, shrimp, and crab in a potato salad. If you're a good girl, I'll let you have a bite."

Chapter 49

After a quiet evening, with marvelous food, we walked to a jazz bistro and had a glass of wine each and shared a second dessert of chocolate pecan pie. Across the room, I spied the taxi driver who had driven me from the airport. He was playing guitar with the band. When the quartet took a break, I was surprised when he came across the room to speak to Cheyne and me.

"My man." Cheyne got to his feet and thrust out his hand. "What are you doing in a jazz joint? Your venue is usually rock or blues."

"Arlan's come down with the croup, him, and the band needed a little help," Larondell Duclose explained and moved a chair from the next table to ours and sat down with us. "I can play rock or blues or jazz guitar with the best of 'em." Before Cheyne could introduce us, the big black man turned to me. "How'd the prettiest fare I've had in many a moon get together with this rascal here?"

"I can't believe you remembered me, what with all the people you must ferry around."

"I remember the prettiest ones...and their names." He cocked his head toward Cheyne. "Did Miz St. Cyr tell you about Boze Newmann followin' us from the airport?"

Cheyne sipped his wine and nodded. "From her description, I knew it was him. Harmless but worthless."

"You knew who he was all along?" I asked the cabbie. He never mentioned the man's name at the time.

"Sho." He shrugged. "I know mos' ever'body livin' in N'Awlins. I didn't say nothin' about it at the time 'cause I had no idea why he was followin' you…still don't. Jus' bein' a pest, mad 'cause I got his fare, prob'ly." He took a swig from the bottle of beer he brought to the table with him. "I had a little talk wid him the next day. He won't be botherin' you no mo', no." The diamond stud in his tooth flashed in the bistro's muted light.

Cheyne lifted his glass in salute. "I'm sure the local constabulary appreciates your help."

"I know that's right." Duclose drained his bottle of beer and rose to his feet. "Y'all have a nice evenin' now. I gotta get back to work, me."

Cheyne ordered a second glass of wine for each of us, and we listened to the music for a while, before returning to the garage to retrieve his car. I was enjoying my time with him far more than my evening with his cousin. Cheyne didn't come on to me or make smarmy, sexual innuendoes. The man had class.

Feeling a bit like a giddy teenager, I wondered if he'd kiss me goodnight. So far he'd done no more than hold my hand while we walked along the French Quarter streets. I was going to be more than a tiny bit disappointed if he didn't kiss me when we got home.

The sheriff drove his personal vehicle, a black Lexus SUV, as he turned off the highway from New Orleans onto the road leading to Frenchy's Landing.

I leaned back into the soft leather seats. I wondered how he afforded a luxury automobile on a policeman's salary, but during our evening's conversation, he mentioned a trip to Florida a couple years earlier, where, on a lark, he bought a lottery ticket and won "a nice hunk of change." He invested much of the money in rental real estate, a condo development and a couple of strip malls, so he would have some independent means of support in addition to his salary as a public servant.

The man was full of surprises. No dummy, he had advanced degrees in both criminology and finance. Claude mentioned Cheyne was now studying law at Tulane, and he had a job waiting for him if he took Claude up on his offer.

He pointed to a tract of vacant land to our right. "I bought that property just recently. I'm thinking about putting up some luxury townhouses on it, a gated community. Something designed to be ecologically friendly."

"Is there a market for that right now?"

"More than you might think, and with some decent leadership in Washington, the economy's making a big comeback. A lot of boomers are retiring and selling their big houses. I'd offer a home maintenance and lawn care package, too. There's a nice little creek at the back part of the property that would be perfect for a small, private marina."

I felt rather than saw his eyes cut in my direction and glanced toward him.

"You probably don't need the money, but you might want to consider doing some architectural consulting for me." He gave me a tentative smile. "Just an idea, you know."

Before I could answer, his cell phone emitted the strains of *Bonanza*.

He gave me a sheepish look. "So I'm hooked on old TV shows." He checked the caller ID on his car console and frowned. Instead of answering on the car's instrument, where I could hear the conversation, he took his cell phone from inside his jacket. "Sheriff Delacroix."

I'm nosy, so I tried to hear what was being said, but he had the phone in his left hand, so I heard nothing.

Cheyne listened a moment and pulled his vehicle to the shoulder of the road. "When did he find her? What?" He drummed his fingers on the steering wheel as he listened to the voice on the other end. "What was he doing there in the first place? He didn't mess with anything, did he? Yeah. Okay. I'm almost at Shadow Cove. I'll be there in a few minutes." He drew his blond brows together.

I watched his face. "What is it?"

Cheyne tapped the cell phone on his leg and stared through the windshield into the darkness. "It's Annie Lebeau. Somebody's killed her."

Chapter 50

"Looks like she's been dead for several hours. Smells like it, too." The young dark-haired deputy shifted a wad of chewing gum in his jaw and leaned against the kitchen counter. "Flies're already after her when I got here. Might've happened early this morning... like before daylight. Won't know until the coroner checks her out." He nodded toward the back door, through which flashlights could be seen bobbing in the darkness. "Eliot and Jacques are out back lookin' around. They got here right after me."

Annie's battered head lay in a fly-covered pool of black blood on the kitchen's worn linoleum floor. A tall, ornate ceramic candlestick lay next to her body. The corpse was already ripe in the bayou heat, and the police officers had opened the front and back doors to allow some air to circulate, but the smell of death was unmistakable.

Cheyne wrinkled his nose against the putrid odor and walked carefully around the body, stepping from the kitchen into the living room. Like his deputies, he'd smeared Vicks salve under his nose to counteract the stench. "When did you say you got here, Leshawn?"

A black youth, wearing a black and gold New Orleans Saints

tee shirt, perched on Annie's dilapidated sofa and stroked her tabby cat. "About an hour ago...maybe less. I called y'all right off when I found her. Mama wanted me to bring Tante Annie a mess o' them collards." He nodded toward the greens wrapped in newspaper that lay atop the table in the adjacent dining area.

"Little late for a delivery, isn't it?"

The kid held the cat close to his thin chest. "Yessir. I...uh...I sorta made a stop before I got here."

"Over at the crib of that nasty girl he's been hangin' after." A black woman about forty years old moved to the doorway to the kitchen where Annie Lebeau's body lay. A red minidress hung lank on her skinny frame. She leaned against the door jamb and frowned back at the young man, but she spoke to the sheriff.

"Yes'um," the boy agreed. He exchanged a look with the woman Delacroix knew was the kid's mother and Annie's great niece, Tameeka L'Oiseau. "Okay, if we take Annie's cat home with us?"

"Sure. Just don't mess with anything else." Cheyne looked around the room. "She's been dead a while. You haven't noticed anybody strange around her house lately, have you?"

The kid shrugged. "Not really. Mos' everybody she does bid'ness with is kinda strange lookin', if you know what I mean."

Cheyne nodded.

"'Course, she got some N'Awlins trade, too, folks I wouldn't recognize. And the house is down here off the road...just that trail leadin' down here. She's always got people comin' and goin'...like on bid'ness, you know." He wiped his nose with the back of his hand. "You reckon they used that big candlestick thing to kill her?"

"Looks like it," Cheyne answered. "The door was unlocked? Didn't look like anybody'd broken in?"

"Yessir...uh...nosir. I mean...yessir, the door was unlocked, didn't look like nobody'd forced it open or nothin'." The kid narrowed his eyes. "That must mean it was somebody she knew, and she just let 'em in."

The sheriff nodded. "Possibly, or somebody she was expecting on business."

Tameeka moved from the doorway to the dining table and sagged onto one of the chairs, her arms wrapped around herself. "God knows who'd do such a thing to an old woman."

Cheyne knew Annie Lebeau had made plenty of enemies, but he didn't bother to point this out to the woman's relatives. He looked through the kitchen door at the body on the floor. Blood was splattered everywhere and smeared on the heavy candlestick Annie used in Voodoo ceremonies. Apparently somebody bashed her head in with it and pounded her face to a bloody pulp. From the carnage, it looked like Annie tried to fight back. Her attacker must've assaulted her in a murderous rage, bludgeoning her over and over.

The sheriff turned back to the teenager on the sofa and leaned toward him from his towering height. "You tell me the truth, Leshawn."

The kid cringed. "I am tellin' you the truth, Mist' Cheyne. She was dead, jest like I…"

"I don't mean that," Cheyne interrupted. "I believe you about how you found her. What I want to know is have you heard any rumors about Annie dealing?"

Eyes the size of Mason jar lids, the boy swallowed. "You mean dope?"

"Yeah, dope."

Leshawn shook his head, holding the cat tighter. The tabby mewled, and the boy relaxed his grip and stroked the pet. "Uh, uh. I ain't heard nothin' 'bout that." He looked toward his mother. "You heard anything like that, Mama."

She picked at a fingernail. "Nah. I mean, they's rumors, but I ain't never heard nothin' for sure." She snorted. "Don't know why she'd mess wid dope when she got all these potions and all such shit as that to sell. Tante made plenty of money, I tell you that true. She didn't need to go truckin' wid no dope." Tameeka cocked her head and appeared to ponder the notion, then chuckled. "Still, they weren't much that woman wouldn't do for money. You hear what I'm sayin'?"

Cheyne cut his eyes from mother to son and nodded. "You

both…you hear anything, you let me know. Y'all go on home now, and take care of that cat."

Tameeka gathered up the collards. "Okay if I take these greens back home wid me? Ain't gone do Tante Annie no good."

"Yeah. No sense in wasting good collard greens." Cheyne took a turn around the living room. The furniture was threadbare, but a large flat screen television perched atop an entertainment center holding an expensive music system, stacks of CDs and DVDs. A section of the room was set up with an altar, covered by a lace table cloth, with statues of Catholic saints sharing equal space with primitive dolls representing Freda Erzuli, Damballa, and Baron Samedi…Voodoo deities…one a love-hate goddess, another a huge, all-powerful snake god, and the last, the harbinger of death. A cut-glass vase held an assortment of cigars. A bottle of brandy and another of cheap whisky stood along one side. Cheyne's lips twitched. The *hougan*, or Voodoo saints, were known to like liquor and cigars. He fingered the mate to the candlestick lying beside Annie's body in the kitchen.

A square of what looked like paper caught his eye, and he realized it was a photograph. Using just the tip of his gloved finger, he flipped it over…and drew in a sharp breath.

The crime scene people and the coroner arrived, along with a half dozen more of Annie's relatives. One older woman got as far as the front door and set up a wail. The deputies corralled them on the front porch.

Despite the late hour, word of the old Voodoo woman's death was already spreading through the bayou, and Delacroix knew the place would turn into a zoo pretty soon. A new set of headlights flashed across the front of the house, when a news van from a New Orleans television station lurched to a stop in the dirt front yard. Cheyne signaled to a deputy. "Keep the news hounds at bay."

Chapter 51

I faced Sheriff Cheyne Delacroix across his cluttered desk. I had no idea why I was here, and the deputy who rousted Sharla and me out of bed shortly after daylight would tell us nothing.

He held up a small, clear plastic bag. "Does this look familiar?"

"What? Why that's my earring." I reached for the bag containing one of the *fleur de lis* earrings I bought my first day in New Orleans, but he laid it back on his desk. "What are you doing with it?"

He didn't answer me. "When was the last time you wore it?"

I leaned back in the uncomfortable wooden chair, mystified. *How had my earring wound up at the sheriff's department?* "Umm. I think...uh...yeah...the night of the party at Shadow Cove." I huffed a short laugh. "The same night I met you, as a matter of fact."

"You haven't worn the earrings since then?" Both his tone and his face remained expressionless.

"No. I have a bit of jewelry I brought with me, so I haven't thought much about it. I guess I haven't worn the same stuff twice." I attempted a thin smile. "One of my admitted vices. I like nice jewelry."

He said nothing.

His behavior was exasperating. I wagged my hand at him. "What's this about?"

Nothing. He rocked back in his chair, and it squawked.

"Why do you have my earring? Where'd you get it? And why did you drag me down here at this ungodly hour?" This was the third time I'd asked this last question, and he had yet to answer.

"Want to tell me where you were yesterday morning maybe around four or five o'clock?"

"Asleep in my bed," I snapped. "Where else would I be?"

"How about later...let's say up until maybe nine or ten in the morning?"

At this point I had no way of knowing that, due to the heat and humidity and the unair-conditioned interior of Annie Lebeau's cottage, the time of her death was still uncertain. Later I learned her house had been closed up tight, and the heat had built up as the day warmed. By the time Leshawn L'Oiseau, her great great nephew, discovered her body, decomposition had already set in. Her death could've occurred as early as four or as late as nine o'clock that morning.

"What's this about?" I was beyond frustrated at the way he stonewalled my questions. "Why do you want to know where I was?"

"Just answer me, please."

Something in his tone made me go cold. I looked to the left and paused. I saw him track the direction of my gaze. My actions weren't lost on the sheriff. I remembered reading somewhere that most law officers know when a person looks to the left...not the right...and pauses before answering, they are most likely preparing to tell the truth. I hoped he was paying attention, because I was telling the honest to God truth. Why would I lie?

"I woke up early, barely daylight. I got up and decided to do some exploring around Frenchy's Landing. I left Sharla a note saying where I was going."

"Where did you go?"

I shrugged. "I went to that little café on the main street and had breakfast."

Delacroix jotted something on a note pad. "Clarice's?"

"I guess that's the name of the place. It has some tables set outside in a little courtyard, and I ate out there. Then I went to a couple of shops that were just opening." I uncrossed my legs and placed my feet flat on the floor, both elbows resting on the chair arms. "I just prowled around a bit. I wanted to see something of my new home town." I fixed him with a steady stare. "Is that some kind of crime or what?"

He leaned back in his chair, which squawked again like an angry crow. "Then what? Did you make any side trips, like out into the swamp?" He made a churning motion with his hand. "You know, just to get the lay of the land." His tone was laden with sarcasm.

The sound of the squealing chair reminded me of the one I left behind in Seattle. I'd rather enjoyed knowing it bugged my coworkers. I also wondered if the sheriff didn't oil the aggravating piece of furniture for the same reason I hadn't greased my chair. Maybe Delacroix used his chair the same way, as a source of annoyance to people he was questioning, perhaps to distract them, trick them up. But I had nothing to hide. "I just rode around, trying to get my bearings...but, no, I wasn't about to venture into the swamp. God only knows what's out there, and I don't want to get lost and be some alligator's lunch."

His cold flat gaze made me stop speaking. We stared at each other for a moment, neither saying a word.

Okay. I was getting more than a little pissed off. "I'm not telling you another blessed thing until you tell me what this is about." I waved my arm in his direction. "And tell me where you got my earring."

The chair let out another loud squawk, as he leaned forward and placed his arms on the desk. His shirt sleeves were rolled up, and golden hairs on his thick forearms glinted in the sunlight slanting across his desk. He let several beats pass before he answered. "I told you last night that Annie Lebeau was murdered. It happened sometime early yesterday morning." He tapped the plastic bag with his finger. "This earring was found under her body. That's why I had one of my deputies haul you in here bright and early this morning before the news spread all over the bayou."

I sucked in a breath. "Wha...." I was literally speechless. I'd been more than annoyed to find two deputies pounding on my front door shortly after daylight and demanding that I get dressed and accompany them to the sheriff's office. They gave me only enough time to put on a pair of jeans and a tee shirt. I wore no makeup, and my hair was yanked up in a ponytail.

The officers would tell neither Sharla nor me why I was being rousted. Sharla said she would follow us and was now waiting in the outer office.

Unable to think of anything to say, I finally noticed that Cheyne was unshaven and wearing the same clothes he'd worn the night before, during our date. He must have been up all night.

He held up the bag containing my earring and pulled his mouth into a tight line. "Nobody had to tell me who it belonged to. I remembered seeing you wearing it."

"Surely you don't think I...." A tremor of fear raced up my spine. "I would never...I mean, I was angry at her, but I'd never...."

Delacroix stared me down, unblinking. "I can't overlook the fact that I heard you talk about killing her, even beating her to death." He tapped his forefinger on the desk. "There were other witnesses, Sharla, your cousin Robert, Claude."

"I need to talk to Claude. I need a lawyer. Why I'd never...," I babbled.

He still said nothing.

I felt tears well in my eyes. "I was angry. That was just talk. You really...honestly...you don't believe I could have killed her. Do you?"

"Somebody did, and you had as much reason as any number of other people."

"But I'd never...." I cocked my head at him. "Wait. I did say something about beating her...but I was angry. It was just talk." My words sounded strangled. "Oh, no...was that how...did somebody... oh, my God?"

"Somebody used a heavy candlestick she used in her Voodoo

ceremonies to pound her head to pulp. A relative found her last night on her kitchen floor."

My hands flew to my mouth. "Oh, no. How awful." I could barely speak. "I swear to you, Cheyne, I had nothing to do with it. I'd never do such a thing. Why...why...I don't even know where she lived."

He snorted a mirthless laugh. "Not hard to find out. Everybody knows where she lived."

I shook my head. "Not me...and I simply wouldn't...." I paused, swallowed. "Come on, Cheyne. You know perfectly well I didn't kill her...don't you?"

He watched me closely for a few heartbeats. "I honestly don't want to think you did it, but how do you account for your earring being found under her body?"

I chewed my lip. "I don't know." I sat quietly for a few moments. "You know, my house, Shadow Cove, is like Grand Central Station. I don't know how many people have been in and out of that house since I arrived. Somebody must've sneaked up to my room and stolen that earring." I gave him a thin excuse for a smile. "Maybe I should put a guest book in the entrance hall for people to sign." I stared at the floor. *Why is somebody doing this to me? I haven't done anything to hurt anybody...except inherit a plantation and a fortune.* "But why would anybody do that? Take my earring and leave it at the scene of a murder? I mean that's what had to have happened."

Delacroix shook his head, then picked up a ballpoint pen and toyed with it. "Okay. So the earring went missing sometime after the party where I met you."

"Obviously, but I didn't know it was missing."

"Where do you keep your jewelry?"

I shrugged. "In my bedroom, like most women. I brought a little travel pack with me for the jewelry I brought. The rest of the stuff is still back in Seattle, in a bank vault."

"There's not a safe at your house?"

"I don't know. I never asked." I looked off into space. "We had one in our house in Seattle, but I never even thought to ask Sharla if there's one at Shadow Cove."

"So the earrings were just lying in one of those jewelry travel packs?"

"Umm…no. As a matter of fact, I just laid them on the dresser." I put a finger to my lips. "In fact, the store where I bought them gave me a little velvet bag. The earrings were lying on the bag on the dresser."

"On the bag…not in it? Right out in the open? Where anybody entering your bedroom could see them?"

"Yes, I guess they were." A shiver ran through me, and I crossed my arms. "I would never imagine somebody would come into my home, into my bedroom, and steal something."

He fiddled with a small plastic bag on his desk, saying nothing. Finally he picked up the bag and handed it to me.

I saw a photograph inside, and my breath caught in my throat. "That's me. I must have been only three or four."

"I recognized you immediately, right down to the widow's peak and that little dimple in your chin."

"Where did this come from?"

"I found it on Annie's Voodoo altar. Apparently whoever paid her to put that hex on you had an old picture of you." His lip twitched. "Your face hasn't changed much since you were a little girl…just lost some baby fat. She'd have no problem recognizing you from that picture."

"Do you suppose the person who took my earring also stole the picture…maybe from an album in the house? I've seen several old albums in the library."

"Could be."

"Or it could be a relative who already had the old picture."

"Possibly. Sooo…." He tapped the pen on the desktop. "Who all has been to your house since the night of the party? Who can you remember?"

I thought a moment and rattled off names, including his own, while he wrote on a pad. "You, of course, and your cousin Courtland. Claude and Wills have been in and out." I made a face. "You were there when my cousin Robert came by to invite me to eat with them.

Remy Thibadeaux stopped by, for no particular reason." I smiled. "I think he has the hots for Sharla, even though she's a bit older than him."

Delacroix snorted a laugh. "Remy has the hots for anything in panties, including a couple of transvestites down in the Quarter, from what I've heard. Who else?"

"Well, the men refurbishing my front door." I pondered. "Umm…Doralynn Thibadeaux and her daughter Katie. They came by to invite us to a barbeque at their place." I cocked an eyebrow at him. "I don't think Katie likes me very much."

"Probably because of Court. She has her eye on him and is jealous of every woman he looks at. Not that she has a snowball's chance in hell of landing my cousin."

"She might steal my earring out of spite, but I can't see her killing anybody."

"You never know…add anger and jealousy together." He wrote something on the pad. "Anybody else?"

"Marcel Rutledge, our factor, brought some papers by for me to sign." I looked off into space. "Lucy Lesieur brought some homemade dessert thingies by. Just being neighborly, I guess."

"Maybe I should've asked who hasn't been to your house."

"I haven't seen the Pope yet, although Father Gee did come by for dinner one evening."

"Don't be surprised if the Holy Father puts in an appearance. Any of your Renard relatives?"

"Nope. Just St. Cyrs. Umm, my Aunt Simone came by with Court's mother."

"Any hired help?"

"Oh, sure. Moline and her daughter and another young woman. They show up every now and then to do housework. I haven't figured out their schedule yet, if there is one. And the yardmen, but they don't come inside."

"And you probably didn't pay any attention to who went to the bathroom or which bathroom they used while they were in the house, did you?"

I felt exasperated. "No. Of course not. And they all seem to know their way around the house better than I do. I can't very well follow them around."

We sat quietly while Cheyne read over the list he'd compiled. "Anybody on here seem to dislike you...other than Katie, of course, and we know what that's about?"

"I haven't been here long enough to make any enemies."

Cheyne looked up from the list. "*Cher*, you had enemies before you got here."

I swallowed the lump that suddenly clogged my throat. "Are you telling me you don't think I killed Annie Lebeau, and that somebody's trying to frame me for it?"

"That would be my guess." He leaned back in his squealing chair again. "I never for a moment suspected you, if you want to know the truth."

"Then why'd you drag me out of bed this morning...barely gave me time to brush my teeth?"

"Merely procedure." His smile was cold. "And maybe I want somebody to think I'm looking at you as the killer. I just don't know who that somebody might be."

"You aren't getting any ideas about using me as bait or something like that, are you?"

"Of course not." He twisted his lips in wry smile. "I'm just thinking maybe if the actual killer thinks I'm focusing on you, he... or she...might let down his guard and do something stupid." He heaved a sigh. "I'd like to be subtle about this. Not get somebody all excited...let them slip up and make a mistake in trying to keep their tracks covered."

Chapter 52

Sharla had dressed and followed the deputy's car to the Bayou Ombre Sheriff's Department. She was waiting when Cheyne escorted me from his office.

She wrapped both arms around me and turned on the sheriff. "What the hell are you doing rousting us out of bed when it's barely daylight?" Like me, she was clad in jeans and a tee shirt, *sans* makeup, her hair sticking out in all directions. "What's this all about? I've already called Claude, and he's on his way out here."

The sheriff held up his hands. "Sharla, calm down. Hush."

"Don't you hush me, Cheyne Delacroix. What's this bullroar all about? I know it's got something to do with Annie Lebeau being killed, but why've you got Laurette down here, like she's some common criminal?"

An obviously angry, fortyish black woman, standing at the receptionist-officer's desk in the waiting room, halted in mid-rant, her multiple chins quivering. Her manicured claws were dug into the skinny arm of a tearful teenage girl. Both gawked at the spectacle

Sharla was creating. "What? She say Annie Lebeau got herself kilt?" The loud woman turned back to the officer at the desk.

"I can't tell you...," the female deputy began.

"That white girl kilt Annie, you reckon? She a St. Cyr. Just come to town, her." She pooched out her full scarlet lips. Despite the hour, Erlene Beauchamps was in full makeup, her hair a marvel of the hairdresser's construction skills, her flowered caftan accessorized with the just the right bangles, necklace, and hubcap-sized earrings.

"I don't...," the deputy stammered.

"Sharla, come on." The sheriff grabbed her by the arm and hustled us out the door.

Her anger clearly set aside for the moment, the big woman let go of the teenager and snatched up the huge purse she'd dropped on the deputy's desk. "Come on here, girl. I deal wid you later. We need to get back to da house. I gotta call some people, me." In a swirl of voluminous caftan, Erlene Beauchamps trundled her weight in the sheriff's wake, the young girl trailing behind.

"Keep your voice down," Cheyne admonished Sharla, leading us across the parking lot and stopping beside Sharla's vehicle. He glared at the large black woman and her charge, as the two women climbed into a small red Cadillac. "Just what we need. Damn Erlene Beauchamps's got the biggest mouth in the bayou." He shook his head, then told Sharla. "Take Laurette home. She can tell you all about it." Hands on hips, he leaned toward us. "Sharla, right now, I'm not in a position to trust much of anybody, but I'm going to trust you to keep Laurette out of harm's way. If you talk to Claude, do it in his capacity as a lawyer...hire him...whatever."

Sharla looked from the lawman to me. "What's going on? I mean, do we need a lawyer?"

"That's up to you. Like I said, it wouldn't hurt to retain Claude's services officially. That way he's obligated to keep anything you tell him confidential, not that I'd ever worry about him running his mouth when he shouldn't. He's a clam."

Sharla's cell phone rang. She fished it out of the side pocket of her purse. "Just a minute." She looked at Cheyne. "It's Claude. Does he need to come here? He's only a couple of minutes from town."

"No. Just have him meet you at the house. He doesn't need to be seen here at the office talking to Laurette." He heaved an exasperated sigh. "Shit. By now Erlene's probably told half the town Laurette was in here for questioning about Annie's death." He nodded his head toward where the black woman was backing her car out of a parking space, her cell phone pasted to her ear. The little Caddy listed to the driver's side, the tires squashed by the woman's heft. "I can't believe that biting sow hadn't already heard the news." He looked at the two us, his lips a tight line. "I had a plan. Now I have to start damage control."

I hadn't said a word since leaving Cheyne's office...hadn't had the chance, with everybody else yammering. Now I sagged against the side of the big Escalade. "I thought you said you wanted people to think you were looking at me as the killer." I glared at him.

"I was hoping to use a little subtlety here," he answered. "Sort of let the news leak out. Now everybody in town will be running their mouths, thanks to that damn woman." He nodded toward the diminishing sight of the lopsided red Cadillac.

"What?" Sharla turned toward me. "What's this about you killing Annie?"

Chapter 53

We arrived home to find Claude already inside the house, a pot of coffee brewing in the kitchen. He set out the fixings for breakfast while asking about the trip to the sheriff's office.

By now I'd learned he had a key to the house. Sharla assured me he was the only one with a key, other than herself and me, and he could be trusted to keep the key safe. I felt somewhat relieved to know that, in spite of a constant parade marching through our home, only one non-resident had access to the house.

"First things first, before I say a word," I began. "Cheyne said I should retain you as my lawyer to insure that everything I say is kept confidential."

The dapper attorney drew his silver eyebrows together. "I *am* your lawyer. I'm on a permanent retainer. What's this all about?"

I brought my hands to my face and held them on either side. "I'm as confused about this as you are."

Sharla walked in a tight circle. "Confused doesn't cover it. It's a stinking mess."

"I'm not confused about anything." Wearing an apron over his dress shirt, his tie tucked inside, Claude held his hands out to his sides, an egg in each one. "I'm totally in the dark. I don't have a clue as to what you're both dithering about."

"Somebody's trying to set me up for Annie Lebeau's murder."

Claude clinched both hands into fists, breaking the eggs. "Ah, shit." He threw the eggs into the sink and turned toward us. "That's nothing short of ridiculous. Why the dickens would you kill Annie?" He looked over his shoulder at us, as he washed his hands and wiped them on a dish towel. "I mean you were annoyed with the old hussy, but that doesn't mean squat. Everybody who knew her was pissed at her about something."

"You're officially my lawyer?" I eyed him. "For everything?"

"Certainly, *cher*. I'm at your disposal for whatever you need. Everything you tell me will be strictly confidential."

"On the phone, you said you already knew about Annie getting herself killed," Sharla interrupted.

The lawyer waved aside her comment. "I was just sitting down to breakfast when you called me. Dihanne, my housekeeper, had already heard the news and told me."

"She'd already heard it in New Orleans?" I gasped.

He shrugged. "Bad news travels fast, especially on the bayou telegraph. Always been that way. Servants hear the worst first. Then it was on the morning news, of course. Annie was a local fixture."

"What are they saying? Any idea about a suspect?" Sharla leaned against the kitchen counter. "Anything about Laurette? Had Dihanne heard anything?"

"No. Nothing about anybody in particular. There are so many people with grievances against the old girl…people standing in line to kill her." Claude broke eggs into a bowl. He flapped a hand at us. "Y'all're messes. Go hit the showers and do something about putting yourselves together while I fix y'all some breakfast. Then we can talk about this sorry business."

Like most gay men, he expected women to look their best at all times. There was no excuse for a woman not having herself put together. Death, hurricanes, murder charges, no excuses.

I was sure the baleful expression on Sharla's face mirrored mine.

"Shooo. Get fixed up." He paused and turned to me. "And for the record again, yes, I repeat, I am officially your attorney in whatever capacity you need me for." He gave me a crooked smile. "And more than that, *cher.* You can always trust me not only as your lawyer; you can always trust me to be your friend, to keep your confidences. After all, I am your Uncle Claude, trust me as such. " He flapped his hand at us again. "Now get."

Chapter 54

After the women went upstairs, Claude leaned back against the countertop, his elbows resting on the granite surface. His curiosity was aroused by the sheriff's emphasis that Laurette needed to be able to trust him with any confidential information. He knew everybody was aware that he had his finger on the pulse of whatever happened in the bayou, as well as in New Orleans. He also hoped he had a reputation for impeccable trustworthiness. He'd been looking after the interests of Etienne St. Cyr and his immediate family for as long as he could remember. Why would Cheyne suggest Laurette needed him to be more or less sworn to silence?

Most everybody on the bayou could be considered a suspect in the old Voodoo woman's murder. She hadn't been likely to be voted Miss Bayou Congeniality. She did a lot of business with people from New Orleans, too, widening the circle of suspects. One of them could've been ticked off at her.

He'd never given much credence to all the Voodoo claptrap, but he knew a lot of people were convinced it was real. Even Sheriff Delacroix believed there was something to it.

As for Laurette being a suspect in Annie's death. Claude rubbed his chin. *"Merde,"* he muttered. He got the bacon out of the refrigerator, while he pondered the possibilities. *Maybe Delacroix already has an idea who killed the old woman and is keeping things close to his vest, hoping to flush out the perp. Cheyne Delacroix's a sneaky fils de putain…but an honest one.*

Chapter 55

"I gave Cheyne the names of all the people I could remember coming to the house since that big party we had, and that was the last time I wore those earrings." I cut the *pain perdu*, Creole style French toast, with my fork.

Claude had already eaten breakfast at home, so he leaned back in the kitchen chair and sipped his strong chicory-laced coffee. "I remember overhearing somebody comment on the earrings, but that could mean nothing."

"Laurette mentioned that she'd bought them as estate jewelry, so there's probably only one set, and somebody zeroed in on that information." Sharla crumbled some bacon and dropped it on the floor for the cats milling around the table.

"That's true." The attorney agreed. "Good observation. That would mean the police finding the earring might suspect Laurette."

"Uncle Claude, I wouldn't think I'd been here long enough to make any enemies." I took a long quaff of my orange juice, enjoying the jolt of sugar that coursed through me.

Claude echoed the sheriff's earlier remark. "*Cher*, you had enemies before you got off the plane."

"I know that's right." Sharla snorted. "The rest of the damn St. Cyrs would love to see her in jail and see all this property divvied up amongst them."

I stopped eating. "So you think it has to be a member of my family? I barely know them, and they hate me that much?"

"It's not so much that they hate you," Sharla pointed out. "It's that they love money, and they're a greedy bunch of bastards."

Chapter 56

Bayou Ombre Sheriff Cheyne Delacroix rocked back and forth in his squeaky desk chair, pondering his interview with Laurette St. Cyr. Not for a moment did he suspect her of killing Annie Lebeau. As for that vipers' nest she called a family, he could think of any number of them who were capable of murder.

They all wanted to get their hands on Shadow Cove Plantation and sell off the prime property. His cousin Courtland made no bones about wanting to acquire the place and chop it up, just like he and his father had done their own ancestral estate.

Court had been playing up to Laurette. Wooing her was the old fashioned word. If he could press his court…no pun intended… and perhaps even marry Laurette, then the property would be his. Court…charming as Satan himself…suitor or ruthless opportunist?

Cheyne thought back to the car he'd seen leaving Court's house the day he'd attempted to visit Annie Lebeau. The driver had ducked, obviously not wanting to be recognized by Cheyne. He wondered what part, if any, the driver of the car played in Court's plans.

"Skreeek!" He leaned back, and the chair shrieked. He twisted his lips in wry smile, pondering his suspicions.

He hoped Claude Landrieu was as loyal to Laurette as he seemed to be. What about Nicole Dubois? Was she Laurette's friend or foe? Did a neighbor have a bone to pick...something Cheyne knew nothing about? Almost any member of Laurette's family could be considered a suspect. Would one of them kill Annie and try to frame Laurette?

Chapter 57

Courtland Delacroix sipped a glass of white wine. He perched on the wrought-iron bannister enclosing the second floor gallery of his palatial home. The place was a miniature of the Delacroix's original Fleur d'Or plantation house, painted the color of the yellow bricks used to build the ancestral abode. His parents resided in the Nineteenth Century mansion, and they were welcome to it. He preferred a house with all the modern amenities, built shortly before he married Fabienne, when he was shopping for a wife.

The thought of his dead wife made the bile churn in his gut. She'd been nothing but a hot-to-trot slut. Still, he could've made it work, but she was just too willful and independent, and couldn't keep her panties up. Especially around his cousin Cheyne.

What do women see in that Neanderthal? He's raw, crude, but women seem to like the type.

He heard his cousin had wined and dined the lovely Laurette St. Cyr. Poaching on his territory, to his way of thinking. He had plans for that young lady, and he wasn't about to let a clod like Cheyne mess them up.

Court needed another wife. Laurette would be perfect... beautiful, rich, from the right kind of family. He'd determined he wouldn't make the same mistake with Laurette that he'd made with Fabienne. He'd learned his lesson. Now somebody seemed to be trying to throw a monkey wrench into his works...this business with the old Hoodoo woman being killed...Laurette the prime suspect.

He couldn't imagine why Laurette would kill the hag. Plenty of other people had more reason. Even if she didn't do it, she could be found guilty. She was a newcomer, and local juries didn't trust outsiders.

If she were found guilty, the property would be split up among the St. Cyrs.

Before Laurette arrived on the scene, he'd let the family know he was willing to buy as much as they wanted to sell...if it came to that. After seeing Laurette, he'd changed his mind. Marrying her would mean getting the property without buying it...and, he reminded himself again, he needed a wife.

Chapter 58

I was happy to see Roland Dubois and his wife and daughter at Claude's house. My new uncle had arranged a small dinner party, which included his partner Wills.

I spied Courtland Delacroix the moment he arrived, wine bottle in hand. *Why had Claude invited him?* Claude had implied to me that he didn't care much for Court, even though he admired his building skills. My lawyer knew Court had his eye on my property. He also knew I had no intention of selling to anyone. *So why is he here?*

Instinct told me I was being deftly maneuvered into keeping company with Court. But the maneuvering would not be done by Claude. So who was doing this? Perhaps Wills was playing matchmaker. But why? Perhaps Wills was simply a romantic.

We gossiped and chatted while a maid passed around crystal glasses of wine and a tray of canapes until the housekeeper announced dinner was served.

A pair of silver candelabra and a crystal bowl of freshly cut roses and gardenias decorated the center of the table, their heady aromas blending with the smells of the gourmet foods wafting from the kitchen. Place cards in silver frames indicated where each of us was to sit.

"I can't believe all this hoo-haa about you bein' a suspect in Annie Lebeau's murder." Roland speared a gigantic shrimp in remoulade sauce with his cocktail fork.

"Neither can I. I was totally aggravated at the woman, but I wasn't about to murder her."

"Even though somebody really needed to kill her," his wife, Giselle, put in.

"Mama! What a thing to say." Nicole scowled at her mother. "The wife of a former cop and mother of a future cop."

The older woman shrugged. "I'm just saying."

"Considering some of the other skeletons we have in the family closet, we don't need a murderer," Nicole persisted.

Her father waved his hand in dismissal. "A family without skeletons is a bunch of bores, and we have our share of both."

"More skeletons than bores, I would bet," I tossed into the conversation.

"I know that's right." Sharla pointed her fork around the table. "We've all got some, and our families are all mixed up in mischief going back to the year one…or at least until the founding of N'Awlins."

"*Mais ye*, and some of it was more recent." Roland raised his wine glass. "I had to laugh at the article in the *Times-Picayune* a couple weeks ago about all the local families who'd been involved in bootleggin' during prohibition. It ruffled quite a few feathers." He laughed. "Like it was supposed to be some kind of surprise."

Claude saluted with his own glass. "Your family did all right during prohibition."

"We didn't have a pot or a window until whiskey was outlawed." Roland chuckled. "Then my great-great uncle got into business with your great-great grandpa and Laurette's …great-great or however many greats…uncle or cousin."

"Who counts?" Claude joined his laughter. "They all made money."

"You mean they were bootleggers during prohibition? My

family?" I was astounded. I thought my family had made all their money legally.

Everyone looked at me as if I'd grown an extra head, and I realized they all knew about it...including Nicole, who was close to my age.

"Sure," Claude said. "Everybody was doing it. And the St. Cyrs had that system of tunnels under the cemetery to hide the goods in until it could be shipped upriver, so nobody ever got caught."

"Tunnels?" I looked from one to the other.

"Nobody's sure what they were built for, maybe some kind of escape route or something," Sharla put in. "During the War of Northern Aggression, the original Laurette St. Cyr used them to stash all the family treasures, in case the Yankee soldiers came calling."

"Which they did," Claude interjected. "But all they found was a stripped, threadbare house, nothing worth stealing."

"I'm surprised the slaves didn't rat them out," I said. "Or had they all left?

Again, I was speared by incredulous stares.

"Of course they didn't leave," Courtland told me. "Shadow Cove was their home. Where would they have gone? And they were loyal to the family. My family's slaves stayed, too."

"But I thought..."

Sharla shook her head at me. "Contrary to what you've read in history books, most of the former slaves stayed put, especially the house servants. They had no place to go...no way to support themselves, so most of them stayed and worked for their former masters."

I took a big gulp of my wine and returned to the other topic. "But bootleggers...I just can't imagine."

Claude hooted. "*Cher*, Louisiana was founded by some of the biggest rogues in France. I sometimes think corruption's in our genes."

"Our past political shenanigans will prove that to anybody." Giselle Dubois cackled. "And the current ones."

"I know that's right." Sharla raised her glass in mock salute.

"To corruption." Court lifted his own glass.

"Now what've you got, Oscar?" Claude bent to retrieve a piece of foil his white toy poodle had in his mouth. "I swear, anything shiny catches your eye...and foil is not good for that boy." He wadded up the foil and laid it beside his plate. "My keys went missing a couple days ago. Of course, I keep an extra set of everything, so I wasn't late for my court date." He glanced my way. "Except your house key... there's only one of that. Dihanne found the keyring tucked behind this boy's bed this morning."

"They can be little demons, but they're adorable," Sharla leaned down and patted the other of the pair of poodles, this one named Crandall.

"By the way, Court, not changing the subject, but I really appreciate you getting over here so quickly and getting that crack in the courtyard fixed before it got any worse," Claude said. "I wanted to get it sealed before it got all the way to the pool."

"What are friends for?" Delacroix flashed his most charming grin. "I just rearranged a couple of things, so my guys could get over here early."

Wills pointed a finger and me. "See, sugar. That's what I mean. Court can always be depended on to help you."

Oscar and Crandall pranced around the table to me.

"Shoo," Claude scolded. "You two know better than to beg from the table. Now stop pestering Laurette."

Neither animal paid much attention to his admonition. Instead, both dogs stood on their hidelegs at my chair, and I gave each a head pat. The little snowballs and I had fallen in love with each other at first sight.

"They're not pests. They're little sweethearts. In fact, I'm tempted to get a pair just like them, but I suppose I really need larger dogs at Shadow Cove. I don't imagine poodles are much good as watch dogs; although, I've read that it doesn't matter about the size of the animal, as long as it barks."

"This is true up to a point," Roland commented. "A barking dog eliminates the element of surprise on the crook's part, but a big dog is more likely to scare somebody off. Personally, I'd suggest you get whatever size dog you want, but have a security system installed in that place."

"You don't have one?" Nicole seemed surprised.

Sharla shook her head and nodded toward Dihanne to remove her plate. Claude's housekeeper and her daughter had prepared and were serving the elegant dinner. "We've never had any problems with prowlers or anything else."

"Until I arrived," I amended.

"I know that's right, *cher*." Sharla reached and patted my arm. "But I wouldn't trade having you home for anything."

I was seated between her and Court, who reached for my other hand, the right one. I quickly placed it in my lap. I just wasn't comfortable with public displays of affection, especially from a man whose motives I wasn't certain were honorable.

"We're all delighted to have you here, my dear," Courtland agreed, seeming to ignore my snub.

"Oh, absolutely." Wills raised his wine glass in salute. "A toast to our newest bayou belle. And I feel I must apologize for the untoward events that've transpired and must taint your opinion of us."

Claude lifted his glass and quickly put in, "Things are usually pretty quiet out on Bayou Ombre. Most of the crime takes place here in N'Awlins."

"And we sure Lord know we have plenty of that," Giselle added.

"I know that's right," Wills agreed, with a nod in my direction. "Sad to say, we're not the safest city on the planet."

Wills sat across the table, sandwiched between Nicole and her mother, with Nicole situated directly across from Court. Roland and Claude occupied the chairs at either end of the table.

Earlier in the evening, I noticed Court and Nicole standing in the dimly lighted courtyard together. He had a hand on the small of her back and was whispering to her. I saw her turn and look back toward the house, but I wasn't sure if she could see me, where I stood just inside the open French doors to the living room. In any case, she said something to Court, who shook his head. She laughed, tossing back her golden mane, and came back into the house. I'd moved aside so she wouldn't know I'd seen them. A curious *tete a tete*. I recalled they appeared quite cozy at the party at Shadow Cove, too.

I wondered if Courtland Delacroix flirted with everyone. And I also wondered how receptive Nicole was to his flirtation. Moline hinted that he needed another wife. Was he shopping or what?

Perhaps it isn't me Court's supposed to be wooing. Perhaps it's Nicole, and I'm misreading the signals.

I glanced at them over the rim of my wine glass.

"Not changing the subject, but are you trying out for a part in the troupe's next production?" Court asked Nicole.

"I don't think so. I'm pretty tied up right now with my tests."

A tiny mental bell dinged. I remembered both of them mentioning they were involved in some amateur theatricals. Perhaps that was the connection between them...not a romance. Not that I minded Court being interested in another woman, but I suspected he was playing up to me to get his hands on Shadow Cove...and that rankled.

"The next play is a murder mystery, isn't it?" Nicole's mother commented and then laughed. "How *au courant*, what with Annie being killed."

"Hey, let's talk about something besides crime here. I get that all day," Nicole suggested, as Dihanne began placing small bowls of creamy spinach soup in front of us. "Laurette, how about I make reservations for the two of us at my favorite day spa? Get our hair trimmed, nails done, a facial, a girls' day."

"That sounds like a super idea," Sharla accepted the invitation for me. "You two can spend the day doing *jeune fille* stuff."

"I'd love to, and my hair does need a little trim," I said.

"We'll have a great time. Let's make it day after tomorrow." Nicole's smile was white against her light tan skin. "If that suits you."

"Will that give you time to get a reservation?" Her mother asked.

"Oh, sure. They know my schedule gets a little crazy sometimes, so they always make room for me."

Giselle raised her eyebrows. "And, like your daddy, you always over tip."

"There is that." Nicole wrinkled her nose at her mother.

Chapter 59

A light fog had rolled in from the creeks surrounding the bayou by the time Sharla and I arrived back home. The Louisiana fog was nothing like Seattle's murk, which could be thick as cotton batting. Here the layers of mist shifted and slithered around the enormous trees lining the highway, parting and revealing the road. The lights in the houses along the way peeked in and out of the drifts like mischievous lightning bugs. The fog wasn't so thick I couldn't see to drive.

At one point, a deer loped across the road in front of us, and I could see the red eyes of animals in the underbrush lining the two-lane roadway. I turned off onto Shadow Cove's oyster shell driveway and crunched around the fountain and flower bushes in the circular bed. We'd left lights on inside the house and on the front verandah. The outside lights on the garage were welcoming in the diaphanous fog. I pulled the little Caddy SUV into the garage, feeling snug and safe, as the big garage door rumbled shut behind me.

"I feel like some cocoa laced with brandy," Sharla suggested, getting out of the car.

"Okay, let's shower and put on our nighties first. Then we can kick back and relax."

After my shower, I opened the French doors and walked out onto the gallery, watching the tendrils of fog wafting silently on the scant night breeze.

It wasn't late, only a little after midnight.

I smiled to myself. I never realized I was a bit of a night owl, since I'd always had to get up early, either for school or for work. Left on its own, my body clock didn't wake me until around eight each morning, so I was already getting into the habit of going to bed a little after midnight most nights.

A twinkle in the distance caught my eye. I leaned forward over the bannister. In the dark and the fog, I couldn't tell how far away the glittering light was, but I knew the creek made a sharp turn on the far side of the family graveyard, perhaps a half mile away.

The light was in the exact spot where I'd seen another brief gleam a few nights earlier. I stepped back into the room and turned off the lamp in my bedroom. If there was somebody out there, they wouldn't see my silhouette.

Why is somebody on the river this late at night and this close to Shadow Cove?

I saw another flash...twin red lights. They looked like tail lights...like the lights on the back of Remy's airboat.

The glints danced between the drifts of fog for a few seconds and winked out.

The night was silent. I heard nothing from that direction, other than the muted night sounds, swamp creatures prowling, and these noises, too, seemed muffled by the fog. Were the lights boat lights... somebody simply fishing at night?

I rubbed my naked arms, feeling the cold dampness of the mist. I went inside and locked the doors to the gallery.

"Probably just somebody out gigging frogs or fishing," Sharla assured me when I met her in the kitchen. "I don't know much about doing either, so maybe that's just a good spot, out there near that old boat dock."

I took a swig of my brandy-laced cocoa. "You're probably right."

She shrugged. "No other reason I can think of for somebody being out on the creek at night."

"You've never had anybody bother you out here?" I was a city girl, still not used to the isolation of the bayou.

"Never." She laughed. "All those stories about bootleggers at dinner tonight has got you spooked." She sipped her own cocoa. "The only unwelcome guest we've had is Annie Lebeau, and somebody solved that problem for us."

"It's scary knowing there's a killer loose here in the bayou."

"I'm betting whoever killed her is from N'Awlins...came out here, took care of business, and hightailed it back to the Big Easy. Probably some Voodoo customer whose spell didn't work for him."

Chapter 60

I was looking forward to my day with Nicole. I liked her a lot and hoped we could be good friends. Truth be told, I'd never had close girlfriends. Mama was my best friend. I still wondered at the way Court flirted with Nicole, when he seemed so focused on me the evening we had dinner. Maybe it was just male ego. Maybe he was one of those men who had to have the attention of every woman in the room. And Nicole Dubois was one of the most beautiful women I'd ever seen. I felt a bit like a little mud hen next to her nearly six feet of golden splendor.

Jealousy did not play a large part in my psyche. For the most part, I was happy with who I was. I didn't possess spectacular looks, but I was far from homely. I was smart, graduated at the top of my class in high school and was magna cum lauda in college. People seemed to like me well enough, although I was not a social magnet, like my mama. I was okay with me.

I dressed in a pair of knee-length jeans, with rhinestone *fleur de lis* crusting the back pockets, and a white eyelet peasant blouse. High-heeled, rhinestone-embellished sandals completed my look.

I'd ditched most of my conservative Seattle clothes since arriving back home. New Orleans style was more flashy without being trashy, and it suited my taste.

I started out of my bedroom, but again I felt that curious sensation of not being alone, like someone was watching me. A chill swept over me. I whirled around and looked toward the French doors. Nobody was there. I checked the lock...I don't know why I did that. People seemed to meander in and out of my house at will.

Since my earring had been stolen, I'd fixed myself a makeshift hidey-hole for my jewelry under the vanity in my bathroom. No more leaving it on display. I fully intended to have a safe installed soon.

Picking up my purse, again I felt drawn toward the painting of my long-dead ancestor, for whom I was named. I walked over the fireplace and looked up at her face, placid, with its enigmatic smile. "Are you trying to spook me?" I asked aloud. I cocked my head to the side and studied her features. The resemblance between us was uncanny. "Are you a guardian angel? Or a haint?"

I laughed at my foolishness and turned to leave.

"Faites attention."

I jerked back around at the sibilant sound. My hand flew to my mouth. My breath caught in my throat. I flicked my eyes to the dim corners of the room, saw nothing. Nobody lurked. Yet, I'd heard the words of caution clearly. I knew I was alone in the house. Sharla had gone grocery shopping, and this was not one of Moline's cleaning days.

Fear crawled over my skin, prickling, cold.

I stared at the portrait.

"I'm going nuts here," I muttered and fled the room, taking deep breaths to get myself under control. I shook my head at my own silliness. I had a great day planned, and here I was letting myself be spooked by nothing. Everybody knew old houses made funny noises...and that was all that happened...just the house creaking, a draft blowing through an uneven door...or something. I hurried through the house to the garage.

I opened the door to the small gold Cadillac SUV I'd decided to use until my Cayenne arrived. Sharla was welcome to the monster Escalade, too much vehicle for me.

A funky stink assaulted my nose. "Damn." I knew I hadn't stepped in anything since I'd just left the inside of the house, but the odor was rank. I didn't have time to investigate where the smell was coming from, so I just turned the AC on Max and strapped myself into the driver's seat. Perhaps the car just smelled bad from being closed up...but Sharla and I had used it only a couple nights earlier. Surely something hadn't gotten inside died...or done its business.

"Whew." I snorted, holding my breath and hoping the odor would dissipate; otherwise, I feared my hair and clothes would absorb the stench.

Backing out of the garage, I navigated the roundabout in front of the house and headed down the long shell driveway. I turned onto the two-lane country road leading to the highway. The day was sunny, and the humidity was lower than usual, a good day to get hair done. Nicole had made lunch reservations at Redfish Grill before our stint at the spa. I was looking forward to some raw oysters or maybe those barbequed crab claws.

The rickety bridge where I spotted the alligators on my first trip back home lay directly ahead. Something slithered across my sandal, causing me to jerk my foot from the accelerator. I glanced down at the floorboard.

"Oh, Jesus," I squeaked.

A long water moccasin glided across my foot to the passenger's side. The serpent coiled itself in the footwell in front of the seat.

Before I could slow down and get out of the car, another dark brown snake slipped out from beneath the passenger's seat and fixed its slanted eyes on me.

I sucked air. Terror swept over me.

I stomped my foot toward the brake, but missed and hit the gas pedal. The car hurtled toward the shoulder of the road.

"Shi-i-i-t!" This time, my foot connected with the brake, and the car swerved, the tires screaming.

A third snake crawled over my ankle. A series of breathless

squawks escaped my mouth, and I stomped my feet on the floorboard, kicking at the reptile.

The car swiveled from side to side on the pavement, hitting the rough edge and almost tipping over. I sawed at the steering wheel, panicking, not knowing which way to turn.

I could hear myself screaming.

Something slithered across the top of my seat, brushing the back of my head. I lurched forward, caught by the seatbelt, trapped.

"Oh, God! Oh, God!"

I jerked the wheel, and the Caddy caromed toward the opposite side of the road, down into the ditch, then back onto the pavement. The car whipped sideways, the tires squalled as I hit the brake pedal with both feet.

Rubber burned off the screaming tires.

Another snake coiled in the passenger seat. The repulsive creature opened its mouth showing the white interior from which it got its name, cottonmouth water moccasin.

The things were poisonous.

I hurled myself toward the door. Caught by the seatbelt, I couldn't escape the snake's impending strike. Another serpent crawled onto the seat, distracting the first one. I scrabbled for the seatbelt latch, planning to jump from the vehicle while it was still moving if I had to. I'd risk broken bones to get away from those terrifying snakes.

How the hell had they gotten into the car?

The bridge abutment appeared in my peripheral vision. The car hurtled toward it. I couldn't take my eyes off those hideous snakes, coiling one on the other. I let go of the seatbelt and jerked the steering wheel again. I must have hit the brakes.

The car bucked and tilted on the berm of the ditch.

Kicking with my feet, I hit the gas again.

The car spun out of control. Small shrubs and plants slashed against the sides as the Caddy careened in a complete, dizzying circle. The vehicle bumped and lurched over the uneven ground.

My hands were frozen to the steering wheel, my feet scissoring on the floorboard, hitting neither the gas nor the brakes. The car rocketed completely off the road, into and out of the ditch, closer to the bridge. With sweaty hands I scrabbled at my seat belt clasp again, but my wet fingers could get no purchase on the metal. I tried to hit the brake again, missed and stomped on the gas pedal. I flailed at the steering wheel with both hands, shrieking.

I was slung left and right, backward and forward, as the Caddy humped and bucked toward the creek. I stomped at the brake again, and my foot hit the edge of the pedal and slipped off. The left side of the car struck something, knocking me toward the snakes in the passenger seat. Then the vehicle bounded sideways and hit something else, and I was thrown toward the door. A large object smashed into the windshield. I scrunched my eyes shut as shattered glass sprayed over me.

The airbag deployed.

I threw my hands up in front of my face.

I felt the car become airborne, plunging over the creek bank.

The front hit something, and I was hurled against the seatbelt.

My head smashed against the side window.

Chapter 61

Remy Thibadeaux recognized the small gold Cadillac tumbling over the embankment. Automatically, he grabbed his cell phone and punched in 911. He swerved his airboat from the middle of the creek and plowed toward the vehicle churning the waters ahead of him.

Out of the corner of his eye, he saw a pair of alligators start toward the Caddy. He wasn't too worried about the reptiles. He kept a rifle holstered beside his tall seat.

"Right here at the Boudreaux Creek Bridge," he told the operator, his voice surprisingly calm. "*Mais, ye, cher.* There's a woman in the driver's seat. We need po-lice, the ambulance, all of it. I'm on it. I'll try to get her out. The car's banged up, but it looks like I can get the driver's side door open."

Remy slewed his shallow-draft airboat alongside the car and shut down his engine. He jumped out and waded toward Laurette's car, keeping a watchful eye on the gators hovering about fifty feet away.

The murky water swirled past his knees, and the car was canted forward, its nose in the water. The left-hand rear door was bashed in, and the driver's door was badly dented, but Remy was strong as an ox. He wrenched the door open, and Laurette would have tumbled into his arms had she not been held fast by the seatbelt.

Remy leaned across her body to release the seatbelt. "Godamawty! Goddamn!" He jerked back as the snake shot out at him. The venomous reptile missed him and hit the water, swimming rapidly away. Another snake slithered out from under the car seat and into the water. Remy cursed some more but risked reaching around Laurette to loosen the seatbelt.

Her unconscious body fell into his arms, and he got a grip on her. His gray eyes were wide with fear as three more snakes crawled out of the car. Laurette wasn't heavy, maybe a hundred ten pounds, so it was easy for Remy to pick her up. She was splattered with blood from cuts caused by the broken windshield. He couldn't tell if she'd been bitten by any of the snakes.

In the distance, he heard the howl of the ambulance, as he awkwardly climbed the creek bank, with Laurette cradled in his arms.

A sheriff's vehicle screamed to a halt on the shoulder of the road, and Remy saw Cheyne Delacroix jump out.

The policeman shuffled down the embankment and helped Remy carry Laurette to the top. "What happened?" Cheyne helped Remy lay Laurette on the ground.

"Shit if I know. I was coming down the creek, me, and I saw her car flying off the road into the water." Remy flopped down on the grass. "Goddamn, Cheyne, the car's full of water moccasins."

"What?"

Remy panted. "I'm tellin' you, the fuckin' car's full of snakes." He huffed. "I don't know if they bit her or not. I just hurried up and got her out of there. Scared the shit outta me."

Another sheriff's car pulled in behind Cheyne's vehicle. The deputy got out and hollered. "I'm callin' for a tow truck, y'all. Ambulance is right behind me."

Chapter 62

I lay in the hospital bed, where I'd spent the past two nights. The IV was removed earlier this morning, and the doctor said I could go home today. A two-inch cut on my forehead was bandaged, and small patches of gauze covered the other cuts and abrasions on my face and body. I managed to escape the accident with no broken bones or serious injuries...or snakebites. However, the terror of knowing somebody tried to kill me had not abated. Bile churned anew in my stomach when I realized how close I'd come to being killed. I bit my lip and fought down the urge to cry. *Who on earth hates me this much?*

Cheyne insisted the hospital keep me for a couple of days for my own safety. He knew as well as I did that the snakes had not gotten into my car on their own. A sheriff's deputy was on duty 'round the clock outside my door. The sheriff himself stood over by the window, silently, waiting to escort me home as soon as the doctor released me.

I could hardly wait to get out of there. I hated hospitals.

Sharla perched on a chair at the side of the bed, and Claude stood at the foot, his arms resting on the footboard, a large Styrofoam cup of Coke held loosely between his hands. Sharla had brought me some clothes. The folded tee shirt, cropped pants, underwear, and sandals lay on the bed at my feet.

An enormous bouquet of flowers rested on the table beside the window, courtesy of Courtland Delacroix. I guess Court had heard me say I liked stargazer lilies, because the arrangement contained several. Their scent was strong, but I wasn't complaining, since their odor obliterated that "hospital" smell in my room.

Smaller arrangements were banked on the other furniture and on the floor. Flowers, from my St. Cyr cousins, my Renard grandparents, aunts and uncles, the Duboises, the Lesieurs, Doralynne and Paul Thibadeaux, arrived early this morning. They all must've seen the incident on the evening news or heard it on the bayou gossip telegraph. "This place looks like a funeral home," I grumbled. "I'll let the hospital keep the flowers and give them to other patients."

"I'd keep those live plants. We can put them in the garden," Sharla suggested.

"Okay. I don't need a houseful of reminders of that wreck." I shifted against the pillows propped at my back. "I wonder if one of the people sending me the get-well flowers was already thinking in terms of funeral wreaths. I can't help but suspect one of them tried to kill me."

"I know that's right," Sharla agreed, furrowing her brow. "You can't trust anybody." She reached for Claude's Coke and helped herself to a sip. "Your car looked like the loser in a demolition derby, so I guess those damn snakes were too scared to bite you. God knows what would've happened if Remy hadn't been coming along right then."

Claude's expression was as somber as his voice. "That's exactly why Cheyne put the quietus on visitors. Nobody's been allowed in to see you except him, Sharla, Father Gee, and me...and Remy, of course. We can pretty much discount his having anything to do with this, since he was the one who rescued you. Not even family members are allowed in here. I wouldn't trust any of them as far as I could throw them, but then I never have."

"Nothing like a warm, loving family," I remarked. "Y'all warned me." I wondered if indeed it had been a family member who tried to kill me. Of course, they were the only ones with a motive, money. On the other hand, I didn't know but what there were some other machinations afoot by people outside my family who could want me dead for the same reason. Still, the only way anyone else could get to the money was through my family, if I were dead…so it all came back to a family member, but which one…or two…or three. I'd been warned they were a vicious, wily bunch, ruthless when it came to a dollar.

I shivered as my mind drifted to the possibilities of who put those snakes in my car. After almost two days in the hospital, much of my fright had been replaced by anger, and I was determined to find out who'd done this to me. I was equally determined to see that whoever was perpetrating the attacks on me received the full force of the law.

Everyone at Claude's dinner party knew I was planning to meet Nicole, and most everybody knew the Cadillac SUV was my vehicle of choice. *Could Nicole have collaborated with one of the others at the party to get me out of the house, or had the timing just been random?* I didn't want to think of Nicole in this context, but neither did I want to suspect any of the others of trying to harm me. Then there was the matter of the carjacking. No one at Claude's party could've been involved in that…or could they? I had no idea how any of these people might be connected to one another in ways of which I was not aware.

Cheyne left the window and came to stand behind Sharla. "We're getting fingerprints off the car. Those damn snakes didn't climb inside by themselves. He tapped his fingers on his hips. "What I want to know is how did somebody get inside your garage without one o' y'all knowing it. My deputies checked all the outside doors for any signs of tampering and didn't find anything. So it almost had to be somebody with a key."

"Laurette and Claude and I have the only keys." Sharla looked toward the lawyer.

"I've been thinking about that." Claude paced, running a hand through his silver hair.

In spite of the crisis, he was his usual dapper self. I had yet to see the man with a hair out of place or a wrinkle in his clothing.

"Remember I mentioned the other night that my keys had gone missing?" He glanced at Sharla and me. "You know when y'all were at my house for dinner?"

"*Mais, ye*, I remember," Sharla answered him. "But they turned up where...in the dogs' bed, didn't you say?"

"At the time, I thought nothing of it...just one of the dogs got them off of the night table beside my bed." Claude stopped pacing and shook his head. "Somebody must've gotten those keys from my house and made a copy of the key to Shadow Cove." He looked in my direction. "Just like somebody got that earring from Laurette's dressing table."

Cheyne raised his eyebrows. "The same person?"

Claude nodded. "That's what I'm thinking. Too much of a coincidence."

"Who on earth would do this stuff to me?" I couldn't imagine anybody wanting to kill me, but that's exactly what had happened. "If I'd been trapped in that car with those snakes, down the embankment where the car might not've been seen right away, the snakes could've killed me." I shuddered.

Sharla patted my arm and reiterated. "Thank God Remy came along when he did."

Claude turned toward Cheyne. "I keep trying to remember who all was at my house those days the keys were missing...and it was only for a day or so." He tugged on his lips with his fingers. "As it happened, the time was just a tad hectic. I was winding up a case and going a little nuts with a crazy client, and Court's people were doing some work on the courtyard, fixing some cracks." He sighed. "And the damned air conditioner went on the fritz and had to be serviced. Dihanne called her brother, who owns the AC company we use, so that shouldn't be anything to worry about."

"Those workmen...did you know them? Court's I mean," Cheyne asked.

"No. In fact, I wasn't even home, but Court's people are usually pretty reliable. He doesn't hire trash. Besides, Dihanne said he came by and checked to see how their work was coming along." Claude shrugged. "Wills was in and out as usual. Nicole Dubois dropped by to pick up some materials I had for her for one of her law enforcement classes, something for one of her term papers. Wills and I entertained a few people at a small cocktail party the night before y'all were there." He directed the last remark to Sharla and me.

"People you know well?" Cheyne turned a straight-backed chair around and straddled it. "People who might know Laurette?"

"I don't know if they actually know Laurette...but they might know about her."

Sharla emitted a short laugh. "And we don't know who all they might know, do we?"

"There is that," the lawyer answered. He cocked his head. "Come to think of it, David Marquis, one of my guests that evening, is a business associate of Robert's. His wife's thick as thieves with Reggie."

"I know Valerie Marquis," Sharla said. "Snotty little social climber, worships Reggie." She gave a short laugh. "If Reggie farted, she'd blow Valerie's brains out."

Cheyne hummphed.

"I know that's right." Claude glanced toward me. "Your cousin Angeline's husband's sister was there, too. Jason's sister, Paulette, is married to a man who happens to be one of my clients."

"Oh, wow," I said. "That's almost family."

"Especially in the South." The lawyer cast me a wry look. "For what it's worth, Edwin Tanner and his wife were there, too."

"Tanner?" I raised my eyebrows. The original Laurette St. Cyr was married to a man named Kyle Tanner.

"A distant cousin, probably four or five times removed," my uncle explained. "I told you there were some Tanner relatives in the woodpile. As far as I know, none of this branch of the tribe has any dealings with the St. Cyrs." He pulled a face. "But I could be wrong." He cut a look at Cheyne and nodded. "Can't hurt to check."

The sheriff had taken a small notebook out of his pocket and was writing down names. "May I ask why you were entertaining these people?"

The attorney shrugged again. "Actually, it was just a small cocktail party to celebrate winning a case."

Cheyne grunted.

"What the case involved is confidential," Claude told him. "I can't see it having any bearing on what happened to Laurette."

"Except that some of the people at the party are loosely connected to her," Cheyne qualified.

Claude gave him a thin smile. "Well, hell. You know how N'Awlins is. Everybody's related to somebody or in business with somebody or in bed with somebody."

Cheyne huffed a laugh. "True."

"I'll be happy to give you the names of all the people who were there." Claude finished drinking his Coke and tossed the cup into the trash basket. "Anything to help find out who did this to my girl here."

Chapter 63

"For the life of me, I cannot believe you pulled that stunt with the snakes. Hell, you could've been bitten." Courtland Delacroix swirled the wine in his glass as he paced the floor. The French doors to the verandah were open, allowing a flower-scented breeze to waft through his home.

"I've lived around the bayou my whole life. I know how to handle a snake, and we both know moccasins aren't nearly as aggressive as rattlesnakes."

"Still, you don't need to be doing shit like that. What happened with Annie was one thing. She saw us...but this, this business with the snakes. Laurette could've been killed, and I don't want that."

Court's guest drummed nails on a polished side table. "I saw how you look at her."

"So I'm a good actor. That's all it is. An act. Stop being so damned insecure and jealous."

"I'm sorry." A pout.

"I thought we'd agreed. I'll do what needs to be done to get close to her." Court picked up his visitor's hand and kissed it. "You're the one. You know that. Just be patient. I don't want her dead. She's worth a lot to us alive...for a while at least."

"I don't think I can bear the thought of you being with her."

"It'll only be for a little while. You have to trust me."

A tearful sniff.

"Come into the bedroom, *cher*. I'll show you how much you mean to me."

Chapter 64

"What are you doing?" Sharla plopped onto the kitchen chair across from me.

"I'm making out a list of all the people I can remember coming to the house before Annie Lebeau was killed." I turned my paper sideways so she could see it. "Then I'm writing down the names of all the people Claude remembers coming to his house just before his keys went missing." I leaned back in the chair and eyed Sharla. "You know, the person who took the keys had to bring them back. I need to ask him who came to his house twice."

"Hmm. You're right. I'll do that. Every amateur sleuth needs an assistant." She picked up the phone from the counter and tapped in Claude's number. She'd taken my note pad and was jotting something down.

I listened with one ear while getting Cokes for each of us from the fridge. One of the cats came in through the new doggy door and wound itself around my ankles. The animals had learned to use their new escape hatch quickly and seemed to enjoy being able to come and go at will. The fence people had finished the new enclosure around a portion of the backyard only the day before my incident with the snakes. They even put razor wire around the top and charged it with low voltage, just enough to get an intruder's attention and to keep the cats from trying to climb over it. Neither human nor animal was getting over that fence without a hair-curling.

"I'll accept for both of us, unless Laurette has a hot date. Um, hmm. *Je t'aime, aussi, cher.*" Sharla returned to her chair and took a swig of Coke before commenting on the phone call. "Okay. As Claude said, Wills was in and out, but that's pretty common, since he practically lives there. He thinks Court returned to the house to check on his workmen, but he'll check with Dihanne to find out for sure."

I tapped my forefinger against my lips. "Umm, is it just me, or does it seem odd that Court doesn't have a couple of foremen or supervisors who oversee his jobs? Most of the building contractors I met back in Seattle were basically project managers. Someone handled the grunt work for them."

Sharla shrugged. "Maybe it's because he considers Claude a special client. Just like with us, when his guys are working here, he's likely to drop in and check on them." She shook her head. "Maybe he just gives special attention to certain people, you know, his regulars."

"You could be right. Who else made a return trip?"

My sleuthing assistant consulted her list. "Nicole came back to return the materials Claude loaned her for a class."

"Nicole again," I pondered. "She's training to be a cop, so she should be trustworthy."

Sharla cocked that eyebrow and said slowly, "You'd think, but then about the only people we can eliminate are you and me...and Claude, of course." She looked back at the pad. "Valerie Marquis took some leftovers home from the cocktail party Claude mentioned and returned the plate she used the very next day."

"Who's she?"

"The woman Claude mentioned being asshole buddies with Cousin Reggie."

"Oh, yeah, I remember now." I leaned back in my chair and

mulled this. "Do you suppose she's good enough friends with Reggie to swipe Claude's keys and get a copy made of our house key if Reggie asked her to?"

"*Mais, ye.* They piss through the same quill, as my mama'd say."

I laughed. "My mama'd say the same thing…and I never did know what it meant."

"Me either." Sharla toyed with her Coke glass. "Funny, I never would've thought of that. Valerie would do anything Reggie asked her to, just to suck up, and taking leftover *hors oeuvres* home would give her an opportunity to steal the keys and then use returning the plate as a cover for bringing them back."

"Uh, huh, and I have no doubt my cousins would do me dirt."

She saluted me with the glass. "You're quite the Miz Sherlock."

I sat quietly for a moment and reread the list.

"What's that frown about?"

"Nicole." I looked up at my friend. "I hate to think anything bad about her, but I saw her more or less flirting with Court the night of Claude's party. I saw them in the courtyard together, and it was pretty obvious they were talking about me." I caught my bottom lip with my teeth. "I saw them being pretty cozy at that dinner party we had here at the house, too. You don't suppose she and Court are up to something, and she's playing up to me for some reason other than being friends, do you?"

My mentor pulled a face. "I don't want to think that, but I have to admit, I don't know her that well. And Courtland Delacroix could charm the panties off a nun."

"What about Cheyne?"

"What about him?"

"I saw him having a little flirt with her at the party here at the house." I twirled my hair around my finger. "It might've been nothing, but I overheard a snippet of their conversation, and I heard her say something to him about my being a good catch."

"Whoa. Now that's interesting." Her eyebrows climbed to her hairline.

"I didn't hear his reply, but he leaned over and whispered

something to her." I stopped speaking for a moment, not sure what to say next. A cold knot was forming in my stomach.

"And...there's more, eh?"

"Well, I didn't hear any more, but when he said something to her, she gave him a little nuzzle and glanced toward me and laughed."

"Oh, my." Sharla rested her elbow on the table and propped her face on her hand. "I'll have to confess something. I've always noticed Nicole flirting with everything in pants, and I've wondered to myself just how that was going to work out with her planning on being a cop."

"Um, hmm. I was hoping she and I could be friends, but this has me wondering." I drank some more Coke without tasting it. "I wonder if she's trying to use me because of some relationship with Court...or with Cheyne." I picked up the pen and fiddled with it. I didn't care if Nicole was carrying on with Court, but the idea of her having something going on with Cheyne rankled. "I just have to wonder if she's playing a game with one of them, and I'm involved in this game as some sort of pawn, without having a clue as to what's going on. If that's the case, I don't like this situation for shit. I also have to wonder why Court and Cheyne both seem to be vying for my attention. I'm not exactly what you'd call a femme fatale."

Sharla chuckled. "You sell yourself short, *cher*. You're beautiful."

"I'm also a realist...a very rich realist," I reminded her.

"There is that." She got up and took something out of the freezer. "I'll make some chicken for dinner tonight...don't know what, maybe one of my original concoctions."

I didn't look up from the list I was studying. "Everything you cook is good."

"You know, I have to wonder about what you said about Cheyne, you know flirting with Nicole?"

"Oh?"

"Umm...he's a really good guy, but he's not a saint, and he just about has to beat the women off him."

I felt a rush of heat run up my neck. I didn't like hearing this. Not that I had any reason to be jealous, but still.

"He's been known to get around, and I wouldn't be surprised if he'd enjoyed a little flirt with Nicole." She put the frozen chicken in the sink to thaw. "I've heard rumors about him and any number of women."

"That's nice to know." I smacked the pen down on the table.

"Now don't go getting all pissy on me. The man's hot as hell. You can't expect him to live like a monk just because he's single."

She stopped speaking, and I knew she was taking in the pout I could feel covering my face. "Oh, shit. You've got a case on him, haven't you?"

"No. It's just that..." I shook my head, unable to meet her eyes.

My new best friend, or aunt or whatever she was, walked behind me, leaned over, and wrapped her arm around my neck, placing her face next to mine. "To tell you the truth, *cher*, I'd rather see you interested in him than in Court. He's a far better man...but I repeat, he ain't no saint."

The gesture was all too familiar. Mama used to do the same thing with me when I was upset. I ran my hand up her arm and leaned my cheek against hers. "I guess I'd just like to think he was paying attention to me because he thought I was special somehow... not because he was up to something or after my money."

Sharla pulled back and kissed me on top of the head. "If it's any consolation, Cheyne doesn't have a rep for being a tomcat...just a healthy male." She walked back around the table and sat down again.

"I just don't know what's going on here. I don't know who I can trust...except you and Claude. I've never had anybody try to harm me before." I felt my throat closing up. I wasn't a whiner.

Sharla crossed her arms on the table and echoed my earlier thoughts. "This is getting curiouser and curiouser. There's definitely some kind of game afoot, and we're going to have to keep our guards up, not that I have anything to worry about. It's you they're after." She speared me with those turquoise eyes, eyes filling with tears. "But then they might realize I'd lay down my life for you, so they'd have to go through me."

Chapter 65

Cheyne wondered how much of the conversation with Roland Dubois he should keep to himself and how much he should tell Laurette.

Roland still had his sources within the New Orleans Police Department. His little shop was near the precinct house in the French Quarter, so cops often stopped in for coffee and gossip. The shopkeeper and the Shadow Bayou Sheriff sat across from one another at one of the small bistro tables and sipped the espressos Roland had brewed for them.

"The description sounded too much like Robert St. Cyr to be a coincidence." Roland tapped his finger on the rim of the small cup. "And I wouldn't put anything past that snake."

"Sorta backfired on him when his fancy car got shot up, didn't it?" Cheyne's smile held no warmth.

"Hmph." Roland nodded. "I heard he'd gotten rid of the car. Reggie wouldn't even allow him to put it in the garage." He cackled. "Those two are real pieces of work. They deserve one another."

"If he really was behind it, did the dude the NOLA cops picked up say what his motive was? I mean taking the car with Laurette and Sharla in the back seat?"

"*Merde.*" Roland twisted his lips. "He and his sidekick just figured it was another white dude acting squirrelly. Whoever it was…Robert or whoever…gave them orders not to harm the women, just scare them fartless." He held up a forefinger. "And mainly he emphasized that they not get a scratch on that car."

"It had to be Robert." Cheyne sipped his coffee.

"Umm, humm. That's what the po-lice think, too. The pair of carjackers were just supposed to drive around a few minutes, not long enough to get caught, and then dump the car. They had another ride stashed near where they were supposed to leave the Maserati, a side street in Metairie. They got part of their money upfront, then they were supposed to get the rest when the caper was successful."

"Which ain't gonna happen now, podnah."

Roland chuckled. "Nope. That got fucked up for sure."

"Serves 'em all right…the carjackers and Robert." Cheyne toyed with his small spoon. "How'd the cops get onto them in the first place? Did the one who got shot squeal?"

"Not right off, although they picked him up again after the *numero uno* thief got arrested, and he unloaded everything he knew when he learned his partner'd been busted."

"What happened?"

Roland shrugged. "Just the usual crap. No honor among thieves, and the one who made the deal and got the first installment of cash started running his mouth, bragging in one of the titty bars." He nodded a greeting to a customer who wandered in and headed for the bar area. He had an associate helping out today, so he and Cheyne continued their conversation. "One of his ex-girlfriends works in the place and heard him jacking his jaws and called the law, just to jerk his chain."

"Payback?"

"Literally. This fool owned her some money, so she was getting even by siccing the po-lice on him."

Cheyne saluted with his coffee cup. "That's how a lot of police work gets done."

"Um, hmm," Dubois agreed. "Are you going to tell Laurette the New Orleans cops suspect Robert of planning this little escapade?"

"I was sitting here pondering just that." Cheyne was quiet for a moment. "After that ordeal with the snakes, I feel like I need to give her a heads up."

"I agree...even though the bad guy may not be Robert." Roland twisted his lips. "Personally, I can't see him doing something like that stunt with the snakes. He's such an idiot he'd probably wind up getting bit himself."

Cheyne barked a laugh. "I was thinking the same thing. That boy could fuck up a wet dream."

"I know that's right. He gives new meaning to the term 'worthless as the tits on a boar.'"

"Of course, that doesn't mean he didn't pay somebody to do it." Cheyne pointed out.

"You suppose he's actually nasty enough to try to get Laurette killed?"

"Ordinarily, I'd say no. He's just a jackass," Cheyne answered. "But greed can make a man...or a woman...do strange things."

Chapter 66

"Why that sleazeball son of a bitch." Sharla snarled. "I oughta go into N'Awlins and whip his butt personally."

"There's no guarantee that it's him. The description sounds like him, though, but the cops don't have any concrete proof," Cheyne told Sharla and me.

We sat at the kitchen table drinking lemonade and eating beignets.

"I didn't like him and Reggie from the get-go," I said. "They're both so phony, and they have greedy-gut written all over them." I took a deep breath, pondering my next words. "Cheyne, do you suppose he paid Annie Lebeau to do that hex thing on me…and maybe he put those snakes in my car?"

"I can't see him doing anything himself. He would've paid somebody." He wiped powdered sugar from the beignets on a paper napkin. "That voodoo crap and the carjacking were scare tactics. The snakes…" His voice trailed off.

"Somebody meant to kill me."

"Did you get any fingerprints off Laurette's car?"

"Nothing we could use." Cheyne shook his head. "By the time, the cops, the medics, the tow truck people...hell, I don't know...Jesus himself might have handled the car. The fingerprints were a mess. And I'd bet whoever put those snakes in there wore heavy-duty rubber gloves to protect himself from a snake bite."

"Or herself," I added.

He nodded. "Right. I've been thinking about that. There's no reason whoever is doing this might not be a woman...or a woman could be involved."

I wanted to ask him about Nicole Dubois but held my tongue. I wasn't sure about his relationship with the beautiful cop-in-training...or her relationship with his cousin Courtland.

He pointed both his hands at us, making pistols of his forefingers. "Now I know you're going to share this with Claude, and that's fine, but don't any of y'all go jumping to conclusions. My gut instinct's telling me there's more afoot here. I feel certain Robert did this business with the carjacking, but the other stuff...I just don't know. I think there's more here than meets the eye. There's something strange going on with all this mess."

"I know that's right," Sharla said. "And I tend to agree with you. If Robert is behind it, he wouldn't do any of the dirty work himself." She held her glass of lemonade in both hands and emitted a short laugh. "In fact, I'm surprised Robert even thought of that carjacking scheme. That boy has trouble figuring out how to tie his shoelaces. I think there's somebody else involved...maybe more than one somebody. After all, there's a lot of money at stake here."

"Yeah. I think it's a team effort on somebody's part," Cheyne said.

"By the way, have you ever found out anything more about that fire at the maintenance barn?" Sharla asked.

Our sheriff shook his head. "Nothing concrete. We checked the tire marks at the scene, but all we could tell was the tires were fairly new and the vehicle was a big pickup, F-150, Dodge Ram, like that."

"What about the gas can?" I asked. "Any fingerprints?"

"What prints might have been on the can were smudged." He

drank down the rest of his lemonade. "They wouldn't mean anything anyway unless they were on file, and we can't just pick somebody up on suspicion, with no sort of trail leading to them. I figure it was one of Annie's nephews, cousin, whatever." He emitted a short laugh. "Funny thing…we know they're all sorry as owl shit, but very few of the Lebeaus have ever been arrested for anything. They always have alibis."

"And we may have our suspicions about who hired Annie, but we'll never prove anything, right?" Sharla cast him a baleful look. "The Lebeaus are slick as eel snot."

"I know that's right." Cheyne rested his thick arms on the table top.

"I guess Annie's voodoo business is one less thing for you to worry about," I commented to Cheyne.

"For now." Cheyne glanced at his watch. "I need to run. I have a conference call with some people in an hour." He pushed back his chair and smiled at me. "Walk me out, *Ma'amzelle?*"

"*Bien sur, M'sieu.*" As I rose from my chair, I didn't miss the sly look Sharla tossed my way.

Cheyne took my hand in his as we walked down the front steps to his sheriff's vehicle parked in the circular driveway. "I don't want you going off by yourself until we get this mess solved," he told me. "At this point, I don't trust anybody other than Sharla and Claude."

"Neither do I…except you of course." I leaned against his car and looked up at him.

"You have no idea how much that means to me." He took both my hands in his and pushed them behind my back, pulling me into his warmth. "I care very much for you, *cher*, and I want to keep you safe."

"Any ideas about who you're keeping me safe from? If it's Robert, I think I can handle him." My breasts were pressed against his massive chest, his warmth spreading to me.

"Robert's an idiot, but don't go underestimating him." He chuckled. "I'm keeping my eyes on several people…maybe too many. I just don't want you wandering off by yourself…even to go into town. Take Sharla with you."

Most of his words were lost on me. I was still dealing with his declaration that he cared for me. I felt my own heartbeat speed up at the notion that I just might be important to this man. "If you suspect somebody, I'd like to know who you're talking about. I want to know who to watch out for."

I felt his laughter rumble in his chest. "You're a persistent little hussy. But, no, I won't tell you right now, because I have no proof... just don't be alone with anyone except Sharla or Claude."

"One of those cop feelings?"

"Something like that...but it makes no sense right now...even to me. So just do what I say." He had his arms around me and played his fingers up and down my back.

Before I knew what was happening, he brought his head down and kissed me. His cousin Courtland's practiced kisses had curled my toenails, but I'd never felt anything like the heat that surged through me. Without thinking, I wrapped my arms around his neck and pressed myself against him from my head to my thighs. I felt like I'd never get close enough to him.

His cell phone rang and the radio in his vehicle squawked simultaneously.

We both jumped.

"Well, poop." Cheyne groused, echoing John Sandford's Virgil Flowers.

Chapter 67

Despite Cheyne's warnings, there was no way I was going to stay cooped up inside the house, even with a killer on the prowl. Besides, I should be safe enough on my own property.

The tunnels mentioned at Claude's dinner party intrigued me. Sharla said she had no idea what the original intent of the tunnels had been. I wondered what had happened to them. Had they been sealed up, collapsed maybe, or were they still accessible?

Sharla told me she'd never tried to go into them, didn't like close spaces. Along with the other papers dating to the Nineteenth Century, she found a map of the tunnels and tucked it away in a library cabinet. I fished it out and spread the yellowed paper onto the desk. Part of the paper had been damaged, so all I could see was where the tunnel led to or from, depending on your perspective. The map showed a small house or cottage, maybe just a summer house, about a quarter-mile from the cemetery. The ink was faded, but the tunnel appeared to lead from the building toward the cemetery. There was nothing to indicate the other end, whether it terminated somewhere in the graveyard or inside the house itself.

I sat down and studied the old map. *How would I build the tunnel?* Were I the original builder and intended to use the tunnel for storing valuables, I would put the entrance in one of those old crypts. Were the entrance inside the house, it would be too easy to find, and there was always the danger of a house catching fire, so I was betting on a crypt entrance. *But which crypt?*

As an architect, I wondered how the tunnels had been shored up to keep them from caving in or filling with ground water. Buildings in Louisiana had no basements because of the chance of flooding. The ground stayed wet year round. The plans showed what looked like a gravel field built around the tunnels, which would have siphoned off some off the excess water, much the way utility manhole systems are constructed in low-lying areas.

I carefully rolled up the map and put it back inside the cabinet next to the fireplace.

Sharla was in the garden talking to one of the yardmen, who was hosing down the lawnmower, getting ready to leave for the day, so I left the house without telling her where I was going. I didn't plan on being gone long.

The cemetery fence was less than a hundred feet from the house, and a paved pathway led to it from one of the side verandahs. The wrought-iron gates were never locked, nor were the entrances to any of the crypts. Out here in the boonies, there was little chance of anybody vandalizing one of the gravesites. The largest tomb was topped by a six foot tall, ferocious-looking angel, wielding a sword. This was the tomb where my father lay. I entered the knee-high wrought-iron fence surrounding it and placed my hand against the cold marble, as if communing with my daddy. I felt tears well in my eyes, but knuckled them away.

The next tomb was guarded by a more placid angel with wide-spread wings. The weathered marble indicated this might be the oldest burial site. I peered closely at the names inscribed and the Eighteenth Century dates for births and deaths. I was right. This was the tomb of the earliest St. Cyrs.

I looked around at the array of angels, weeping angels, dancing angels, sleeping angels. Angels and gargoyles, on the same tombs. For some reason, this struck me as funny, and I laughed out loud, spooking a squirrel who high-tailed it away from me.

A particularly beautiful tomb was decorated with a statue of Aphrodite, chubby cherubs cavorting at her feet. I read the name, Veronique De Lesseps St. Cyr, beloved wife of Etienne St. Cyr. I studied the date. She must have been the mother of my namesake, the Laurette St. Cyr who saved the plantation after the Civil War…make that the War of Northern Aggression, I reminded myself with a smile.

Statues of Jesus and the Blessed Virgin abounded.

I gave the largest crypts a cursory examination but saw nothing that looked like an entrance to a subterranean chamber. More than likely, the entrance would be inside the tomb itself. I didn't particularly want to go inside them alone. I'd wait on Sharla to explore this end of the tunnel with me. If she didn't want to go inside, she could at least keep watch at the doorway to make sure it stayed open while I explored.

I wended my way through the graveyard and found another small gate in the fence on the other side. The metal screeched as I opened it.

The path from the gate was overgrown with weeds, so I was glad I'd traded my flip flops for loafers. The farther I got from the big house, the more unkempt the terrain became. A wild tangle of vines impeded my progress, and I was careful where I put my feet. I'd had enough scares by snakes for a while. Through the thick underbrush and trees trailing Spanish moss, I thought I saw the outline of a small, white building. This must be the building shown on the map.

I pushed aside some limbs and found a narrow path through the bushes. I followed it, walking carefully so as not to get tripped up by the vines running along the ground.

The house vanished as the path wound around a copse of trees. Ducking under some low-hanging limbs, I almost tripped over a pile of rocks, what looked like ancient building debris. I skirted the rubble and pushed aside another limb. The house suddenly loomed in front of me, only a few yards away.

The white stone or marble building looked like a miniature

Grecian temple, complete with columns and a frieze above the entrance way. Looking back toward the big house, I could see nothing but jungle. That accounted for why I hadn't noticed the small house from my balcony. The trees and the tangle of vines impeded the view, allowing me to see only a portion of the creek from the vantage point outside my bedroom and nothing much lying beyond the confines of the cemetery.

Stepping high over the weeds, I made my way to the front portico and carefully climbed the broken steps. I looked all around, thinking I would like to restore the place and use it as a summer house. It was charming, like something out of an Eighteenth Century Fragonard or Boucher painting.

Looking down, I noticed there seemed to be a break in the tangled shrubbery on the creek side of the porch, like the tall weeds had been mashed down by somebody walking on them. I went over and stooped to examine the area. A footprint stood out in clear relief in dried mud on the stone floor…and another one. The prints were large…a man's footprint.

Someone had been here recently. Why? Who? Perhaps just one of the groundskeepers, but why would he be out here, since they obviously didn't keep up this part of the estate?

I laughed to myself. Maybe he got caught short and had to come out here to take a quick pee, but why would he? There was a bathroom in the building housing the yard equipment.

A scantily defined path led from the building toward the creek. I gingerly stepped off of the porch into the mashed weeds.

Ruts formed by tires were branded into the soft ground.

I followed the tracks and discovered what appeared to be a little-used road from alongside the building, paralleling the creek bank. Looking in both directions, to my right I noticed the road vanished around a curve into the trees. The shorter distance to the left led to the creek. I chose the shorter leg and followed the path, finding that it ended at a dilapidated dock.

We hadn't had any rain for a few days, so I could see tire marks clearly in the soft earth. The tire marks were wide, the treads easily discernable. Somebody had driven a vehicle, probably a large pickup, down to the dock. Why?

I looked back toward the outbuilding, thinking about the footprints I'd just found. If somebody had been walking around down here by the creek, he would've gotten the mud on his shoes and tracked it back to the little house.

I paused and chewed my lip. Before coming to Louisiana, I'd never seen a boat like the one Remy used when he rescued me from my snake-ridden car. The flat-bottomed, shallow-draft watercraft was powered by an engine using an airplane propeller on the rear. Sharla told me the boats were popular in bayous and swampy areas because they could be easily navigated in shallow water and they were good not only for fishing in the shallow creeks but for hauling stuff up and down the narrow rivers and inlets of the bayous. She said Remy told her the crafts were especially popular in Florida with the drug dealers plying the inland waterways. This information prickled a notion in my mind, but I didn't want to go there.

Fists balled on hips, I surveyed my surroundings, squinting against the sunlight dappling the water. A light breeze rippled my hair, caught up in a loose ponytail. A white marsh bird startled me, erupting from the cattails and swooping upward, its feet barely skimming the weeds. The bird glided low across the water, landing and paddling away from the dock.

My laugh was tinged with nervousness. I hadn't realized I was just a tiny bit anxious out here all alone until the bird spooked me. The silence around me was complete, for a city dweller, the sense of aloneness was not exactly comfortable. I reminded myself that nobody knew I was out here...which could be good or bad.

I turned in a circle, as if to reassure myself I was alone...just me and the bird and whatever other critters might be lurking in the tall grasses. Gazing back in the direction of the big house, I estimated I must be over a quarter-mile from home. The lights I'd spotted from the gallery outside my bedroom could well be originating right here. The flickering lights might be boat lights, people fishing or frogging, but what were these tire tracks doing here?

I hiked back to the little stone building and walked a ways past it in the opposite direction. I followed two rutted lanes as they curved away from the creek, wondering if at one time the roadway and the now decrepit dock had been used to transport goods to and from the plantation.

Trees grew thick on either side of the trail, and I was sweating and swatting at no-see-ums, those tiny aggravating insects I'd grown to loath since returning to Louisiana. Tinier than gnats, they would swarm all over a person, coming out of nowhere and then vanishing as quickly as they appeared.

I puffed air to get them away from my face and fanned with both hands. Up ahead, I could see the trail intersecting with a wider unpaved pathway. I walked a little farther, until I could see the new path winding through the trees back toward a shell road leading to the cane fields. I recognized the road from the little hut made from palmetto fronds and wooden uprights Claude told me the field workers used as shelter from Louisiana's infamous sudden downpours. He'd driven us along the distant roadway a few days earlier, so I knew where that one led.

I could've gone forward and followed the road back to Shadow Cove, but I remembered it wound its way through the fields for two or three miles.

I didn't want to walk that far, so I turned around and started my trek back, the shorter distance. I must've walked over a mile from the little house. I was hot and thirsty...and tired. My ordeal with the snakes must've burned up a lot of adrenalin my body had not yet replaced.

Chapter 68

I trudged back to the small stone building and climbed the steps to the porch. Perhaps there was a chair inside, and I could rest a while.

I pushed open the wappy-jawed door to the interior. The one large room comprising the place was awash with leaves and cobwebs. The interior was cool, and the unprotected windows funneled the breeze.

My sweat was drying in the wind, and I pulled my shirt away from my chest and fanned myself, wishing I had brought a bottle of water with me. It was hotter than I realized.

Something metallic on the floor caught my eye. I knelt and picked it up. A wrapper, candy, chewing gum? It was fresh, not faded with age

I wondered if some kids were using the place to make out. I rested on my haunches and ruminated again on the flashes of light I'd seen. The lights could be from boats…but that didn't account for the tire tracks. There could be a simple explanation.

Lovers, teenagers? Maybe.

I might be intruding on some horny kids' hideout. If that were the case, a fence would take care of the problem. I really didn't like the idea of unknown people coming onto my land, no matter how innocent and harmless the reason.

A space across from me on the littered floor looked clean, or at least more bare than the rest of the place. I rose from my crouch and examined it.

"Oh, my." I leaned closer. There appeared to be some kind of opening in the floor, a place where the stones looked uneven. Could this be the tunnel entrance or exit or just the result of the building setting over the past century and a half? I searched about for something to use to pry up the stone.

I couldn't believe my luck. Nestled against the wall was a long iron pry-bar.

My heart thudded, and I hefted the thirty-inch rod in my hands. This was no antique. The shaft was not grimy or rusty. It hadn't been left here by some long ago workman. I wondered if someone had been careless and left the rod behind recently...and had used it for what.

Sometimes I'm too nosy for my own good, but this was my property. I grabbed the bar and approached the uneven stone. Poking the bar under the edge, I leaned on it.

The stone lifted with surprising ease, silently. It appeared to be hinged, a sort of lid or trapdoor. I pushed the door open all the way. I got down on my knees and peered into the hole revealed by the trapdoor. "I'll be damned."

Right below the lip of the hole, I spotted a light switch. I flipped it, and a string of lights illuminated the dark space below...the tunnel. A metal ladder was propped against the wall. Like the pry-bar, the ladder was clearly not a relic of yesteryear. The Ace Hardware logo was easily legible on the side of the shiny metal.

I propped the bar across the entranceway to make sure the door couldn't slam shut and slithered over the edge. I climbed down the ladder and into the tunnel. Behind the ladder, I could see what looked like a set of stairsteps that had crumbled. "Hmm." I wondered what had caused them to give way, maybe the Depression era bootleggers had damaged them.

The air in the tunnel was funky and several degrees cooler than the air above ground. The atmosphere was damp. A trickle of water oozed along the bottom, but I was wearing sturdy loafers, so I stepped down and tested the floor. It was firm, brick-paved, and cantilevered so water would flow down the middle. I looked closer. Grates inserted into the brick allowed water to sink into the gravel below. I felt of the walls, also brickwork. This was quite a sophisticated system.

The place was well-lighted, so I ventured deeper into the subterranean passage.

About twenty feet from the ladder, I spied plastic-wrapped bundles, the size of bricks, of a white substance, arranged against the wall.

I eased forward and examined what I knew from watching movies and television crime shows were packages of what could only be cocaine ...right here on my property. "What the hell?" I whispered to a pair spiders scuttling out of my way. The stacks of dope extended several yards along the tunnel walls.

Somebody was storing drugs in the tunnels, and I had a feeling I knew who it was. Claude had told me about my second cousin Junior Couliette's cottage industry and his suspicions that my Aunt Denise's husband was involved, as well as Cousin Sissy's husband. And I was betting the wives knew as well, along with Cousin Robert. The whole frigging family was in the drug business and using my property to stash their wares. No wonder they wanted me out of the way.

"Well, hell," I muttered, my words echoing along the passage. I should return to the house, but I still wanted to see where the tunnel led. I could see the lights all the way to what I supposed was the end and wondered when the place had been wired for electricity and who'd done it...bootleggers or drug dealers.

A desk and two chairs sat not far from the stacks of dope. This looked like a makeshift office. For some reason this annoyed me even more. These pukes had set up housekeeping for their business. I opened the desk drawers but found nothing, just a blank pad of paper and a ballpoint pen, a few paper clips, but then I wouldn't expect the drug dealers to leave any sort of paperwork around…probably kept their records on their computers.

I shut the drawer and resumed my trek toward the end of the tunnel. It was uniformly about six feet wide, and its ceiling was over a foot above my head, six and a half feet high. The passageway was mostly empty except for a few pieces of dilapidated furniture, a couple of chairs and small tables that looked like they might've come from a bygone century.

I walked for at least ten minutes, then spied what looked like an end to the tunnel. My hair stood on end. I must be right underneath the cemetery. All those aboveground crypts were right over my head. This notion gave me a chill.

A set of steps were built into the wall of the tunnel, like I'd found at the other end, only these were intact. The lights didn't follow the stairs, so I tested the steps and found them sturdy enough to support my weight. They didn't feel like they were about to crumble under me. Placing my hand on the wall, I carefully climbed upward.

The light was sufficient that I could make out the outline of a doorway at the top. I felt around for a handle. I found it and tried to move it up and down, but it seemed stuck, so I took off my shoe and beat on it. I felt it give and put all my weight on it.

The handle dropped down, and I almost lost my balance as I stumbled against the door. I slipped my shoe back on, then pressed my shoulder against the doorway and shoved. It was heavy and felt like metal, cold. I managed to scrape it open a few inches but could see nothing but black. A mustiness assaulted my nose. Scant illumination filtered from the string of lights behind me, just enough for me to see that I was looking into some kind of chamber.

I squinted into the stygian interior and perceived a smidgen of light coming from above me. Vents, tiny slits near the roofline let in air and light.

My eyes adjusted, and I could see the outlines of sarcophagi. "My God," I mumbled. I was right. The tunnel ended in one of the tombs, but I had no idea which one.

No way was I venturing farther inside the realm of my dead

ancestors. What if the door closed behind me and I got trapped? I'd explore more later...with Cheyne. For now, I stepped back and tugged the door closed behind me, using both hands, as the heavy metal screeched like a terrified swamp creature. The door latch clicked, and I sighed with relief.

Right now, I wanted to get out of there and call Cheyne. He needed to see this stash of drugs.

I stepped back down the stairway, hugging the wall until I reached the bottom. Then I took off down the tunnel until I reached the end where the dope was stored.

Clambering back up the ladder, I crawled over the lip of the entrance way and closed the hatch, tossing the pry-bar aside. My earlier exhaustion had dissipated. My heart was pounding, and I wanted to get Cheyne out here as fast as I could.

Feeling in my jeans pocket for my cell phone, I realized I'd left it in my bedroom. I hissed a curse and stomped my frustration.

I'd have to go back to the house to call Cheyne. Family loyalty be damned. I wanted him to arrest these thieving slimeballs. Their butts were going to jail. These vultures had tried to kill me.

Hurrying down the steps from the little house, I gingerly high-stepped through the overgrown shrubbery and retraced my way back to the cemetery. I snatched open the gate and rushed through into the graveyard.

Moving at a quick trot, I rounded the tomb trimmed with garlands of carved flowers, topped by a kind-face angel, the one holding the body of my namesake Laurette St. Cyr and her husband Kyle Tanner. A gust of icy wind engulfed me, and I stumbled against the side of the sepulcher. I slapped my hands against the cold marble to keep from falling.

"Tu es en danger, ma petite." The sibilant voice slithered over me.

"Uhnnn." I panted, jerking my hands away and backing away from the crypt. Blood was pounding in my ears.

"Faites attention." The same warning I received before I was attacked by the snakes.

"Oh, my God." I crossed myself, then whirled and ran as fast as

I could, zigzagging through the city of my dead ancestors. I raced across a small pavilion encircled by smaller tombs, and rounded the last one.

"Awwkk!" I collided with a hard male body.

Courtland Delacroix grabbed me by both arms. "What on earth are you running for? Sharla told me she saw you going out toward the cemetery."

I had no idea Sharla had seen me from her spot in the garden. "Come back up to the house. I've got to call Cheyne."

"What's going on?" He didn't let go of me.

My breath was coming in pants. I didn't have time to talk to him. I pulled my arms free. "I've got to call Cheyne."

"Wait, wait. What is it? Tell me what's happened. Is someone out there...did someone try to hurt you?" His eyes mirrored his concern.

I waved toward the little house, hidden deep the thick trees. "Drugs. The tunnel below the cemetery is full of dope."

An alarmed expression crossed his face. "What? How'd you...."

"I found the tunnel. My cousins are using it to stash cocaine," I interrupted him.

"Your cousins?" He grabbed my arms again.

"You heard me. I've got to call Cheyne. They've been moving the stuff at night. I saw lights...thought it was just fishermen, but it's not."

"You know it's your cousins...for sure?"

"Yes. I know about Junior's drug business, and I've got to get Cheyne out here fast."

He cut his eyes toward in the direction of the summer house, his expression closed. "Junior. That fool." His grip on my arms tightened.

"I don't know who all's involved, but I've got to call Cheyne." I jerked away from the hands gripping my arms and ran toward the house.

"Wait. You're right. We need to get the Cheyne here quick." He caught up with me and grabbed me again with one hand and whipped out his cell phone. "I have his personal number right here. I can get to him faster than you. I'll call him. Go on into the house."

Chapter 69

I was gasping, as I ran through the backdoor into the kitchen.
"What is it?" Sharla held the phone to her ear. "Just a minute,
cher. Laurette just came running in, looking like she's seen a ghost."

"Sharla." I paused to catch my breath.

"What is it, *bebe*? What's wrong?" Her expression of alarm must
have mirrored my own.

"I...I got into the tunnel under that little house..."

"You what? What were you doing...?"

"What's she saying...something about the tunnel?"

I heard Claude's voice coming through the phone Sharla held
away from her ear.

"Tunnel's full of dope, cocaine, I think." I managed to wheeze
the words out. "Stacks and stacks of packages. Maybe millions of
dollars' worth."

"Whaa...?"

From the phone Claude hollered. "I heard what she said. Don't
do a thing, *cher*. I'm on my way."

Sharla stared at the dead phone for a moment. "You found cocaine in the tunnel?" She didn't seem surprised.

I bobbed my head.

Her expression turned cryptic, like she was processing what I'd told her.

What was going through her mind? "The lights I've been seeing on the river at night, in that direction. They must be off-loading the stuff and hiding it." I grabbed a glass from the cabinet and stuck it under the water dispenser on the refrigerator.

"Junior."

"You know about him?" I gulped the cold water.

"*Mais ye*, but he's slick. Nobody's caught him."

"I found a road leading from that old boat dock back through the trees to the cane road."

Her expression gave away nothing. "You've been a busy little bee, you."

Her tone struck an odd chord, and fear lanced through me. *Have I misplaced my trust? Does she know what's going on…is she part of it? Should I be afraid of this woman I've come to love?* I concentrated on trying to breathe normally and finished my water, while she said nothing more. I fought to keep the fear out of my voice. "That's been going on right under our noses."

Sharla watched me silently.

A door slammed.

Sharla's lip ticked up, and a peculiar glint sparked in her eyes as Court came into the kitchen putting away his phone.

"Court just called Cheyne. He found me in the cemetery, and I told him what I'd found." The words spewed from my mouth.

A peculiar look passed between the two of them…knowing, conspiratorial even. A cold fist gripped my stomach. Confusion swirled in my head. *Am I being played for a fool by these two? Sharla hadn't seemed all that surprised about Junior hiding the dope on my property. Who am I supposed to trust? I've seen the viciousness Sharla's capable of when we were nearly carjacked. Yet, she said somebody would have to go through her to get to me.*

"Did you get hold of Cheyne?" Sharla's tone was flat.

"Help's on the way." His words were clipped. "Those bags of coke aren't going anywhere."

Sharla puffed out a breath and sank onto a chair, leaning her arms on the kitchen table. "Laurette finding the stash has messed up that playpen." She looked toward me. "How'd you find it?"

"Just being nosy." My voice sounded hollow. "I went exploring, found an old boat dock not far from that little house, by that shallow inlet. I could barely see it because of the underbrush." *They know all about the house, the tunnel. They know Shadow Cove better than I do.* I fought to keep my breathing even, fought down the urge to bolt from the house and run. On the other hand, I didn't want either of them to see my fear. *Cheyne's on the way…isn't he?* "The dock's rickety, but it might be sturdy enough to serve the purposes of Junior and his buddies. They can slip in there late at night and hide the dope until they're ready to move it."

Both watched me silently, while I babbled.

Court moved to the coffee pot and poured himself a cup. He walked over to the windows overlooking the bayou behind the house and stared out, saying nothing, just sipping his coffee.

I saw Sharla tracking him with her eyes, her expression unreadable. Something cold slithered up my spine. *I had misread someone. But who? Sharla? Court? Both of them? Even Claude perhaps?* I licked my lips. My throat felt tight. *I'll keep them talking until Cheyne gets here…if he gets here. I'll wait my chance and run. I don't know who to trust, so I'll distract them and run, hide in the cane fields.* "I guess I was just intrigued by those tunnels y'all talked about," I blathered. "I never for a million years thought something like this could be going on."

"How far did you go into the tunnel?" Court turned back toward us and asked me. His brilliant blue eyes shifted toward Sharla and narrowed.

Another wave of terror swept over me. *What if he's part of it? What if he hadn't called Cheyne?* "Not far. Why?" I lied. I gauged the distance to the back door. *Could I make it and outrun them both if I had to?*

He shrugged. "Just wondering what else might be stashed in there."

"Like what? Dead bodies? Like maybe Junior's been killing off the competition and hiding the bodies there?" Sharla raked her fingers through her hair, making it stand on end.

Thank God I hadn't tripped over any corpses…of course, I hadn't gone into the crypt at the end of the tunnel.

"I suppose it's possible," Court conceded, his tone pensive. "It would be a good way to make somebody disappear." He stared into his coffee cup. "And not that many people know about the tunnels… just a few of us." He eyed Sharla like a predator trying to decide whether or not to attack.

My confusion was complete. *What the hell is going on with these two? Are they friends? Enemies? Conspirators? Had the circumstances surrounding the drug business made them reluctant allies? What?*

Her laugh was mirthless. "All this time, I've felt so safe out here at Shadow Cove, and there were drug smugglers using the property. If I'd blundered into them, they'd've killed me, yes."

Her words caused a tiny frisson of relief to trickle over me. *She's not involved.* I managed to get my lips unglued. "A couple of times when I've seen those lights, I've been tempted to investigate," I said. "But I'm a coward at heart."

"Sometimes cowardice can save your life." Sharla got up, tucked her fingers into the back pockets of her jeans shorts, and ambled over to the windows where Court had been standing. "I wonder what's keeping Cheyne. His office is only a few minutes away."

"He was in a meeting." Court looked at his watch.

Was it my imagination, or did Court's tone sound sharp? And there's something odd in Sharla's voice, and she keeps narrowing her eyes ever so slightly every time she looks at Court. They both seem nervous, but then being in proximity to all those illegal drugs would make anybody antsy. I felt woefully out of my element in trying to discern what was going on.

Court glanced at his watch. "Excuse me, ladies. I need to make a short trip down the hall."

I assumed he was going to the bathroom.

Sharla rubbed her bare arms. "Cheyne should be here by now. I'm calling him."

She wants Cheyne to arrive as much as I do. Her words assuaged my momentary distrust of her. I chewed my lip and watched as Court disappeared around the corner, pulling his phone from his pocket. "He's probably on his way...I hope."

Rising from my chair, I stepped to the sink and turned on the hot water. I washed my arms off up to my elbows, noting that I'd acquired a few more scratches to add to the ones resulting from my car wreck. I splashed water on my face and used paper towels to dry off. My hair was coming loose from its ponytail, so I undid it and finger-combed my sweaty locks before tugging my hair back up onto my head with the scrunchy.

Sharla had her back to me, tapping her fingers on her hips.

"What's wrong?"

She turned toward me, her smile thin. "Beyond the obvious?"

I shrugged. "You seem...I don't know."

"I'm trying to get my head around this. The dope." She looked toward the hall where Court had vanished. "And Court." The last words were a whisper. "I'm scared."

"That makes two of us." I glanced at the clock. "You know, you're right. Cheyne should be here by now. I wonder what's taking him so long."

"I'm calling him," she repeated.

Court reentered the room. He must have heard us. "I'm on it. No need to bother Cheyne." He held his hands out palms downward. "You need to chill, ladies."

A ragged edge in his tone caused a flutter of fear in my stomach. *Something's off...what is it?* I watched Court cut his eyes toward the clock. Over twenty minutes had passed since we came into the house. A cold clamminess broke out on my forehead. I shivered.

I heard the front door opening. Cheyne. *But how did he get in without a key?*

Before I could move, Court headed for the entrance hall. "We're back here in the kitchen," he called.

The answering voice did not belong to Cheyne Delacroix.

Sharla slid her eyes toward me, an unfathomable expression on her face. "What the hell," she whispered.

"What's going on?" I aped her tone.

"I don't know." She twisted around and groped on the countertop. "Where's my phone?"

Chapter 70

Court entered the kitchen accompanied by Wills O'Neal, Claude's lover.

I looked from the two men to Sharla, whose expression mirrored her surprise...but surprise tempered with another emotion...a sort of resignation. A look that said something she suspected had been confirmed. *But what?* I was totally baffled.

She gave the men a long look and nodded.

Court's smile was rueful. "You knew?" He said to her.

"Not much gets past me. You should know that by now...or by Claude." She looked at Wills.

"What are you...?" Once again, I felt like Alice falling down the rabbit hole.

"You didn't call Cheyne. You called Wills." Sharla accused Court.

"What can I say?" He held his palms out and shrugged. "A man does what he has to."

"You are a consummate asshole," Sharla barked. "I've always suspected it, but now you've proved it."

"This is all very well, honey, but we've got to do something about these two in a hurry." Wills reached into his jacket and pulled out a gun.

I sucked in a breath.

"I'm not the only one who knows about you two," Sharla said. "So you're going to have to kill a lot of people if you want to keep things quiet."

Court raised his eyebrows.

"What?" My words came out on a gust of breath.

Sharla's half smile was bitter. "Court will do anything to keep his daddy from finding out he's gay. And I do mean anything, including murder. His daddy would cut him off without a penny...kick him out of the business."

Court looked down at the floor and shrugged.

I felt the air leave my body, like a balloon with a slow leak.

Sharla snarled. "Katie Thibadeaux saw you and Wills gettin' it on in the graveyard. She told me, and she told her daddy." She shook her head. "You certainly did destroy all her girlish daydreams."

"That stupid little cow." Wills snorted. "Court wouldn't touch her with somebody else's."

Sharla's mouth twisted in an expression of exasperation. "For God's sake, Court. So you're gay. What the hell's the big deal? So your daddy would disown you. You could start your own business, be your own man. It's not worth killing somebody over."

An odd look glided over his face, something more evil than a smirk...and I knew before the words were out of Sharla's mouth.

"You've done it before, so another time should be easy. Is that it?"

I took my eyes off the gun Wills held long enough to look in her direction.

"You killed Fabienne, didn't you? How many people do you think she told about you?" She cocked that eyebrow. "Don't you think she told her boyfriends...including Cheyne?"

She snapped the sheriff's name like a whip.

Is she goading him or buying time? Either way, I clenched my teeth to keep them from rattling. *That gun pointed at me keeps getting bigger.*

"Fabienne had a mouth on her, and she liked to run it," Court growled. "I told her we could have an amicable agreement. I'd give her whatever she wanted, and she'd let me be. She could have her lovers, and I could have mine. I know several couples who do that."

"Too bad your daddy isn't more amenable," Wills remarked. He kept moving his gun between Sharla and me, as if he didn't know who he wanted to shoot first. He looked toward Sharla. "Court's daddy's a homophobic bastard."

I managed to get out a few trembling words, helping Sharla stall, I hoped. I'd heard Claude say on the phone that he was on the way. *Oh, God, I hope Claude isn't part of this.* "If Court could get close to me, persuade me to marry him, then he wouldn't need his daddy's money. Is that where I fit into y'all's plan?" I turned toward Court. "Did you really think I was stupid enough to fall for that crap you were laying on me?"

"I needed more time." He grinned. "I was working it."

"What about your flirting with Nicole?" I seethed. Sharla was right. He was an asshole.

"A mere diversion. I had to keep up my reputation as a ladies' man." He nodded toward Wills. "We need to get them into the tunnel and take care of them there. Junior's boys are scheduled to pick up the dope tonight. They can haul the bodies off, leave them in the swamp to be found...or not."

"That's pretty damn sloppy, Court," Wills said. "We need a better plan."

"We don't have time to plan. It was working out fine, if this little bitch hadn't gotten nosy. Now we have to take care of business fast," Court snapped.

Wills grimaced. "I don't know. I've been thinking about this all the way out from the city. We could kill them right here...make it look like a home invasion. No sense in blowing a good deal with where we hide the dope. With the rest of the family in charge, we can keep on as long as we like."

Court appeared to ponder this notion. "One thing I love about you is your ability to think on your feet, shift gears in a flash." He chuckled. "Even planting that earring on old Annie Lebeau..."

"You killed Annie?" My words came out as a gasp. "Why?"

"Katie wasn't the only one who saw us in the cemetery," Court answered. "That old mule actually had the gall to try to blackmail us."

"Enough of this chit -chat," Wills interrupted. "We need to get this show on the road. Nobody knows I'm here, and nobody knows she found the dope in the tunnel."

Claude knows, I silently reminded myself, while renewing my prayer that he wasn't involved in any of this.

"We need to get rid of both of them fast." Wills nodded at Court. "I've got some surgical gloves in the car. We can take care of them and then go through the house tearing up things. Steal the jewelry and dump it in the bayou, so it looks like somebody was preying on a couple of women living out here alone. The sun's going down, so it'll be dark soon. When they're discovered, it'll look like a couple of thugs came out here after dark and killed them."

Court barked a blood-chilling laugh. "I may just have to be the one who comes by tomorrow morning and finds the bodies." He bobbed his head. "*Mais ye, cher.* This might work fine. When we finish up here, you high-tail it back to N'Awlins and take Claude out to dinner, be the ever-lovin' boyfriend and act like nothing happened."

So Claude isn't part of this. I cast a glimpse at Sharla, who gave me a tiny shake of her head. I didn't want them to know Claude had heard what I said about finding the drugs in the tunnel before Sharla hung up the phone…and neither did she. Claude would know something had happened…but more than likely, he'd buy whatever story Wills cooks up. I hadn't said anything about Court being here. Court and Wills might pretend they just got here and found us. They might kill Claude, too. My heart was pounding like a jack-hammer. My knees trembled. *Oh, Claude…Uncle Claude. You said you were on the way…but where are you? And can you manage these two when you get here? We have to keep them talking.*

While they were yammering, Sharla moved closer to me where I stood beside the counter. "What makes you think I didn't tell Claude about you two…about what Katie told me she saw?"

The colour drained out of Wills's face. "Did you?"

"Well, hell. If she did, we'll have to take care of him, too." Court's voice was hard.

"I'd really hate to do that, you know." Wills swallowed. "He's really a decent sort."

Court's head swiveled toward his lover. "What's this shit? Are you pussying out on me? We're in this together."

I felt Sharla's arm move next to mine and caught a glimpse of her hand gliding across the countertop toward the hot coffeepot. The two of us might be able to take them.

"I'm not totally without feelings, Court," Wills snapped. "I'll do whatever is necessary. You should know that by now."

"Then let's get this done," Court snarled and nodded his head toward me.

Wills swerved his gun in my direction.

Suddenly, Sharla was between the gunman and me.

The coffee pot was flying through the air, scattering hot coffee. "You won't kill my baby."

I heard Sharla's scream at the same time the gun boomed.

A red flower exploded above her heart. She slammed into the wall.

"Sharla!" I shrieked. "Maa-maa!" A truth blasted through me with the power of a gunshot.

I saw Wills flailing wildly as the coffee scalded him. He jerked the gun's trigger reflexively, and I heard one of the kitchen windows blow out.

Another shot rang out, and Wills flew backward across the kitchen, the top of his head exploding.

I was slammed against the countertop, as Cheyne flung himself through the doorway from the back hallway and knocked me aside, firing another bullet at Wills.

Claude ran through the door from the dining room and collided with Court, who was scrabbling to get the gun Wills dropped to the floor. From the corner of my eye, I saw Claude grab an iron trivet from the counter and cold-cock the other man with it.

Court when down without a sound.

I fell to the floor beside Sharla.

She was gasping for air, crying over and over. "I couldn't let him kill my baby. I couldn't let him kill my baby."

I held her close to me. My heart was going crazy. I couldn't let her die…couldn't lose her.

Epilogue

Sharla was propped in the hospital bed, her shoulder thickly bandaged. I perched on the chair beside the bed, holding her hand, my face pressed against her fingers. It seemed like years had passed since the shooting, but it was only day before yesterday. I spent all day yesterday and this morning in the room with her, watching her sleep, before going home and napping this afternoon. The sedation had worn off only a short time ago, and her voice was a slur. "*Ma bebe.*"

"Tell me," I barely whispered, fearing what she was about to reveal, yet longing to hear the words I knew would unlock secrets.

"I'm your mama."

I choked down a sob. I'm not sure when I first suspected the truth. There was just something in the way she looked at me, the way she'd smile at me and reach out and touch me. When we were alone, she'd often fold me into an embrace and just hold me. On those occasions, I always felt something twist inside me. There was a closeness, a flesh calling to flesh, that I couldn't explain. No matter how much I loved Celine, or how much she loved me, there was some primitive connection missing. A feeling that surged through me the first time Sharla touched me.

Now it made sense. I was born of this woman's body. Half of me was her. My mother.

We both remained silent a few minutes. When she spoke again, her voice was weak. "After a couple years of marriage and visits to God knows how many doctors, Celine had to accept the fact that she was never going to be able to have children of her own." Sharla licked her lips. "Seeing as how we were sisters, half anyway, I agreed to artificial insemination by your daddy."

"That's why I was born in that private clinic in Savannah?"

"*Mais ye, bebe.*" Her smile was wan. "We went to visit relatives nobody'd ever heard of, so I could have you." She chuckled and grimaced at the pain it must have caused. "Celine had waddled around for months with a padded belly, pretending to be pregnant. The story was you arrived prematurely while we were in Savannah." She smiled and cocked that eyebrow. "Due to complications, Celine had to stay there a while, which accounted for you looking like a full-term baby...which you were...by the time we got back home."

I heaved a sigh. "And nobody suspected anything?"

"Not as far as I know." She shook her head. "Claude, of course, knew from the beginning. He handled the legalities...or illegalities, I should say."

This didn't surprise me. "Do my Renard relatives know?"

Sharla made a face. "Now that was some kind of acting on the part of Celine and me, but we kept it from all of them."

"How about your mama?"

"There was no way I could keep the secret from my own mama, but she would never tell." She wiggled in the bed. "Claude, could you raise the bed just a tad?"

I noticed her voice seemed to be getting stronger, and she managed a smile in the lawyer's direction.

My uncle got up from his chair and adjusted the bed, then helped her lean forward while I plumped her pillows. Her wound wasn't as bad as it looked at first. The bullet had gone through her shoulder and missed anything vital.

"So you lived all those years with the St. Cyrs, first looking after me, then taking care of them," I said.

"Umm, hmm." The eyebrow went up again. "I have another secret I need to tell you, and only Claude knows this, too."

I waited.

"The night your mama and daddy had that awful fight." She took a breath. "I'm afraid I was the subject of the fracas."

"Oh?"

"You're daddy wanted another child...same as before.'"

I bit my lip. "And?"

"Your mama'd gotten some hare-brained idea that your daddy and I were carrying on." She raised a finger at me. "Which we were not. I want you to understand that. I will confess I had certain feelings for Etienne." She gave a small shrug. "After all, I'd given birth to his child. But he was never in love with me...nothing of the sort. He was fond of me, and I kept my own feelings to myself. Our relationship was never anything improper...never."

I doubted not her words were true. "How did you feel about having another child with him?"

She stared off into space. "It was so long ago. I wasn't totally averse to the idea, but I wasn't crazy about it either." I held a glass of orange juice for her, and she took a long sip. "In the long run, I probably would've done whatever he wanted."

"But it didn't happen, obviously."

"No. Your mama just got wild with the very notion...and of course, she would've had to be considered. It couldn't happen without her cooperation. She started accusing him of all that rot...and then they had that fight..." Her voice trailed off.

"And I know the way it all ended." I raised her hand to my lips and kissed it.

"It nearly killed me when she took you away with her." Sharla's voice was tight, as she fought back the tears. "My only consolation was knowing she loved you as much as I did and would keep you safe and would see that you had everything you needed." She gave me a wan smile. "And I knew in my heart you'd return some day. I guess that's what kept me sane...knowing I'd see my baby again."

"The important thing now is that I'm back where I belong at Shadow Cove...with you, Mama Sharla." I looked at Claude, who'd returned to his seat over by the window. I'd ridden into town with him. "And you, Uncle Claude."

"You have no idea how happy we both are to have you back home with us." He saluted me with his cup of Coke.

"I know a few people who aren't so happy." I changed the subject and laughed.

"No." Claude joined my laughter. "Your cousin Robert is mightily put out, and I'm sure Junior is more than a tad perturbed at losing all that dope the police confiscated."

Sharla sniffed. "I still can't believe that little turd managed to weasel out of being charged with dealing."

"Yeah, Court ratted him out right and proper," I said. "But Cheyne said Junior lied his way out of it, saying he knew nothing about any of it and neither did any other member of the family."

"Junior and his daddy wanted to retain me as legal counsel, but I bowed out…gave them all some guff about how I didn't trust myself to be able to give a proper accounting due to my relationship with any number of the people involved." Claude snorted. "No way was I getting mixed up in their dope problems when I knew they were all guilty as sin. If they're even charged with anything, which I doubt, the attorney they hired will get them off."

"Why are you so sure?"

He and Sharla both looked at me as if I'd just cut the cheese in front of the Pope.

"Because the lawyer they hired will do the same thing I would've done…played the St. Cyr card…all the family political and social connections. Plus, they have absolutely no evidence tying Junior and the rest to the drugs. It all looks like it was Court's operation…which is what they're claiming. And that boy is in deep doo doo, seeing as how Cheyne heard him confess to killing Fabienne. Drug dealing is the least of his worries when he's facing a murder one charge."

"What a shitass he turned out to be," I said.

Claude snorted. "And then there's Robert. The police could get nothing on him either. He admitted to paying Annie to annoy you… as he put it…but said he meant you no real harm, just wanted you to leave, so the rest of the family could split up the inheritance. And I firmly believe he hired those two little thugs to carjack you and Sharla."

A light pinged on my brain. "I just remembered something… what that little creep said…the one in the driver's seat."

"What are you talking about?" Claude asked.

"I just remembered it. As he was getting out of the car, he called

Robert a dirty name and said he was going to cap his ass for this…his exact words." I looked at them both in silent amazement. "I just realized what he'd said. He knew Robert…and I'll bet Robert hired him."

"I'll be damned," Claude said. "I'll bet you're right."

"Robert's a sneaky snake." Sharla shook her head. "They couldn't be charged with kidnapping?"

"No, seeing as how they never moved the car with y'all in it, and they abandoned the vehicle."

"And they never ratted on Robert for hiring them," I commented.

"No. They gave a vague description, but it was like 'all you whities look alike.' They admitted they'd already been paid half the money for the caper, and I imagine Robert will be hearing from them again for more money for keeping their mouths shut. He hasn't seen the last of those two. As my mama always said, 'you mess with a turd, you're going to get some shit on you.'" My uncle smirked. "The best part is knowing the pure hell Robert is getting from Reggie for spending all that money on the little creeps and getting his car trashed…and mostly for embarrassing her to her high-toned, society friends."

"I know," I agreed. "If any two people ever deserved each other it's Robert and Reggie."

Claude looked at his watch. "Cheyne should be here any minute. He said he'd be by as soon as he could get away. Going to take you out for a muffuletta. He invited me, but I told him you two could go alone and bring me a carry-out. No sense in my being a third wheel, and I'll enjoy keeping Sharla company while she has her dinner."

"Too bad you couldn't sneak me some wine." My mother made a face. "Anything to make the hospital food palatable."

Claude had said little about Wills, his former lover. I knew he silently mourned both the man's deception and his death.

"I wish y'all were coming with us."

"Soon enough, *ma cher.*" Claude nodded his head. "As soon as Charla's well enough. We'll have a double date, us."

Sharla wagged a finger at me. "You hang onto Cheyne. He's a good man." She touched her ear. "*Vous ecoutez votre mama.*"

"*Mais ye, mama*, I'm listening."